TALES FROM THE UNCONSCIOUS

CHRISTOPHER GIBSON

Tales from the Unconscious

Gibson Konsult AB

International Psychoanalytic Books (IPBooks)
New York • IPBooks.net

Tales from the Unconscious

Published by IPBooks, Queens, NY
Online at: www.IPBooks.net

Copyright © 2021 Christopher Gibson

ISBN: 978-1-949093-92-6

For My Family

Contents

Book Two
Provocations

Book Three
Audacities

Preface

———•———

Preface is an old term from the study of rhetoric. It is in a sense an explanation or defense, but primarily it is an introductory address. Here, the writer should say why they wrote their book and what it's about, and justify their authorship.

This is a story book about psychoanalysis and therapy. I started writing stories to illustrate psychoanalytic ideas when I became aware that I *thought* about clinical papers more than I *felt* them. In other words, it was more of a cerebral process than a heartfelt one. These stories were originally intended to be used (and indeed were used) in seminars with people in related professions, students, and anyone interested in psychoanalytic ideas. I wanted to find a way to introduce a topic in a lively manner that would capture the audience's interest. People from various walks of life are curious about psychoanalytic ideas, and there are many texts on the subject. Some people have a lot of experience of psychoanalysis; others have only a passing knowledge of Freud and his colleagues. As a teacher, I wondered how to present relevant material. I took my lead from

Freud, who recognized the need for an artistic approach to his work. He wrote the following in *Studies in Hysteria*:

> '...It still strikes me myself as strange that the case histories I write should read like short stories and that, as one might say, they lack the serious stamp of science.' (Freud, S (1893), p. 160)

And he went on to comment that it was the nature of the material that led to his use of a literary format. It was unavoidable in his view.

I thought about the engagement we have with stories on television, in the theatre and cinema, in books and magazines. We can learn something new from these creations when we link a story with other aspects of our lives. For example, it is not unusual for parents to use a story rather than an injunction to help children learn. The injunction 'You must wear your cycle helmet' may achieve a different result than a story of a giant who forgot his helmet when he went cycling, with noisy and colorful consequences as he fell off his bike!

Tales from the Unconscious consists of three books that present ideas around a theme exemplified by each title. The book as a whole attempts to illustrate the vagaries of our inner lives and makes links to the theories of psychoanalysis and psychoanalytical psychotherapy. The basic theory is the same in both methodologies, and the similarities between the two are considerable. They are both open-ended processes of self-discovery via free association in a professional therapeutic relationship. This method was pioneered by Freud, who grasped an essential need in humans to be understood more than to be loved.

Expectations is a collection of short stories about love— unrequited, failed, impossible, and cruel. In the second book, *Provocations*, the theme is the provocative arousal of emotions in another person. *Audacities*, the third book, is about an audacious act—suicide—that affects many lives.

In my experience we are capable of unlimited love and of its opposite: hate and cruelty. We control ourselves through what we call civilization, which can break down under stress. Once a suicide has occurred, civilization seems to leave the field: repetitions occur and people around the suicidal victim lose their balance and are capable of great injustice. This is particularly so if they hide the truth and allow others to suffer the unconscious knowledge they carry of the self-murder of a relative, friend, or even therapist. Although we try to keep our love dominant over our envy, life does not always work out as we wish. Or maybe it does work out according to some of our darker, unconscious wishes. When we are motivated by hatred, nothing is sacred.

When you read a story, notice your reaction to it: you may identify with it, be annoyed, or feel indifferent. It's not unlike looking at a piece of abstract art: what happens inside us when we look at it is the most important part of the experience. In other words, we understand the art by knowing our feelings about it. And art and love are adventures in which we hope to succeed, but we should be prepared to lose and fail.

'Freud's main conclusions (were)... of the predominating part played in the mind of man by the irrational and by conflict respectively.' (Jones, E. (1940), p. 14) I have tried to demonstrate Jones' point with these stories.

We know from experience that childhood stories have their roots in the unconscious and may lead us to feel and think differently about ourselves and our world. According to psychoanalysis, stories have their origins in dreams and phantasies, and they are as real for the unconscious as the experiences of the other senses. They are symbols and metaphors that cast light on childhood, adolescence, and adult experiences. Hopefully, they will transport the reader from familiar ideas to the esoteric world of the unconscious. Art also has the ability to get inside us and to show us who we are at the moment. Psychoanalysis has the same effect and, as with a piece of art, you should feel free to interpret or discard these stories as you wish. My experience as a teacher of emotionally disturbed children and adolescents has shown me the benefits of the story format in presenting an idea or theory, because stories often awaken buried traces of experience in the unconscious. A story can reach the heart more effectively than a theoretical explanation. Some of these feelings may seem unimportant but eventually may lead to other associations. I hope that they provide questions rather than answers.

Postscript

After each story is a postscript with a quotation or two and a few lines of comment to indicate a possible direction in psychoanalytic theory. But I don't want to take away your freedom to think as you wish about each piece, so I haven't written much more. As you will see, I've used quotations from Freud and Shakespeare most often. Shakespeare gives us lots of reasons to value stories as a route to the unconscious and to psychoanalysis. Even Freud is reputed to have commented that, in his ruminations about the unconscious, he found that the poet had been there before him. If someone talks about a world leader or their line manager at work behaving like King Lear we know what they mean. And if we want to vividly and briefly describe a parent's neglect of their teenager's need for support and direction we can refer to *Romeo and Juliet*.

In the postscripts I could try to explain in detail what these stories are about but I think the reader's response would be diminished if I did that. I don't want the reader to lose the spontaneous experience of the feelings provoked by considering the text. The postscripts do not give the comfort of an answer; rather, they may produce discomfort by being unfinished. In every story there are secrets that even the writer is unaware of. Hopefully, the free associations you have in relation to what you read will open your mind to unconscious phantasies that may influence your thinking. If I say too much, then a story will continue after I had intended it to end. You may need to let each story reside in your mind for a time before you know what you think about it, like a piece of music that reverberates after the end of a concert. What you remember will be what is important to you. Let each story influence you; it is not so much what it is about but the effect it has on you and your understanding of yourself that is important.

NB. The word 'fantasy' is used for conscious images with feelings and the word 'phantasy' is used for unconscious images and experiences, as seen in dreams for example.

When I've referenced a quotation or book, I've put the date of publication and the title. In the case of Freud, I have put SE, meaning the *Standard Edition* of Freud's works, published by the Hogarth Press and The Institute of Psycho-Analysis, London.

References

Freud, S. (1893). *Fräulein Elisabeth von R*, pp. 135–181. SE II: *Studies on Hysteria*. London: Hogarth Press and The Institute of Psycho-Analysis.

Jones, E. (1940). Sigmund Freud 1856–1939. *International Journal of Psycho-Analysis* 21:2–26.

For quotes from Shakespeare:
Clark, W. G., and Wright, W. A., (Eds) *The Complete Works of William Shakespeare*. Garden City, NY: Nelson Doubleday Inc.

For quotes from the Bible:
Jones, A. (Ed.) (1974). *The Jerusalem Bible*. London: Darton, Longman and Todd.

Finally, I have to say who this writer is, and why he thinks he is qualified to write these stories.

Christopher Gibson trained in the psychoanalysis of adults, children, and adolescents at the British Psychoanalytical Society's Institute of Psychoanalysis. He is a training and supervising analyst of the Swedish Psychoanalytical Association.

He is a teacher and former headmaster of a school for children and adolescents with emotional problems. After qualifying as a psychoanalyst, he worked at King's College London University, Brent Adolescent Centre, and the Anna Freud Clinic.

In 1998, Christopher and his psychoanalyst wife Jill Lindqvist Gibson moved, with their family, to Gothenburg, Sweden.

He practices in Gothenburg and is a visiting supervisor in child, adolescent, and adult psychotherapy, the criminal justice system, addiction clinics, and outpatient care. He holds monthly 'continuing professional development seminars' for psychotherapists, psychologists, social workers, and therapists. He has been a visiting teacher of psychoanalytic psychotherapy at Ersta Sköndal Bräcke Högskola, and The Psychological Institution, Gothenburg University.

Christopher Gibson is the author of *Bardzo Zmienna Czarownica* (2017) *(The Changeable Witch)*, Instytut Studiow Psychoanalitycznych, Warsaw

Acknowledgments

My gratitude to Jill Gibson for her support for this project and comments on each story.

Thanks to Doug Watts of Jacqui Bennett Writers Bureau critique and editorial service, www.jbwb.co.uk, for his corrections and comments on these stories as they arrived over recent years.

Expectations: Thanks for detailed work to Linda Nagle, Devil Editing, 3 Belgrave Street, Wallasey, CH44 1BL, UK. Tel: +44 7533 315 375; Email: lin@indelible.org.uk

Provocations: Thanks to Mike Bailey, Email: mtb20@btinternet. com, copy-editor and writer, for his corrections and insightful comments.

Audacities: Thanks to Derek Collett, Email: dmc1965@zen.co.uk, for his corrections and thoughtful comments. Derek has also harmonized the style and contents of the final combined draft of the three books

The Sermon

———◆———

I was standing in the pub with a few friends, one of them being Bill. Good old Bill: overweight, sweating slightly, with his crumpled off-white shirt hanging out of his trousers. He was always ready with a good word or a joke. I said,

'The trouble is some people just don't care. It's not their problem if the guy down the road gets drunk every night or can't feed his kids. But that's not right. Someone should do something, shouldn't they? I mean...'

The group stared at me expectantly but I fell silent as my thoughts suddenly vanished and my words dried up. Fortunately, Bill broke the mood. 'Very profound, George. You should write a book. Why don't you have another beer?'

A few people chuckled, attention switched away from me, thank God (or Bill), and the conversation moved on.

Don't you hate that kind of situation? You recognize it, don't you? You start saying something apparently meaningful but you don't know how to finish the idea, or even the sentence. So you look down. You hope someone else will release you from the attention waiting on your next, supposedly brilliant, remark. The one you have suggested by your demeanor that you are about to deliver.

Unfortunately, it's not in your mind, it doesn't exist, and probably never will. Unless it's the one you wake up with in the middle of the night. The retort you should have used. If you write it down, in the morning you will find it is utter nonsense. How boring I would be if I wrote a book.

I left the pub at the end of the evening without saying any more. I wondered what would make the next thing I said interesting or amusing. I thought I'd probably remain silent for some time.

But now I break that silence. I hope you find it helpful.

Book One

Expectations

Introduction

————◆————

Expectations. Dictionaries agree that an expectation is something looked forward to, whether feared or hoped for. Synonyms of expectation are *anticipation, assumption, belief, eagerness, hopefulness, prediction,* and *suppositions.* In these stories, it is expectations of love that are the focus of interest.

The aim of this collection is to bring psychoanalytic ideas to your attention by describing different kinds of relationships, including distortions and failures of love. They represent the kind of fantasies that feel real in the transference–countertransference experience of an analysis.

From our memories, both conscious and unconscious, come our expectations of love, happiness, and destructive relationships. Love takes its shape within our unconscious.

What is expected in love and in analysis? What love is offered by the analyst through their devotion to the task, and what love is desired that needs to be thought about instead of realized?

'It (Psychoanalysis) is in essence a cure through love.' (Letter from Sigmund Freud to Carl Jung, 1906, Jones, E. (1955) p. 485, cited in Loewald, H. (1960) p. 32)

Freud is apparently talking about the love involved in the analyst–client relationship. I think he refers to a commitment to listening to the other person as they search for self-knowledge, via free association, in a relationship with the analyst. This relationship includes transference and countertransference, i.e. the transfer of feelings to the other person; via this experience, unconscious patterns of relating reveal themselves, and can be described and understood. 'Moreover it is transference that provides the strongest proof, the only unassailable one, for the relationship of neuroses to love.' (Ibid., p. 32). It is in the transference and countertransference response that we see the patterns of the history that has led to the neurosis.

The client uses free association to release these thoughts, and by 'free association' we mean to talk without thinking in order to avoid the natural censuring necessary in everyday life. That's a lot of ideas in a few lines, which I hope will be clarified by the stories. They give various pictures of the kinds of fantasies that arise in analysis and analytic therapy.

In the so-called transference, memories of love, wishes, regrets, and hatreds are experienced anew with the analyst. The analyst feels these experiences and has feelings towards their client, which are called the countertransference response.

The analyst's aim is to understand these experiences without enactment.

'...what turns the scale in (the patient's) struggle, is not his intellectual insight... but simply and solely his relation to the doctor.' (Freud, S. (1917), p. 445)

If the analyst listens properly, and describes the relationship in the consulting room, it is hoped that the other person feels understood.

The first story, 'What on Earth is Transference?', will give you a better idea of what I mean, and the poem 'Ravished' is an example of a countertransference problem. The rest of the stories describe some of the variations of love and hatred that may appear in life and in analysis. Love is to be found outside the consulting room, with someone else, when transference conflicts have been sufficiently resolved.

References

Freud, S. (1916–1917). *Introductory Lectures on Psycho-Analysis, Part III, General Theory of the Neurosis, Lecture XXVII, Transference*, p. 445. SE XVI. London: Hogarth Press and The Institute of Psycho-Analysis.

Loewald, H. W. (1960). On the Therapeutic Action of Psycho-Analysis. *International Journal of Psycho-Analysis* 41:16–33.

Sutherland, J. D. (Ed.) (1965). *The Letters of Sigmund Freud and Karl Abraham, 1907–1926. International Psycho-Analytical Library*. New York: Basic Books.

1

What on Earth is Transference?

———◆———

This is an unlikely story, but I'm trying to explain something, so you'll have to trust me, and go with it.

Percy, a twenty-five-year-old freelance journalist, walked into Jim's office.

'What on earth is this transference thing, anyway?' he asked. 'I'm writing an article for a Sunday paper about psychoanalysis, and this word keeps coming up in the reference material. The writers seem to assume that the reader will know what it means.'

His colleague, Jim, an experienced newspaperman on the edge of retirement, looked up from his work, his bald patch shining in the florescent ceiling light. He put his cigarette on the edge of an overfull ashtray, and rolled back in his office chair.

'What? Do you think I've got nothing better to do than answer your dumb questions?'

'Oh, sorry, I didn't realize you were busy.'

'You didn't ask. I'll give you a short answer to your transference question. It's… Er, well, basically, as far as I understand it, it's the experience of being convinced the other person is who you think they are.'

'And you are not who I think you are?'

'For the sake of this answer, I'll ignore that. The idea is that you transfer to me an image, and experience of, for example, your mum, dad, first schoolteacher, whatever, and treat me as if I'm that person.'

'Sounds a bit far-fetched, if you ask me.'

'I'm not. You're asking me. For example, when you came into this room, you talked to me as if you expected me to drop everything I'm doing, and answer your question, as though I'm the parent of a young child. If I ask myself the questions *Who do you think you are?* and *Who do you think I am?*, and vice versa, then I might understand who is being transferred to me.'

'And what do you mean by vice versa?'

'If you didn't knock, as you didn't, I might think, *Oh no, not Percy just now. I'm busy. He's a nuisance.* Or if you did knock, and I was not busy, I might think, *Oh good, Percy. A friendly face. Nice to have a chat.* You might be either of those: a nuisance who comes into my room without knocking, or a friendly face come to distract me with something interesting.'

'So, the transference of experiences goes in both directions?'

'Yes, of course. You might be thinking that I'm in need of cheering up, or you might not. Alternatively, you might think that, because we're friends, you don't need to follow the rules of politeness, like knocking, and asking if I am busy.'

'Why are you being so shitty?'

'There you are—*am* I being shitty, like some frustrating mother? Or is what I'm saying reasonable, given the context? You have to sort that out, but be sure I'm not who you make me into.'

'OK, but I can't do that all day long.'

'No, but it's a useful tool in its place. Psychoanalysis is an attempt at self-knowledge through understanding these moments of contact between two people in a consulting room. Like all great ideas, it's simple.'

'OK, where's the catch? Not many people are indifferent to psychoanalysis. Why is it loved by a few, and ignored by most?'

'The catch is that most of the feelings I described are unconscious, says the theory.'

'Ah-ha, the great escape. Everything is unconscious, so the theory can't be challenged.'

'You're responsible for your unconscious. It's yours.'

'But if I dream, it's just a dream, nothing to do with me.'

'Sorry, no, it's created by your mind.'

'Oh. Well anyway, where do I find evidence to confirm this theory about transference?'

'Small children will tell you the truth, and if you want a metaphor, use the Post Office.'

'What do you mean by that?'

'I'm not saying it again, you've had enough time. Now get out of my office, I'm busy.'

'And who is being transferred to me now? What irritating figure do I have the pleasure of being?'

'Get out.'

'So, who are you, you miserable old sod?'

'Out!'

Percy went back to his office and pondered the conversation.

He decided to visit a school in search of the truth.

Would he really go to a school and talk to a child? He's a journalist, of course he would. Now please read on.

Percy met Isabella, aged six and three-quarters. Isabella was playing with a family of dolls.

'These children have been very bad, so the mother is going to hit them.'

'Oh, my goodness.'

'Yes, they bite people. I bit my teacher on the arm, like this.' She demonstrated on her own arm. 'She was soft and tasted like cream.' Isabella giggled. 'Then I was taken to see a talking lady.'

'A talking lady, you say?'

'That's where you get taken if you bite teachers,' she said. 'I thought she was a crocodile.' Isabella gathered up all the doll children.

'And then what happened?'

Isabella buried the children up to their ears in sand and stood the mother and father figures over them. 'The lady talked nicely. She had clean toys and a clean room. Until I got there.'

'You are bright, Isabella.'

Isabella pulled the children out of the sand and put the dolls to bed.

'The crocodile turned into a lady. I didn't bite my teacher again.' Isabella played, fetching and carrying bits and pieces for her doll's house. 'But I might bite you, because you're in the way.'

Percy went away. *I've learned something*, he thought. *Strong feelings can be transferred to other people, who are then perceived as the image of those feelings...*

If Isabella has transferred to her therapist angry feelings represented by the image of a crocodile, then the lady becomes a biting crocodile. Of course, it's Isabella who bites, but she pushes that idea onto the therapist.

But what of Jim's Post Office metaphor? Percy went to the local postal sorting office. He met a postman, who had a large sack in his hand. He asked the postman what the word 'transfer' meant to him.

'You're joking of course… The transfer? Oh, my God! We've got a right one here, Ronny, one of those posh ones.'

Ronny walked over. 'What is it, Ken?'

'This bloke here, dead posh he is, and all that. He doesn't know what a transfer is. There's one born every minute, isn't there? He'll be telling me next he doesn't know what a metaphor is neither, I shouldn't wonder.'

Ronny shook his head.

Percy looked at the floor.

Putting on his fake posh accent, Ken said, 'A transfer is the movement of the post to another place. A letter can have all sorts of content when it goes to someone else. When it arrives, it can have many different effects: the receiver of the letter opens it and they have an experience of the contents. In other words, you could say, as a metaphor, that they experience a transfer from someone else. Understand?' Ken's posh accent came undone as he finished. 'Sort of thing… Get it now?'

'Can it really be so simple?'

'All the best ideas are simple, mate. Now roll your sleeves up and help us if you're staying, or go away.'

Percy couldn't understand why everyone sent him away.

'I'll have to sleep on it.'

'Yeah, that's right, off you go. Sweet dreams. Who are you, really?'

Postscript

I will put here a few ideas that give an idea of the theory that is the basis of the above story. My aim is to aid a discussion about the subject. But as I said in the Preface, I don't want to say too much and hinder your free associations. And anyway, what Jim says echoes this paraphrase from the theory of psychoanalysis: transference is a phenomenon that feels real; it is an unconscious projection of feelings a person has about people they have known who remain present in the mind as memories and fantasies. The idea is that, in the transference, long-buried experiences of infancy which have been covered by years of accumulated experiences re-emerge and are experienced as completely real and pertinent to the current situation. For a thorough description of the Freudian view of transference, see Laplanche, J., and Pontalis, J.-B. (1980).

The story above was a simple account of transference, and it is alarming at times how concrete it can feel and become if it is acted out; this is because the experience is so real. It is evidence of the continuing presence of our infantile prototypes, which re-emerge and dominate the new relationship with the analyst.

By 'acting out' we mean that a feeling is acted on instead of being thought about and described in words. The client and or the therapist have a phantasy they do not recognize as such, and believing it to be real, they act on it. This was described by Freud in 1914. We have to remind ourselves that transference and countertransference are fantasies that feel real. Otherwise, an analytical relationship can go badly awry.

References

Freud, S. (1914) Remembering, Repeating and Working-Through (Further Recommendations on the Technique of Psycho-analysis II) SE XII, Hogarth Press and the Institute of Psycho-Analysis

Laplanche, J., and Pontalis, J.-B. (1980). *The Language of Psychoanalysis*, p. 455. London: Hogarth Press and the Institute of Psycho-Analysis.

The next story is an illustration of the problems of acting out feelings, conveyed through a client's thoughts in the moments before the end of her therapy

2

Ravished

———◆———

He met her in his consulting room and they engaged in an analysis, an attempt to understand her performance anxiety. She talked about her suffocating upbringing and the lust-filled eyes of wayward relatives. In adolescence, she had made a break from home.

'I used drugs and sex without limits. I let someone use my body.'

Unwittingly she was her boyfriend's slave. She believed she was free from home but she was shackled by dependence. Painfully, she understood her lust, and her weakness for those rough adventures:

'It was only rebellious fun, until it went too far.'

One day she awoke with her repellent, sleeping abuser in a smelly room, with crusted food and empty bottles strewn about the floor. She felt like shit, and she understood that his perversion was strangling her mind. She'd repeated her childhood experience.

'I got up and left, wearing last night's party dress and high heels, at breakfast time, carrying a plastic shopping bag. People looked at me. I felt ashamed. *Imagine what she did last night... I was a used woman.'*

She tried to rebuild her life, make new friends, but guilt interrupted her development. In therapy, her free words released her from self-blame and disgust. Gratefully, with warm eyes, she met her therapist's gaze.

He thought it was love and forgot 'the transference', that trickster in the consulting room who insists that fantasies are real, and that wishes should come true. Overwhelmed by need, he forgot his role. He searched the internet for her. He checked her birthday and congratulated her. He imagined her in his arms just for a moment. How could that hurt? But this is ridiculous, he told himself, and not what I want. I'm a professional with more important things to think about. However, when she said,

'I think it's time for my therapy to end. You've been so helpful, and listened to me kindly. I've learned a lot about myself, but now I need to move on,' he was forlorn, then gratified by her tears of sorrow. The last day came. He wanted her, but not the responsibility for that act. He didn't move, or maybe he did, but only a bit, perhaps.

'We've been meeting for how long?' she asked.

'Three years.'

'It's gone by so fast. I'm sorry I have to leave. I've had colorful dreams, and shed many tears. I feel as if I've thought more than I'm aware of. I think better of myself and my life is easier to accept, but there is something I haven't said, though I don't know what...'

He said, 'An ending can be like this. Of course, there are regrets and unresolved feelings, it's inevitable. Now our session is over.'

She thought, here we are. In the final moment, he looks sorrowful, I'm sad and grateful. Did he move? Am I looking for that? Does he want to hug me? We've never touched before. Perhaps he wants me to initiate it. It's hardly a crime and I want to be close, to know him in another way. He looks expectant, we share an awkward smile.

Why is this happening now? The story is in the unconscious, he would say. Has this always been our unspoken story? Today is the end of a piece of work, my therapy, and my money. It's his job, a relationship too, but professional, he would say. I'm in his hands, metaphorically at least.

I've wondered about his body under his expensive formal attire. I've had a dream or two about him, maybe three. I'm ashamed. I've never spoken to him about it and he hasn't asked. Does he have dreams about me? Are his little smiles just for me? What do they mean? Does he enjoy fantasies about me? Or does he even know them? What about his unconscious? We've never talked about that. If I hug him, how should it be? Of what intensity? I've a second to decide. If I move, will he move too? A big 'thank you', that's all it is, just once. I'm kidding myself. After a hug, this person will be gone, and there will be a stranger in his place. Do I want another beginning?

I'll give only a brief cheek-to-cheek, with arms lightly around his neck. A sort of hello-and-goodbye hug. Or will it be a goodbye-and-hello hug? I could let my chest touch his, softly. Or shall I push? And what shall I do with my hands? I want to feel his shoulders. I didn't know I had these thoughts, but I felt there was something. No, this fantasy is too much, it's more than a hug. I want to keep this therapy in my soul. I'll shake his hand politely, with thanks. That's the decent thing to do.

He's smiling. What's happening? Does he know my thoughts? He moves towards me. I'm clutching him and pushing back, from head to toe. I'm breathing him in: cologne, sweat, his home, clean clothes. His rough stubble presses against my cheek, his hands slide down my back, over braid and band. They hesitate on my hips, millimeters of fabric separate us: my clothes made in Bangladesh; his suit made in Italy. Ruined.

Postscript

This is a story of the enactment of transference and counter-transference feelings. Transference is described in the first story of this collection and I can summarize the theory of countertransference in the following way: countertransference consists of all the analyst's feelings for the client, including those awakened by the transference. When they are understood, they may give a deeper meaning to the therapy. Freud became aware of the struggle with romantic experiences and wishes in himself, and in his colleagues. He put his thoughts down for the benefit of everyone in a paper called 'Observations on Transference-Love'. 'Our control over ourselves is not so complete that we may not suddenly one day go further than we had intended. In my opinion, therefore, we ought not to give up the neutrality towards the patient, which we have acquired through keeping the counter-transference in check.' (Freud, S. (1915), p. 164) And he encourages his followers to keep their countertransference under control. Otherwise, the patient would have succeeded in acting out what should have been remembered, described, and understood. Freud was clear that an enactment of love wishes by the analyst would be a success for that part of the patient that wants a love affair but she would have lost her analyst and all the work they had done. His paper is well worth reading.

Enactments occur when feelings between the couple in the consulting room are so strong that they block their ability to think. Then action replaces thought. We see in this story that both parties attempt to think but are overwhelmed in the end by feelings that have no words.

The remedy for this situation is for the analyst to insert a thought between a feeling and an action. A feeling is something to be understood and put into words. In this case, the analyst's job was to understand his client's tendency to allow a man to use her, but he appears to have repeated her fantasy in the form of action.

Reference

Freud, S. (1915). *Observations on Transference-Love (Further Recommendations on the Technique of Psycho-Analysis III)*. SE XII. London: Hogarth Press and the Institute of Psycho-Analysis.

The next story plays with the hidden unconscious experiences that may affect conscious action. It may give a helpful insight when you are wondering how the scenario described above could have come to pass.

3
An Unconscious Love Affair

————•————

The following little story is an attempt to illustrate unconscious communication between two people. The unconscious is represented by a person beside each of them who is unwittingly experienced, but not seen.

Doreen worked in a large insurance company. It was a dull place, although many of her colleagues were nice. Her friend Cathy was having an affair with one of the managers.

'Love is like a nice meal, isn't it?' said Cathy.

'There are so many flavors and sex is the dessert,' said Doreen.

'You have to let the hormones have their way. Who is going to stand against them?' they giggled over lunch.

One day, Doreen was alone at lunch. Cathy was busy.

'Is this seat taken?' said Ted from the accounts department.

'No, not at all. Please sit down.' She'd always had a thing for Ted but put it out of her mind, because she knew he had a family too. However, love doesn't always accept civilization's limits.

Unknown to her, her romantic feelings, personified, slid out of her mind and sat in the chair next to her. There, they met Ted's feelings,

19

also displaced from his mind onto the empty chair opposite. Unknown to Doreen and Ted, the two unconscious figures enjoyed a warm and intimate conversation of their own.

Ted and Doreen always took a four-seat table. Soon, they were meeting regularly for lunch. Doreen wondered why none of their colleagues tried to sit with them, as though the seats were taken.

'How are you, Doreen?'

'Fine. Actually, very well.' *Her other self said to Ted's: I'm particularly well, now that I can sit with you even for this brief time.*

'How is the project in your office going?' asked Doreen.

'Excellent. It feels good to be so involved.' *Ted's other self said: it's wonderful to be with you.*

'The soup is nice today. It's rich and warming,' said Doreen.

'My salad is crisp and firm.'

Doreen said, 'When we sit together, I feel empty, as if a part of me is missing.'

'Yes, I too would like to talk about our... sorry, I mean *my* situation. It feels awkward between us at times, but it might be me, of course.'

'I don't know. Life is like this sometimes, isn't it?' said Doreen.

The unconscious aspects of Doreen and Ted wanted to express themselves in another reality. They often tried to get back into the minds and bodies next to them, in order to be amorous. One day, Doreen had an idea, although she couldn't identify the source—not consciously, anyway. Her hormones were running the show for the moment.

At lunch, after their usual, slightly embarrassed, 'Hello, how are you?' Doreen lowered her eyes. 'We are quite reserved and a little awkward with each other, aren't we?' she said. 'I had an idea when I woke up this morning. I don't know where it came from, but it felt like fun to think of it. It's a game and it may lighten the mood.'

'That sounds interesting,' said Ted. His unconscious said: *I will follow you. I am desperate to practice procreation with you.*

Doreen continued. 'Let's pretend we are in an old-fashioned friendship, like in an eighteenth-century novel or something. We'll be reserved and charming, but hint at other feelings.' She looked up into his eyes.

'Just for fun, you mean?'

'Yes. We will keep whatever we say to each other locked in our hearts. It won't change anything at all. Like a kind of romance in the politest form, but not, if you see what I mean.'

Unknown to him, Ted's unconscious pushed back into his mind for a moment and prompted the following response.

'Good idea, I'll start. Doreen, I love you very much, and I have an abiding wish to be intimate with you.'

'Wait a moment. This is supposed to be a slow opening of our souls to each other.'

'Sorry, we'll start again.'

'We can't, you've revealed everything.'

'But I thought we were pretending?'

Indignant, Doreen picked up her lunch tray, and left.

Doreen was now alone at lunchtimes. She regretted the consequence of the game, and resolved to meet Ted if a new opportunity arose, so that she could try to return to their old friendship. However, as we know, relationships remade soon continue from where they left off. A few weeks later, they happened to meet by the only empty four-seater table in the cafeteria. Doreen smiled politely and sat down.

Ted had now put his unconscious out of the way, or perhaps he was simply ignoring it as best he could. He was formal and polite. 'I'm so sorry for the inappropriate language I used last time. Please accept my apology.'

'Yes, of course. It was also my fault. What a relief it was just a game.'

But her unconscious hopped back into her mind for a moment—it's only natural—and prompted the next comment. 'I might have pretended to say the same to you.' She laughed, embarrassed, and composed herself. Her unconscious moved out of her mind and sat on the chair beside her again, opposite Ted's. She went back to her meal as usual. *However, their unconscious figures sitting beside them were delighted to meet again. Their romance flourished like a fertile and unruly garden. They shared their dishes, feeding each other and playing footsie under the table. Sometimes, they leaned forward to kiss.*

Doreen looked forward to lunch with Ted each day, even though the cafeteria menu was hardly outstanding, and she could have eaten elsewhere. One Monday lunchtime, after another weekend of trying to keep him out of her mind, her unknown figure, her unconscious, slipped back into her mind. Then, she found it impossible to resist an inner pressure for fulfilment. She heard herself say, 'I don't know what led you to say that you loved me a while ago?'

The figure from Ted's unconscious, overwhelmed by his hormones, of course, slipped from the chair beside him and back into his mind, to stay. He found himself saying, 'It's always good to have time with you, Doreen. I feel so alive.'

'Yes, I feel like that too.'

Ted pushed his dessert into the middle of the table. Doreen did the same. The bowls of fruit clinked together.

'It feels easier with the truth out in the open,' said Ted.

She let him rest his fingers on hers, and said, 'I feel as if I am kind of agreeing with myself about you. And it's sad, too, because we cannot act on our feelings, but maybe...'

'Are these seats taken?' asked another voice. Two people from the audit department, with lunch trays, stood beside them.

'No, not at all. Please sit down,' said Ted and Doreen together.

'Thank you. Will you be eating those desserts?' asked one of the newcomers. 'They look very good.'

Postscript

We can close our eyes to the things we do not want to see, but it is more difficult to close our hearts to the things we do not want to feel. Although, of course, we can deny them.

What is unsaid in the consulting room may have a powerful effect anyway as the unconscious pushes to be heard, and desire appears to have no limits. What is denied in one arena will find its expression in another. The psychoanalyst Georg Groddeck (1866–1934) was a proponent of the theory that we are lived by our unconscious, or IT, as he called it. (Groddeck, G. (1949)) Indeed, Freud found his idea useful and incorporated it in his thoughts. He pointed out Groddeck's belief in the deep power of the Unconscious, which he called the IT, which lives us, and in his view is unknowable and uncontrollable. (Groddeck) is never tired of insisting that what we call our ego behaves essentially passively in life and that, as he expresses it, we are 'lived' by unknown and uncontrollable forces. (Freud, S. (1923), p. 23)

In the imagery of the above story, the phantasies that the would-be lovers have are denied access to their consciousness because of a wish to be civilized and faithful to existing partners. In other words, those wishes are repressed. However, according to the theory of the unconscious, the erotic wishes do not disappear; on the contrary, they continue to grow and find their expression in another way.

And there are the hormones of course: what do you think about their influence on the unconscious? Although this is a playful story, it is quite important in this collection because it introduces the idea of one unconscious communicating with another, and that is a theme which flows through the three books in one form or another. In addition, I've tried to show that the unconscious of one person is affected by the unconscious of the other.

References

Freud, S. (1923). *The Ego and The Id*. SE XIX. London: Hogarth Press and The Institute of Psycho-Analysis.

Groddeck, G. (1949). *The Book of the It*, London: Vision Press.

The next story is alive with this idea and with the conflict with social values caused by apparently illicit desire...

4

Desire and Longing

———◆———

Hello, and welcome to a weekly radio magazine on love in which we feature people in new relationships. I'm Miranda Evers (M), and today's guests are two women. For professional reasons they prefer not to give their real names. They call themselves Althea (A) and Cathy (C). Welcome to the studio.

A. Thank you. Actually, I think we should use our real names, but we don't agree.

C. We have to think of our children and husbands, not to mention our clients.

M. And you have families?

A. Yes.

M. But you are willing to share your relationship with me—sorry, I mean with the listeners?

C. Yes, absolutely.

M. You released a book this week about desire and longing. It opens with some provocative sentences about love, new love in particular. You say it has a kind of magic about it that can make a

25

person mad. Is it madness? Cathy, can you tell us how you met and how you manage this relationship?

C. Yes, I think I've felt mad at times. But I'd prefer Althea to start; she's mentally better organized than I am.

M. My producer is reminding me to describe you both. Cathy, you're wearing a flower-patterned summer dress, and your blonde hair cascades beautifully over your shoulders—divinely pretty.

C. Thank you.

M. And you, Althea, with your intense black hair in a pageboy cut, are wearing a fitted, light-gray trouser suit and white silk blouse. Strong and elegant. Appropriate to your profession, I imagine.

A. Yes, we are psychotherapists.

C. I thought we weren't going to say that?

M. Cathy, you look surprised by Althea's revelation, but there are many therapists in this city. Why shouldn't a few of them be in love with each other? I mean, it isn't as if it's abnormal.

C. No, all right.

A. In answer to your question, may I quote from our book, to give a sense of the quality of our experience? It's easier to read, I think.

M. Yes, please go ahead. But can you give us some context first?

A. Yes, we met at a conference, as we usually do now, once a year. It's often impossible to be close to each other. I didn't know how she was feeling about us after a long break, and there are always so many people around who we're sure would be critical of our relationship.

C. We both feel the same. It's unavoidable.

M. Thanks. Why don't you read, if you're ready?

A. Actually, you should read it, Cathy, as you are speaking in this piece.

C. I walked towards the train station, and home. My hat was crooked and I could feel rainwater on the back of my neck. I thought my feelings for Althea could never be returned. Then someone touched my right shoulder and a hand slipped under mine, taking the weight of my bag. 'You need some warmth, I believe,' Althea said as she turned me around gently. A taxi was waiting. She opened the back door and nudged me with her hip. I slipped into the back seat of the car, and she followed.

'But I'll miss my train.'

'Then I'll buy you another ticket, later. You'll have to help me now, I don't have my glasses. Can you read out the address on this piece of paper for the driver?'

The car began to move slowly forward.

'I love to hear your voice, it's like music.'

Althea kissed my cheek. I felt afraid and excited. Maybe we could open our hearts to each other after all. She put her arm around my shoulders. Through my winter clothes, I felt the easy fit of our bodies. The taxi driver adjusted his mirror.

M. Well, that's a stomach-tightener—a mysterious rendezvous.

A. We wanted to set the scene by describing a romantic moment.

M. Continue with your thoughts, Althea.

A. I'm a therapist, I'm bisexual, I now realize, and I'm in love with Cathy. Weird? No, we are people, and Cathy is the world to me. We wrote the book because we felt we'd go mad if we didn't have an outlet for our secret experience. And we wanted to offer other people some relief from the loneliness of loving and not being with their loved one.

M. Good therapeutic reasons.

A. Cathy and I are married to other people, and we have children. But you know, in a marriage you live in a capsule of feelings: you love your husband, and your children. Sometimes you stand aside and realize that your soul needs more. You don't love your family less. But you need a person to touch you in another way. It could be a woman or a man.

M. A man?

A. The gender is not important, or the age, or background for that matter, if they catch your soul.

M. That's not me, but go on.

A. When we meet, we are sometimes intimate, but that is not the primary reason for meeting.

M. Wow, I'd be all over her.

C. Please, Miranda, I don't understand. Why are you saying this?

M. Just joking. You sound like my producer.

They looked through the glass wall of the recording/transmission booth. Staring back at them was an unsmiling, dour middle-aged lady with horn-rimmed glasses.

M. Never mind. Please go on, Althea.

A. There's something else, deeper. We think we can manage the conflict of being committed to several hearts at once. But possibly not; maybe our relationship will be torn to pieces by social pressure and guilt.

C. Unless we married each other, of course, and even then, a few people still hold out against reality.

M. Yes, I recognize that.

C. Are you gay?

M. No, yes, I mean, we're here to talk about you. I was agreeing with your point. This is awkward... Tell us how your relationship started.

A. Three years ago we saw each other for the first time. I was having dinner with some friends in the Armenian restaurant, not far from here. Do you know it?

M. Yes, I thought we could all go there afterwards. Sorry, I'm getting a bit involved.

A. As you no doubt know, the restaurant has long tables. The kind you can dance on.

M. Or make love on.

C. Must you? What kind of presenter are you?

M. The naughty kind. This is a pre-recording, so we'll cut a lot out. The producer is nodding—er, no, she isn't. Oh God, we're live.

C. She doesn't look happy.

M. Apologies to our listeners. I'm only joking. Go on, Althea, I'm sure we have a liberal audience.

A. At the other end of our table sat Cathy with her friends. Occasionally, we glanced at each other. Our group left first. I put her out of my mind.

M. And there are your families, of course, you haven't talked about them.

A. Yes, that's right. We've made our choices in life, and stability is paramount. I mean, you can't tear up a safe environment for children because of a chance that something else might work. Call me old-fashioned if you wish.

M. This relationship isn't old-fashioned.

A. At an international conference six months later, we were part of a small group discussion. I don't know who caught whose eye first. Later, on a pretext of discussing a paper, we sat alone, and talked for hours. At some point, I tried to touch Cathy's hand, but she pulled back.

C. Yes, I did, you were too fast. I wanted to be sure it was true.

A. She said, 'No, don't, I don't want to lose you.' I just loved her immediately.

M. Cathy, would you like to come in here?

C. Yes, thanks. After that, there was a slow development. We started writing to one another, and the letters became filled with verbal caresses. We talked about our conflicts of loyalty, and guilt towards our families and colleagues, but our feelings enfolded us. When we meet, we can sit together without talking for ages, each unconscious talking to the other, I suppose.

M. That's something to take in: one unconscious talking to another. I haven't heard that said before. I imagine it's a concept from your profession.

C. Yes, it's worth thinking about. It's the process involved when, for example, two people feel for each other without being conscious of it. But they gradually become aware of the truth as they observe and understand each other.

M. I wonder if it's happening here.

C. Of course, in some way, the unconscious is ubiquitous and a part of every contact between people. But back to our story. We agreed to attend another conference together. We thought it wouldn't seem unusual. Sorry, I seem to be doing all the talking— you carry on, Althea.

A. You don't usually, it's nice to see. It was winter. I arrived in Vienna, the station was crowded, I walked alone through the busy streets. We stayed in separate accommodation for fear of collegial judgment. That night, I lay awake looking at the obscure shapes of furniture in the room, listening to the sounds of the city. I imagined I could feel Cathy's back pressing against me. I wanted her so much. I couldn't eat breakfast. I went out early into the half-light of a gray morning. Maudlin thoughts filled my mind. I wondered if Cathy would attend my funeral.

M. This sounds like another part of your book, both romantic and tormenting.

30

C. Sometimes when I think about her, I feel a terrible emptiness that pulls in my gut.

A. It's mutual; the feelings of longing are almost unbearable.

C. I think we both became depressed, denying our feelings for the sake of everyone else.

A. As I approached the conference building I saw Cathy standing on the edge of a group of friends, her shoulders hunched. Everyone seemed pleased to be there despite the cold. I imagined approaching her from behind and putting an arm around her. As I got closer, feeling was becoming action, it was unstoppable. I knew I would kiss her, in front of everyone.

C. Lucky you didn't.

A. It could have been innocent; people do kiss in friendship.

C. But not like you do it.

M. Oh, that sounds delicious.

C. Miranda, please.

M. What? Sorry, joking. Althea, go on.

A. When the group broke up, you looked around, and gave a brief smile. We saw each other again in the lobby. I was sure everyone knew I was only there to meet Cathy.

C. Yes, I thought others would say things like, 'Look at them, so terrible. It's still a perversion, you know, whatever Freud and the gay lobby say.' Paranoia gripped my throat. In the auditorium, the multitude of voices sounded like an orchestra tuning up.

A. I tried to look around discreetly, pretending to check my cell phone. I think we both heard the presentations without listening. I was trying to plan a move to get physically closer to her.

C. Then, at the coffee break, we could talk to other people and stand back-to-back. But when we faced each other I was speechless.

31

I'm laughing now but it wasn't funny then. It happened again at dinner.

A. Yes, that meal dragged on with jokes and pretend flirtations. I was choking on my food. I messaged Cathy from the table to say 'I'm leaving'. She didn't answer.

C. I couldn't. I didn't want to be seen leaving with you.

M. You are both describing a paranoia that is strangling this relationship. You have no idea what people think. Most of the time we are all wrapped up in our own needs.

C. You sound like the therapist. You are absolutely right, we don't know. Probably no one cares.

A. I imagined we could find reasons to leave. A pair of migraines came to mind, ridiculous and funny.

C. We could have asked if anyone had a tampon.

A. If we got out, I thought we'd surprise a taxi driver with what would happen next.

C. What was going to happen next?

A. Come on, you know.

C. In a cab?

M. You seem to be enviably playful in your relationship.

A. She's teasing me. It was a relief when the other people were dulled by the wine. But we went home separately anyway. In the morning, as I checked my train ticket, I wondered if Cathy's plane had taken off.

C. I wandered around the duty-free store trying to remember which aftershave to buy. At the gate, I wished I'd paid the extra for a fast-track pass.

A. I walked to the station; it was raining again, of course. I looked forward to a big hug with my children, and the routine of my work. We know we may have to give up this relationship. Other people will be hurt if we disappear into each other. Out of love for them, we try to be discreet.

C. Instead of caressing, you mean.

A. Yes, of course that's what I mean.

M. That sounded bitter.

A. Sorry, but it's stressful going over this.

M. How did you ever make a real connection? It's in the book, I think. Can you read it for us, Cathy? It's you speaking, I believe.

C. Of course. *After yet another conference, in which we avoided being seen together, I was alone in my hotel room, shutting off my feelings, packing my bag efficiently. There was a knock at the door. Althea stood outside, her cheeks wet from tears.*

'I was about to call a taxi.'

'Or to be with me,' Althea whispered, moving forward. She put the flat of her left hand against my chest and pushed, pulling the door behind her. It closed with a reassuring clunk. She kicked off her shoes. With her free hand, she loosened her coat, and let it fall to the floor. I was backed into a chair by a small table. She was smiling at me as I sat down.

'I smell coffee,' she said. 'I'll organize it.' As she moved to the kitchen area, I noticed that she glanced at my unmade bed. I felt excited. The cups and percolator clinked. I watched her hips. She turned. 'You're looking at me.'

'Yes, I am.'

Althea returned to the table with the cups, a little coffee in each. 'It's enough for now.'

'I want to see your eyes.'

She leaned forward, her nose almost touching mine. I looked at her soft hazel eyes, and every beautiful eyelash...

M. It's warm in here. I'm glad my producer is laughing too. How can we conclude this without bursting into flames?

A. I've never felt so alive, but in the end it's impossible. The pain of separation is terrible and trying to be normal with the family is a constant strain. I suppose the conclusion is that everyone will get hurt, sooner or later.

C. But, as humans, we strive constantly to fulfil ourselves in all aspects of our sexuality.

A. So we're stuck here, hoping we can turn this into a good friendship.

M. I hope you can, but it's time to end this program, and although I say that with some relief, we wish you every success. Goodbye, listeners. I hope you have enjoyed the insights from these two honest ladies. From all of us in the studio, have a good week. Phew, that was something. Shall we go to the Armenian restaurant?

A. I have to go to a meeting for a while.

C. Yes, I'm not sure. I mean, what are we doing?

M. All three of us could meet up later. My place isn't far from here.

A. I think that sounds complicated.

M. Is this mic on? Oh, fuck. No, God, I've said 'fuck'—live on air.

C. Is that a wish?

The producer raps on the glass wall and Miranda leaves the booth to talk to her. Cathy and Althea can hear an angry exchange.

A. Cathy, seriously... are you going with her?

C. We need to open our relationship.

A. We've lost the opening question about madness. This is a wild suggestion. We shouldn't open it up like this surely?

C. Why not? It's a dream come true.

A. Oh, yes—and whose dream would that be?

Postscript

'So are you to my thoughts as food to life,
Or as sweet-season'd showers are to the ground;' Shakespeare,
Sonnet LXXV

And so does each of the lovers think of the other. And in the whole sonnet is the story of this couple; the love, longing and doubts, that eventually make a relationship untenable.

With regards to sexuality, and contrary to popular belief, Freud did not take a position against homosexuality on moral or medical grounds, as the following quote indicates.

'Homosexuality is assuredly no advantage, but it is nothing to be ashamed of, no vice, no degradation, it cannot be classified as an illness.' (Freud, S. (1935))

Regarding this story, to be overwhelmed by passion has its joys, as everyone knows, but passion may be short-lived if friendship does not have a central place in the relationship. Shakespeare understood this and he puts in into words with Friar Laurence's speech in *Romeo and Juliet*. He admonishes Romeo and Juliet to love with moderation, and points out that the love that lasts does not go forward with haste. 'Therefore, love moderately. Long love doth so.

Too swift arrives as tardy as too slow.' (Shakespeare, *Romeo and Juliet*, Act 2, Sc 6, ll. 13-14).

Another person's desire is not the same as their love. It does not mean that they value us and, if we are not loved back, despite strong wishes for the other person, we will suffer.

In this story, conscience in both ladies forms their behavior and, in the end, it shows that their relationship is unsustainable.

A question about this story: where is the depression that belongs to a situation like this? We should expect both Cathy and Althea to experience considerable suffering, accepting that their relationship cannot go on, or at least must be only a friendship. This is masked in the story by the excitement of Miranda, who is intoxicated by the sensuality described in Cathy and Althea's relationship. However, she, too, will have to give up her wishes, and experience sadness that she cannot be part of their world. Every time we give up something we have to tolerate the emotional consequences of a loss. A certain depression is normal and healthy in mourning. It is unhealthy when it turns inward and inhibits creativity. (Freud, S. (1917)) He illustrates the difference by pointing to the self-hate that characterizes what we call a destructive depression, and he calls melancholia.

References

Freud, S. (1935). *Letter from Sigmund Freud to Anonymous, April 9 1935. Letters of Sigmund Freud 1873–1939*, pp. 423–424. Ernst, L. Freud (Ed), Basic Books 1961

Freud, S. (1917). *Mourning and Melancholia*. SE XIV. London: Hogarth Press and The Institute of Psycho-Analysis.

And what happens when expectations of love and the longing to be desired are frustrated, even temporarily? What depression awaits? The next story illustrates a teenager's reaction to such a situation...

5

An Expectation Frustrated

———◆———

'Do you want to go to the pictures on Thursday?' asked Joe, Tracy's new boyfriend. 'I'll be there by five-thirty, and the film starts at six, OK?'

That was a few days ago. Now, sixteen-year-old Tracy was standing outside the Odeon, wearing new jeans and a tight sweater. Also, especially for the occasion, new, floral-patterned, matching underwear. Her hair looked lovely, and her make-up was discreet but effective. Tracy was in love; she arrived on time, at five-thirty.

17.40: 'Where is he? Where is he?' Tracy moved from foot to foot in the cool April breeze. She thought of his warm body and remembered the nice things they had done together, things they had laughed at, how he had touched her. Each memory brought a tingle of delight; something good stayed within her soul. She tried to be like him and enjoy what he enjoyed. She had changed toothpaste to his brand so that she could taste him when he wasn't with her. He now drinks her kind of tea!

When they lie together, forehead-to-forehead, they sometimes doze off.

They are lying in the deep forest. She is his princess; he is her knight in shining armor. From time to time they hear the cries of evil creatures in the distance. She feels safe with him as long as his armor gleams. But what if it lost its shine?

'He's the most loving bloke I've ever had,' said Tracy.

'Of how many?' asked her friends.

'Not so many, but he touches me softly, and he looks at me, really looks.'

'You're joking,' said her friends. 'We know Joe, lovely Joe with the—'

'Shut it, you're just jealous. He's better than my last bloke, anyway.'

'All right, all right, just saying.'

'Well, fucking well keep it to yourself. He's mine and he's perfect.'

'Oooh…'

Tracy looked at her phone: ten minutes to six. What if he was late? 'Don't think it. It's not possible,' she said aloud. 'He'd rather die. I know him better than his mother.'

Another wonderful memory crossed her mind: their first kiss. The memory dispelled all doubt.

17:55: *He'll be here any second*, she told herself, looking down the road again. Wouldn't it be wonderful if he came right at this moment?

On the cinema steps, two contradictory thoughts were coming together, and Tracy couldn't tell them apart: the wonderful idea of the perfect lover who never frustrates, and the disappointments of an ordinary boyfriend with human failings.

17:58: *But he said he would be here on time. He promised.* She checked her cell phone again.

38

17:59: *Will we be in the cinema this evening?* she wondered, as she felt tears filling her eyes. *How will this evening end?*

The church clock opposite the cinema struck six times. When it stopped, the silence was crushing. Her stomach felt empty.

18:02: Perhaps the train was late. He lives a bit outside town, after all. Could there be another girl? No. Maybe someone was sick on the train and he's helping them, so he can't use his cell.

18.08: He would never do this to her deliberately, surely. Or was he a complete bastard?

18.12: Did he think she was smothering him? Perhaps he wanted more space. *Please don't let it be that.*

By six-thirty, Tracy had been standing on the cinema steps for fifty minutes, thinking back to the times they had shared and becoming despondent. Some of the passers-by knew her and said hello. She felt humiliated. She couldn't answer.

Fuck it. She decided to walk home. At the first junction, on the opposite side of the road, she saw a couple holding hands. Momentarily she was lost in good memories, even as she felt jealous of them.

For an absentminded moment she was back in the dark forest. Her prince's armor was not shining any longer. Dark creatures from the depths were crawling forward towards her and Joe. She was no longer his princess.

The pedestrian light was green but she didn't walk. The cool April breeze awoke her to where—and why—she was. The light changed. It was red again, and she started to walk. A car hooted. She jumped back in alarm. 'I hate him,' she shouted. 'No, not you, just go!' The driver shook his head and drove on.

Tracy felt even more stupid. 'I'd like to cut him up,' she muttered, an uncomfortable rush of adrenalin accompanying her dark passion.

'Damn him.' The light turned green. She ran across the road. 'I'll get him. He'll suffer.'

She'd go and see her friend Magda. They'd help themselves to her mum's booze. They'd drink until they were plastered. *But then I'll just feel worse.* She decided to go home after all.

As she approached her house, she saw the flickering blue-and-white light of the TV through the window. Maybe her parents would go to the pub later. They could take her too, those friendly faces, pleased to see her and smiling pleasantly. As she went indoors, her stomach tightened in anticipation of her parents' questions. She opened the living-room door. The welcoming warmth of the hearth fire enveloped her, and her rage subsided for a moment.

'Hello, love, everything all right?' asked her mum without turning from the TV.

That's odd, thought Tracy, *they're usually more interested.* 'Joe didn't turn up. I stood outside that bloody cinema in the freezing cold for fifty minutes and now I am really pissed off.' Tears welled in her eyes.

'Oh, what? That's a shame. Joe was here all the time. The train was late. He said something about a signal failure, and his phone died. He's had a bad day. He thought you'd be here.'

Tracy was speechless.

'Jack, Jack, are you listening?' said Tracy's mum.

Jack turned from the TV. 'What?' He looked at his wife, then at the door. 'Oh, hello Tracy, did you get the message from Joe?'

'No, she didn't. How could she?' said her mother. Turning to Tracy, she said, 'I told him to get in touch with you an hour ago.'

'Why couldn't Joe...? Never mind... Where is he, my so-called boyfriend? I'll kill him.'

'Oh no, dear, you shouldn't do that, he's very tired.'

'It's a bit of a cock-up,' said Tracy's dad.

'Jack, language! She's your daughter.'

'Sorry, we can go to the pub if you like, girl.'

'She doesn't want to go to the pub now, do you, dear?' said Mum, turning back to the TV. 'She's got other things to sort out. I sent Joe up to your room to rest, love.'

Tracy bounded up the stairs, angry and relieved. 'We'll go to the pub later. I don't care how tired he is.'

She was Joe's princess once more, but he had a lesson to learn about how princesses combine with angry creatures to become real people.

The bedroom door banged against the wall as Tracy swept through. Joe woke up. Tracy struggled to pull her new tight sweater over her head.

Joe yawned. 'I like the floral print.'

'Help me get this off, or you're double-dead. You're a bloody idiot, like my dad.'

She threw herself down on her occupied bed.

Postscript

In the Shakespeare play *Romeo and Juliet*, as the couple separate for the first time, Juliet asks Romeo to keep in contact with her 'Art thou gone so, love, lord? Ay, husband, friend,/ I must hear from thee every day in the hour,/ For in a minute there are many days.' (*Romeo and Juliet*, Act III Sc, 5, ll, 42-44). A meditation on that last line could go a long way in a discussion on the subject of separation and loss. For example, what do babies notice and feel during an absence of the mother, however brief?

Absence makes the heart grow fonder, or so the saying goes, if it doesn't cause the relationship to collapse because the separation is too long. In this case, the difference between the time when Tracy expected to see Joe and their real meeting wasn't so long. But, as Juliet says above, a minute can feel like days when one is in a state of longing for relief from pain, or for the presence of a loved one.

To be furious with a partner is a part of the love–hate dynamic of every durable relationship. In Shakespeare's Sonnet CXVI he makes the point that love is enduring and does not change because there is a temporary upset in communication. 'Love is not love which alters when it alteration finds.' It is worth reading in full.

In the next story, we see the negative effects of the hunger for love…

6

Bungalow Days

———•———

I'm a psychotherapist and, a few months ago, a young guy came to see me. He arrived early for his appointment and, when I opened the door, he rushed past me into the house.

'It's straight ahead, is it?' He sounded out of breath. Before I could answer, he'd gone into the consulting room and sat down.

'Never mind about my name or address, I'll tell you later. I live one minute at a time. I have to tell you my story—now.'

'Good morning, you're sitting in my chair.'

'Sorry, sorry,' he said, and moved to the alternative chair. He wore a bright green T-shirt and jeans, and his hair was unbrushed. His eyebrows were raised, and his eyes wide. He reminded me of a four year old who has rushed home from his playgroup to relate astounding news about another child who had done something shocking, like eating an earthworm—a live one.

'I've moved home because I lost the love of my life. She left last year. Now I'm tearful again, sorry. Tissues? Oh, here beside me, thanks. Why did she leave me? Am I boring, or clingy, or too romantic? I don't think so.'

43

'Are you able to slow down a little?'

'Can't keep up? It's your job. I advertised for a house exchange and took the first thing I saw, a suburban bungalow in need of renovation. I know it sounds like social suicide to leave a fashionable part of town, but it was necessary to make a break.

'The bungalow owners had been hoarders. They died by suicide pact, after the local council threatened to clear the house because of the health risk. They drank all the booze in the house and took all the pills they could find at the same time. Because they never threw anything away, there were quite a lot. Pills, I mean, and everything else of course. Their children wanted to be rid of the property. Maybe they were depressed too, or ashamed, or both.'

'Are you ready to tell me who you are?'

'Yes. No. Later.'

'The house needed a lot of work: a new roof, damp-proofing of the walls, and it stank. Rats ran through the rubbish, which filled the rooms and corridors from floor to ceiling. I invited the local history society to go through the house: they were delighted and took loads of old stuff.'

'It sounds like the house is a mirror of your feelings. Is that why you're giving me details, to inform me about you?'

'Yes, hmm, interesting, you read that in a book, did you? To continue, in the middle of the back garden, in front of a fishpond, stood an ageing caravan. It was the only uncluttered living space, so I moved in there. I began to feel better as I worked on the renovation. I knew I was running away, but I didn't care.

'On my free days, away from my work in an IT company, I helped the builders. One cold, rainy morning, I walked to the front of the house with an armful of ripped wallpaper to throw in the rented container. I used seventeen containers, you know. At the nearby bus stop, I saw a young woman sitting on a suitcase. She appeared to be crying, so I walked over and talked to her.'

'The next bus won't be here for some time, and it's raining. Can I help you?'

'No, I'm fine. But thank you.'

'OK, but if there is anything, I'm working in the house over there. I am just going to make some tea. I'll go back to work.'

'Actually, I'm not fine. My name is Maria.'

'And I'm Simon.'

'Maria and I sat in the caravan for the afternoon, drank tea, and ate bread and jam. Her aroma was lovely. I suppose we were both desperate for kindness and tenderness. She told me her story.'

'I went to a house up the road this morning.' She pointed, actually the wrong way, but it didn't matter. *'The people had advertised for someone to rent a room. This is the right area for me and my job. I stood on the doorstep, with my suitcase and stuff. I know it's a lot to have with me but I'm desperate. My partner hits me. I don't want to live with him any more. I took everything I could carry. I've nowhere to love, I mean live.'*

'We both smiled at her slip of the tongue, and she continued.'

'When they opened the door, the man said, "Oh, you're…"'

'Black, I said. He wasn't smiling. He closed the door. Through the ill-fitting letter box, I heard a whispered conversation. The door opened again. A short lady with a tight mouth said, "Sorry, the room is taken, by a white girl… uh, I mean another girl." She shut the door. I started

crying. After a few minutes, I gathered my stuff and walked away. I sat at the bus stop. I don't know where I'm going.'

'You're here now, and soon, as luck would have it, I'll have a room to rent.'

'Can I trust you. Are you sincere?'

'The bungalow has three bedrooms. I need to rent out one of them, to help with the bills. I'd also like the company; I'm alone, you see.'

'What happened to you, then?'

'I'd rather not talk about it please, it really hurts. My partner left my old house. So I moved. I'll tell you more later, maybe.'

'OK. But tonight, can I sleep here, please?'

'It depends how you feel. We're sitting on the only bed. I use the other parts of the caravan for storage. We can divide the bed down the middle with a rolled-up blanket. The house will be ready in a few days, I'm sure.'

'She smiled, and I wondered if we were sharing romantic thoughts. I should have been more careful. Later that afternoon, I continued work in the bungalow and she organized her things in the caravan. Later, we went to the local pub for a meal and a few drinks—The Green Man, do you know it?'

'No, I...'

'Maria and I chatted, and laughed, it was nice. Back in the caravan, we undressed discreetly, not easy in a caravan, and went to bed. Neither of us had made too much of how big the rolled-up blanket between us had to be. We were both restless. Rain pattered on the old caravan roof. With unseen smiles, in our fiberglass-and-fabric cocoon, we heard the chatter of the drops of water. Within a few minutes, her arm touched mine, I stroked her back, her foot slid up my calf. Silently, we conspired to remove the blanket obstacle and lay entwined, warm against the cold, damp world outside. We murmured and caressed, in a wordless union. Weary after the day's events, we slept. A little later, we woke again and came together, more impassioned. We knew we'd started an undying love. We had always been one. We needed no words.

'At some point in the early afternoon we had breakfast, and drank coffee, looking into each other's eyes. To the apparent embarrassment and excitement, I believe, of the builders, we shared the newly restored shower in the bungalow. The following day, we both had to go to work and survive a nine-hour separation. My work colleagues were delighted to see me in good humor again. Over the next few days, struck dumb by love, Maria and I fitted smoothly together in every activity. What one had missed, the other did. We were a duo in the caravan, preparing for our new life in the bungalow, which didn't seem boring any more. After some sublime days, it was ready. The interior was simple and elegant, made for a new beginning; our previous partnerships were forgotten, apparently. I came home from work to the longed-for change of residence. Maria's stuff wasn't in the caravan. I felt put out; I'd assumed we'd move in together but, as usual, we hadn't talked about it. On the bed was a note. I have it here. I'll read it to you.

'*My dearest darling Simon,*

Our heavenly journey is taking a new course, inward, a reminiscence.
I've been in contact with my ex-partner.
After a long conversation he has apologized profusely.
He has promised me another life.
I know him best and we talk, a lot.
He needs me in ways you do not.

I've moved back to him.
Forgive me, Simon.
You must know that I'll always love you, inside, forever.
These days are now a heavenly memory.
I hope you will have a good life filled with the kindness you
have shown me.
All my love,
your Maria

'How could she think he needs her more than I do? I was so furious that I rushed outside, picked up a heap of waste paper lying in the garden and stuffed it into the caravan's narrow entrance. I threw in some turpentine from the painting equipment and lit it. Our love nest was soon ablaze. Flames rushed into the sky. I stood in front of the caravan's gas tank in the hope that it would blow up. It just fizzed. Desperate, I jumped into the inferno. The pain was excruciating. I awoke from my suicidal fantasy, leapt out through the burning back wall and landed face down in the fishpond. The water helped reduce the pain, but I couldn't die.

'A neighbor called the emergency services. By the time they turned up, there was not much left. I was still in the fishpond trying to drown myself. I spent a few days in hospital, and was given a psychiatric assessment. They decided I'd been "temporarily disturbed by recent personal stresses". They recommended me to you.

'I couldn't stand being alone in the bungalow, so I went back to work. I cried a lot, which annoyed my work colleagues. They were nice to me and finally I was feeling something real. I cried copiously over Maria, she who, in the end, dumped me. They were sympathetic, although some people thought I was tedious.'

As the therapist, I thought I should interject. 'It sounds as if, like the previous owners of the house, you've failed to mourn. You've tried to hide your previous sorrow in a renovation and a new romance.'

'Another book you've read, is it? For God's sake, let me finish. Now, I have to make the best of my bungalow. I like being near the countryside. I've found a new guest for my extra room on a university student lodgings website. She's a studious girl. We're friendly, and we talk. It's nice to have female company.

'I've come today because something ironic has salted my wound. It also gives me sadistic satisfaction, and I don't like that in myself. Last week, I read in the local newspaper that a white man had beaten up his partner. They had recently reunited after previous violent episodes. The boyfriend is now in prison. She lies comatose in hospital. I checked: it is Maria. I can't tolerate the memories of the lovely times we had, now wrecked, possibly forever. I hate myself for gloating over her misfortune. That's why I'm here. Can you help me?'

I took a deep breath.

Postscript

Simon lost his love and had to find another as soon as possible to reduce the pain of his loss. He took the first house he could find in exchange for his own 'social suicide', which he repeats in reality when he loses a woman again. He took the first person he saw in the same emotional state as himself and, because she was also in need of care and consolation, he wanted her even more. By loving her, he could give love to the sad, lonely, unwanted part of himself. Was that his unconscious motive for getting involved with Maria?

49

And Maria's situation is similar to his, which is why they don't need words: they see themselves in each other.

And this is a manifestation of mania. Mania is a defense against pain and depression when a loved person is felt to be missing and lost forever. It involves denial, which is omnipotent, and any alternative love object is idealized and clung to. And mania is what our main character is suffering from. His love life is empty, and as we know there is nothing that takes the taste out of life quite like unrequited love.

And keep in mind—as I said in the Preface—that every story has secrets that even the writer is unaware of. In other words, the story will speak to you.

The next story shows one person's alternative solution to his separation anxiety...

7

A Muse in Paddington Station

———•———

In Brunel and Wyatt's splendid Victorian railway station, built long before computer-aided design—what an achievement—I sit in a cafe, on an August evening. I'm admiring the symmetry of the ironwork-and-glass roof, eating a donut, and watching travelers. People in transit crowd the concourse, making journeys from one unknown place to another. What's their future? How was their past? In my loneliness, I relish the painful feeling of being excluded from their lives and the constant changes in the scene.

Strange? Masochistic? Of course. I rest my eyes on an attractive person and feel at ease in her imaginary presence. Unwittingly, she gives me a moment's relief from my anxiety. She looks at the departure notices, lifts her bag, and walks away. I follow her with my eyes, but she's gone, and sadness envelops me until the next interesting person comes into view.

Depression, anxiety, infatuation, and excitement: are they cousins in a destructive internal army? They seem to use the same chemical weapons that burn my interior without mercy. They're involved in many an emotional ambush: the feeling that I have an exam the next day or of waiting for a loved one to arrive or phone. And like a gang of ruffians, they're inevitably present after a separation, pulling at my insides with unseen hands. Sometimes, for a moment, I forget my love has gone, but one of those characters is around the next corner waiting to hit me with memories that will set fire to my extremities. I've no idea how that experience has become so delicious.

'Is this seat taken?' says a female voice.

'No. Please.'

'Thanks. Warm day today, wasn't it?'

'It is, I mean was, yes.'

'I see you're writing; I'll be quiet.'

'Thanks.'

Sitting a meter from me is a young woman in a white cotton shirt. I can inhale her breath. She strikes me as being considerate, and charming; indeed, even the way she crunches her crisps is endearing. Adrenalin speeds through me and I feel unsteady, as though I'm falling off my chair. A new love is offering me another life. I'm flying, but will I crash? She slurps her iced cola adorably, and I want her with me, always. She looks at my notebook; she smiles. I lament the Christmases we never spent together, the birthdays, the holidays by the seaside. All I've ever wanted is to be with her. I see it clearly in my fantasy. What am I doing to myself with this tsunami of longing? She speaks…

'Hi, I'm Tracy. Sorry, but I'm a compulsive chatterbox, me. What are you writing about, anything interesting?'

'Oh yes, sorry, I'm Gordon. Pleased to meet you.'

'Unusual name these days. What are you writing about?'

'Yes, it was my mother's choice. And nothing.'

'Nothing? You're a philosopher then, are you?'

'No, I'm just doodling with words.'

'I like doodles, can I see?'

'Er, well… I suppose… No, if you don't mind. The notebook is a bit private.'

'All right, suit yourself.'

Now she takes up one of those plastic rice pots with a fruit flavoring in a side compartment: Tutti-Frutti. She's that, all right. She's having trouble with the foil top: shall I help? No, she's done it. Slowly, she mixes red jam with the white rice.

'What are you thinking about?'

'Nothing.'

'There's a lot of nothing in your life, ain't there?'

'I suppose.'

'You suppose! You're a funny one, ain't yah?' She spoons a small amount of rice into her mouth. 'How did she cope?'

'Who? Cope with what?'

'Your mum. How did she cope with nothing in your life?'

I feel exposed and embarrassed. I can't speak, so I try to continue with my writing. I'm distracted as Tracy eats her snack: how delicious she is, a perfect, un-botoxed person. When she disappears from my sight, she'll do things unknown to me, but familiar to her. I hope each of us will wonder what the other is doing. My lungs will fill with air, my heart will beat, she'll breathe out, her eyes will see what I cannot. Perhaps she has work to do, or someone to meet, a child to collect and cuddle, a kindness to offer a partner. But she's with me right now, and soon we'll embrace with our eyes.

'You look very involved for someone thinking about nothing. What are you writing? Come on, let me look, please. I want to see what nothing looks like.'

Her laugh is so intoxicating that I let the notebook slip into her beautiful hands. She reads silently, seriously. What have I done?

'Who are you writing about? Have you been writing this now? You have, haven't you?' She looks into me with an investigative eye. I didn't know she could be like this. I lower my head.

'You don't know me—or anyone here. It's random people you look at, ain't it? That's what gets you off, but they're what you make them, you say it yourself. If you climbed into my life right now, what would happen?'

'I'm not answering that.'

'What about all the friends you'd have to meet, the new family, voices, accents, tastes, other people's habits—no laughing matter—or the jealousies? What's it got to do with you how I eat my fucking crisps, you bastard? And what's this about Tutti-Frutti? "The virgin white rice and the blood-red jam." Fuck off.'

Ouch, that really hurt. She's disappearing in front of me. 'I'm not answering that either. Leave my fantasy alone.'

'With me, you'd have to commit totally, or risk leaving scars behind, as you make your humiliating exit. No, come to think of it, you wouldn't leave any scars, but you'd be carrying a few, believe me, Gordon.'

I nod furiously, hoping to assuage the ire of my recently intended, who is now blowing reality over me. I wish I could explain that it isn't her as she is now, obviously. Although I think she's understood that. The first feeling at a new meeting is the one I want. Followed by the sense of being left out of something better; so much richer, warmer, desirable.

'Are you stealing feelings from me, is that your game?'

'It has to be like that. We can never meet again.'

'You've got something right—finally.'

'But I'll have the burning, tingling pain of regret. There's a flash mob of potential but impossible partners in the station all the time. They attract me and briefly calm my soul.'

'What potential have you got then, Gordon? Have you got any at all, do you think?'

The way she's looking at me is definitely aggressive, and I don't want the rest of her Tutti-Frutti over me. 'In this station, there are so many beautiful structures—I mean *people*—to admire and never possess. They live far away, in unknown places.'

'You'd like to phone one of them though, wouldn't you?'

'I suppose.'

'You suppose? And she'd be there on the end of the line, with no idea of what's going on, and you'd like to ask her if you could meet and, if so, would she be the same as when you saw her at the station? That's what you mean, ain't it?'

I nodded.

'I think you might be a bit bonkers. Whoever she is, she's probably got someone, and it might be another girl. Ever thought about that?'

'That's the beauty of it. Someone else has the privilege of being her love, and I can suffer being left out.'

'There's something you want in everyone, isn't there? Especially when you decide who they're with.'

'Yes, I suppose that's accurate.'

'You suppose? I see you've eaten a donut.'

'It's my second, actually, they're good here.'

'So, you're a greedy little Mummy's boy? And who took her away from you? If you were anything to do with me, God forbid, I'd definitely knock this out of you, sunshine.'

I smiled; she didn't.

'Bye, Gordon. Don't wince, I'm not going to hit ya. You're a sad case.'

Tracy walks towards a platform. Another person approaches her, they embrace, link arms, and continue walking, and which train is standing there? The night train to Penzance. So romantic, could it be better? My pain is terrible and exquisite. I'm out of their lives, completely. I'll never reach them, even in my dreams, although my thoughts about them are eternal.

The next bearer of a new life comes into view, with an Icelandic flag on her backpack. Warm feelings well up from the deep.

Postscript

Carson McCullers, in her book *The Ballad of the Sad Café* (McCullers, C. (1951)) describes the experience of hidden love and forbidden love when she describes a character who is in love but must hide it. She describes her character as creating an inner world where the secret is cherished. This is what Gordon has done: he lives in his own world, recreated over and over each time he loses one person and finds another. However, there is always a triangle that he cannot avoid: the other person has a life that he is not a part of. And in the story, we see a hint that that is how his problem began: Tracy wonders if his mother gave more attention to someone else.

A repetition of some excitement related to frustrated love and desire is illustrated above, but did you see anything else? It is not unusual to replace the suffering related to separation with another symptom that is felt to be more manageable. For example, a fear of traveling instead of confronting the pain of loss. If we cannot experience legitimate suffering, then we will be ill with other complaints.

In our infancy, we all develop ways of approaching love and hate which we repeat in later life. When a child has intense expectations for love, and a repetitive need for the provider of that love, it suffers from anxiety over and above the normal. Gordon is reliving this painful situation by repeating it in adult life. We carry our infant with us and that small person inside demands to be comforted. If we lose our love, we are defenseless against suffering.

Reference

McCullers, C. (1951). *The Ballad of the Sad Café*. Boston, MA: Houghton Mifflin.

The next story illustrates the efforts of a small group to counter the frustrations of triangular love by using a creative solution to their needs for satisfaction…

8

Triangular Love— The Problem of Three

———•———

Oliver and two friends, Ilse and Raj, were standing on the steps of the local priest's house at four o'clock in the morning. They rang the bell again and again.

'Let's go,' said Raj.

'We're not giving up that easily,' replied Ilse. 'You're the same in bed. Come on, be a man.'

'But I'm Oliver's boy.'

'You're not. Stop being so gay. You're a fake.'

'No, I'm not a fake. Anyway, Oliver says he likes my skin better than yours.'

'If we are going to have a baby that's shared three ways, you'll have to do manly things to me. Just be clear about that.'

The safety chain rattled as the front door opened and a tired lady of about forty stood before them, wearing a white linen nightgown. 'I hope there's good reason for a call at this time of night.'

'We want to talk to the priest,' said Ilse.

'I'm one of the priest's housekeepers. I'm Sister Mary Rose.'

'That's novel, a nun in a priest's house!' said Oliver.

'It's not unusual. There's another Sister here, too.'

'Three of you?' asked Raj.

'Yes.'

'Fortunately, we want to talk about that,' said Oliver.

She gave a generous yawn. 'I had to get out of a warm bed.'

'We've not been to bed yet, so it isn't so bad for us,' said Raj.

'Well, I never, how nice for you all. Come in then. I hope this is serious.'

'Absolutely,' they choroused.

'Come in! You can sit here in the visitors' parlor while I get him out of bed—I mean, knock on his door, silly me. It may take a few minutes; we're not used to visitors at this hour.'

After a time, during which they heard mumbled protests from further inside the house, the priest appeared, trying to fix his clerical collar. Sister Mary Rose followed him, fussing to help. He pushed her hand away.

'This is Father O'Malley,' she said as she left the room. Through the door, they heard her say, 'What are you doing out of bed? Come now and help me in the kitchen. Stop arguing.'

The priest looked at the door. 'You can ignore that. What do you want at this unholy hour? I hope it concerns a death, or a serious illness at least?'

'We'd like to get married,' said Oliver. 'We're trying to solve an old problem.'

'Who wishes to get married? There are three of you. And which old problem are you referring to? Perhaps there are several?'

'Yes, we know, that's the point. We want to be married to each other. We've heard stories about how difficult it is for three people in a love relationship. We want to make this relationship function, so we thought that if we make vows before God, it might help.'

Father O'Malley cast a glance at the door. 'That sounds a little naive, if you don't mind me saying. Sometimes it's a possibility, but not in your case. Anyway, who's going to be intimate with whom? Do you follow?'

'Yes, we follow. We're young and curious,' said Ilse, 'and we're people first, genders second.'

'And what do you mean by that, young lady?'

'She means,' said Oliver, 'that we love each other equally, and who is with whom at any given moment isn't relevant. We share each other.'

'And what did you think about the children of this arrangement?'

'I will grow them, and they will help me get them started.'

'But who will be the legal father?'

Ilse sighed.

Oliver continued, 'One of us two, me and Raj here, will inseminate Ilse, by chance of course. I mean we'll never know whose sperm made the connection.'

'I will,' said Raj, looking wistfully at Oliver.

'Stop it! Oliver, tell him, he's not to keep on saying that. I'm supposed to get it all.'

'Disgusting. Is this really your plan?'

'It will have a symmetrical beauty: there will be no competition because we won't know who the father is. We'll share the mother with the baby. So, we avoid the father's competitive relationship with the baby, and the mother will have enough,' said Oliver.

'Enough what?'

'Enough of people,' said Raj. 'She'll have plenty of men.'

'And you know all about that,' said Ilse.

'But it sounds like there's a competition between the three of you already. Have you been in a situation like this before?'

'No, but we've read all about the Oedipus story that applies to everyone and we want to try to avoid those consequences,' said Oliver.

'I'm sure we'll work it out,' said Raj.

'It's an old myth and has nothing to do with life as it is,' said Father O'Malley, looking at the floor. 'The church and religion are the eternal reality. What you're saying is naive, inappropriate, and outrageous!'

There was a knock on the door. Sister Mary Rose and a sisterly companion came into the parlor. She, too, was wearing a flowing linen nightgown, which gave them a matching angelic quality.

'This is my other housekeeper, Sister Mary Annunciation.'

They each carried a tray bearing tea, milk, honey, and a plate of buttered toast, partly covered by a white kitchen towel.

'We thought you might need some comfort in difficult circumstances,' said Sister Mary Rose, 'to soften the pains of life. Reality isn't easy, is it?'

The trios looked at each other.

'Quite unacceptable,' muttered the priest, looking at the fully laden trays.

'Not at all, Father,' said Sister Mary Rose, 'the tea is fresh, and the toast is warm under the cloth, as you like it.'

Postscript

This story takes a humorous look at an unlikely situation. A priest with two women and a triangular relationship, the members of which want a three-way marriage. According to the Oedipal story, the child, believing itself to be left out of the parents' relationship, wants to join in on equal terms. *What is good for the goose is good for the gander* is an old English expression. And in this story, the children, represented by Ilse, Oliver, and Raj, are saying, 'If mother and father can be satisfied with an alternative solution, why can't we?' The three friends are trying to avoid the feeling of competition and of being left out of something nice by marrying in a triangle; the priest recognizes that it will not work, although he seems to be in a similar situation.

Is the Oedipus complex universal? The child's exclusion from the parents' sexual relationship is a painful reality for the child, and, according to Freud, the analysis of clients' Oedipal complexes via the transference and countertransference relationship is the central task of psychoanalytic psychotherapy. '…the Oedipus complex is the nuclear complex of the neuroses, and constitutes the essential part of their content. It represents the peak of infantile sexuality, which, through its after-effects, exercises a decisive influence on the sexuality of adults. Every new arrival on this planet is faced by the task of mastering the Oedipus complex; anyone who fails to do so falls a victim to neurosis.'

(Freud, S. (1905), footnote added in 1920, on p. 226)

Do you agree with Freud's idea?

Reference

Freud, S. (1905). *Three Essays on the Theory of Sexuality*. SE VII. London: Hogarth Press and The Institute of Psycho-Analysis.

In the next story, we move to something more painful, the enactment of destructive Oedipal wishes across the generations through incest and the effect of that trauma on one person's creativity...

9

Sandra's Wish

---◆---

In the following story the italics represent Sandra's unknown inner world, represented by her dreams and unconscious phantasy.
Sandra is the narrator of her story. The single therapy interview described is a metaphor for a long therapy.

∽

*O*ne of the small children in Sandra's room climbed onto her bed and said, 'You're going to talk today, and make us real.' Another indistinct figure disturbed these warm images. Dark, ghostly, threatening, it rubbed up against her. She felt dirty.

I woke up with a throbbing head and dry mouth. Gray light seeped through the grubby drapes. I dozed. I thought of my first flight in an airplane. It took an age to rise through the mist. I was surprised to find a sunny day above the clouds.

The dark and flowing figure, which looked like Sandra's grandad, expanded until it filled the room. The children receded, and the dark figure whispered, 'Silence.'

A bony body turned over in the bed and pressed against me. I didn't want to look. Was it someone from the pub? Kev, or Jack? I nudged whoever it was and said, 'You're too rough.' I got up and grabbed my dressing gown.

'Sandra, that needs a wash.'

'I like my smell.'

'That's just as well, isn't it?'

'You're in my bed.'

'You needed the company.'

'You took what you wanted.'

'Maybe.'

'A woman knows, Kev, or is it Jack? I can't see properly; my eyes haven't focused yet.'

I went downstairs to the bathroom behind the kitchen. The floor was cold, but the warm water that drenched my hair was a comfort. I remembered my appointment today with a therapist. Would it make a difference? I'll talk, his sad eyes will observe me, and he'll say, 'Hmm, that was difficult for you.' I'll weep, and he'll push the tissues towards me. I'll get a bill—for what? Tissues? I wrapped a towel around my head.

In the kitchen, I found two half-cleaned mugs. I put a heaped teaspoon of instant coffee and two of sugar in each, then filled them from the hot water tap. The milk was out of date, but fuck it. Small lumps of undissolved coffee floated on the surface of each overfilled mug. I took some aspirin with a sip from both mugs.

My hands were full, and my towel was slipping over one eye, but I managed the stairs. I pushed the bedroom door open with my hip. 'Kev, you'd better get up, I'm going.'

'I'm Jack. Get to the optician.'

'It's too early to see last night's sin.'

'Cynic. This coffee isn't hot.'

'That's OK. You've got to drink up fast anyway, I'm going soon.'

'You made it from the bloody hot water tap again, didn't you? You're weird, Sandra; you want sex, maybe. You say you want to die—'Please don't leave me!'—then your lukewarm coffee guarantees a quick exit. Where are my fucking jeans?'

'I want sex, but not your way.'

'You did last night.'

'I was drunk. God, I need a ciggy.'

'No need to raise your voice, and you're not having my cigs.'

'The packet's empty anyway.'

'Thief. And another thing—about your weird dreams—anyone would think there's a mob of people in your head. You should talk to someone.'

'I'm going to meet a therapist today.'

'You've done that before. You say nothing. This coffee is shit.'

The threatening figure brushed her skin again, making her feel cheap and worthless.

'Don't forget your underpants. I'm not washing them.'

'You don't clean anything.'

'Wow, Kev—Jack, I mean—you've got your jeans on at the second attempt.'

'Fuck off.' He pulled on his worn leather jacket.

'So iconic, Mr Cool.'

'Lose some weight,' he snapped, and slammed the door so hard that it bounced back open.

'Yeah, that's right, have a bang with a dirty girl, and leave. So what if I'm deluded? What difference does it make? I wanted children, visitors for tea, and chickens in the garden. All those wishes are fucked up now, though.'

'Idiot,' he spat as he stomped down my garden path.

Why do I get involved with these men? I wiped my eyes on the bedsheets and found a dress that looked half decent.

I ran out to the bus. The driver waited, proving that some people can be kind. I thanked him; it's worth giving nice people a smile. I sat looking out of the window to distract myself from my anxiety about the coming interview. I love the trip into town: the country landscape, the variety of houses. Children would enjoy this ride. The bus filled with people I didn't recognize. I began to feel lonely, and butterflies fluttered in my stomach. Another day, another therapy session.

The dark figure swirled around her head. 'Silence,' it commanded.

I remembered Kev or Jack pushing into me, and I felt sick. In town I changed to another bus and traveled to a tidy suburb. The analyst worked in a modern apartment block with an attractive exterior. I rang the bell but, when I heard footsteps, my muscles weakened, my curiosity evaporated and, as the door opened, the beautiful landscapes I'd seen from the bus were lost; before me now was only a gray interior and a gray man.

'Sandra? Hello, I'm John Spencer.' I think he said that; I didn't catch the name. 'Good morning. This way, please.'

I followed him into his gray room. There was a colorless Persian rug on the floor. But his eyes were lively, like a summer sky.

I imagined he'd read the referral letter from my doctor. I'm a forty-nine-year-old, childless spinster, who works in a biscuit factory. I asked my doctor to help me make an early exit, reminding him that 'It's legal in Switzerland.' This therapist probably thinks I'm hopeless.

Note from the writer: Now, if you think this story is crazy, it is about to get worse. As I said, the italics represent unconscious phantasies inside Sandra's mind that have an effect on her. She is now meeting the therapist and his unconscious will be aware of her phantasies and will react to them. He will respond in ways he may not have expected. This story is based on an idea from psychoanalysis that one unconscious communicates with the other in all encounters. See, I told you it's crazy. Now read on.

Sandra held a baby. Two young boys and a girl with warm brown skin rushed forward in the therapist's apartment. Around Sandra were friends from the biscuit factory, teachers, previous lovers, and even the children's grandparents.

The therapist's butler announced, 'MS SANDRA and HER INNER WORLD of MEMORIES and EXPERIENCES accompanied by SEVERAL GENERATIONS THEREOF.' And so the therapist's unconscious became aware of Sandra's inner wishes and even, eventually, the dark figure that tried to prevent her from speaking to him.

I forgot to take off my coat. Was I frightened? Ready to escape? I don't know. My voice was going to squeak; I knew it. I felt pressed to the floor by unseen hands. My life was crushed.

Sandra's friends and children disappeared. The dark dream figure whispered again 'You cannot speak' and leaned into her as if to crush the life out of her.

The therapist, whatever-his-name-was, looked concerned. 'Can you tell me about yourself?'

'I expected you to sit at a desk and hide behind a barrier of questions.'

'No, I don't have a list.'

'And you smile. Sorry, I'm nervous. I can't breathe, and I've still got my coat on.' I heard the clock ticking. I didn't want to waste my time. I thought I'd better just talk. 'A teacher in my school, years ago, walked up and down the examinations hall. I was stuck on a question. He whispered to me, 'Write down what you're thinking.' I did, and it worked. Funny to think of that, and I didn't catch your name.'

'That sounds like a helpful memory. And my name is John Spencer.'

'Thanks. I'm frightened, Mr Spencer. The subject of this exam is me and my lost hopes for my life.' I paused; he waited. 'I remember being held down by boys at school. I couldn't breathe then, either. I thought it would be pointless to be here today. I only cry. When your door opened, I felt like I had on the bus: with people, but alone.'

'It took courage to get here and ring the bell.'

'And you want an early memory, I suppose? You all do.'

'Who's all?'

'You therapists. What do you want it for?'

He smiled again, and I thought I'd go on. 'All right, an early memory: I was standing at the gates to a mental hospital, my dad's second home. Cynical, aren't I?'

He didn't answer.

'I was looking at an ice-cream van. It wouldn't start. Some people pointed at the open back door. The driver closed it and the van drove away. I felt deprived of an ice-cream and a dad.'

Mr Spencer was quiet, but he appeared interested.

'Look, I'm just saying what you want to hear, aren't I? The truth is my life is shameful. This morning, I didn't know who was sleeping next to me. I take men no one else will have. I get drunk, they fuck me, I make coffee no one should drink, they leave me.'

'You're used and alone; with boys in school, on the bus, the mental hospital, waking up this morning.'

'Am I complaining? You realize I'm a hopeless case, I suppose? I use the blokes too, so I don't know why I go on about it. Yes, I'm alone. My mum was always pregnant. Grandad had his hands on my body whenever he had the chance; Dad couldn't or wouldn't stop him. The ice-cream van is a metaphor for me and the old man, I suppose.'

The swirling figure that had excluded the family and friends from the room was wrapped around her.

'Are you repeating your grandad experience with the men you take home?'

'I suppose. But why would I want that?'

Children came back into the room and the dark figure released its grip on her.

'I work in a biscuit factory. The manager likes my quick mind, as he calls it. He keeps me on the factory floor to solve tricky problems. He knows I won't ask for promotion. I'm afraid I'll just jump into the huge mixing machine and make a cookie of myself. Silly idea. It's a determined machine, like my merciless grandad. I feel stupid making a joke of my death. I got drunk at the last Christmas party. The manager held me down over a desk in his office and touched me, and I felt something. I didn't want it in that situation. Is that what I'm doing again? I struggled free of him, but now he leers at me. It's so shameful. I need a cigarette. I want to stop hurting and living this shitty life.'

The children crowded around Sandra. The baby was in her arms. The dark figure was trying to push past the children and get at Sandra's body.

The therapist didn't say anything, so I continued. I described the biscuit factory: the mixing, the cleaning, spreading the biscuit dough, the baking, the timing, the packaging—on and on I went. He looked tired, as if he'd like to sleep, poor chap. I'm sure I saw him pinching his thigh to stay awake. Then he said, 'Is there something else?'

'I'm so angry. My grandad, he came through my back door. I was his ice-cream. I wanted to be his favorite. I didn't protest. I have a terrible idea that, somehow, I liked it too. The shame is awful. I feel worthless. I always have.'

I began to cry, of course; tears fell into my lap. 'I so wanted to have children. There are none. My brothers and sisters are far away. They have better lives. My cold house belonged to my dead parents; I can't move on with my life.'

The children were smiling. Sandra's relatives and friends moved closer. The dark figure was smaller, pushed to one side, cowed and defeated.

'When I came in here, everything looked gray, even you. Now I see how colorful everything is—your Persian rug, for example.'

He looked worried, as if he thought I was going mad. Maybe I am; I know I was distracted for a moment. But I felt something inside I couldn't explain: optimism. A possibility occurred to me.

'I'm getting out of that cookie factory. What a relief to say it. Grandad said it was a good job. He worked there. I dared not leave, but now I will. And if I can't have children, I can care for other people's. I thought no one would want someone like me, but they might.' I stood up. He looked surprised. 'That was the last time for Kev or Jack,' I said under my breath.

'Sorry, what did you say?'

'Goodbye and thank you.' Finally, a meeting with a therapist that helped me. I didn't look back.

A year later, I was in my garden playing with my foster children, Amanda, six years old, and her brother Sam, eight. I'm sure I saw John Spencer drive by, and I waved. Perhaps he noticed the chickens, but he didn't stop for tea.

Postscript

In this story I've illustrated, in italics, Sandra's internal world. It's a living world. Her memories and images of her experiences and wishes which, in psychoanalytic language, are called her 'objects' are in constant movement and relation to each other and they affect her feelings moment by moment. This is an idea developed by Melanie Klein and her followers. She worked on the assumption that we live in two worlds: the real world and an internal world of phantasy and dreams made up of all the experiences we have ever had. This internal world, particularly in childhood, feels as real as the outside world. In our dreams or in psychosis this inner reality, even for children, is felt to be quite concrete. In this story I have tried to make visual that which is usually hidden, namely our inner world of phantasy, which continues like an endless theatre play in our minds twenty-four hours a day. This is the world of dreams—dreams that sometimes push forward and express themselves in unexpected ways in our conscious world: a slip of the tongue, a night dream, an unexpected solution to a problem, a creative expression, and, in this case, Sandra's decision to be a foster mother instead of living out her childhood role as an abused woman. Psychoanalysis tries to find ways to release a person from the power of the irrational aspects of the inner world. And, in the case of Sandra, the rational did achieve some control over the destructiveness of her trauma memories: she decided to repair her maternal capacity by fostering children.

For a description of Melanie Klein and her followers' theories see the first reference below and for the development of that work see the second reference below.

References

Hinshelwood, R. D. (1989). *A Dictionary of Kleinian Thought*. London: Free Association Books.

Spillius, E. B. et al. (2011). *The New Dictionary of Kleinian Thought*. London: Routledge.

And, in the next story, an alternative solution to Sandra's remake of her life...

10

Politeness Rules

———◆———

I left my London workplace on Monday evening. The first day of the week was over, thank God. The sidewalks were gleaming, and slippery with freezing rain. A late autumnal gloom obscured the traffic. Shoulders hunched and head down, I was crossing the road towards Charing Cross station when I heard someone shouting, 'Out of the way. Out of the way.'

The front wheel of a bicycle hit the inside of my right thigh, and my knee twisted as I fell under the weight of the body that had struck the left side of my torso. The bike's handlebars drove in under my ribs. As I lay in the gutter, stunned and breathless, rainwater seeping into my clothes, I could feel smooth skin against my cheek and detect the aroma of perfume. A soft, warm body lay on top of me, breathing heavily, and the wet hair that tickled my neck smelled of coconut conditioner. The situation was not unpleasant, apart from the pain in my leg and the pressure on my bruised ribs. Instinctively I asked, 'Are you all right? I hope you're not hurt.'

The young woman who wriggled off me said, 'My God, I'm so, so sorry. Are you all right?' She pulled herself to her feet. 'I'm thoughtless. I was in a hurry. It's a borrowed bike. I had my head down trying to stop the rain getting down my neck. The wind was blowing through gaps in my clothes, you see. I know I was riding too fast. The bell doesn't work. Sorry, but that's why I shouted.'

I had something to say about each of those comments, but the words wouldn't come out. I could see the feet of several people and I looked up into the bright flashes of cellphone cameras. I imagined that, in shared doorway shelters, they would upload us both onto the internet, for all eternity.

She kneeled and bent over me. She was wearing an oversized woolen coat. There was no make-up on her sweet, anxiety-lined face. 'My name is Angela but people call me Angie. You can too, if you wish.'

'Oh, thank you. I'm Michael.' The situation was without precedent in my life and I felt recklessly informal. 'You can call me Mike.'

The clouds released more rain onto our wretched tableau. 'I don't wish to be a bother, but I'm in some discomfort, and I don't think I can get up. I wonder if you would be kind enough to call an ambulance?'

'We've done that,' said one of the impromptu camera folk, getting a close-up view.

The traffic was disturbed by my situation and a lot of honking and shouting accompanied our dialogue. A policeman arrived on a bicycle. He looked at me, and at Angie. 'I'm PC Merryweather,' he announced. 'A right old mess on a rainy Monday evening, isn't it? Look at this traffic.' He waved his arms at a bus. 'Get over into that lane,' he told the driver. 'You can see there's been an accident here. Come on, come on.' The bus inched past. He returned to me and Angie. 'Is this your bicycle, miss?'

'Yes, I suppose it is, in the circumstances.'

'Suppose? And do you suppose you are responsible for this man's "circumstances", young lady?'

Rather brusque, I thought, but I couldn't find the right words to defend her.

'Yes, yes. I... I am indeed responsible for what has happened to him, as you say.'

Without waiting for any more explanation, Merryweather looked at me. 'Yeah, he's alive,' he said into his radio, and was answered with unintelligible chatter and static.

The cameraman unwisely continued his documentary footage. 'And you can get that out of my face, and his, sir.' To the rest of the assembly he said, 'All right, all right, time to move along, ladies and gentlemen. I think you've seen enough of other people's unhappiness.' A compassionate response, I thought, which reinstated the constable in his role as a reasonable public servant.

'Right. Now, sir, luckily I was around the corner when the call came. The ambulance will take a while to get to us in the rush-hour traffic, I shouldn't wonder.'

'Thank you so much, Constable. I appreciate your efforts.'

'That's fine, sir, I'm only doing my job. No point asking you if you are wet through; the ambulance will be warm and dry, I imagine. But it depends on who was in there before you, of course. They might have been dead.'

He turned to Angie. 'Now then, miss, some of us have better things to do on a Monday evening. However, you can start by explaining this situation and, in particular, the machine you were riding on.'

'Well, I... I... I needed to get to Parsons Green in a hurry.'

'I think you were going the wrong way, miss.'

76

'I don't think so… Really?'

'Yes, miss, and it's a long way on any bike and, on this contraption, you won't be getting there at all.' He squeezed the brake levers. 'Not much resistance there, is there?'

'No. I borrowed it from a friend.'

'A friend let you ride on this? And no bell, either. Interesting friends you have, miss.'

'No need to be rude, Officer.'

'You're not in a position to say that, miss. According to the law, your situation is precarious, to say the least.'

I wanted to leap to the young lady's defense. I wanted, at the very least, to say, 'I'm here too,' but that seemed sarcastic.

'My… my boyfriend's ill. He phoned me. It just happened. I was rushing from my university class to get back to him. I think I might be pregnant.'

A troubling and desperate line, I thought.

'You should be doubly careful then, shouldn't you, miss?'

I guessed that her tears were unseen in the rainwater that ran down her face.

More passing internet voyeurs were filming the scene. To his credit, the constable reacted. 'You lot what's doing the filming can scarper. This is not the moment. Off with you. Go on, hop it.'

For a moment, we three—Angie, Merryweather, and I—newly of social media interest, already with a number of 'likes', I imagined, maintained our respective positions, wet through, looking at each other and the bicycle. The air became blue; mercifully, the ambulance had arrived. Merryweather gave his objective summary to the ambulance crew. 'This one ran into that one.'

'How did you manage this then, love? You needed a new boyfriend, did you?' asked one of the ambulance men.

Angie began to sob.

'Now, now, I can conduct the interview,' said Merryweather. 'Just joking.'

I wanted to join in this conversation but, as the victim and newly proposed boyfriend who was being prodded by the London Ambulance Service, I felt I had a silent role.

'He seems OK; better move him quick, though—we're getting soaked here. We'll take you in for a check-up, mate, all right?'

I cried out as I was lifted into the ambulance, but it was more as a result of the *anticipation* of pain than actual pain.

'Sorry, I didn't mean to hurt you. I'm so sorry.'

'It's quite all right. I'm sure you didn't mean it—difficult weather conditions, I know.'

Fortunately, the ambulance was warm, clean, and dry, and apparently no one had died in there recently.

Early next morning I was lying where I had been placed—in a corridor at Charing Cross Hospital. As I slipped in and out of a light sleep, a young woman—who seemed familiar—arrived.

'Thank God I found you. You look, um, not too bad. A bit tired, perhaps.'

'Oh, it's you. Yes, thank you. Yes, I didn't sleep much.'

'Not in pain or anything, are you?'

'No, not so much now. But what happened to you after I was "removed" from the scene?' I tried a laugh but my ribs hurt.

'That rude PC Merryweather said he'd be in touch with me soon. There's something so threatening about that statement, don't you think?'

I nodded.

'I wept all the way home, pushing the broken bike. For shame, I avoided telling my boyfriend. He was not ill really, he just wanted some attention. He rarely gives me any. As usual, he didn't ask about my day. On this occasion I didn't mind. Later, I discreetly inquired about you at several hospitals by telephone. They said they couldn't reveal any information to non-relatives. After a sleepless night I got up early this morning to come and find you. This is the third place I've been to. I'm so sorry.'

'You shouldn't apologize any more. I walked out into the road. I know this is terribly rude of me, but I don't remember your name.'

'It's quite all right, you've had a lot to think about. It's Angie. You're Michael, aren't you? You said I could call you Mike.'

'Absolutely. You look tired, too.'

'I'm exhausted. Do you mind awfully if I lay my head on your bed, just for a minute?'

'No, of course not. Not at all.' She put her head down by my knees and closed her eyes. For half an hour I struggled with a dilemma: I wondered if it would be all right to stroke her dark, coconut-smelling hair. She was very sweet, after all. A nurse came by. 'What's she doing here with her head on your trolley? Come along dear, you can lie on this extra one.' She helped the sleepy Angie from her chair, and onto a nearby trolley.

'Thank you so much,' she managed before she fell asleep again. As she dozed, I studied her relaxed face and motionless form. I now felt ambivalent about her unconscious attempts to do damage to herself and me. I didn't know how to fit her into my life, at least not consciously. Should I be angry, resentful, or grateful for the opportunity to meet?

The doctor finally examined me, and proclaimed, 'Your right knee will need support for a while; the ligaments are damaged. You can go home after lunch and a cup of tea.' And, turning to the nurse, he said, 'I won't disturb the sleeping patient. She seems to need the rest. I'll examine her later.'

The nurse smiled at me. 'He's tired, too,' she whispered as they moved on.

Angie woke with a start. 'How long have I been asleep? When are you going home? I'll help you.'

'I'm leaving soon.'

'Wait. Wait for me to get back. I won't be long.' She rushed out.

After a dry hospital lunch and the obligatory cup of tea, I was bandaged and ready to leave when Angie came back into the corridor.

'I'm back, and I've a car to take you home.'

My better judgment told me to decline her offer and take a taxi instead, but politeness ruled. 'You're too kind. I'd love a ride home. Thank you so much for taking the trouble.'

I hobbled down the stairs. Angie helped me into a large black car. The paintwork gleamed, and it smelled of leather and polished wood. 'Where did the car come from?' I should have been suspicious, but it didn't feel right to doubt her.

'It's a lovely antique, isn't it? My boyfriend says it's an old Rover, and it's in good nick. He looks after it all the time. He says he doesn't know how much it's worth any more, it's so good. I think he loves it more than me. I'm sure he won't mind us using it for half an hour. You don't live far, surely?'

'He doesn't know you have it?'

'No. This is all so embarrassing. I'll tell him in my own time. But I want to make everything right with you first.'

'I see. I understand.'

She drove carefully and I was grateful. But, at a crossroads well known for accidents, a large old truck drove straight through a red light. It hit Angie's boyfriend's priceless object. The car was ruined. She and I were now involved in another road accident, and this time we shared an ambulance back to the hospital. On two trolleys, head to toe in the corridor again, we awaited judgment on our respective conditions. I was awake and, as it turned out, uninjured. I received a biscuit with my tea on this occasion, as it was not a mealtime. Angie slept.

The swing doors at one end of the corridor opened abruptly and I heard a loud male voice. 'Where is she...? Angie?' In stormed a bearded man, wearing jeans with some oil stains on them, and a torn green sweater. His hair was disheveled and his eyes wild. He was carrying a black plastic bin bag, shaped like a huge teardrop.

Angie awoke, and peered at the newcomer and then at me. 'Michael, may I introduce my boyfriend, Graham. Graham, this is Michael.'

'I don't fucking care. What happened to my car? Don't answer, I know what happened. The police have been on to me. And why were you driving it? Don't answer, I know. It's because you're a fucking idiot. From this moment on, you are not my girlfriend, understood?'

'And I reciprocate. I want a man who is concerned about my well-being after a road accident. I don't give a damn about your car, anyway. Get out.'

I judged, rightly I think, that this was not the moment to say, 'You're even more attractive when you're forceful.'

He dropped the black bin bag and grabbed her handbag from the end of her trolley.

'Now look here,' I said.

'Who the fuck are you? Stay out of this.'

'I told you, he's called Michael.'

'Michael, eh? You've landed yourself a right old problem here mate, I can tell you. She's capable of some mediocre shagging but, otherwise, she's devoid of intellect and judgment.'

'How dare you!'

'I went into your internet bank account. You didn't pay the car insurance, bitch. I specifically asked you. Now the car is really lost, and the police will be after me. But when I tell them what you did, you can pay up.'

'Now that's enough,' I said, as sternly as I could.

'Like I said, after the hopeless shagging, there's no brain behind that pretty face, remember that.'

'I won't dignify your personal comments with a defense, and leave my computer alone.'

I chipped in, 'Actually, I think the law says that you have to make sure the insurance is up to date for your vehicle. If you entrusted the task of payment to a person who, in your view, is unreliable, that's your responsibility.'

'And what are you, a fucking lawyer?'

'Something like that.'

Angie beamed. 'I'm so lucky I ran you over with my bike.'

I wasn't sure how to respond, so I said nothing. It's usually the best course.

'You what? Fuck it, here's your shitty stuff.' He kicked the black plastic bag under her trolley, and threw down her handbag.

Two men from hospital security arrived. Graham said, 'And who the fuck are you, Laurel and Hardy?' They escorted him to the door, and he left without a scuffle.

'I'm glad that's over. Now I'm really tired,' said Angie, and went back to sleep.

The ward sister said, 'This bag can't stay here.'

'I can take her stuff in my taxi.' I went home. I was angered by the events of the last twenty-four hours, but now that Graham, the ex-boyfriend, was full of fury, I felt better. I was relieved it seemed to be over.

The next day, I went back to the hospital to visit Angie. It seemed like the decent thing to do.

'I thought you wouldn't want to see me again. I don't have a serious injury. The old bastard's car was strong. Only my left leg is bruised. It can't take much weight.'

'You can come home with me to collect your things.'

'Thank you so much. I insist on paying for the taxi.'

'Don't be ridiculous. I'll give you a cup of tea with a home-made biscuit. You can use my phone if you need to call a relative or friend.'

'I'd love the tea. And you make biscuits? Quite the Renaissance man, aren't you?'

We limped out of the hospital, supporting each other, and sharing two good legs between us. In the quiet of the taxi, Angie said, 'I'm so sorry about my behavior that started all this. So foolish of me. You must think I'm an idiot.'

'Please don't mention it again, it's nothing at all. At least we had the opportunity to meet. You've been absolutely charming.'

I noticed in the taxi driver's rear-view mirror that he was smiling. With his help, we arrived at the front door of my house, a recently acquired bungalow in a leafy south London suburb. Angie and I tried to help each other through the front door. Our combined width was an obstacle. I fell forward. Angie lifted her leg to get over me, but her injured leg could not support her. She fell onto the living-room floor and hit the corner of a coffee table. Unfortunately, I had placed it where one can hit one's head if one should fall when injured or drunk. Otherwise, it was convenient for teacups and the paper detritus of daily life.

'Ouch.'

'I'm so sorry, the table is stupidly placed,' I said as I crawled forward to comfort her.

'Not at all, it is a lovely table, and clumsy me.'

I started to laugh and, despite her pain, so did she. We were now on the rug by the fire. I put my arm around her again. 'This is nice,' she said, still holding her forehead, 'but it would be cozier if the gas fire was on.'

'One of us will have to get up and light it. I think it would be safer to stay here on the rug. By the way, are you pregnant?'

'With him? You're joking, surely? Why do you think I ran into you?'

Postscript

Is there really no such thing as an accident? Freud put into words what everyone knew: there are no accidents and no coincidences. Even thoughts and feelings that appear from 'nowhere' carry important, unconscious, meanings.

How important are good manners for the regulation of our lives? 'Manners Maketh Man' said William of Wycombe (1324 -1404). In other words, good manners develop civilization. In this story, I am making a little comedy out of the situation and the couple's polite attitudes to each other. However, good manners, even during such a dire series of events, help to prevent the breakdown of the emotional atmosphere between the couple. There are no outraged accusations that could stop a chance acquaintance growing into something deeper. In an earlier version of the story, it ended with Michael saying to their children, 'that is how your lives started', but I thought I would leave the current version of this story to your imagination—and anyway, that ending seemed too sweet.

How is politeness viewed in psychoanalysis? It is regarded as an important part of maintaining a trusting working alliance in the consulting room. Detached observation is not the only part of our repertoire as fellow human beings in the consulting room. Good manners help to maintain an atmosphere of respect.'Edward Glover (1888-1972) advised, "Once the patient is off the couch the situation existing between patient and analyst is governed by the everyday rules of politeness and consideration" (Glover, E. (1955))

This story also raises the question of the choice of partner. How does it happen? It must be complex, and yet it seems to be random. Can such an accident as the one described also include an unconscious choice of partner?

'Why do you think I ran into you?' says Angie at the end. She's joking, but could that contain any truth? Keep that thought in mind for the next story, which is short and may be surprising—or not—I won't say any more…

Reference:

(Glover, E. (1955), The Technique of Psychoanalysis. New York: International Universities Press. p. 104) in Lindon, J.A. (1994). Gratification and Provision in Psychoanalysis Should We Get Rid of "The Rule of Abstinence"?. Psychoanal. Dial., 4(4):549-582

11

Safe Landing

———◆———

'2 6C? I believe that is my seat.'

'Yes, but do you mind if I stay by the window? It helps me to see the land below.'

'Of course, no problem at all. I only read anyway.'

'Just so you know,' said the lady now sitting next to me, 'if I can't cope with a situation, I usually faint. It's my protection from strong feelings. Please help me if that happens. My name is Jasmine, by the way.'

'Absolutely, er, yes, I'll help you. I'm Derek. I'm sure this flight will be fine. If I can't cope, I always say what I'm thinking deep down—silly, really. We all have our own little ways to manage, don't we?'

The journey was calm. We chatted. I liked her. She was wearing modest clothes: a pink top, dark trousers, and jacket. The tailoring outlined her body without being provocative. However, the smallest amount of skin that was visible, the light brown triangle below her chin, at the top of her chest, seemed alive with promise. When she looked at me, her eyes were warm and attentive. I was in love.

I dismissed the thought; we couldn't be closer than temporary traveling companions.

We leaned into each other's shoulders from time to time without apparent intention, but the pressure increased all the while. As we approached our destination, the loudspeaker came to life. 'This is your captain. We are beginning our descent and may experience strong winds with turbulence on our way down. Tighten your seat belt an extra notch and notice your nearest exits.' The chatter of pilot and control tower continued for a few seconds. The cabin was silent.

'Oh, my God,' said Jasmine. 'What kind of message is that?'

'Reassuring? Maybe, in a way—at least he cares if we get out.'

She fainted. I put my arm around her shoulders. I could feel the reassuring warmth of her body. 'This could be quite a ride,' I whispered, and it was. The airplane shook as we descended through thick cloud, veering from left to right.

I held her firmly, caressing her cheek with my free hand. The engines whined, as the pilot tried to hold the plane level. It was exciting and terrifying. I held her hand against my cheek.

We descended lower and lower, until we hovered over the ground, swaying from side to side. The plane was misaligned with the runway as the captain kept its nose into the wind to maintain lift before touchdown. Would we land sideways and break up, scraping and sliding into a funeral pyre for the voyeuristic pleasure of the morning newspapers? The runway lights sped past. We were running out of tarmac, surely.

I stroked her shoulder. I pushed my nose into her hair and breathed deeply. She smelled divine. 'I know you can't hear me, Jasmine, but I want you to know that I love you. And if we survive, I'll marry you, directly, without question.'

The nose of the aircraft swung parallel to the runway lights. The left undercarriage wheels touched the runway, then the right, and then the nose wheel. We were safely down. The airbrakes rose on the wings, the reverse thrust roared, the wheel brakes engaged, my seatbelt tightened.

I gave her shoulders an extra squeeze. 'You can wake up now.' I touched her cheek.

She lifted her head and faced me. Her smiling eyes met mine. 'Thank you for holding me.'

I felt embarrassed. I took my arm from her shoulder. 'We'll be in the airport building in no time. I hope the baggage isn't delayed. Then we'll go our separate ways. It's been a pleasure to meet you, and I'm glad I could be of assistance.' I searched the magazine holder in front of me, in case I'd left something personal where it shouldn't be.

'You know, on this occasion I heard everything. And yes, I will marry you, absolutely.'

Postscript

The proverb from life at sea, 'Any port in a storm', comes to mind in connection with this story, and it means the following '(*idiomatic*): In an adverse situation, when one lacks good alternatives, it is appropriate to avail oneself of any possible refuge, aid, or helpful course of action.' (Wiktionary)

And it may mean, as in this case, that we are blind to the reality of the person we are with and believe that we are in love, when actually we are simply desperate. How many relationships start in this way? One or both partners trying to solve a life crisis, in this case a potential near-death experience, by rushing into a marriage that is not really suitable for either party. This could become tragic if they wake up to what they have done after a child has been born.

In this vignette, something of a romantic feeling, an infatuation, was developing anyway it appeared, and this, plus a near-death stress, led to Derek's impulsive proposal, coupled with Jasmine's immediate acceptance. This couple seem to have mixed up the infatuation which may arrive in a situation of dependence and true love, which grows over time. Sometimes, as we all know, there are difficult situations in life from which we would like to extricate ourselves. Even if the solution does not seem much better than our present reality, we would like to change our circumstances. It is as if a change could solve the problem and, of course, it might. The next story is an illustration of just this phenomenon…

12

Mr Blanc's Soul Change

———◆———

I was wandering in a part of town known for its variety of unusual shops when I came upon a place called The Most Famous Swap Shop in the World.

You know what a 'swap shop' is, surely? A place where you can exchange something you don't want for something you do.

I went in, but there was no one there. I could hear the sound of a radio in the back of the shop. On the counter was an old-fashioned bell, which I pinged.

I heard movement. The radio chatter stopped. A shabby drape of faded green velvet covering the doorway was drawn aside. Through the opening came a man wearing a stained, brown warehouse coat. His hair was awry, his glasses dirty and slightly crooked. Several days' worth of stubble covered his jaw.

He stood behind the wooden counter, the uneven surface of which was sprinkled with what looked suspiciously like bloodstains. 'Yes, good morning. Yes, how may I help?'

'Oh, er, good morning. This looks like an interesting place. Why is it the most famous in the world?'

'Look, I'm not here to explain myself. But, in the interests of business, I can tell you. We are famous for doing exchanges of parts of people.'

I must have looked surprised. He continued, 'Some people think it's gruesome, but there is a demand, you know.'

At that moment, another person came into the shop. His head was bowed; he wore a long grubby raincoat and appeared stressed.

I backed away from the counter, intrigued. The newcomer looked up at the shopkeeper. 'My name is Blanc, B-L-A-N-C,' he said, 'and I work in a library.'

'Yes, nice to meet you. I'm the owner of this establishment. Smithers is the name, not to be confused with smithereens, as I'm not broken into small pieces.' I wondered if his explanation was a joke, but he was straight-faced. There was a cough from behind the velvet drape.

'Sorry, dearest,' said Smithers, half-turning towards the drape, 'I should say that this establishment is jointly owned by Mrs Smithers and myself. How can I be of service to you today?'

'I see. Well, I've come about an exchange or, to put it more precisely, a straightforward change.'

'It's not straightforward, I can tell you that for nothing. Which do you want: heart or mind?'

'Actually, I was more interested—in fact, *desperate*—for a change of soul.'

'What?' Then, half-turning again to the curtained door behind him, Smithers shouted, 'Did you hear that? A change of soul.' There was no answer.

To his new customer he said, 'We don't do that. As I said, we only deal with a change of heart or a change of mind. We can do your delicate bits if you wish, but there is an extra charge.' He looked down and brushed a piece of dust from the top of the counter in front of him.

'No, no, it's a soul I want,' said the drab Mr Blanc. His voice was now firm, in stark contrast to his humble physical presentation. 'I'm not comfortable with my soul. I feel out of place—boring, in fact. I'm desperate. You can't do swaps, can you? You haven't got another soul on your books that is too lively and wants to make an exchange to a quieter body?'

'No, never heard of it. I can show you a few dead ones we can move you into, though: we've got a baby, if you can tolerate the parents—difficult people indeed. That would be a long job, though; you'd have to go to school again, teenage development, and all that sex business… nasty. There's a motorbike guy available, but he crashed his bike, so you'll be limping a bit.'

I can't say I found the options appealing, and I thought the potential customer looked distressed.

Smithers continued, 'Don't look like that. You know everything has a downside. We've got a few oldies, ex-pensioners, quiet people with ordinary interests. They would just need a bit of cosmetic surgery, but you may not last long, of course.'

'The body is not the point, really. As I said, I want a new soul.'

'Let me get this right: you want to keep your body and change your soul?'

'Yes.'

'All kinds come in here, mate. I could tell you stories that would make your hair stand on end. But I've never heard of that one.' He shouted into the back of the shop again. 'Soul change?' There was no reply.

'Well, I just thought that you might have a spare soul somewhere in the shop. Please, can't you help me? I'm so boring.'

'No. Look, I'm sorry you're boring, truly I am, but if you change your soul, you would become that other person. You'd never know that you used to be *you*, the man talking to me now. So, you'd have nothing to compare, would you? You wouldn't know who you were, what you were doing in this shop, or why you should pay me. Soul change? Sorry, it can't be done, mate. You're always going to be you. No way out. Accept it, that's the way for you.'

Mr Blanc, head bowed, glanced at me from the corner of his eye, his sorrow palpable. He had an unsmiling face and gray skin, as if he rarely saw the sun. 'Sorry to have troubled you,' he whispered as he left.

Smithers turned to me. 'See what I have to put up with? This is a thankless task, trying to help people and all that.' He shook his head. 'I know what's happened there. I'll bet that, since he was a little boy and read a lot of stories, he really believed that a person could change in the twinkling of an eye. Like they do in fairy stories. If a frog is kissed by a princess. I reckon that, deep down inside, those ideas have pushed him towards this futile search.'

I found it difficult to disagree with Smithers, and I left the shop bemused by both his occupation and his insight.

Mr Blanc Meets Eve

Some weeks later, I was walking in a dull part of town. It was an overcast day, and even the sparkly shopfront displays reflected in the wet sidewalk did nothing to lighten my mood. As I passed an undertaker's, I glanced in through the tall glass windows and noticed an array of photos showing various funeral arrangements. The wood-paneled office was softly illuminated with uplights. In the middle of the room, facing out over the street, was an armchair. A young woman sat there, dressed in a short skirt and cotton jumper, her legs crossed. She had an insolent but oddly enticing look on her face and she was eating a large red apple. Was this a clever front for a brothel, I wondered?

Mr Blanc, the very man who had been looking for a change of soul in the swap shop, brushed past me. I couldn't believe the coincidence. His head was down in his self-deprecating manner, and I suppose he didn't see me as he darted into the funeral parlor. Curious, I went in after him. I pretended to be waiting to talk to the young woman, who I already thought of as Eve.

She looked hard at the despondent man who had just come into her office, clearly annoyed at having been interrupted in her apple-eating pleasures. I half-expected that at any moment she was going to ask him 'What the fuck do you want?', like a delinquent teenager. She ignored me, of course.

'Yes?' she asked, her face filled with disdain.

'I'm Mr Blanc, and I'm looking for a new soul. I've been to the swap shop on the other side of town, but they can't help me.'

She sighed heavily. 'My name is Eve,' she said, casting a suspicious glance at me. 'You work in a library, don't you?' she asked Mr Blanc.

He nodded.

Eve looked him up and down. 'I think the other place called about you. I'm not surprised they couldn't help you. There aren't many souls walking around on earth who'd want to move into you. If you don't mind me saying.'

'I do mind, actually; I find that offensive.'

Surprisingly strong for him, I thought.

'When was the last time a young woman—or man, for that matter—was really interested in you? Can you remember?'

The soul-searching Mr Blanc looked embarrassed. To my surprise, he started to cry. He wept, he sobbed, he was distraught. 'I work in a library. I'm the manager. It's a lovely quiet job, endlessly interesting and educational. But all my staff say I'm boring. They laugh at me. I must have a new soul.'

'Oh no, what have I said? I've upset you, haven't I?'

'I've had a lifetime of insults,' continued Mr Blanc. 'I've never been able to get things right. I mean to be more cheerful, like other people. I thought if I could change my soul, that might help.'

'I'm really sorry. I'll tell you what,' said the young woman, lowering her voice, 'I've an idea that might help you. Come with me.'

Mr Blanc looked hopeful.

In the oak-lined office was a door, camouflaged by the matching wall panels. She opened it; steep stairs led downwards.

'Do you mind if I follow? I have a similar request,' I said, lying completely.

'All right, then. Two idiot birds with one stone, I suppose.'

I didn't respond, not wanting to spoil the opportunity. We followed her down, quite a way. At the bottom of the stairs was a large room with a low ceiling. On a multitude of metal tables were naked dead bodies.

She said, 'Choose one of these, a good specimen. I'll move you into it. I'll burn yours later, under another name. Maybe you will feel better about your soul when other people feel better about the way you look.'

'How will you move my soul over?'

'Never mind. I have my methods. You won't be disappointed.'

'Aren't you forgetting he will still be the same person?' I interrupted.

'Who asked you? I'm selling the body.'

Mr Blanc looked dejected. 'That's true, isn't it?'

I should've kept quiet.

In the corner of the room was a narrow but comfortable-looking couch. Above it, an old-fashioned white telephone was hanging on the wall. 'What's that for? It seems out of place,' I asked.

'It has its uses. The couch used to belong to a psychoanalyst, but he doesn't need it any more, if you know what I mean.' She nodded in the direction of an old body on one of the metal tables.

'And the white phone?'

'None of your business,' she said firmly. 'But come to think of it,' Eve continued, turning to Mr Blanc, 'I may be able to help you get your wish.' She threw the last of her apple behind her. 'It won't take long, believe me.'

'What do you mean?'

From her body language I realized this might be a private moment, so I said 'I'll wait upstairs,' and departed. I shut the wood-paneled door firmly behind me. Other people's special moments can be an embarrassment, don't you think?

Soon Eve came upstairs, alone.

'What have you done with him?' I asked.

'He got his wish,' she said. 'I separated him from his soul and a new one will be along shortly. I've got friends in the old graveyard.'

'I'm sure you have. Is that what the white phone is for?'

Before she could answer, Mr Blanc came up the stairs and into the office. He was unaware that he had walked through the door. Now he was a ghost of himself.

Eve said coyly, 'We had a moment on the couch, the earth moved, and he left his body. Mr Blanc's soul will have to go to the place his exchange-soul comes from. He can try it out anyway.'

'So, it is possible?'

'We'll see. It's the best I can offer.'

Then, turning to Mr Blanc's ghost, Eve said, 'You'd better go to the old graveyard. There are a lot of souls there. You've missed their breakfast meeting, but you'll be in time for the ghostly lunchtime assembly.'

As Mr Blanc left, a man of his own age ran through him and into the office. He was wearing the sort of seventeenth-century clothes I'd seen in pictures of Shakespearean characters. He was a lively person with a twinkle in his eye.

Eve took the newcomer downstairs, forgetting to close the door. After what sounded like an ecstatic moment, a rejuvenated Mr Blanc's body bounded up the stairs. He smiled and winked at me as he left. Fascinated, I followed. 'Do you mind if I come along?'

'Not at all,' said the new Mr Blanc, 'you can join the party. We're going to have some fun in that workplace of mine.'

That afternoon, and late into the night, there was a jolly commotion in the library. I remained an impartial observer. An extraordinarily flexible Mr Blanc entertained his staff with tales of his hitherto unknown exotic life. He used old English words, several of them obsolete, or so obscure that they had to look them up in dictionaries. Later, he demonstrated some of his special techniques. They were very surprised. The dour demeanor of yesterday's Mr Blanc had changed in the twinkling of an eye. Just as the story books say it can be—if you get a kiss from the right princess, of course.

'It looks like Mr Blanc, but he seems to be someone else,' said one of the exhausted librarians. I left late in the evening, unable to take any more observation, but I returned the next morning to see the results of his antics.

Mr Blanc Meets Himself

In the city library, the staff said they were suffering headaches, and pains in places where they had not felt them for some time. I inquired after Mr Blanc. They said he had collapsed at some point in the early morning and been taken by ambulance to the local hospital. They informed me that he appeared to have died ecstatic, of emotional overload, and been sent to Eve's funeral home.

I went to see Eve. She was in her armchair, eating yet another red apple.

'Good morning, Eve, you may remember me from yesterday.'

'Yes, absolutely. Looking for anything?'

Mr Blanc's original soul floated through the door. Eve took another bite. 'Yes?' she said, chewing hard.

He said, 'At the breakfast meeting in the graveyard, I was bored out of my ghostly mind. My new friends are not interesting, and a few were downright tedious.'

'Now you know what it feels like to meet you in the morning.'

I thought that was a little harsh. Mr Blanc looked shocked. What he had always known landed in his soul with enough force to give him an insight. 'There's something I'm missing. I have to appreciate what I have and what I can do; there's no point running after what is outside my capabilities.'

'Yes,' said Eve, 'I know all about that. I had a psychoanalyst down here, remember. I did my best, but he wouldn't stop talking. Come with me.'

They went downstairs. I followed. There we found the exhausted, and badly shaken, seventeenth-century version of Mr Blanc.

'Look at the state of my body. It looks like it's been in a plane crash. What have you been doing?'

His seventeenth-century replacement, who was not quite dead, said, 'I don't know how you cope with so much beauty in your library. It's an impossible job.'

'The subject matter is the books, not the people looking after them.'

'You don't see it, do you? But whatever, I want out of this arrangement.' He looked at Eve. 'Can you do this for me? Be a darling, separate me from this body. I'll go quietly to my mates in the graveyard. I won't bother you again, not for a while anyway.'

'Make it a long while. What's in it for me?'

Mr Blanc's original soul began to weep.

'No, stop. I hate men's tears, even if you are a spirit.' And to the seventeenth-century Mr Blanc she said, 'All right, just one more time.'

She looked at the original Mr Blanc's soul and me. 'Excuse us, please.'

'Of course.'

Mr Blanc and I sat upstairs in the waiting room, reading magazines. After a few minutes we saw the seventeenth-century soul on his way out.

'So soon?' I inquired.

'She can really separate you.' He passed through the front door and limped off in the direction of his old friends. Mr Blanc's original soul floated downstairs for his reunion with himself. I went back to the library.

The tired staff were lost without the fastidious Mr Blanc. However, just when they thought they would give up for the day, he entered. He was moving with his usual formality but, unusually, his head was up, and he was smiling. He carried a bag of fresh croissants, and a large Thermos of coffee.

'We usually have tea.'

'Not today. Gather round.' He distributed the welcome breakfast. 'Now, I'm aware that yesterday there were some exotic seventeenth-century goings-on here. They may be regretted—or possibly not.' He paused, but no one responded. 'I'm not the man I was two days ago. One day, I'll write a book about my experiences. For now, I want you to accept my apologies.'

No one had asked for an apology.

'We have to get back to running an efficient library. I'm going to do my best to make the workplace more interesting. To help counteract my tedious demeanor, I want you to appoint me a lively deputy, who will advise me on how to keep the workplace pleasantly engaging.'

Without hesitation, they pushed forward a bright, newly recruited young woman. 'I'm Eve's best friend,' she winked.

Postscript

Freud, in his book *The Future of an Illusion, Civilization and Its Discontents* (Freud, S. (1929), p.76), thought that the pleasure principle governed humans' relationships with the world, and he added that our search for comfortable satisfaction is frustrated at every turn by the rules of reality. He did not think that it was in the plan of creation that we should be happy in the ordinary sense of the word. But possibly we will get some satisfaction from accepting reality.

Mr Blanc, according to Freud, has to accept that the unhappiness in his life is to be tolerated. Freud thought, as Mr Blanc discovered for himself, that unhappiness was easier to find and comes from

100

several sources: 'from our own body... from the external world, which may rage against us... and finally from our relations to other men.' (Ibid., p. 77) The story is an account of him making these discoveries. He has to face up to who he is, and that he has a useful part to play in the community. In this context, that would be running an efficient library. And, of course, we don't know much about his love life, apart from the couple of incidents with Eve. But the arrival of Eve's best friend on the library staff gives a hint that his empty love life might change in the future.

'Self-love, my liege, is not so vile a sin, as self-neglecting.' (William Shakespeare, *Henry V*, Act II, Scene 4). This little quote emphasizes the point that, in Mr Blanc's case, the poor chap could not see what might be valuable in himself. Instead, he focused on what was lacking. In the end, he resolved the problem by accepting himself and the help of someone else, Eve's best friend, who could possibly liven up the work atmosphere. As Shakespeare says, it is a sin to deny one's talents by neglect.

References

Freud, S. (1929). *The Future of an Illusion, Civilization and Its Discontents*. SE XXI. London: Hogarth Press and The Institute of Psycho-Analysis.

Clark, W. G., and Wright, W. A., (Eds) *The Complete Works of William Shakespeare*. Garden City, NY: Nelson Doubleday Inc.

In the next vignette, we come across another attitude to reality and the quiet love that underlies devotion to a task...

13
The Family Doctor

One day, during a school history lesson, I heard about the terrors inflicted by the Nazis on the nations of Europe. People with numbers tattooed on their arms were starved, frozen, executed, burned. We pupils became horrified voyeurs as we perused grainy photos. A few days later I was sitting in our doctor's waiting room with my mother and one of my younger brothers, two-year-old Jimmy. I was twelve.

The doctor was tall and dark. He didn't look familiar: his face was long, his nose was more pronounced than most, his skin color was darker than I'd ever seen before. A man of few words, he was suitably formal, with a dour and somber manner. My mother said this was a sign of his commitment, and that he was an excellent doctor from another country. I felt jealous that my mother admired him.

It was the 1950s, so I was wearing my school uniform for this visit. I had the customary sharp crease in my gray school trousers. It was made by rubbing soap on the inside and ironing the outside of the trouser, so that the long, straight fold stayed in place. To preserve the precious creases, despite my cough and temperature, I decided to stand rather than sit in the small waiting room. It was late afternoon. Jimmy was complaining. Mother was tired and showing signs of exasperation.

Earlier in the week we had made an extra visit to church to see a large crucifix that had been added to the new building. It hung high above the sanctuary. I studied it. I asked about the features of Jesus' tortured face.

'Jesus was a Jew. Some Jewish people have those features,' my mother said.

'I thought the Jews were His enemies.'

'The Jewish people have suffered greatly over the years,' she said. She seemed embarrassed. I pressed her with questions. She tried to explain the complexities of the socio-political history suffered by the Jewish people, and that there were Jews like Jesus who helped everyone. I was confused about the relationship between the crucifixion, the not-so-kind Jews, and the Romans who had carried out the execution. Could these two religious groups have acted in an unholy alliance?

In the doctor's quiet waiting room, my little brother was grizzling. I bent forward to take a magazine from the table in the middle of the room. Jimmy thought this was interesting and moved towards the table too. Our mother stretched out to hold him back. The outer door opened, and the cleaner came in. She carried a large bucket of steaming water; soap bubbles spilled over the edges, a mop leaned precariously on one side. Jimmy moved towards it with his arms outstretched.

The cleaner, a burning cigarette clenched between her fingers, was looking for an ashtray. I had seen one on the windowsill and, being the polite schoolboy I was, I picked it up and moved stiffly towards her.

Jimmy was close to the bucket. My mother stretched in front of the cleaner to block Jimmy's access to the soapy water. She, in turn, held her cigarette up and away from Jimmy and leaned awkwardly towards the ashtray. The top of her mop slipped under her overall's shoulder strap, tipping the bucket.

I was trying to stand straight to preserve my trouser creases and leaned further forward with the ashtray. We were a group in an ill-fated dance.

On the other side of the waiting room, the surgery door opened, and the doctor entered the room. I realized that he looked like the Jesus on the cross in church.

He observed the unfolding calamity. He reached out an arm towards Jimmy, who was now leaning on the edge of the bucket. Too late: the bucket went over, and Jimmy slipped. The cleaner, trying to avoid him, fell onto my mother. Cigarette ash landed in Jimmy's curly hair.

I also went down, turning my body and trying to hold the heavy glass ashtray off the floor. My trousers became soaked and covered in soap bubbles. Jimmy screamed, as did Mother and the cleaner. The nurse came in to help us.

I was shocked. The doctor seemed calm. His bare forearm was close to me. I saw small, roughly tattooed numbers in a row. I looked at his face. He'd noticed my attention; he looked embarrassed. The school history lesson meant something else to me now. Our doctor had been tormented by the Nazis, but he carried on here with us. Gratefully, and with shame, I knew that even a spectator is not innocent. I couldn't explain it but, as an onlooker, I'd become a part of the horror.

Postscript

I wrote this from a memory of my childhood. We lived on the edge of London and, after the Second World War, a doctor from another European country had settled in the area and opened a general practice. My mother did indeed admire and respect him. There were a number of children in our family, and sometimes the doctor made home visits to diagnose an illness. He was always calm and kind, as I remember, with a sad look in his eyes. The incident in the waiting room described here is partly fictitious and written to illustrate my point of view about being a participant observer in another's suffering. In school, I had seen pictures of the torture and killing of civilians during the war. In the waiting room was a group embroiled in an ill-fated dance. Everyone had his or her accidental, but unavoidable, part to play. Through this event, I understood a little more of the doctor's experience. When I put together the pictures I'd seen in school, his features, and the historical events alive in my mind, I felt that even observing a situation gives one a responsibility. I'm thinking about our human tendency to gloat over pictures of others' suffering, as we are invited to do in the news reports every day, as opposed to our need to mourn a disaster.

When I wrote this story, I was remembering one person's courage, which moved me then and has remained with me ever since.

In the next story is an illustration of the courage of two people facing the truth about their lives.

14

Miss Eleanor, Her Little Dog Mitzi, and 'Mike the Bike'

———◆———

M iss Eleanor's breakfast lacked butter. She didn't usually go to the local gas station to buy butter, but the grocery shop was too far away. Anyway, she was not sure it was open at this early hour of the morning.

Miss Eleanor, seventy-six years of age and a retired psychoanalyst, took her little dog, Mitzi, to walk the few hundred yards from her apartment to the gas station. She crossed the road carefully.

On her way, she thought, *I'll also look for a packet of dark-chocolate digestive biscuits. I seem to be running out. They are always good to have in the larder. I find them comforting. I don't think I've ever really analyzed my wish for this particular oral pleasure: how strange.*

On the gas station forecourt was a large motorcycle. She had always been afraid of—and fascinated by—motorcycles. She stopped for a moment to admire the chromed tubes and the worn leather saddle.

Years ago, a male friend used to give her a ride on his motorbike. She remembered the excitement and the fear of death that tightened her stomach as she climbed on the back. The excitement of forbidden fruit, of course. No helmets, the wind blew through her hair, and the open road beckoned. Those days were gone, and everybody in them.

A memory tried to reach out from deep inside her mind. She felt it in her heart, but could not form a word. She could not remember what had happened to that chap. She must have put him away into a corner of her mind, a long time ago.

Pulling herself out of her thoughts, she refocused on the task at hand. *Butter, I need some butter. And biscuits; it's expensive in this place, but I cannot eat my breakfast without the butter at least.*

Miss Eleanor went into the gas station, which included a minimart. Standing at the counter paying for petrol and some goods was a tall, broad-shouldered man with blond hair. In her imagination he was handsome, but she would have to wait until he turned round to assess him fully.

The man appeared to be looking at the girl who was serving him. Miss Eleanor noted that the girl was young and pretty.

The phone rang and the girl answered. 'Yes, this is Jane. Oh, hello Dad. Yes, I'm fine, just a little busy at the moment. I'll talk to you in a few minutes.' She looked up and smiled at her customer. By the way the man shifted his stance, he seemed annoyed. Had he been having other thoughts about the girl?

Jane continued with the till.

Why had her dad called? Of course, it's early morning. A young woman shouldn't be on this shift alone really. He's concerned; she's somebody's daughter! I wonder if this biker can think that thought? Would he like to see *his* daughter in this situation with a hungry biker?

'Sorry to keep you waiting,' said Jane.

'That's all right,' said the biker.

Miss Eleanor, standing behind him, noticed that he seemed to straighten himself up. *What a surprise, he's polite! What has happened to him? And now I'm being prejudiced. Why shouldn't he be polite?*

She wished she had worn her other glasses because there was something written on the back of this large man's leather jacket. She stepped closer to read it. Mitzi went closer, too, and began to smell his lower trouser legs and heavy motorcycle boots. *What freedom*, thought Miss Eleanor, *to get so close you can sniff around someone's legs without it being, well, the source of a social misunderstanding, so to say.*

Now closer to him, she looked at the writing on his broad back. Written in bold letters, with a golden hammer logo, were the words: Tor's Brothers MC Club. *Those peaceful, intelligent people, the Swedes, and their well-organized country! Well I never!*

Jane took his money and gave him his change.

He said, 'Thanks. Have a nice day.' At that moment, Tor's Brother stepped back from the counter. The little dog squealed in pain. The man moved quickly onto his other foot, standing on Miss Eleanor's foot. Miss Eleanor thought she would faint, the pain was so fierce.

'Boots! Your bloody boots!' she shrieked. 'You wretched man!'

The wretched man lurched forward and swung round.

Shocked at what had come out of her retired psychoanalyst's mouth, the pain was so intense she thought her foot was broken. Miss Eleanor felt quite dizzy. She sat down hard on the floor, half in a faint.

Jane stood rooted to the spot, her hand over her mouth.

Tor's Brother crouched down over Miss Eleanor. She saw an angel. She looked into his pale-blue Nordic eyes. He looked concerned. She saw his blond hair. He was so nice. *Do such people feel empathy?* she wondered. But this was not the moment to think this way. Her foot hurt like hell.

Miss Eleanor saw water welling up in the MC gang member's eyes. Could it be true? He was, yes, he was crying!

Water ran down his face. 'I'm so sorry,' he said. *When was the last time he had said that?* wondered Eleanor. 'I'm feeling a bit stressed.'

He paused for breath. 'You look like my mother. I'm so sorry.' He breathed again. 'My girlfriend had our baby last night, and this morning. She suffered so much. I never realized she was so strong. I don't care about people I hurt, you know, it's my business.' His tears continued to flow.

Where is all this coming from? thought Eleanor. *He's had a trauma, surely. He's in shock. He's been holding himself together all night and now this unexpected accident has released years of pent-up feelings. But did he have to tread on a psychoanalyst to experience this catharsis?*

Tor's Brother continued, 'I usually just ride away from other people's pain. I don't care.'

Eleanor thought he would fall over her in his grief. *He has really suffered with his girlfriend, the new mother*, she thought. *He didn't realize it until this moment. But my foot, my poor foot, and Mitzi... what about us? Must he have a therapy session now?*

'I sat by her head in the delivery room. I tried to hold her. She shouted at me, "You're suffocating me, you bloody idiot!" She hasn't said that before. I tried to move. "And you're not sitting down the other end, neither, you dirty bastard!" She's never said that before either.

'The language that came out of her last night was unbelievable. I've never heard her say such things. And no one, not anyone, has ever dared to threaten me like she did. Then she said, "Can't you kiss me?" I couldn't; I didn't know what to do.

'But the midwife was cool, very cool. I haven't met anyone like her before, either. She was tough and kind. Kind to me, seeing how I was and all that.' He shook his head. 'I'm going to say "thanks" the next time I see her.'

Miss Eleanor began to cry.

'Oh, God, you and the dog. I'm sorry. I'll help you. I've seen people die, but I've never seen anyone being born before, and it was a girl. Her first breath and cries: I couldn't believe it. It was like my bike when it starts up, you know you feel alive when you hear it, just amazing. I couldn't stay there blubbering so I came out, and landed here. Now you're crying, and the dog.'

Jane was standing in front of them, with her hand over her mouth.

Tor's Brother blurted out again, 'My girlfriend had a baby. We had a baby, a little girl.' He sobbed, 'I'm the dad of a daughter. I know what it feels like!'

'Well, er... congratulations! This is truly wonderful!' Miss Eleanor managed to say through her pain and tears. 'I mean the new baby. You must both be very proud.'

'I'm so clumsy. I am so sorry. So sorry I hurt you.'

She could hardly believe it. She'd thought she was going to be murdered for standing so close to a Tor's Brother; for getting under his feet, for Mitzi sniffing his jeans and boots, for reading his Tor's Brothers inscription, and for calling him a wretched man!

But his concern, the story, the new baby, the tears, his repeated apologies touched her. She wanted to say those stoic English things like, 'It's quite all right; it was entirely my fault; I should have been somewhere else; so rude of me to stare at your back... it was just a bit of butter and some biscuits I wanted.' *But now he looks as if he's trying to pull himself together. He straightened up when I offered my congratulations. As if that confirmation made it real.*

'Can you call an ambulance, love?' he said to Jane.

'Yes, yes, and I'll ring my dad. I think he knows the local vet. He'll help us,' she answered through her tears. 'I can take the dog. I'll look after her.'

As the ambulance doors closed, Miss Eleanor heard the biker say, 'I'll go back to my girlfriend's place for a kip, then I'll come and see you in the hospital, darlin'.'

In Accident and Emergency, Miss Eleanor lay on a bed and cried. Not so much from the pain in her foot, but because she felt a terrible ache deep inside. She couldn't define it. It felt like a forgotten story rising inside her.

How kind everybody was! Her young doctor was charming. He explained everything. He offered her some very good pain relief. She took what she was offered with gratitude. It was great! The mental freedom! She felt a little wayward.

She cried again. She could not understand what was happening to her. There was something about these men: the one who had hurt her and now the one who treated her. Mixed with the excitement and pain, something was coming out of her unconscious. Or was it someone? The drugs took over and she slipped away to happy thoughts. Summer days by the seaside with her parents. So long ago. Then she wondered how Mitzi was. *Probably OK. I imagine that pretty checkout girl, Jane, has nice parents*, she thought in a haze.

When Tor's Brother came into the room, he introduced himself. 'I'm Mike,' he said.

'You look anxious, Mike,' Miss Eleanor said, aware of sounding rather too bright. 'I'm sure I'll be all right. It was an accident. And anyway, this medication is wonderful.'

'It isn't that. When I got back to the girlfriend's place I fell asleep on the sofa. I woke up a few hours later because I thought I heard a dog whimpering. Or a baby? I was having a dream about a screaming woman, then I lost it. I can't remember it, I want to.'

He looks like he is in a panic and he needs to talk. I can't do that now. I don't know if he knows he needs to talk. I'm not in a state to do it anyway. 'That was uncomfortable,' Miss Eleanor said. 'To have such a dream, I mean.'

Mike changed the subject. 'How are you now?'

'The foot has a small crack in a bone. It's been taped up and I've been told not to walk for a while. But the hospital needs the bed. So I wonder if you could help me get home? I'll take the crutches they are loaning me.'

'Yeah, I'll help you. It's the least I can do.'

I'd love to go on that bike, she thought. *It would be, well, rather wonderful. His broad back, the Tor's Brothers MC Club logo pressing against my chest. The thunderous noise and vibration. No, I'm a silly girl, old wishes in even older skin. I'll take a minicab.*

Mike rode behind the cab to her apartment. He paid for the cab and helped her up the stairs. She called him 'My angel'.

'The mother of my daughter won't like that. Mike will do.'

Mike the Bike, she thought, a little embarrassed by his mild reprimand. *This must be a change for him. I imagine he's quite familiar with women when he wants to be.*

He gave her a kiss on the cheek, and said goodbye.

Miss Eleanor hobbled to the window and looked out. She saw him sit on the bike. The starter motor whined for a moment and the sound of thunder echoed around the blocks of apartments. As he set off down the road, the noise was deafening.

That wretched Tor's Brother! My goodness, did I say that? She couldn't be angry. She really wanted him to come back for a visit, to see how she was managing. Maybe he would, or would he? The painful memory she could not quite get hold of squeezed her heart. Her knees weakened. *What is that? Who is that?* She began an uncomfortable rumination. *Most people seem to have left me: age, illness, or death.* She didn't want to feel sorry for herself, although her foot ached. After a mental struggle with her sorrow, which took a little time, she put the kettle on to make some tea. Through the bubbling of the boiling water she heard the telephone ring.

'I'm not sure how to say this,' said the vet, 'but there is a young man here standing at the reception desk. He's wearing a leather jacket. He arrived here on a large and noisy motorcycle. And I have to say, he is rather...'

'Yes, I know,' said Miss Eleanor. She was in love again. Unexpectedly, she remembered a forgotten face. A young man from years ago. It was like yesterday, or today even. The image took a few seconds to take form. The sound of his old bike. His enigmatic smile, the silk scarf wrapped casually round his neck. With a chilling shock, she remembered how and why it had ended. She had put it away soon after it happened. His crash, no helmet. She had not seen him again. They said there was another girl with him at the time, a shop girl from a perfume counter. The protocol for funerals—and who attended— was different in those days. Particularly among her class of people. Her parents didn't approve of him anyway. 'He's a fling,' they said. 'You'll get over it. You'll soon forget.' Dutifully, she did, but she buried her bitterness, too. Now her stomach felt hollow.

'Hello, hello?' said the vet on the telephone. 'Are you still there?'

'Yes, yes.' With a struggle, Miss Eleanor pulled herself back to now. Tears pricked her eyes. *What a lot of water today*, she thought.

'He says he's here to collect Mitzi. Is that all right?'

'A kindness, a good deed,' whispered Miss Eleanor. 'Yes, that is quite all right,' she said as calmly as she could. 'He must have gone back to the garage to ask Jane where Mitzi was taken.'

'What did you say?' asked the vet.

'Nothing. He's being kind, that's all.'

'Yes, all right, but this is a little irregular. However, Mitzi is ready to go home. The damage was not as bad as we feared. There is a bit of bruising and tenderness. I've given her some sedatives and she is sleeping now. You can give her one more tablet tomorrow if you think she's in pain. She will probably stop limping in a few days.'

'Thank you so much. It'll be all right to let the young man take her. Could you loan him a travel box, please? I will return it. Oh, and give him your bill, if you please. I will pay it as soon as I can get to the bank.'

Mike paid the bill in cash, without question. The vet handed over the sleeping Mitzi. Cradling the travel box in his arms, Mike turned to leave.

The vet saw the inscription on his back: Tor's Brothers MC Club.

'Your Miss Eleanor is an interesting lady,' she said.

Mike turned and smiled. He didn't do that so often.

In the meantime, Miss Eleanor had tidied her hair and made some tea. She'd found the last of her dark-chocolate digestive biscuits. With all the commotion at the garage she hadn't managed to buy any more. She thought her wretched young man might like a chocolate digestive. A celebration of life: his daughter was born and she herself was alive! And kissed on the cheek! Not assaulted for rudeness to a Tor's Brothers MC member!

She remembered her first boyfriend, again. 'The fling', as her parents rudely called him. With a shock, she remembered he had liked these biscuits. *But I must have remembered this before, in my own psychoanalysis, surely? The work of that analysis is clearly incomplete, as they all are, I suppose. These biscuits were his favorite; it was our only indulgence. We didn't do anything else. It was another time. So many years ago, there was another morality then. How silly*, she thought. *Perhaps his perfume-counter girl gave him these biscuits, too, or some physical equivalent. Now I'm being mean.*

She realized that she had not given Jane in the garage a thought. *The accident must have been a shock for her also, and she has been very helpful. I feel jealous of her too. How these old prejudices stay hidden in the mind. I'll have a chat with her later. I'll take Mitzi with me to thank her.*

Miss Eleanor wondered, not for the first time, why she'd never met the right chap, and built a family with him.

She wanted to shout out, 'It wasn't a fling… I loved him!' She'd had lovers over the years. She'd known passion. She wasn't inhibited. That wasn't the point. There was just something about that first man and his motorbike that stayed in her heart like a metaphor for what was good, fun, and wild.

Then there was his possible betrayal, the other girl and, on top of that, her own parents' snooty attitude. *Will I ever forgive them all?*

Is that it? I have to forgive unconditionally to move on? Is that the message? She wondered if she was being unconsciously reminded of an even earlier loss, a betrayal she could not get over. *Mike the Bike has awoken something. Even if he is not conscious of it. I helped a lot of people in my career. I had to say goodbye and good luck cheerfully to other people's children.*

She listened to the silence in her apartment. *Now I'm alone, feeling the minutes pass, I don't like it. It's hell sometimes. I have to forgive them all every day, despite their silence, or I can't live. Most of all, I have to accept what I chose to do.*

She heard Mike's bike. *Here comes Mitzi's ride. Not quite so loud this time, no extra twist on the throttle!* She looked out of the window and saw the broad-shouldered man carefully pick up a travel box. She felt a little faint again. *Mitzi's had more than me! She's ridden behind him. I'm jealous!*

She turned back to the tea table, with the last of the dark-chocolate digestive biscuits. Would she ever buy them again? Did she need to? She had hardly ever wondered why she always kept a packet of those biscuits in the house. *And I'm a psychoanalyst,* she thought ruefully. *There must be a lot more to think about. We all carry the scars of unforgivable sins and we all have an unconscious. We have made our history.* She comforted herself with that humbling thought.

Mike came into the apartment. 'How's the foot feeling?' He sat down heavily on the sofa while Miss Eleanor shuffled to the table to pour some tea.

'I'm fine and I'll be even better soon, I'm sure. It'll be so nice if you can come to visit some time.'

'Yeah, I'll come with the daughter and the girlfriend. It's strange, I thought I remembered a bit more of the dream when I was on the bike behind your cab, but it wasn't that. I thought that my mother must have gone through what I saw my girlfriend suffer last night—strange, eh?'

My God, thought Eleanor, *he's continuing his therapy session with me.* She was tempted to add, 'And you felt grateful,' but she knew she had to let him come to that conclusion in his own time.

He changed the subject. 'Mitzi is easy to have on the bike. She slept the whole way. Even the exhaust pipes didn't wake her up. But I imagined the small babies I was waking up with the noise. I'll have to get some silencers,' he said. 'But what will the other blokes in the club say? Pussy bike or what? Sorry, that was rude.

'Babies! Shit... I've got one. I said I'd be back in the hospital half an hour ago.' He jumped up, mumbling an apology. 'I'll be here again, another day.'

'Goodbye, Mike,' she called after him as the door closed. *He has a girlfriend, a baby, and a new life. Mitzi has had more than me—a ride on his back.* She remembered, fleetingly, being carried round the parlor on her father's back. She remembered hoping that her mother felt left out.

I wonder if he'll return? She hoped and fantasized: the wind in her hair, the open road. She was back there, with him, her fling, lost but not forgotten.

She remained sitting at the table. She dropped another sugar lump into her cooling tea and watched the tiny ripples reach the edge of the cup. *Everything is experienced in such detail and in slow motion when you are suffering*, she thought. She picked up another chocolate biscuit. *Maybe it takes a whole life to work out your losses: birth, boyfriends, and everything else. They show themselves again when you least expect it.*

She had taken one bite of the now sticky biscuit in her hand. *How difficult it is to eat biscuits when you are crying. What to do now? Suffer it until you get to the other side? This emptiness feels as if it will never end. All the possibilities of one life, so clear when you are old. The life I've made, or the life with him if he'd lived? It might not have worked out anyway. It's so easy to regret. So much harder to be grateful to yourself for the life you made.*

And it took Tor's Brother to awaken my long-buried distress. Perhaps this is the start of something new.

'Don't be ridiculous,' she said to herself sharply. She tried to kick-start her usual defense, hiding from pain. But something had risen from her unconscious and could not be hidden again. She poured a little warm tea.

Now it's too late for breakfast and I still haven't got the butter. Oh, silly me! But I'll get my old address book out and ring a friend today. Let's hope they are alive. She laughed at her dark humor. And she wanted to think about writing a paper on forgiveness.

She heard the bike's thunderous start. She thought about her rescuing angel waking up small children, and helping her to face her private hell. *Mike the Bike. Who does he think he is? Who do I think I am?*

Postscript

In an earlier version of this story, the Tor's Brothers MC Club was called the Hell's Angels. However, it was pointed out to me that the latter society are, understandably, protective of the copyright on their name. I looked for other names, but the most likely ones were taken by other groups of motorcyclists. So I opted to invent a name that fits with Scandinavia, where I live. As far as I know it is not in use by any other group. I haven't met any brothers of Tor.

The story tries to illustrate a process that occurs when a minor trauma triggers a reaction and opens hidden feelings: when Mike accidentally hurts Eleanor and Mitzi, he becomes aware at a deeper emotional level of the events of the night before. He thinks about the creativity of his girlfriend, the skill and courage of the midwife; he is in awe of them. Then, he recalls memories of his mother and childhood.

For Eleanor, the tall man who causes her pain reminds her of another aspect of the long-buried loss in her adolescence. They both have a painful insight about themselves that helps them to think about their present situation in another way. For each of them, the original loss was too heavy to feel and think about, so it was denied, repressed, and forgotten. Mike pushed his feelings away, as he usually did in his 'professional life' when he made other people feel pain instead of him. Eleanor appears to have used her early loss more creatively by her choice of profession. That is, she helps other people with their mourning.

In the next story is a metaphor for what makes an analysis function, how we listen...

15
Molly Mop

————◆————

Molly, a middle-aged lady with a friendly face and graying hair, was a cleaner. She wore an old cotton overall decorated with large flowers. Her work slippers were threadbare.

Molly's daily responsibility in the town's hospital was the central corridor. It was the longest and widest in the building. The doors of many departments populated its length. Early in the morning, she would start at one end with a bucket of clean water, floor soap, and a strong mop.

By the end of the day, she had reached the other end of the corridor, used four buckets of water, and drunk thirteen cups of tea. The tea was given to her by the thirteen departments she passed on her slow journey down the corridor.

After work, she would say, 'Oh, my back. Oh, my poor legs. I'm going home now. I'd like to put my feet up, but I've got so much more to do.'

In the course of her day, she would meet a number of anxious patients who littered the corridor. They were strewn there by the departments, each of which decided that a certain patient did not belong with them. Each time a patient started to walk towards another department they heard the sound of a door closing in front of them.

If Molly was nearby, she would say, 'This is a bit of a nightmare, ain't it.' It wasn't a question or a complaint, it was a description.

'Yes, it is. Do you work here?'

Molly always avoided giving an answer. She didn't want to embarrass a stressed person when she clearly looked as if she was working there. 'I'm doing this for the moment, what about you?' she would say, simply and kindly, apparently to pass the time. Then she listened, open to anything, nothing, and everything.

The wandering patient would then gratefully tell Molly why they were there, how difficult life had been, how much they had suffered, how long they had waited.

Molly listened, and she mopped. Gradually the patient's story would become calmer and more thoughtful. When they passed the next department, the secretary usually noticed her, the door opened, and Molly was offered a cup of tea. If she was with a corridor patient, she asked for 'A second cup, please.'

By the time they had finished a cup of tea—or two—the patient would say, 'I think I don't really need to spend my time in this corridor. I can go now.'

If they said, 'What would you do if you were me?' Molly would continue to clean the floor and, after a few moments, she'd say with a kind smile, 'You ain't got to the end of your story, have yah?' The corridor patient would say, 'No, I don't think I have,' and carry on talking about their lives, until eventually they heard themselves say what they needed to know. Then, they would leave.

In the various departments, the staff noted that the patient waiting lists were not growing. They wondered what was happening in the corridor; did the patients actually find their way to the right place? The administrators thought that perhaps some research was required. Molly continued to mop and listen.

Sometimes Molly and a patient, in their slow walk down the corridor, reached a department she thought could be appropriate for them. She would say, 'Hang on a minute, stay by me mop and bucket. I'll only be a moment.' She would go inside and say to the administrator, 'I think the patient out there belongs in here. Can you have a chat with them? And may I have a cup of tea, please?'

One day, when she came back to her bucket after she had placed a patient, Molly found a small child trying to use her mop. Molly said, 'You can use a mop that's the right size. Come back tomorrow and I'll have one for you.' The little child looked at Molly and said, 'I've got secrets.'

When the child returned, Molly had a small mop available. They worked together cleaning the corridor. From time to time, the child talked to her in quiet tones and Molly listened carefully. The child's mother, who sat opposite them on one of the many seats for the comfort of corridor patients, changed seats to be near them as they moved along. Occasionally, an adult patient would join the trio and the four of them would move along slowly until the adult patient decided to leave or they reached the correct department.

After several weeks, during which the child whispered her secrets to Molly, the child's mother said, 'School and home life are much better and, outside this corridor, my child is talking aloud again.' Molly nodded discreetly to the mother, while the child continued to mop.

In the next few months, Molly began to breathe heavily; working was a strain. She lost weight. One day, towards the end of her shift, she, the child, and the mother were outside the last department door.

Molly said, 'I think it's time for me to go.' The little child smiled and squeezed Molly's hand. 'Goodbye and thank you,' she said, and went on her way with her mother.

Molly went through door number thirteen. The administrator said, 'You're welcome, Molly. Here's a cup of tea.'

The doctor smiled. 'We're ready for you, Molly,' he said, and she walked into a brightly lit consulting room, where she could put her feet up—finally.

Postscript

'Give every man thy ear, but few thy voice' (William Shakespeare, *Hamlet*, Act I, Scene 3, ll, 68). Molly lived by this good advice. I suppose this could be the beginning of a story. But it's a vignette to show that many people can listen in a way that gives the other person's unconscious an opportunity to discover something about themselves. Freud learned his method of free association by accepting his patients' critique. In the case of Frau Emmy von N, he listened to his patient's complaint that she did not want to go on answering his questions. She wanted him to listen to her without interruption. 'She then said in a definitely grumbling tone that I was not to keep on asking her where this and that came from, but to let her tell me what she had to say. I fell in with this, and she went on without preface.' (Freud, S. (1893), p. 63)

Whether an individual's analysis is based on Freudian psychoanalysis or some other form of talking cure, the evidence from our personal experience is that talking helps alleviate emotional symptoms, lessens anxiety, and frees up our minds. Psychoanalysis uses the most powerful tool, namely the relationship in the consulting room. We all have the experience of being emotionally upset and, after talking to someone who listens, who then makes a few comments that link our experience to other parts of our lives, we feel understood, and hopefully understand ourselves better. That is part of the evidence for the value of psychoanalysis and similar therapies—it is inside us, we know it already. Everyone needs a Molly.

What happened to Molly? In this little sketch of a 'corridor therapy', we don't know. There are people like Molly, who understand how to listen. For example, it is not unusual for a child in school to share a worry with one of the people working there, possibly the teacher, but maybe the dinner lady or the person supervising the playground. What is the value of their conversation? Why do children feel better after such a contact?

Reference

Freud, S. (1893). *Frau Emmy von N. Case Histories from Studies on Hysteria.* SE II. London: Hogarth Press and the Institute of Psycho-Analysis.

The next story illustrates another kind of expectation, one that is satisfied by the love that makes thinking possible…

16

Jamie's Question—Where do my Thoughts Come From?

—————•—————

J amie was nine years old, an advanced little boy with a question: 'Where do my thoughts come from?'

'They come from your head,' said Mum.

'God's magic,' said Dad.

That's like the answer to where do babies come from, Jamie thought, *and Mum is pregnant again. God's been busy.* Jamie asked his grandma the same question.

'God gave you thoughts, dear.'

'Like God gives babies, Grandma?'

'Yes, but it's the bubbly wine that mixes things together.'

'You mean a mixture of my mum and dad?'

'We don't talk about that, Jamie. But there is another little person coming to us soon. A baby girl, I shouldn't wonder.'

'I don't want to think about her.'

His big brother was jealous of Jamie's cuddles with their mum. No point asking him.

When he posed the question to his teacher, Sister Judith, she said, 'Thoughts are in your mind, child. And your mind is in your brain. We talked about the brain a week ago! Stop dreaming.'

At the next break-time, Jamie was too busy thinking to play. He wandered back into the school building. There was a bad smell in the boys' toilets.

'Never mind me, son, you carry on,' said the caretaker. 'I'm just clearing a blockage. I was in the army. I was a POW. You know what that is, don't you?'

Jamie did indeed know this story; all the boys had heard it several times. He was quiet because he didn't want to be rude; his mum had said he should be kind to the caretaker. 'He's had a trauma,' she said.

'Prisoner of war, that's what it means, son. It's hot in Burma, and smelly, much worse than this toilet. But I'm not worth any less than anyone else.' He pushed hard with his brush. 'Another thing, son: in these toilets, everyone is the same. Do you follow me? No one can avoid sitting on one of these, at least once a day and, when they do, they're the same as you and me. Everyone hopes they can do their business without a stink and some believe they won't create the tiniest whiff.'

Jamie tried to change the subject. 'Where do thoughts come from?'

'Same place all this stuff comes from: your insides.'

'But how do they start?'

The caretaker continued to poke around in the toilet. Jamie moved to leave.

'Now that's interesting. I've read books, you know. All the smelly stuff in here comes out of a complicated system, like your brain, I suppose. Food goes in and comes out looking like something else, but it's still the same stuff.' The caretaker raised his hand, as if to scratch his head, but looked at his gloves.

'Hmm, judging by some people's thoughts, it all comes from the same place. Oops, mustn't let politics come into this, eh, son?'

Adults always seem to go too far, or not far enough, thought Jamie.

'My dad says it's God's magic.'

'Well, that would be simple. My pay packet might look a bit healthier if God's magic could be called up, eh?'

Here we go again: grown-up humor.

'No offense, son, I shouldn't be talking about my pay packet in front of you, should I?' He pushed and shoved his industrial-strength brush. 'That's beginning to sound like something, ain't it?' His voice echoed out of the toilet bowl. 'Thoughts come from inside, made from what went in. All very complicated, eh?'

Jamie wasn't sure if he followed.

'What's your name, son?'

'Jamie.'

The caretaker appeared not to hear him. 'You know memories from years ago, like in the war? It's all in there in your head, like in another world. It's all there, mixing around. Just like yesterday, every detail. It's never history, really, is it?'

He added a flexible extension to his brush and sent it around the U-bend. 'The blokes who survived, they had something in their heads that made them go on. You know what I mean, son? We were starving all the time, but I just thought about me mum. I have to be thankful for her.'

Jamie was bemused.

The caretaker started up again. 'I remember Burma every day. It's a torment. Have you noticed, in a dream, even the past becomes the present? Amazing. I wonder how that happens?' He sniffed. 'Anyway, better get on, this isn't solving itself.'

Jamie sort of knew what the caretaker meant, especially thinking about his mum. On the other hand, he also knew what was coming next.

'The Japanese, son, the Japanese...' Mercifully, at that moment, the bell rang for the end of break-time. 'You go back to your business, son, learning from the holy nuns,' came the voice echoing out of the toilet bowl. 'No bad things come out of them. Only my pay packet, of course.'

Jamie backed towards the door at what he considered a polite speed. He wanted to avoid hearing again about the horrors of jungle warfare, and he didn't want to irritate Sister Judith. 'You know, son, Burma... the heat... the smell of dead bodies.'

Jamie made it into the anonymity of the busy corridor. The door closed. He walked towards his classroom, thinking. Ideas come from another place, like Dad says, but not heaven. It's from inside—like all the shit and mess, and thinking about your mum.

By the door, the stout frame of Sister Judith awaited him. 'And what time do you call this, Jamie? Have you been wandering around in your head again?'

'Yes, Sister—er, no, Sister.' He was never sure how to answer her trick questions. He slid past her into the room and met the loving eyes of Sarah, the girl who sat next to him. Her early-pubescent body leaned towards him. What should he feel?

The caretaker had once likened his problems with 'her indoors' to crossing a minefield in Burma. But he couldn't remember the rest of the story. Sister Judith's brisk approach to imparting knowledge brought Jamie's mind into the present, for a little while.

He sank into a formless daydream while the morning's teaching droned on. It wasn't long before he awoke with a jolt. Sister Judith was standing beside him. He could feel the heat of her body through the layers of her habit. He smelled the clean, dry aroma of washing powder, and something else both attractive and repellent. He tried to focus—what had she been talking about? He looked at his sometime savior, Sarah. But she had her head down.

'And where are we now, mister, in dreamland? And where on earth is that—or perhaps you're in outer space today? You disappear into your fantasy realm a bit too often, young Jamie. One day you'll get stuck there, and a fine mess you'll be in then.'

'Yes, Sister; no, Sister...' *Oh God, what's the right answer?*

Sister Judith took a breath, and then, mercifully, an unfamiliar noise on the other side of the room distracted her. She left Jamie's side with a message for Sarah. 'Tell him what's happening, my dear, and try to keep him grounded.'

'Yes, Sister.' Sarah looked delighted and moved closer to Jamie. He felt her arm a millimeter from his; it was disturbing. She offered him a little volcano: an illicit, cone-shaped, cherry-flavored sweet. He knew he shouldn't take it during lesson time, but he popped it into his mouth.

Sarah held him with her eyes, then she looked down at the volcano book. He felt lost, but she caught him with her words. 'Open at page seven, Jamie, and you'll see V...o...l...c...a...n...o...s,' she said, articulating each letter slowly, 'cooled lava cones that ooze hot material.'

'Good, Sarah! Thank you!' Sister Judith had reappeared.

Jamie tried to hide the little volcano under his tongue. It was sweet and bitter; he hoped his cheeks weren't pink.

'You seem to have got his interest, Sarah.'

'Yes, Sister.'

'Back here now, Jamie? With Sarah's thoughts about volcanos? Not thoughts from your other world? You'll be lost there, remember that.'

Sarah turned away with a sigh. Jamie was disappointed and relieved. He dared not wander off again and try to work out where his thoughts came from; neither Sister Judith nor Sarah would tolerate that. He read the book; it described the lava bottled up inside the planet. It was a wonder that the earth wasn't warm and soft, *like the nice parts of my mum*, he thought. He dared not say that out loud.

Soon it was time to end lessons for the day. At home, Jamie quietly ate his food. He said a dutiful 'hmm' and 'good' to questions about his day in school. His parents seemed satisfied with those responses now, although it had taken him some time to train them.

Jamie went to bed, still puzzling over his question. He thought about his day: the caretaker, Sister Judith, Sarah, the volcano lesson, Mum being pregnant, his big brother—who hated him just for being here! He turned off his bedside light and pulled up the covers.

Jamie found himself walking away from his house, without shoes. He trod carefully on the gravel road and, soon, he stood in front of a dark forest. Strangely, he knew where he was. The trees parted, and in front of him was a crooked path. He came to a clearing and saw a beautiful sweet shop. He recognized the sweets called little volcanos, which were cherry-red and pink. He ate some; they were nice, then bitter. He felt pleased, and guilty. He saw Sarah's eyes and felt his mother's arms around him.

Sister Judith's voice called out, 'You can't eat those.'

A little girl came into the shop. She looked hungrily at the sweets.

Jamie knew it was his baby sister. This is my dad's fault, *he grumbled to himself—him and his bubbly wine and God's magic. He hated her and he was filled with guilt.*

He felt hungry; his stomach was empty and burning. He was falling and falling. Someone he needed was missing. He called again and again: 'Mummy.' He was having a thought; he couldn't explain it, but he knew it was true.

He began to rise, up and up. Dad was lifting him. His mother took him in her arms. The warmth of her soft body and sweet aroma soothed him. 'What a nightmare you've had,' she cooed.

'I was nasty to my sister. I don't want her,' Jamie mumbled. 'She took sweets. I took them too, pink and red. I knew I shouldn't, they belonged—'

'—to her,' said his big brother, who had come into the bedroom. 'What's up with the little pisser?' Their mother patiently ignored him, and he went back to bed.

'Mum, I've a secret.'

'You can tell me in the morning, dear.'

'I know where my thoughts come from,' he said.

'That's wonderful. It's a special secret.'

'He's hot,' said his dad, changing the bedsheets.

'Help me put him back in bed. He's almost asleep,' said his mum.

Jamie slept immediately. His forest was not lost: it was a part of him. He knew without words that thoughts came from his longing for something he needed. He woke up happy. After breakfast, all the family rushed out into the world as usual.

Jamie said 'Good morning' to Sister Judith.

Sarah offered him a little volcano. He blushed, and her friends giggled.

Postscript

This story is an attempt to understand how small children develop a mind, using the theory of W. R. Bion. (Bion, W. R. (1967)) Small children require love, food, warmth, and explanations of their inner experiences. Bion thought that the hungry baby had an expectation of a breast, which is essential for survival. If the breast is absent then baby develops an internal image he named 'no-breast', and baby may react strongly in protest. However, Bion said that if the baby can tolerate the frustration of the absent mother—and the degree to which this is possible will vary from child to child—then the experience can be turned into a thought. It (psychoanalysis) all began by one person listening properly to another, as we have seen in the stories *Molly Mop* and *Jamie's Question*.

Reference

Bion W. R. (1967). 'A Theory of Thinking', in *Second Thoughts*. London: Karnac Books.

Epilogue

We can end this book with the thought that love is expressed as a devotion to the truth.

Book Two

Provocations

Introduction

————◆————

This is a collection of stories from the anarchic world of the unconscious, in which the theme is the provocative arousal of emotions in another person. Dictionary definitions of **provocation** can be paraphrased as follows: the act of provoking to anger or aggression; an incitement that arouses or stimulates. In criminal law, provocation refers to words or conduct that incite a person to attack another. Provocation is action or speech that makes someone angry, especially deliberately, as in goading another person to violence; or it may be an action which arouses sexual desire or disgust. This behavior involves the familiar mechanism of projection as used in psychoanalysis, where provocation is defined as 'an operation whereby qualities, feelings, wishes or even objects, which the subject refuses to recognize, or rejects in himself, are expelled from the self and located in another person or thing' (Laplanche, J., and Pontalis, J.-B. (1980), p. 349)

In psychoanalytic theory, projection is also called projective identification, a psychoanalytic term for the placing of a part of oneself in another and the identification of that part with the other person. 'Projective identification is an unconscious phantasy in which aspects of the self or of an internal object (either good or bad) are split off and attributed to an external object.' (Spillius, E. B. et al. (2011), p. 126) Sometimes the phantasy is accompanied by behavior that induces the victim to behave as predicted by the person projecting. Racism is a good example, i.e. in a situation where another race, usually immigrants, is perceived as greedy and only here to steal our resources. We hope that so long as they are greedy, we are not. This means that we refuse to recognize greed in ourselves and, by projecting it onto immigrants, we separate ourselves from it and elevate our self-esteem.

Projection is also a part of ordinary communication, in which we express our emotions by means of facial expressions, tone of voice and those mysterious intuitive instincts which enable us to know how the other person is feeling without the use of words. In psychoanalysis, the exploration of the unconscious leads to the uncovering of our envy and hatred, which is interesting, awful, and fascinating. The following stories mainly describe situations in which aggressive projection dominates. Psychoanalysis is dedicated to the understanding and exposing of such barriers to our creativity, and to the release of loving feelings from negative fantasies.

To sum up, we can say that a projection is governed by the qualities of the conscious fantasy and the unconscious phantasy driving it. *Remember that the word 'fantasy' is used for conscious images with feelings and the word 'phantasy' is used for unconscious images and experiences, as seen in dreams for example.* Aggressive projections are governed by aggressive fantasies or phantasies of different qualities and the energy in the projection is determined by the quantity of hatred, sadism, and vengefulness in the person delivering it. This book is a collection of examples of these kinds of behaviors.

Why teach using stories? Psychoanalysis is a personal exploration of one's mind through free association. I write stories to try to clarify some aspects of the technical language of psychoanalysis. In a clinical paper which shows the relationship between the analyst's theory and his description of his patient, the listeners are observers of two parties, with a passive third party in the lecture hall. Unless they are familiar with similar work, the audience may not be able to relate the analyst's paper to their own experience. On the other hand, telling the audience a story creates another kind of relationship, because listeners can identify with characters in a narrative. When this happens the teacher and audience can relate their emotional experience of the story to the understanding of their own lives and work. I hope these stories will help the reader to take a glimpse into the inner world of the unconscious, 'by which we are lived' (Groddeck, G. (1949)) My advice is to read with an open mind until the tale speaks to you. Like watching a film, listening to a piece of music or looking at a piece of art, allow yourself to note your reactions and thoughts.

This book, like *Expectations* and *Audacities*, started as part of my attempt to make the teaching of psychotherapy more interesting and relevant. The books are written for anyone who is interested in psychoanalysis and for use in a teaching situation, where a story can be taken as an introductory example of a state of mind and the related theory. I want to leave the reader or teacher free to add their own theoretical perspective. We know that clients are more inclined to change when their free associations lead them to insight, rather than the therapist trying to put their own ideas into the client's mind.

References

Groddeck, G. (1949). *The Book of the It*. London: Vision Press.

Laplanche, J., and Pontalis, J.-B. (1980). *The Language of Psychoanalysis*, p. 455. London: Hogarth Press and the Institute of Psycho-Analysis.

Spillius, E. B. et al. (2011). *The New Dictionary of Kleinian Thought*. London: Routledge.

1

The Changeable Witch

———•———

Once upon a time, many moons ago, in a dark forest on the other side of an ocean, there lived a changeable witch. From the outside, her house appeared small; if you looked through the window, you would see a modest sitting room with soft furnishings and colored rugs on the floor. But if you went inside the dimensions would appear huge, with high ceilings and spacious rooms one after another furnished with masses of exotic fixtures and fittings.

The witch possessed a kindly smile and twinkling eyes. She had two black cats, no mice, and definitely no rats. I would like to describe her to you, but all I can say is that she looked like a witch—and to leave it at that. For what she looked like depended on the feelings of the person looking at her. Three people standing in front of her would describe three different witches.

Like an old grandmother, it seemed that she had lived in her house forever. People visited and asked her their unknowable questions, looking for unthinkable answers. Usually, they went away thoughtful and grateful, but not always.

The witch would offer them tea. She didn't interrupt or ask questions and, as she listened, she became more and more like the person talking to her. When her visitor had finished speaking she would say something like, 'What you say is interesting, but I think you've lost track of what you were asking.'

'Really? I'm waiting for an answer. How long will this take?'

'It will take the time it takes.'

'Why do you look so strange? You didn't look like this when I arrived.'

'Hmm, keep looking at me. I have felt your story, and I understand that you feel many things, some hard, some soft, some warm, and some cold. When you get home, light a fire, make some tea, sit down, and quietly repeat all you've said to me. And, above all, remember who you have seen here today. After a time, your inner self will show you the answer to your question. But it's up to you of course.'

'What question? When will I understand?'

The witch would smile and get to her feet. The meeting was over.

Sometimes people were furious. 'I'm never coming here again. You know nothing, and anyway you look awful.'

But when the visitors went home, lit a fire, made some tea, repeated what they had said to her, and remembered how she looked, before and after the conversation, then their inner selves, so deep and eternal, did indeed reveal their question and the answer was clear.

'Now I see who I really am! How could she understand me so well?'

And the old witch, sitting in her rocking chair in the middle of the darkest part of the forest, looked just like herself again. She smiled, drank her tea, and fell asleep with her cats.

∽

One fine spring day something different occurred. The changeable witch was dozing in her rocking chair on the wooden porch at the front of her cottage. Sunshine warmed her face, and the earth smelled of the last of the winter snow and of fresh leaves. An unseen fly was buzzing, while her black cats stretched on the floor by her feet.

Suddenly, the witch felt heavy steps in the forest, but there was no one to be seen. After a few moments she felt the steps again and said to herself, 'A very large person is crashing through the forest towards me. I wonder what they want?'

On the other side of the clearing a man appeared. He was slightly built and approached her with his head bowed. He wore a crumpled coat, which had once been beige.

The witch closed her eyes and felt the presence of a determined and angry man.

'Good morning,' he said. 'I'm looking for the changeable witch.'

'What a coincidence, I am she. How do you do?' she said with a smile.

'Are you annoyed with me?' he demanded.

'Why do you think that?'

'The way you're looking at me. My name is Gerald Crumble. My wife sent me.'

'Welcome, Gerald.'

'I'm not used to walking so far. It's warm, isn't it?' He opened his coat.

'What's written on your shirt?'

'Nothing. My wife ironed it this morning.'

'But it says,

This man thinks he is thru with his wife
But really, he is thru with his life.'

'I don't see anything.'

   'This IS interesting.'

   'Is it?'

   'You are interesting, I mean.'

   'I really don't think so.'

   'You'd better come onto my porch. Please have a seat. Would you like some tea?'

   'I'm not sure. Yes, all right.'

   A tea tray with a pot, milk, sugar, two cups, saucers, spoons, and a plate of biscuits appeared on an occasional table beside her.

   'I'll be mother,' she said, and poured the tea. 'Milk and sugar?'

   'Please.'

   'These biscuits are home-made. My own. They taste of whatever you wish, and they'll last as long as you need a sense of well-being.'

   'I am a little peckish.'

   The changeable witch studied him as he stirred his tea. She felt that there may be something in the coming conversation that would alter her shape drastically.

   'Please excuse me for a moment.' She went inside.

   Mr Crumble looked around, squinting in the sunlight. A bird twittered nearby, and a cool breeze carrying the scent of fresh snow stirred the new leaves. He breathed in. The biscuit was filling, and the tea soothing.

   The witch reappeared, wearing an oversized tracksuit and large training shoes.

   Mr Crumble behaved as if nothing was remarkable.

The witch sat down and picked up her tea; it had remained warm. Mr Crumble noticed his tea had stayed warm too. He felt, unusually for him, that he would like to have a good long talk.

The changeable witch sat back in her rocking chair and looked at him kindly. She was available to him, but she always kept a space in her mind for herself, so that she could think her own thoughts. She was about to explain how she could help him, when he began an account of his troubles. And what a lot he had to say...

'My wife is so bossy, she's forever ordering me about, and the kids are too demanding. I don't think much of their schools—the teachers are downright incompetent. I'm snowed under at work and my boss is just ridiculous. He's an interfering control freak.'

Mr Crumble went on and on in this vein, though he didn't say he sometimes thought about killing himself.

The witch felt everything. As he spoke, her body began to grow larger and the private part of her mind was inundated with his complaints.

'My wife never shuts up. She says stupid things and complains all the time, trying to make me feel bad too, and it drives me mad.'

Mr Crumble didn't say that he sometimes imagined taking the sharpest knife from the kitchen drawer. Nor did he say that he thought the witch was getting bigger. Her face was changing; she was looking more like a man. He thought he must be seeing things. He decided not to look at her any more—it was rude to stare anyway. He looked down at the floor and his violent fantasy continued in silence. *I take the knife in my hand and grab her from behind. She screams and gurgles as she struggles. The kitchen wall is painted red.*

The changeable witch felt all this and saw red too. She saw that Mr Crumble looked delighted. The part of her mind that belonged to her was overwhelmed by the feelings attached to his story.

143

Mr Crumble woke from his daydream. 'Where was I?'

'Something red,' said the witch, in a deeper voice.

She's reading my thoughts, the bitch. He turned away. He dared not look at her. He continued to complain about his work, the kids, and his monster of a wife.

The witch had now grown extremely heavy. She crashed onto the floor to the sound of splintering wood. The special place in her mind for her private thoughts was almost overcome.

'I'm sorry,' Mr Crumble muttered. 'I hate to complain so much. She's not so bad, I suppose—the wife, I mean. I like her really.'

But secretly he told himself, *I like the thought of red everywhere, it gives me such a rush.*

'My wife says she will leave me if I hit her. She says she will take the children. Oh no! Not the children!' His eyes filled with water. 'Sometimes I think about using a kitchen knife on myself, but I wouldn't do it, for their sake. At least, I think I wouldn't do it.'

The changeable witch was now so big her body filled her tracksuit. *He's got to look at me soon or I will be stuck like this. He must see the monster his rage turns him into. But he's hiding his eyes, trying to look small and humble.*

The witch continued to grow, her eyes murderous; she was choking on the little man's hatred. The porch creaked under the weight of her enormous body and she groaned in pain. The seams of the tracksuit and trainers were stretched to their limits.

'I don't want to overstay my welcome,' said Mr Crumble. 'I think I should leave you in peace and let you get on with your day.'

The witch tried to say, 'Look at me! I'm dying!' But her head was pressing on the ceiling, and he couldn't make out what she was saying.

Mr Crumble, head down, took his grubby coat. 'So sorry, do excuse my intrusion. It was delightful to meet you. Thank you for your time. The tea and the biscuits were excellent. I feel so much better.'

As he walked away, he felt as if he'd escaped from something awful. Then the thought occurred that he'd lost something. He felt in his pockets but couldn't think what it was he'd left behind. He felt weak and foolish and imagined what his wife would say. 'Why didn't you stay to the end? You're such a coward. You should have waited and listened to what the lady had to say!'

He walked on, the biscuit effect weakening. A bird sang a melancholy song, and the sounds of small branches that crunched under his feet seemed to be little voices that condemned him. He felt sorry for what he had done, but he couldn't turn back. Was he going the right way? After half an hour he came to a clearing and a fork in the track. A sign read, 'Calm'. It pointed to a pub.

The Greenwood Arms had black wooden beams and crumbling plasterwork. Ivy grew up over the front door and onto the roof. The chimney smoked reluctantly. Mr Crumble felt lost, as if a part of him was somewhere else, but he couldn't work out where.

So he did what any Englishman would do in such a situation.

At the cottage the changeable witch was furious. She needed her spell book and her magic wand. But she'd grown too big to reach them. Maybe she had a spell in her memory. She could not think; she felt utterly helpless.

'He must come back and see these bloody red feelings.'

As she flailed about, she cracked a wall. 'Oh no,' she whimpered. 'What have I done?'

One of her cats said to the other, 'Listen, she's talking to herself, she's become him.'

'Who?'

'That Crumble character.'

'We'll have to get him back, or we'll never get our supper.'

They padded off the porch.

'No, don't leave me,' she cried.

She felt bereft. Abandoned and lonely—and filled up with someone else's bad feelings.

'I could kill someone!' she cried. 'Oh God, I've turned into him!'

Mr Crumble sat at the bar, watching as the barman slowly pulled him a pint.

'I'm not sure about drinking in the afternoon. What will my wife say?'

'C'mon, Mr Crumble. This will make a man of you,' said Gerry the barman.

'How do you know my name?'

'Just a lucky guess. You look sort of crumbly.' Gerry smiled. 'Lets you out once a year, does she?' He winked at his other customers.

'Something like that,' said Mr Crumble, adopting the familiar role of victim.

'Hey, don't be so serious, we're only joking.'

Mr Crumble nodded politely.

Gerry studied him. 'You look a bit pale, if you don't mind my saying. What have you been up to?'

'Not much,' Mr Crumble mumbled, staring at the cloud of rich dark ale gathering in his glass. His guilt about drinking behind his wife's back was increasing. 'But something is missing, I've lost something.'

Gerry turned off the tap, removed the frothy head of the beer with a knife, and waited.

The pub fire burned slowly. After a long winter the chimney was not drawing well, and woodsmoke hung in wreaths, obscuring the details of the other faces in the room.

'I've been into the deep dark forest to visit the changeable witch.'

The pub fell silent. Some customers noticed the entrance of two black cats, who curled around Mr Crumble's legs.

Mr Crumble continued, unaware of the change of mood in the room or of the cats. 'I mean, I did all the talking, she just sat there looking at me. Then it became embarrassing. She began to get bigger. Do you know what I mean?'

Everyone nodded.

'She swelled up enormously, so I stopped looking at her. It seemed rude.'

'You did what?' exclaimed the other customers.

'I... I stopped looking at her.'

'Then what?' said Gerry, as he topped up Mr Crumble's glass.

'Er... well, I heard a loud noise, her chair broke, and she fell off. So, I thought it best to... well, you know how it is.'

Beer was flowing over the edge of the glass. Gerry quickly turned off the tap, then crouched down, looking for the bar cloth.

'I just left.'

'You what?' Gerry shouted from under the bar.

'I left, but I shouldn't have, should I? I'm beginning to understand that.'

Gerry popped up, cloth in hand. 'That's why you don't feel right.'

'I'd better go back, I suppose.'

'Indeed. I'll look after your pint.'

Mr Crumble exited the pub, struggling to pull on his coat. He felt foolish: what would he say to his wife? The forest looked forbidding. 'I have to do it,' he told himself, but he didn't move.

Some of the other customers emerged, glasses in hand, to see him off. They nodded towards the forest.

Mr Crumble sighed and started to walk. It was cold and silent among the trees and he wanted to turn back. But for once in his life he didn't give up. He walked on, one cat ahead of him, one behind.

It was just as well he didn't look back, because the Greenwood Arms had disappeared.

As Mr Crumble pressed on, crunching over fallen leaves, he was seized by the fear of monsters springing from the trees to rip him apart. But he didn't give up and he walked on down the path, darting anxious glances left and right. Finally, he came to the witch's cottage.

The little house had been crushed flat and there was no sign of the witch. The cats prowled the ruins looking for their home.

'Hello, I'm back,' he called out. 'Hello!'

He heard a grunt and saw, coming towards him from the edge of the clearing, a huge angry-looking person in a tracksuit.

'My God!' he exclaimed. 'It's the witch and she looks like me.'

He sat down with a bump, staring with amazement at the figure in front of him.

The changeable witch seemed to be shrinking.

'Please excuse me, Mr Crumble,' she said. 'Oh dear, I must mend my cottage and change my clothes.'

'Of course,' said Mr Crumble, and started to look away. Then, remembering what had happened earlier, he looked back.

The witch scrabbled around in the ruins until she found her spell book and cast a spell. Suddenly her home was whole again. The porch was where it should be, the chairs were mended, and there was even a tea tray with biscuits on the occasional table. The witch went inside and came out properly dressed—for a witch that is.

'Sit down if you please, Mr Crumble, we have some business to finish. It won't take long. Here is your tea.' She handed him a fresh cup, full of warm tea. 'Better than your pint, for the moment anyway.' She winked at him.

Mr Crumble was charmed. He wondered how she knew about the Greenwood Arms. He took the cup and sat down, aware that he felt different.

The witch looked at him with twinkling eyes.

'Look at me and, please, don't look away.'

Mr Crumble nodded.

'I've felt your story. Everything in your life to do with love is far too... well, to be perfectly frank with you, Mr Crumble, it's far too bloody! I think you have lost something.'

He realized that she wasn't making him feel guilty.

'I understand that you feel many things: some of them are hard, some are soft, some are warm, and some are cold. When you get home, light a fire, make some tea, and tell yourself the story you've told me. Your inner self, so deep and wise, so endless and eternal, will show you your question. It's up to you, of course.'

Mr Crumble didn't really understand, but he thought he would do as she said. He was just thinking that another biscuit would be nice when, in the twinkling of an eye, to his great surprise (and, I am sure, to yours) he became aware that he was lying on the couch in the living room of his own home. The window was open and he felt the forest air around him. He could hear voices. Were they the people from the Greenwood Arms? He heard the back door close and the sound of steam hissing from an iron.

The self-effacing, and sometimes a little paranoid, Gerald Crumble, forty-three years old, a draughtsman in an engineering company, lay blinking in the sunlight that filled the room.

On the floor behind him the children, seven-year-old twins Lucy and Jack, played with plastic models of scary monsters and a witch's crooked house. By the window, his wife Maureen was ironing.

He heard Lucy say, 'Can we visit the smiley lady and play with her cats?'

'And can Daddy tell us a story?' said Jack.

'I'm sure he will, but first why don't you run next door to Mrs...'

'You never remember her name, Mummy. She's the smiley-forever-lady.'

'That's true, but it's Mrs Grumpelwinkle, isn't it? Make sure you knock and ask politely. You'll have a story later.'

Gerald roused himself. 'Yes to a story. I'm not sure about her name though.' He fell back into the comfort of the couch.

'So you're awake—you've been asleep for an hour. You must have been tired. You work too hard. I worry about you.'

'Did the children go out?'

'They went next door to the smiley-forever-lady—you know, the one everyone says looks like a kind witch. They want to play with her cats.'

'I've had a really vivid dream. I think I'll light the fire and make some tea. Would you like a cup?'

'Yes, I would, thank you. We've got some home-made biscuits from the lady next door. By the way, I saw that friendly barman from the Greenwood Arms—Gerry, isn't it?—he walked by a little earlier. Why don't we go there one evening during the week? Mrs Grumpelwinkle will take the children for an hour I'm sure.'

∽

In the deep dark forest, the witch sighed with relief. 'That was close; I almost ended up stuck with him.'

She rocked herself backwards and forwards as the last rays of afternoon sunshine warmed her cheeks and the cats played at her feet.

'I think I'll go down to the Greenwood Arms. I believe there's a pint waiting for me.'

Postscript

We don't know how the Greenwood Arms came into being; was it the witch? Even though she was without her spell book when Mr Crumble left her? Probably she'd made the pub so many times that she knew that spell by heart. But it's good to have a few unknowns in the story if there is to be a discussion. Where did Mr Crumble's hatred of his wife come from? From his own heart no doubt, and from his life experience that we are not privy to, but we don't really know much about his wife either, although we can speculate.

The idea for this story began when I had to prepare a seminar on projection and a concept called countertransference. This concerns the feelings a therapist has in relation to a client. If the therapist's personal feelings are strong the experience can be almost overwhelming. At the time I thought the formal description I was writing was boring, so I came up with a version of this story to illustrate the concept. That is, the therapist listens and takes in the client's experience, and feels it. At some point the therapist formulates what the client feels by means of a clarification that helps the client think about themselves. In other words, the therapist's job is to help the client see themselves in a new light. Mr Crumble passes over to the witch all he feels in words and other projections and she is temporarily overwhelmed. He takes time, in the pub with his helpful superego Gerry, to reconsider his hasty decision to run away from her. With help from other customers, who represent other parts of his mind, he returns to the witch and takes in her comments. He goes home and awakens from a dream which has been a part of an unconscious working through of his problem. The reality is that it is he who is persecuted by himself; his wife is caring and the children are playful.

You may ask: why was the witch's house bigger on the inside? What about the words on Gerald's shirt? and the two English-speaking cats? Why did the pub vanish? And what's all this to do with finding an answer to your question, and the answers coming from deep inside yourself? What is real: the dream, the witch in the forest, or the family and home, or are they all real? Is the unconscious as real as the conscious?

However, I'm not going to supply answers. It isn't right for you to question magic any more than you should question your unconscious. They are both unknowable, worthy of respect, and ripe for meditation. You may ignore their messages, but only at your peril. It's up to you, of course.

After all that stuff about projection and countertransference, the next story is an interlude before we tackle the big P, paranoia in therapy. Don't skip *Invitation to the Dance*: it also carries a message.

2
Invitation to the Dance

———◆———

What a great idea it was to hold this conference in a country house. From where I sat on the end of a row of chairs in the packed hall—a ballroom on other occasions, I imagined, where couples danced close together in formal intimacy—I could enjoy a view of the verdant countryside through the floor-to-ceiling windows. The steady rain inspired a gurgling aria in a drainpipe outside, while beating a staccato rhythm on the broadleaf trees in the park.

Due to the inclement weather the windows were shut and the room was becoming stuffy. The lunch had been very good: beautifully roasted beef and plenty of seasonal organic vegetables, accompanied by an excellent claret. By now some conference members were quietly nodding off, even while the afternoon lecturer, who had avoided the wine, was reading her paper. In places her arguments were complex; I knew she had worked hard to perfect her ideas through the small hours of many nights while I had slept. Now I was in danger of dropping off again.

Occasionally, as I'd advised, she raised her voice and changed her reading speed, then paused for a sip of water. At each change of pace several heads jerked up. She continued valiantly until, finally, it was over. I smiled at her: Miriam, my partner, the determined speaker. She smiled back for a second then, interrupted by the chairman, she looked away.

To my left, someone rose in the middle of the row, and I glanced in that direction. She was squeezing past other people's knees as she came towards me. I followed her in my peripheral vision. I had noticed her over lunch and had found her attractive. I had tried to avoid eye contact with her, unsuccessfully. Now she was half a meter away from me, but I didn't look up, although I desperately wanted to. I heard a whispered 'excuse me'—her voice soft and seductive—and through a haze of expensive perfume I detected the warmth of her body. I turned my knees to the right. Was there enough space? As her aroma engulfed me, her nylon-sheathed right leg brushed past me, momentarily pressing against my knee. Did she mean to add a little pressure? Was that real or my wild fantasy? I felt drawn into a paradise of unconditional love. She had already moved on.

Another person followed close behind. The next knee to touch mine was covered in rough material. A denim-clad leg pushed past me firmly and I smelled aftershave, reminding me of my gym. Paradise was gone.

I looked up. Miriam, having escaped the chairman's clutches, caught my eye.

Time for a cup of real country-house tea.

Postscript

How do we humans operate? Some subtle provocation doesn't hurt sometimes, does it? Our feelings can be so labile at times, especially under the influence of wine, good looks, perfume and, naturally, the unconscious. 'Every desire takes before long the form of picturing its own fulfilment; there is no doubt that dwelling upon imaginary wish-fulfilments brings satisfaction with it, although it does not interfere with a knowledge that what is concerned is not real. (Freud 1917) p372)) We are susceptible to the broad and heavy brushstrokes of primal feelings of love and hate which color and sometimes overwhelm our civilized sophistication. These feelings lie in wait to ambush us. In this case most inappropriately, when I was doing something as mundane as listening to a paper at a psychoanalytic conference. But problem solved with a cup of tea.

Reference:

Freud, S. (1917) Introductory Lectures on Psycho-analysis, SE, XVI, (Part 111)

In the next story there is provocation of another kind in a collection of vignettes about paranoia in the consulting room. The client's suffering is provoked by the limits and rules of the situation, and the experience is often provocative for the therapist.

3

Paranoia: Seven Vignettes

———•———

a. The Interview

My doorbell rang for the first appointment, a little early.

'Good morning. Are you the therapist?'

'Yes. I gave you this address when you rang me.'

'Just making sure. You can't be too careful these days, not with all the fake news that's going around.'

'Yes, I see. Do come in and take a seat—no, over there please.'

'Fussy about the seats, are we?'

'It's easier if I sit in the chair beside my desk.'

'All right, have it your own way. You don't want to give up your superior position, I suppose. I hope this interview isn't going to continue in an authoritarian way.'

'I understand. Now, could we–?'

'Do you really understand? We shall see.'

'We only spoke briefly on the telephone, so I need to take a few particulars before we talk further.'

'Particulars, is it now? You'll want the intimate details of my living arrangements soon enough, I'm sure.'

'Just your full name and address will suffice.'

'Oh yes, "suffice", that's a good middle-class word. You've heard it, haven't you, eh? That quote, "sufficient for the day is the evil thereof". Does anyone have the faintest bloody idea what that means? Eh?'

'Would 'unto' help?'

'What do you mean 'unto'?'

'"Sufficient unto the day is the evil thereof."'

'What are you on about? I'm here to talk about me.'

'I'm sorry. Your full name then?'

'Ah, the full name. I knew you'd want all the salacious stuff. You emphasized the word 'full' I notice. You're full of what interests you but you ignore my needs.'

'It sounds as if being here is difficult for you. We can talk about that in a moment, but shall we get to your name?'

'My whole life is difficult. OK, Samuel Adams is the name, sir.'

'Samuel Adams.'

'Yes, sir, or maybe Adam Samuels? I was confused at school. Sometimes they said Adams and sometimes they said Samuels, never the two together, and I'm not sure which is the official version. My mum did the same. She used one or the other, on a whim. Even the taxman has used versions of the two together, if you see what I mean.'

'I think so. You sometimes find it difficult to know who you should be. Let's just take what you said first, 'Samuel Adams', for the sake of simplicity.'

'Look, I know who I am. How would I get here otherwise? And this is not simple, you know?'

'I'm beginning to understand that.'

'Oh, mockery and sarcasm, is it now? Or was it irony, or even a sardonic remark? You can stop that. Sarcasm is the lowest form of wit. It wasn't funny anyway. I imagine you'll be recounting this interview to your friends at dinner this evening, and they'll all laugh at me. That's what I don't like about you middle-class types—everyone else is an idiot in your eyes.'

'And you're not middle class?'

'Yes, well no, my dad was a baker and a good one too.'

'I understood from our telephone conversation that you're a civil servant.'

'In a manner of speaking.'

'Shall we finish with the particulars? Then we can get to the reason you have come to see me.'

'Oh yes, back to the particulars. What is it now, address? You don't need it—you won't be coming to my house. You've got the phone number, but only after I rang back. You're reluctant to answer an unknown number, aren't you?'

'No.'

'Oh yes, I think so. Paranoid, are you? Don't worry, your secret is safe with me.'

Postscript

In the interview above, an anxious man shows his analyst his fear of being investigated—which also means his own fear of learning about himself. In other words, his fear of facing reality.

The man is clearly distressed and paranoid: is it possible to offer him any insight? The nature of paranoia is the greatest obstacle.

Anything that might come towards him, in this case insight, he will regard with suspicion. The paranoid person is beset by delusions which seem so real that they feel compelled to act on them. In these vignettes the person may not be a psychiatric case, but they are acting on a psychotic idea, i.e. it is out of touch with reality.

b. Motivation

Robert, a possible therapy client, was tall and lean, about forty years old. He had a hunted look in his eyes. His face was that of a man who has been thinking about many things simultaneously, without coming to any conclusions. He had filled the interview with detailed descriptions of a traumatic life and finished his presentation with this:

'My wife says I look conservative and progressive at the same time. I'm not sure if that's a compliment. She said that my trademark corduroy jacket makes me look liberal, but my cynical humor about left-wing social policy undermines that. Can you help me?'

I had been silent up to this point in the interview. But there was something provocative in the back of my mind that pushed past my professional restraint.

'I don't know. After all you've said, I somehow doubt it.'

'What do you mean? I've poured out my soul to you for nearly an hour.'

'You've said that, in your infancy, your mother was depressed; in addition, she deliberately dropped you on your head. Your father hated you and your teachers beat you. Your maternal uncle sexually abused you over a period of years. When he was discovered, he committed suicide in front of you with a plastic bag over his head, and you did nothing to stop him. Isn't that so?'

'Yes, all true, and a lot more. I'm glad you've been listening. A lot of people are responsible for the way I am today. By the way, I was only seven when the suicide occurred.'

'That is not a good basis for further personal development, you understand.'

'I know. That's why I'm here.'

'I can help you with your responsibility but not theirs.'

'You're joking. None of this was my fault.'

'I'm sorry to tell you but the prognosis in your situation is very poor. I think progress would be next to zero.'

'This is outrageous! I've never been treated like this before.'

'Rejected, you mean?'

'Yes, exactly.'

'I thought that was the pattern of your life?'

'This interview is out of control. You therapists are not supposed to talk like this. You shouldn't be saying exactly what you think, should you?'

'I'm entitled to an opinion. In your view, you are too damaged by other people. Therefore, I cannot help you.'

'Let me tell you, I've made something of myself. I'm married and we have a new baby. I've a decent job. I came to you to help me get rid of the perpetual torment I feel, as if I'm sitting an exam tomorrow when I'm not.'

'So?'

'I can work at this.'

'In that case, I can offer you therapy.'

Postscript

The client tries to protect himself from admitting his problems by making the therapist responsible for the therapy. However, the therapist will not be able to start a dialogue until the new client accepts control over his own life. 'Thus we still feel our shackles even after they have been removed and do not really know how to enjoy our freedom.'(Freud 1901) It is not uncommon for us to wish to place responsibility for our lives on those around us, particularly our parents. However, psychoanalysis tries to help us understand our responsibility for our life so far. And, in fact, the people we blame are, at least in part, figures from our inner object world, the source of our imagination, who have counterparts in reality. Many people are reluctant to embrace freedom. It involves responsibility, and that is frightening.

Reference:

Freud, S. (1901). Letter from Freud to Fliess, June 9, 1901.

Masson, Jeffrey Moussaieff. The Complete Letters of Sigmund Freud to Wilhelm Fliess, 1887-1904, 441-443, Cambridge, MA, and London, England: The Belknap Press of Harvard University Press.

c. Pizza Paranoia

I'd been talking for some time to my therapist, Mr Jones. He's my second therapist, the first one having died suddenly, which was a shock since he was relatively young. Mr Jones is much older, a man in his sixties, I should guess. According to his curriculum vitae, he has studied a lot and gained a lot of experience. He has the dour expression of a man who has lost something valuable but doesn't remember what it was, a situation I can identify with. I liked him but I felt the same about my first therapist and I'm always unsure. Since that therapist died, I'm wondering if I can trust anyone any more.

Mr Jones wears tailored suits, which I admire. I don't wear such things myself but I appreciate quality. His office is always immaculately clean and he appears correct in all things. That's why the following experience is such a conundrum.

I lay on Mr Jones' couch. He was sitting behind me. Behind him was the door. He was quiet. Then I thought I heard a familiar sound. And the usual aroma of the room—flowers, people, cleaning materials—was disturbed by the smell of pizza.

'I can smell pizza. Isn't it a bit early for pizza?' I sniffed again. 'I've noticed that the door makes a small distinctive sound, and I thought I heard it a moment ago. I don't want to turn round to check on you. You know me, I'm always afraid of everything—even you.'

I laughed. He didn't.

'Uh huh, hmm…'

'I can smell pizza but I know that's impossible. What kind of psychosomatic olfactory sensation is this? Am I hallucinating?'

Silence.

'I could swear I heard you swallow, but I think I'm having a fantasy of you eating pizza. Swallowing would be part of it, of course.'

'Hmm.'

'The smell seems to be stronger now.'

I wanted to turn round to see if there was a slice of pizza in his hand. But, as usual, I felt bound to the couch. I was unable to risk whatever retribution I imagined might come my way if I looked at him. As if I would be looking at the sun god or something—ridiculous.

'I've had lovely pizza on holidays abroad. There's a good pizza place not far from my home.'

'Hmm...'

'I go there often.'

'Uh huh...'

'I had pizza in Naples once—that's where it started, you know.'

'Hmm...'

'You've acknowledged me again.'

Mr Jones was silent.

'Of course, you eating pizza is impossible. You'd have to leave the room to get it and I know that's out of the question.'

Silence.

'You could be using my paranoia against me. You know that I wouldn't believe you would eat pizza during my session. And you know I'd be afraid to turn round and see the truth.'

'It's the end of our time for today, George.'

I thought I heard a familiar noise, like folding cardboard. I sat up on the couch.

Postscript

As we know, the paranoid person is never entirely wrong, and his fantasies may be very convincing. Here we see the client's anxiety, possibly stemming from the untimely death of his first therapist.

What has the client lost that he can't remember? In his fear of everything maybe he has idealized his new therapist to create a person he can trust, but that trust is shaken by an olfactory hallucination, or is it the truth? Perhaps what he has lost is trust in the people he needs. Why would he destroy them?

If the therapist has a pizza slice in the room then he's talking to a boundary-less therapist. If this is an hallucination he has created a powerful resistance to his therapist. Of course, a therapist who sneaks out of the room during the session to take a piece of last night's pizza is not to be trusted. But, in this account, we do not know if the pizza really exists and that is the point. Since this is a vignette for a seminar, I think we should have some doubt in the story, even at the end. But we should believe in the power of paranoid fantasies to be convincing.

d. Desert Air

I was lying on a couch in the consulting room of my therapist, Dr Greengage. He was a friendly guy, although he didn't say much. At times I felt irritated by the absence of his contribution. The couch was comfortable, and the room was warm.

'I guess this session is almost over,' I said. 'I can't think of a new story and there's a good reason for that. I don't have any ideas. There was a time when I had stories queuing up in my head. That was before I started this therapy. Now a new kind of superego awaits my productions, endless criticism from inside my mind. You've got into my head and my mind is a desert.'

'Your mind is a desert?' said Dr Greengage.

'Yes. That means there's nothing there.'

'Really, nothing?'

'Oh, I see what you mean, it's symbolic. Actually, deserts are full of different things: sand, rock, a lot of creatures—desert rats, spiders, snakes—there's water deep under the sand, and oases with date palms. There are nomads with slow-moving camels. And flowers too, after it rains anyway, but that doesn't happen often. It needs a dramatic change to get some things growing, doesn't it? There's a lot in a desert, if you look for it.'

I felt the softness of the couch, which was not like a desert at all. I was comfortable, the atmosphere was soporific, my eyelids heavy.

'Time to finish for today,' said Mr Greengage.

I swung myself off the couch, knowing it was pointless to say goodbye, as he never answered after the session was over. And not so much during it either, for that matter. This analysis was a journey in my own head.

Out in the hall, I put on my coat and opened the front door. I walked down the path thinking, *What does he do for his money? Not much happened today, as usual. Maybe these sessions really are the desert.*

I heard the noise of a window opening behind me.

'Hello, Mr A. I say, you there, Mr A.'

I looked around and, to my astonishment, I saw my therapist leaning out of his consulting room window, holding something.

'Yes, you,' he shouted, 'come here.'

With trepidation, and curiosity, I walked towards him. He'd never done this before. He looked impatient. Was he losing his therapeutic mind? I had to cross the lawn and stand in the flowerbed under the window. Strangely, it was full of sand.

'Who is Mr A?' I asked.

'Sorry, George. That's what I call you in my notes and in a recent paper. Your real name slipped my mind for a moment.'

'Are you writing a paper about me?'

'Oh yes, I've published it. I've had some interesting responses too.'

'How dare you write about me without my permission!'

'Oh, grow up. Don't be such a baby. Everyone does it. Anyway, here's your cellphone, you left it on the couch. Here, take it. I won't chase after you again. I'm not your mother.'

'What about your publication? That's unethical, isn't it?'

He shut the window. 'We'll talk tomorrow,' he mouthed through the double-glazed window.

'No, we won't. You never say anything,'

He turned away, so I started back across the sandy lawn towards the garden gate.

A pale and much too slim young woman was walking up the path—the next client, I assumed. She glanced in my direction. 'Tell him your mind is empty and it feels like a desert. That'll freak him out,' I said.

'George, it's time to finish for today.'

I opened my eyes. My cellphone was lying on the couch by my side. I grabbed it and left.

Postscript

As we know from experience, a dream may serve as a safety valve for our over-burdened brain (Freud (1900), p79) From his tone at the beginning of this vignette, George wants to blame his therapist for his own lack of ideas, but in his short dream his unconscious reveals to him that his creativity is his own responsibility.

George finds that his dream is his responsibility, and he has to take responsibility for his own life. He will not be able to dismiss the insight of his dream as *just a dream.*

Reference

Freud, S. (1900). The Interpretation of Dreams. The Standard Edition of the Complete Psychological Works of Sigmund Freud, Volume IV (1900): The Interpretation of Dreams (First Part), ix-627.

e. Kidnapped by His Mind

My therapist, Mrs Smith, works in a building at the end of her garden. It's built of wood and smells wonderful. Inside is a wide room with a glass wall facing the world outside. Lying on her couch, I have a choice: I can look at the ceiling or the door or the books on the wall to my right—or I can look to my left and out through the window into her beautiful garden. It changes every day: sometimes it appears endless and full of trees, at other times it has flowering shrubs and plants that never cease to bloom. Beyond, I can see her home, a friendly looking Victorian house. In the autumn, dying leaves fall softly—brilliant rich yellow from the oaks and bright red from the maples. During the sessions I mentally wander in that place.

I think my therapist is a creative lady. I can feel it. She listens to me and doesn't say much. In my experience, people with nothing to say talk a lot.

'Mrs Smith, this is a dream I had after our last session. Or maybe it really happened? Perhaps it's both.

'When I was young, I don't remember exactly how old, perhaps between seven and nine, my father was housed in a mental institution.'

In my dream-memory, Mum and I enter an imposing Victorian gothic edifice, part of a myriad of buildings in wide-open parkland. Mum talks to a nurse, who leads the way up wide stairs and down an echoing corridor. She opens the door to a room. The door is a grubby shade of cream, and around the handle are the prints of hundreds of hands. Sitting in a worn armchair by a tall dirty window is a man. He doesn't move. He appears to be looking out of the window. I don't know if he sees anything. I look around a room full of serviceable utility furniture, not yet old enough to be attractive. A worn carpet covers the floor, not quite to the edges.

Mum takes the chair beside the man and gives him little cakes, wrapped in a tea towel. He doesn't respond. She lays them in his lap but he doesn't look at them. She begins to cry and says, 'I'm going to the bathroom for a few minutes.'

I look at the man, my dad. We are sitting in the room together; he continues to look out of the window. The tea towel and cakes rest on his knees. I watch him. Has his mind been kidnapped? Now he seems to be looking at the door. I think he's looking at a chip in the paint. I look at it too. The door opens and catches an upturned corner of the carpet as a nurse comes in. She must have seen my mother go out.

'Is everything all right?' she asks, smiling. 'Your mum is coming back very soon.'

The door closes; my dad is still looking at it. Does he remember me at all? Are all his memories gone? Will they ever come back?

I say to Mrs Smith, 'I don't know what I thought then, but now I think he believed he'd lost everything, including me and Mum. Maybe he thought it was his fault.'

'It sounds like that,' she says.

In the corridor, people walk past, their voices echoing off the walls. I hear distant doors open and close. The door to Dad's room moves slightly. He seems to watch every movement but without interest. Is he waiting for Mum to come back? Forty-five minutes of the visiting hour are left. Will he wait it out in silence? He looks at me—with love, or with hate? I don't know. He's staring at me. Afraid, I turn away and look through the barred window. Leaves are falling slowly and touching down effortlessly on the lawn. They are a comfort. I like to feel I'm one of them.

'I remember all this so clearly, especially the leaves. I suppose I needed a distraction.'

'You said in our last meeting that you look away or even run away from uncomfortable situations. Trying to avoid reality.'

'It's true. It must have started at that time. That's what I'm doing when I look at your garden. I wonder if I'm making you into a fantasy representative of my father?

'Months before, I asked him why he'd moved to the hospital. He said the staff insisted he should go with them. I wondered what would have happened if he'd said no. But he wasn't able to leave. His mind still functioned. It was in there, waiting to be found. I knew even then, without the language I have today, that wherever he went the rooms were all the same: doors had cracked paint and swung open in the same way; the carpet was wrinkled and the decor was unchanging. I couldn't describe it at that time, but I think now that acid ate into his heart and soul, and a great weight bore down on his limbs. Every day he woke up and didn't know where he was. I felt sorry for him and wanted him to be like other children's dads.

'I wanted to say to him something like, "On the way out of the abyss, words will come back to you, Dad. We will take a train ride together and sit side by side, looking out through the window at the passing countryside." How that would have sounded when I was that age, I don't know. These thoughts are melancholy, maudlin perhaps. Poor Dad. I felt sorry for him back then but that's not the whole truth. I also thought he was a cowardly bastard for not fighting with his mind and I wanted to fucking kill him. I still do, to be honest.'

'It's time for us to finish for today,' says Mrs Smith.

I look through the window. The garden is changing from autumn to winter. Everything has bloomed for the last time and the trees are beginning to turn, their leaves floating gently to the ground. The rhythm of the seasons never changes.

I pick up my coat and leave.

Postscript

To give another person your full attention is generous, and uncommon. In this case, the ill father is too self-involved to be mentally available to his child. This sad tale of a client's father's paranoid illness is loosely based on an account I heard from someone I knew many years ago. The consulting room in the garden is one I visited as a student. The story of the patient's mentally absent father is moving but covers up enormous rage, an understandable reaction from anyone when a loved one's attention is turned inwards. However, it can be more pronounced in a child, whose emotional experience is deeper and longer lasting.

The legacy of mental illness in the father is repeated in the client. He remembers it by looking out of the analyst's window at her garden, just as his father did in hospital. His observation of this repetition opens his conscious memory. Later, more importantly, his fury with his father finds words which had been smothered by guilt and a maudlin sympathy for his parent.

f. A Futile Story

When I opened the door, I was confronted by a man sporting a thick blond beard and wearing a beige plastic neck-brace. His pale-blue eyes inspected me through heavy-framed glasses. Of average height and build, with sloping shoulders, he wore old jeans and a gray sweatshirt.

'Mr Mi?' I said. 'Do you pronounce it 'me' or 'my'?'

'Whatever.'

He followed me into the consulting room.

'Actually my name is Sad-As-Mi. I'm also called Sod-Off-Mi by my friends, not that I have many of them.'

I felt sure this was a joke and smiled. He didn't.

'I can see on your face that you're wondering about my name. I see many things. I'm an artist and I've created my name to demonstrate my contempt for Western cultural values. It describes me at the moment—if I change, I'll change my name. Before you ask, I am thirty-five years of age and, yes, I know I look older.'

I decided not to pursue the subject. 'You're here for a consultation concerning a possible therapy.'

'Yes. I was recommended to you by the hospital.'

'I understand. Tell me about yourself.'

'We shall see if you understand. I live in a gray apartment block on the edge of town. It has no remarkable features, but my wife thinks otherwise. She and our children wear brightly colored clothes but they look dull to me, so maybe I'm color-blind. They say we live in a busy and creative suburb. I don't believe it.

'Our children are Sara, who is six, and our son Buster, who is eight. I suppose you want my wife's name? She's called Primrose, like the flower. It's a bit old-fashioned but it suits her lightness of mind. I don't understand what she sees in the world around her. She's one of the producers of the fantasy world that anesthetizes the nation. She works in television.'

He looked at me as if expecting a response, but I was beginning to feel numb. I wondered how his wife and children put up with him. I judged that it wasn't the right moment to ask.

'Primrose earns enough money for us all, so I'm a house husband, as it's called these days. Ridiculous. I'm an engineer by training but I abandoned the profession when the management at work gave up on me. They complained that I was depressed and paranoid. Not true. As I said, I'm actually an artist.

'I keep busy at home. I prepare food, but not breakfast—my wife likes to do that for the children. I do their packed lunches for school and I keep the house clean and tidy. I fret my way through each day, worrying about the fake television news. I'm most troubled by reports of people blowing themselves up in public places. After a particularly nasty attack in a marketplace that killed fifty-three people, I resolved to do something to demonstrate my unhappiness.'

'Wasn't that bombing in the news a few months ago?'

'Yes.'

'It was in another country.'

'We live in one world, or haven't you noticed?'

I didn't comment.

172

'My wife and children came home from our local market that day without saying a word. I couldn't believe they hadn't heard about it.'

'You weren't confusing the two places?'

'I've said we live in one world. You're not listening.'

'But...'

'Don't 'but' me, let me finish. I decided to make an artistic statement of my fury at the bomber's claims to be acting for peace. I wanted to demonstrate existential absurdism so I decided to bomb nothing. And I don't mean not to bomb anything at all, because I was going to blow myself up. So, I suppose that's something— someone, I mean. A contradiction, it could be argued. But not by me.'

He looked uncertain, as if he'd just realized something new. Then he shook his head and continued.

'I found a car advertised as "a rewarding project for an enthusiastic visionary". That described what I was looking for. I thought the price excessive for such dilapidation, but I wasn't in a position to argue, I was in a hurry. I filled it with explosive materials—fertilizer with sugar—and I fixed a detonation device by the driver's seat, all as illustrated on the internet. However, on the day that would demonstrate my thesis 'Random Acts of Suicide Bombing are as Futile as Pissing in the Ocean', I had second thoughts.

'Perhaps anxiety about my impending death made me more aware of my surroundings. I observed my children playing while my wife prepared breakfast. For a moment I saw color in their clothes, and I didn't want to make them sad. Even if I'm a gray man, a father is a father.

'I heard the children complain that their boiled eggs were runny but I ignored them; there is always something wrong at that time of the morning.'

I managed to avoid adding 'not only in the morning'.

'After their meal, they went off with their mother to school and I decided not to die in the bombing after all. I would attach the egg timer to the detonator to delay the explosion so that I could escape the blast. That evening I drove to an out-of-town supermarket, a gray building with a large gray car park. I wanted to create a bang without carnage, or the burning of other cars that were not renovation projects. I planned to phone the local newspaper afterwards to take responsibility for my meaningless action.'

'Now I remember—you're the person the newspapers called–'

'Please, don't interrupt me again.'

'But it's interesting,' I said lamely.

'And for me, it's a bitter memory. However, I think your intervention was badly timed and, in the context, foolish. You'll have reason to regret your last phrase in a moment.'

I didn't respond.

'In the car park I waited until everyone had left. At two in the morning, I set the timer for three minutes and left the vehicle, heading for a big tree on the other side of the site. The bomb went off early and the driver's door hit me on the back of the head. I was surprised but, as I slipped into unconsciousness, I understood why the children's boiled eggs were runny.

'I woke up in hospital and the newspapers were full of stories about me. Articles abounded of irresponsible car disposal—and yes, they called me the 'Egg-Timer Bomber'—that's what you were going to say, wasn't it? Like you, they missed the point entirely.

'My wife and children were interviewed and described by the journalists as 'colorful'. My wife giggled a lot and the children asked for a new egg timer. There were a lot of donations, and we now have

174

fifty-seven egg timers. I found this lack of support for my protest quite hurtful.

'In hospital my only visitor other than the police and my family was a French philosopher. He travelled from Paris to discuss the meaning of my actions. He said that, according to Albert Camus, terrorism has its roots in the absence of hope. It's often the weapon of the poor, born of loneliness and the belief that there is no future, which terrorists project into the whole world. I wanted to talk about Nietzsche, but he wasn't having any of it. I fell asleep during the interview. That's the worst thing, isn't it? When you have something important to say and you're ignored? I became depressed and the hospital gave me your name.'

I wondered who I knew in the hospital who hated me that much. I hoped that sentiment didn't show on my face as Sod-Off-Mi continued his story.

'I didn't want to come here but I had no choice. I'd have served a prison sentence otherwise. I was sent for a psychiatric assessment. The doctor said she found my ideas interesting, but she clearly didn't understand. She just took a lot of notes. The court gave me a fine for disturbing the peace, and for spreading a useless vehicle over a supermarket car park, which I thought was ironic as it's usually full of useless vehicles destroying the planet with toxic emissions. In addition, I was given community service for one hundred hours. How pointless.

'The local creative arts project invited me to join their alternative group. They said I'd made an anti-sculpture because it destroyed itself and they found it interesting. When people say they find something interesting, they actually mean the reverse. Make a mental note never to say, "That's interesting" to me again.'

I wanted to smile, but it would have been false. I said, 'It might be therapeutic to be part of an arts project.'

He sighed loudly. 'Is there any point to this?'

Postscript

Something that is futile serves no useful purpose, and the word describes a feeling in some states of mental ill-health called schizoid disorders. It is a defense against feelings of paranoia.

'Why did he blow himself up?'

'Because he was crazy.'

'How do you know?'

'Because he blew himself up.' (Overheard in a cafe.)

We have all had the experience of seeing a terrorist incident and thinking it was futile and absurd. The idea of human life as absurd was described by Albert Camus in The Myth of Sisypus, (Camus 1955), which explored the human tendency to look for meaning and purpose in a world that is chaotic and irrational, and where we have no choice but to go on trying. Something expressed by Shakespeare in Macbeth, "Life's but a walking shadow, a poor player that struts and frets his hour upon the stage, and then is heard no more. It is a tale told by an idiot, full of sound and fury, signifying nothing." William Shakespeare, *Macbeth*, Act 5, scene 5

The story above arose when, after yet another deadly suicide bombing, I wondered how it would look if a demonstration of futility was the point of the atrocity. Here we see something that is axiomatic for therapists: the paranoid person who is difficult to help because any insight offered is felt to be an attack that they must defend themselves against. The therapist, who might be able to provide assistance, is suspect because she is threatening the client's paranoid defense.

The imaginary encounter above not only contains paranoia but also the omnipotent narcissism that supports it. Sad-as-Mi views the world as his enemy in much the same way as the suicide bomber he denounces. He will not listen to anyone else, only his own internal voice. In the end he has also undermined his chances for successful therapy by rendering it worthless because the therapist doesn't agree with him. In addition, the therapist is too rational; an attentive silence might have helped the situation better. What do you think?

Reference

Camus, A. (1955). *The Myth of Sisyphus and Other Essays*. New York: Alfred A. Knopf.

Clark, W. G., and Wright, W. A., (Eds) *The Complete Works of William Shakespeare*. Garden City, NY: Nelson Doubleday Inc.

g. Passion, Delusion, Paranoia

I kicked off my heels, swung my legs up onto the therapist's couch, and smoothed down my skirt. Now I could begin.

'I know this may seem quite mad, Mrs Rodriguez, but I had the most frightening experience in the airport coming back from holiday. I'm still not sure what it was all about. Perhaps I was hallucinating—I've got some new tablets and they're quite strong.' I hesitated.

Mrs Rodriguez was sitting behind the couch. 'Continue with your account,' she said.

As always, she spoke with kindness and compassion. Although she has a Spanish name she sounds English and she's charming in every way. I think she's old enough to be my mother but she keeps her body in great shape and her dark Mediterranean complexion is very beautiful. She is a lady to lust after—in other circumstances, of course.

'All right, I'll go on. I was waiting in the transit lounge, playing the airport waiting game with myself. It's a children's game but anyone can play. For example, you can ask yourself or a partner: how many people are there in uniform on the concourse? How many people with red coats can you see? How many children are laughing? How many crying?

'A security guard looked at me, maybe he'd noticed me looking around and counting. I tried to look relaxed and pulled my hand luggage closer to me. I sipped my coffee. He moved on.

'Sunlight was streaming through the windows, warming the space; the air conditioning was ineffective. I looked around. There was something familiar about the surroundings and a memory suddenly pulled at my mind.'

What are the chances of us meeting like this? Don't look round! I will sit behind you and drink my coffee. Don't you remember me?

'I sat still. The voice was familiar.'

Come on, think harder. Surely you remember me? How could you forget?

My nerves tingled as the memory gripped my body. I hoped no one noticed me shudder. Years ago, this woman and I had met in an airport hotel. It was an encounter that opened our souls and united them forever. The joy and laughter and pain came back to me.

I remember.

Don't speak any more. No one must see your lips move. I live with other people. I am from a part of the world where honor means everything and disgrace leads to death. Just drink your coffee. If there are people watching me they will think I am talking on the phone. I've been watching you for a few minutes. You are just the same after all these years. I've often wondered how you are. Don't answer. I expect you are playing the airport waiting game.

You are tormenting me. It feels familiar, I...

Don't—you mustn't show any sign you know me. I'll do the talking.

And so she did, like the first time, and it made me happy. But then sorrow crept into my soul.

Don't cry you did that last time. Remember our day together—and our night? I can still feel your lips on mine. I imagine you want to know how I am? I'm OK, life is what it is. Fortunately, you never know what might have happened if we'd taken another road. But you can torture yourself with fantasy if you wish. That dress is gorgeous, very flattering. You have exquisite taste.

'There was movement in the row of seats behind me, on her side. An angry conversation developed, with foreign accents and male voices denouncing her. I half turned; shadows blocked my light. Then, remembering her injunctions, I quickly turned back and tried to act naturally. As I lifted my coffee cup, my hand was shaking. How brave could I be for love? She'd told me not to move. I tried to distract myself—is she drinking cappuccino or latte? We used to like cappuccino. How do you tell the difference? I forget.

'A chair scraped on the cool stone floor. The demanding voices faded away and the airport bustle closed around the empty space behind me. I looked around furtively. There was lipstick on the rim of the abandoned cup. I wanted to taste it, just once more. A blue glove lay on the table, like the pair she used to wear. She'd left me a memento. Without looking, I slowly put out my hand but the cup was gone, the glove too. I turned. The chair was as it had been when I sat down to play the waiting game.

'How many people in uniform were there? What colors were they wearing? Who is crying now?

'The departure board flashed. I was boarding at gate fifteen, which was a ten-minute walk, or was it the other way around? What a country this was! What were the chances of such a meeting? Oh God, why couldn't I remember her name?

'And when you imagine her now, what name comes to mind?' inquired Mrs Rodriguez kindly.

Postscript

I thought of this story after observing two people in an airport waiting lounge. They were sitting back to back on a double bench. Both appeared to be talking into cellphone earpieces. After a time, I noticed that they spoke in turns, as if talking to each other, not as if they were conducting independent conversations. Then one got up and left with some other people. As she went, she cast a longing glance into the eyes of the one who remained seated and had turned to face her.

Who were they? What was it all about? I've no idea. Two unknown people, travelling to different places, continuing their separate lives.

I changed the emphasis in this story to fit the relationship of two people in a consulting room, one on a couch, the other in a chair, who only look at each other at the beginning and end of a session.

Is this story also about transference? (See the first book, *Expectations*, for a story about that, 'What on earth is transference?') Is the speaker really longing for her analyst's physical affection, though she cannot say it directly? Her unconscious comes up with this association, a dream fantasy.

You'll have noticed that the narrator is a woman and that the delusion, or whatever we call it, concerns 'the love that dare not speak its name,' as Oscar Wilde said at his trial for homosexuality. The implication is that the friend at the airport is a previous lover, in a country where such love is dangerous to admit.

Delusion is a term used in psychiatry and usually refers to something a client believes which is untrue but impossible to alter in her mind by logic or even evidence. The speaker is offering the experience as something that actually happened to her. But possibly the point is that it is happening in her transference of love for her therapist.

Reference

Testimony of Oscar Wilde. Available at: https://www.famous-trials. com

A General Comment on These Seven Vignettes

Above are a series of unlikely events, at least in the way described, but they are not far from the psychic reality of the world of dreams. When we sleep for a few hours, we live in a different world. The pain of reality and of who we are, the intolerable 'slings and arrows of outrageous fortune', to quote Hamlet, may well incline us to seek alternative solutions, one of which can be a retreat into symptoms which are a clue to their origin. Therapy tries to uncover, through dreams and free associations, the path from the symptom back to the fantasy that inspired it, and forward again to the acceptance of reality.

The next story is a modern revival of an old battle, the so-called 'controversial discussions' in the British Psychoanalytical Society during the Second World War. It is written like a scene from a play and demonstrates the mutual animosity inherent in the theoretical disagreements of the original discussions.

4

A New Controversial Discussion

———•———

John, still in his pajamas, raised his head from the stack of books he was looking through when he heard the front door close.

'You're up early for a Saturday. Where have you been?' he said, yawning and running a hand through his thinning red hair. Then, frowning, he studied his wife in more detail and added, 'There's something different about you, but I can't quite put my finger on it.'

'Well, well,' Diana rejoined. 'You're quite observant for someone who can't get out of bed at a decent time.'

'Don't be sarcastic.'

'So, what do you think?' She gave a little twirl.

'I'm not sure. Maybe I like it, maybe not. But there again, I don't know what it is yet.'

'Keep trying.' This time, she tossed back her head, stylishly, like a model at a photo shoot.

'Hair?'

'Wow—someone's sharp this morning.'

'More sarcasm, eh? No, I can't say I like it. How much?'

'You don't want to know, but you will soon enough because I used the joint account.'

'I've told you about frivolous expenses.'

'I want to look nice for our dinner invitation this evening. We're going out, remember?'

'But surely you can see that you don't look your best with this new hairdo—*ow!*'

A book hit John's eyebrow.

'Hey, that hurt.' He picked up the book, Bion's *Attention and Interpretation* (paperback, 208 grams), and touched the wound at the impact site. He looked at a smear of blood on his fingers.

'Oh, sorry. Only joking. I didn't mean it to hit you really.'

In his childhood, John's temperament had been described as choleric. Today, he threw what was nearest to hand, heavy artillery: Peter Gay's *Freud: A Life for Our Time* (hardback, 1,396 grams). It arced through the air, but Diana had time to duck and it shattered a flower vase on an occasional table behind her. The sound was horrendous (warzone). The flowers scattered and water ran over the oak parquet floor (collateral damage).

'That was disproportionate and typically male. That beautiful— and quite valuable—object was my grandmother's favorite.'

Second Thoughts (paperback, 291 grams) flew at a pace. John was surprised by her accuracy and upper body strength. He wasn't ready. It was too early in the morning for him and, although he dodged, it clipped his ear.

Now he took up one of Freud's collected works. Determined to finish his foe, he hurled volume XXIV, *Indexes and Bibliographies* (hardback, 750 grams). It hit her shoulder.

A girl who has climbed the social and professional ladder from a suburban housing estate doesn't buckle for a Freud volume. The thin but deadly paperback, *Learning from Experience* (214 grams), flew at him like a frisbee. Once again he lacked the necessary agility and the book hit the top of his head.

'Hey, this is getting serious.'

Diana didn't care, she was insulted and injured. *War Memoirs* (paperback, 511 grams) went his way, but this time he was ready and the book flew harmlessly into an armchair behind him. He reached for another Freud volume, a hardback, but *Taming Wild Thoughts* (paperback, 133 grams), slim and aerodynamic, met him edge on, squarely between the eyes, causing blood to pour from his nose.

Diana threw open the front door and rushed out, screaming, 'Fuck you. I'm not going to dinner with you ever again.'

The engagement was over for the moment, which was fortunate because the psychoanalysts had an extensive library.

John's Freud volume, however, had already been dispatched. It shot through the open doorway, bounced unevenly and then careened off and hit the front door of their immediate neighbors, Mr and Mrs Harry Goldstein. Coincidentally, they also had a keen interest in Freudian texts and other publications by various psychoanalysts.

The door opened and Mrs Goldstein called out, 'Harry, they've had another fight. It's volume twenty-one, *The Future of an Illusion, Civilization and Its Discontents.*'

Postscript

The 'controversial discussions' were a series of scientific meetings of the British Psychoanalytical Society held in October 1942 and February 1944. They sometimes proceeded even as bombs rained down on London. The meetings were an attempt to resolve some theoretical and clinical issues in the Society. The group around Melanie Klein and the Viennese school of analysts argued their respective positions, sometimes with passion, personal comments, and some aggression. Both groups produced seven papers each which are regarded as seminal papers even today. However, they led to a division of the society into three groups: the Kleinians, the Middle Group, and the Anna Freudians, each of whom trained their own students. For the texts of the various papers and a description of the meetings see King and Steiner (1990).

References

Bion W. R. (1984). *Attention and Interpretation*. London: Maresfield Reprints.

Bion W. R. (1984). *Learning from Experience*. London: Karnac Books.

Bion W. R. (1984). *Second Thoughts*. London: Maresfield Library, Karnac Books.

Bion W. R. (1997) *Taming Wild Thoughts*. London: Karnac Books,

Bion W. R. (1997) *War Memoirs*. London: Karnac Books.

Freud S. (1957). *Indexes and Bibliographies*. SE XXIV. London: Hogarth Press and The Institute of Psycho-Analysis.

Freud S. (1929). *The Future of an Illusion, Civilization and its Discontents*. SE XXI. London: Hogarth Press and The Institute of Psycho-Analysis.

Gay P. (1988). *Freud: A Life for Our Time*. London: JM Dent and Sons.

King P., and Steiner R., (Eds) *The Freud-Klein Controversies, 1941-45*. London: Hogarth Press.

Following this story is a collection of vignettes under the title *Goading* which are about an aggressive form of projection and provocation...

5

Goading: Six Vignettes

———◆———

What does the title mean? A **goad** is a piece of equipment used on a farm to guide livestock. It is a type of long pointed stick, and is also known as a cattle prod. To goad a person means to do something to them in word or deed to irritate or annoy them. There is no good reason for the behaviour, the purpose is to get control over them consciously or unconsciously, through the anxiety that the unpleasant experience induces.

a. Moving Stuff

What's a policeman doing here? It's all right, Denise, he only wants to check the truth of my story. He's going now.

'Goodbye, Ron—Officer, I mean—and thank you again.'

Look at him getting on the motorbike. Sexy bottom, or what?

No, I've never said I was bisexual. I haven't thought about it that much, but I think I could be in the right circumstances.

Anyway, to answer your question about why he was here. I was driving as fast as I could within the limit, or so I thought. I could only use one arm, as you know, so I must have done something wrong. He pulled me over.

Stop fussing. Do you want to hear the story or not?

Feel it, the bottle is warm. I'll put it into you before it cools down. Here: hold it yourself, between your legs.

Relax, where's the equipment? Oh yeah, on the bedside table, under my nose.

Denise, stop going on at me.

Was it worth it to get fined for speeding? I didn't get a fine, he was really nice. He stopped me and said, 'Is this your vehicle, miss?' So polite, like they are.

Does this bit go into that plastic thing or is it the other way round? OK, I understand, I think.

Anyway, he wanted to know why I was driving so fast. Then he said, 'Why are you holding your left arm like that?'

'Like what?' I asked, trying to play the innocent.

'You're holding your arm next to your side,' he said.

'It hurts. I damaged my elbow playing tennis.'

'Then you shouldn't be driving, should you?' He sounded all stern and sexy. But I was afraid I wouldn't get to you on time.

'Tell me the truth,' he said.

'All right. This is very personal, so be nice,' I said. He didn't say anything, so I went on. 'In my armpit I'm holding a glass container with fresh semen in it to keep it at body temperature. I'm taking it to my girlfriend. A gay friend gave it to me like this. I didn't collect it personally, if that's what you're wondering.' He remained serious; I have to say he was very professional. But I was nervous and embarrassed, so I continued, 'I want to get home as fast as possible and deliver it to her.'

Then he smiled sympathetically. I was relieved. He told me his first name and let me follow him, with the blue lights flashing on his motorbike. And when we arrived he offered to give us some more stuff, in person. To either of us or both, cheeky sod, should the need arise. Very sporting of him, I thought.

Why are you looking at me like that? You'd only have to turn the lights out and imagine it's me with this equipment. Or vice versa of course.

What? Don't be like that. No, I'm not being cruel and heartless. Of course I love you. Don't cry! Laugh, for God's sake. I'm only joking—sort of.

Just be happy this stuff is here, it's still nice and warm anyway. What a performance. You'd think the Almighty Creator could have worked out something a bit easier, wouldn't you? Are you ready?

Postscript

I saw a news magazine program on television about homosexual couples having children, in which a woman collected semen from a gay friend and carried it under her arm to her partner. This imaginary development of that event is an example of projection carried out in an apparently light-hearted manner which is actually aggressive. The pushing of uncomfortable feelings onto Denise is cruel. It seems the speaker is anxious about the home-made donation for pregnancy that she and Denise are undertaking. She is also anxious about the process of donor fertilization, and the consequences of its success or failure give rise to conflicting feelings. She doesn't admit she is anxious but behaves in a cruel way to her partner, thus projecting her feelings onto her.

She is worried about the policeman, a superego figure, but she flirts her way out of the problem of her speeding and possible late arrival. Although this should be a loving moment, she is unconsciously compelled to goad her partner Denise instead of sharing her anxiety about the new reality on which they are embarking.

b. The Start of a New Life

It was the vomit pouring over me, my newspaper and the pint in front of me that awoke me to the beauty of the vomiter. I wiped my face with the back of my one clean sleeve. With both hands on the table, she leaned over my drink. Her pretty dress was still spotless. And rather décolleté, I was delighted to see. When she looked at me I could see shame in her adorable face. Nevertheless, her intoxicated eyes poured unfocused love into my soul.

'I'm so sorry,' she said, burping up a bit more stuff, and letting it dribble down into my glass. The stench was overpowering. I tried not to move, as I didn't want to feel her stomach contents seeping through my clothes.

'I've been looking at you all evening,' she slurred, her head rolling from side to side. 'Will you marry me? No one else wants to.'

'I'm sure that's not true but yes, of course I will marry you. When?'

'Saturday.'

'Tomorrow?'

'Yes.'

'Thanks, I'd love to.'

She gave a weak smile. 'Oh, no,' she groaned, and pushed herself back. Up came another projectile spume. This time I saw the sick land on my newspaper and my pint. The glass was now half full of beer with a frothy topping of vomit.

All this took just twenty seconds; my quiet Friday evening was over. I was messed up, smelly, and engaged to the nameless culprit.

Two young women rushed over and caught the vomiter under the arms as she fell backwards in a faint. 'Maureen,' they called. One of them said to me, 'I'm so sorry your evening is ruined.'

'I'm going home to get cleaned up. Does she live far away?'

'Yes, but she's here with us, her ex-bridesmaids, drowning her sorrows. She was dumped this evening, just before her wedding. He ran off with her best friend.'

'I think I'm the stand-in. So, no need to cancel.'

'What, you? Look at the state of you!'

'For the sake of this new and promising situation I'll ignore that. We can take her to my house, it's not far. We can get cleaned up together. I mean we're to be man and wife tomorrow, so it won't be immodest.'

The friends, Myra and Nancy, introduced themselves as we lifted Maureen's slight and beautiful frame. I carried her in my arms. Looking at her vomit-stained face, I was again struck by how lovely she was. The stench brought me back to reality. The bar staff of the Rose and Crown appeared with mops and a bucket. 'You lot aren't coming back here in a hurry,' they called after us as we left.

'Tomorrow, for the reception,' I shouted over my shoulder.

Myra looked at me.

'Only joking. I'm sure you've found somewhere better than this. I'm looking forward to it already.'

'No, I just wondered how you knew.'

The smell captured my attention again. I would have to apologize to the staff later to spare Maureen's blushes.

When we got home, the two friends disrobed the lovely Maureen and put her in the shower. I put my clothes and hers into the washing machine. After wrapping myself in a dressing gown, I gave them some towels and one of my large T-shirts.

'We'd better put her in the bed in the spare room to sleep it off. We don't want to give her a nasty shock when she wakes up, eh?' I said.

Nancy looked at me.

'I mean she shouldn't wake up next to me, even smelling sweetly, as I'll soon be after *my* shower. We don't want her to think we've had non-consensual premarital coitus, do we?' They didn't join in with my mirth, so I added, 'I realize she needs her sleep to be fresh for our big day tomorrow.'

Maureen's friends were quiet, then Myra said, 'We'll collect her tomorrow morning. And don't look at her: it's bad luck to see the bride before the ceremony.'

'Absolutely, I know the rules.'

'And that, ladies and gentlemen, was the beginning of our sublime journey of twenty-five years together to date. I'm sure you'll all agree it's an entertaining anecdote. Our thanks to the staff of the Rose and Crown for the lovely meal. And now, please be upstanding and raise your glasses to—Maureen.'

Postscript

'Then the Lord God said, 'It is not good that the man should be alone. I will make him a helpmate." (*Genesis 2:18*)

Here is a revolting and amusing start to a life partnership. Was this divine intervention or a unique opportunity that the speaker grabbed? He didn't have to do anything, just walk into a ready-prepared wedding ceremony with a life attached.

Projectile vomiting is a strong metaphor for the projection of feelings but, ironically in this case, something good is being offered to the narrator: a marriage to fill his empty weekend and a lifetime ahead of getting to know Maureen. It could, of course, turn out to be a disaster. The humor in the story plays on our natural reaction of disgust, and our wariness about being offered a marriage partner in this way, especially one who is drowning her sorrows in drink.

Reference

Jones, A. (Ed.) (1974). *The Jerusalem Bible*. London: Darton, Longman and Todd.

c. The Fall of Rome

I was twelve years old and a lazy idiot, according to some experts. Our Latin teacher, Mr Farrel, was a heavily built, quick-tempered, redheaded Irishman, a bachelor in a Catholic boys' school. The place oozed sexual frustration from all its inmates, every day. Heterosexuality was curtailed and homosexuality forbidden.

Mr Farrel smoked heavily and his hands smelled of nicotine. In addition, he seemed to have a sinus problem and constantly swallowed snot down his throat. Occasionally, he cleared his throat and spat out of the third-floor classroom window while we wrote a Latin exercise, not attractive behavior for a potential mate or for those walking below.

He seemed jolly at times, mostly when he could make jokes at our expense. But he was a teacher of the old school, a devotee of the maxim 'spare the rod and spoil the child'. When he wasn't happy, he liked to use his hands to torture those with learning problems. He threw pieces of chalk, and occasionally even the wooden-backed blackboard duster, at talkative pupils.

No doubt he had been brought up in the same violent way in which he maltreated us. He probably came from a family of a dozen, in a country where inebriated husbands made their wives pregnant according to the Pope's rules and the delight of the celibate clergy. No contraceptives and no terminations, even in life-threatening circumstances, for Catholic families. But I couldn't feel sorry for him.

Farrel referred to those who could not write fluent Latin by now as 'idiots' or 'eejits'. Especial 'eejits' were altar boys, like me, who had learned the Latin responses in the ceremony of the Holy Mass but didn't know what they meant. I was also regarded as being among the 'dregs' of the school, the most deplorable, with the lowest marks in Latin and everything else. This was to be my last day in Mr Farrel's Latin class.

Mr Farrel approached my desk with my homework book in his hand.

'What do you call this, O'Hara?'

'My homework book, sir.'

'Don't be cheeky, O'Hara.'

'No, sir.'

'I call it a mess, O'Hara.'

'Yes, sir.'

'Can you explain these brown stains on the cover and the edges of the pages, O'Hara?'

I looked carefully at the offending brown color on the otherwise pale-blue book. My friend O'Malley called out, 'He took it into the toilet.' Perhaps he wanted to take the heat off me.

There was general laughter; Mr Farrel whipped round, furious. 'I'm going to deal with someone later.'

'It's gravy, sir,' I shouted, trying to rescue O'Malley.

Mr Farrel turned back to me, his cheeks pink with anger. 'You were doing your homework on the dining-room table?'

'Yes, sir.'

'During Sunday lunch, I suppose?'

'Something like that, sir.' I was looking at the floor, and I missed the incoming back of his hand across the top of my head.

'A dangerously cavalier response, O'Hara.'

'Yes, sir. Sorry, sir. I was doing that.'

'What were you doing, boy?'

'My homework at the lunch table.'

'And your parents approved of that, did they?'

'I was doing it on my knee under the table and my little brother leaned over and tipped my plate.'

'I see. So it's the little brother's responsibility, is it?'

'No, sir. Yes, sir. I mean, no, sir.'

'What's the Latin word for responsibility, O'Hara?'

O'Malley called out, '*Officium.*'

'*Officium*, sir.'

'And you're the class parrot now, are you, O'Hara?'

'No, sir.'

He hit me again.

'Yes, sir.'

'Who said *officium*?' he demanded, glaring at the class of uniformed boys before him. They were presumably glad it was me being tortured, not them. But now the unwise prompt put them all in Farrel's line of fire.

'Who was it? Who said *officium*?' You will all remain behind this afternoon for half an hour if I do not get the answer.'

Under that peer pressure, O'Malley piped up: 'Me, sir.'

'You're too smart, keep your mouth shut. You can see me after the lesson. And you, O'Hara, let's try again, shall we? What's 'conscience' in Latin?'

Silence

'It's not difficult, O'Hara, we learned it last week,' and he took a tuft of my hair in his smelly fingers and pulled until I was standing on tiptoes to reduce the pain.

'What is it, O'Hara?'

'It hurts, sir.'

'The idea of pain, O'Hara, is to improve your cognition.'

A few boys sniggered.

'No answer? It is *conscientia*.'

'Yes, sir.'

'And now what does *stultus piger es* mean?'

'Don't know, sir.'

'It means, "You're a lazy idiot", and these are the last words you will hear in a Latin class. You might not care but when you try for your first job and they see that you not only failed Latin, but were thrown out of the class, you'll regret your indolence.'

'Yes, sir.' What Latin had to do with being a bus driver or going to art school I didn't know.

He dragged me by the hair towards the door. I was on tiptoes, my face contorted in pain. I was thinking that 'lazy' and 'idiot' didn't go together. Shouldn't it be one or the other? I mean, if you are lazy it doesn't matter if you are an idiot or smart, the result is the same: nothing gets done. If you are an idiot it doesn't matter if you are lazy. It might even be good, because you wouldn't do so many stupid things. I was amazed at my mental clarity under torture. Perhaps Farrel's method worked after all.

'Open the door, boy.'

'I can't see the handle, sir... you're pulling my head up.'

'Your head will be off if you don't find it soon.'

I thought of people approaching their execution who dragged their feet just to stay alive for a few more moments, perhaps to give God another chance to intervene, but I found the handle quickly due to the agony in my scalp.

'There we are, O'Hara, that wasn't hard, was it?'

'No, sir.' I wish I could have used the Robin Williams line from the film *Good Morning, Vietnam* when he said to his angry sergeant something like "You look like a man in need of a blow job." But such things are only funny afterwards, and anyway the film hadn't been made then.

As the door closed behind me, I heard Farrel say, 'And now the boy who does his homework in the toilet can stand up.'

I didn't hang about. I was relieved I hadn't said anything provocative. I didn't mind being out of the room. I was free.

Unluckily I ran into 'Dithers', the headmaster, Mr Dilkins, in his corduroy jacket, partly covered by his old university gown. 'Wandering in the corridors again, O'Hara?'

'Yes, sir. Er, no, sir. I'm going to the toilet, sir.'

'Ah yes, the late homework. On your way to find your book, are you? Or do you have a loose bowel?'

'The latter, sir. We ate a heavy Sunday lunch, sir.'

'I see, and what has happened to your hair? There seems to be a tuft missing.'

'Latin, sir.'

'Ah yes, Mr Farrel. He's enthusiastic, isn't he? Good to see that in a teacher. He gets results. He describes you as a lazy idiot, O'Hara. Do you think that's true?'

'No, sir. I think it's either one or the other, sir. I mean lazy or idiot. I don't think I can be both, sir.'

'What are you talking about, O'Hara? You think too much. I can't imagine what's going to become of you, particularly without Latin, but perhaps God will be merciful.'

The art teacher took me in.

Postscript

'Spare the rod and spoil the child' (Elfric of Eynsham, 950–1010). He was paraphrasing from the Bible: 'The man who fails to use the stick hates his son; The man who is free with his corrections loves him.' (*Proverbs 13:24*)

Learning through violence has been traditional in many cultures. And, of course, to some extent it works. A little anxiety makes us all take action, possibly creatively if we have a problem that is essential to solve. But when pain and anxiety are too much then nothing happens, because our capacity to think is overwhelmed. In this vignette there seems to be a mixture of both. Some pain makes O'Hara think; too much causes him to lose what he knows of Latin vocabulary.

As we know, excessive frustration leads to anger and the wish for revenge. This seems to be the case in the Latin classroom, where Mr Farrel tries to avoid the suffering in his apparently loveless life. The teacher's empty life is projected onto his pupils, who are compelled to feel that there is something missing from their minds. The real absence in his life leads to a feeling of inadequacy in Mr Farrel. His behavior towards O'Hara causes the pupil to feel angry, rebellious, and inadequate. Mr Farrel is triumphant and has brittle control over the class. His constant spitting out of the window is also a primitive metaphor for his need to remove something sickening from his body—possibly unconscious memories of the way he himself was treated as a child. Or do you have another theory?

Reference

Jones, A. (Ed.) (1974). *The Jerusalem Bible*. London: Darton, Longman and Todd.

d. Fear of Dogs

If you wish to relieve yourself of fear, disgust, or any bad feeling for that matter, how do you do it? Do you 'pass it on', as children say when playing tag? I was mentally organizing a seminar on the subject of projection, as this behavior is called, on my journey home from work. As luck would have it, two outrageous examples of this mental mechanism presented themselves during the journey. The following account is true in every detail, believe me.

A pit bull terrier was sitting upright on the aisle seat of my tram during the evening rush hour. Every other seat was taken and some people were standing. I stopped walking down the aisle and stood still. The dog was looking around at the other passengers. I tried to avoid eye contact, while keeping it under observation. I didn't want to have a staring match with an animal that has a reputation for merciless violence. The other passengers behaved as if nothing out of the ordinary was happening. The owner of the dog sat beside her in the window seat. He was wearing torn jeans and a grubby gray hoody, with the letters WTF printed on the front. Like couples who have known each other for a long time, he ignored the dog, concentrating on an electronic device, while the lovely pit bull continued to look around, curious about her surroundings.

A few minutes before this confrontation, a tram had arrived at the tram stop, but it wasn't the one I wanted. I heard a dog bark and saw a pit bull terrier leading a young man in my direction. I jumped on the tram as the doors closed, feeling as if I had escaped the front page of tomorrow's local paper: 'Innocent bystander mauled at tram station'. A few stops down the line I changed onto this tram and walked down the aisle, looking for a seat.

Since childhood I've been wary of dogs. I've never assumed they were friendly until I know them. Now I was stuck here on a tram in Gothenburg, Sweden, a peaceful country of equal opportunity. Did 'equal rights' include pit bulls? If so, I had missed the parliamentary debate on the passing of that legislation.

I wondered about the dog owner. *Who does he think he is when he lets his dog sit on the seat next to him? Who does the dog think she is? Does the dog decide? Are these questions of any help to me? Shouldn't I be working on an escape plan? I could try complaining to the driver, but she's locked in her cabin at the front.*

The owner's apparent disregard of his dog girlfriend led me to wonder if he had any control over her. Previous experience led me to think that my intervention would end bloodily. It was my belief, or rather my default fantasy, that the owner was also of a violent disposition. I thought with prejudice: *He owns the dog in order to project his violent hostility towards the rest of the community, now represented by the random group of fellow travelers. If that theory is right, then so long as I feel fear he can relax and play with his phone. Am I brave enough to say, 'Excuse me, but the dog should sit on the floor'? No, I'm not.* I didn't believe he would respond favorably to my comments, so I said nothing.

I looked casually in the dog's direction: her tongue was hanging out and she seemed to be ignoring her boyfriend. Another passenger walked past her. The dog was curious but otherwise unmoved. A good sign? Possibly.

My mind wandered for a moment. I thought that *Pit Bull* would be a good name for an energy drink. It projected power, violence, social decay, and a careless disregard for the needs of others. What would the slogan be? *Pit Bull gives you balls* or *Pit Bull sets you up*, or should that be *sits you up* or, in my case, *stands you up?* The copywriting needed more work but it seemed a viable idea. However, I was distracted by a new outrage. It didn't arouse anxiety; rather it offended my aesthetic sensibilities.

A well-dressed man with a tidy beard, apparently distracted by his own thoughts and not at all concerned with the dog, and who was also looking at an electronic device, was picking his nose and putting his finger into his mouth. The disgustingness of the scene outweighed my mental terror relationship with the dog couple. People facing forward could not see the nose-picker but I was facing back, also keeping an eye on the dog. The new scene of unhygienic horror absorbed me. What did the nose-picking mean about the man's relationship with the people around him? Was he a concerned traveler bearing his fellow commuters in mind? Or was he still two years old with no one to forbid him from indulging in nose-picking/eating? Nausea rose in my throat. I had two reasons to get off the tram forthwith: finger in nose and dog bottom on seat, plus the presumed threat of dog teeth.

At the next stop the dog said to her young man, 'Time to get off, dear.'

No, that's ridiculous. She didn't say anything of the kind. The couple didn't move. I retreated down the aisle and stepped off.

I kissed the ground in relief. As the tram pulled away, I heard screams of terror mixed with groans of disgust. The tram driver was laughing hysterically, but WTF.

Postscript

This account illustrates unconscious provocation by others. The dog's boyfriend and the nose-picker were not conscious of what they were doing nor conscious of other people's reactions. If they had been made aware of them then perhaps they would have been concerned or embarrassed, but I wouldn't count on it. I could have intervened but, although psychoanalysis encourages the practitioner to 'make the unconscious conscious', I judged—I believe rightly—that this was not the moment.

When we are bringing up children, we try to make them conscious of the effect of their behavior on other people. And possibly we do the same for a friend and partner. But the general convention is that, apart from extreme situations, we do not enlighten strangers. Or do we? In some cultures it is not uncommon to comment on other people's behavior to their face while, in others, polite silence is regarded as the norm.

I don't think I'll add anything further, except to say this is a true story, though originally in two parts. The essential bit is that about the dog and me—the man picking his nose took place on another occasion, on a bus. But you didn't really need to know that.

e. Unfair Landing

I was out for a healthy walk in the middle of the day along an old railway line. Once, trains had taken city residents to the coast on sunny days on this track but now it was used by pedestrians and cyclists. On the parallel motorway, cars had replaced the environmentally friendlier trains.

Overgrown bushes between the path and the road obscured a view of the traffic, but it could be heard loud and clear. A man was walking ten meters ahead of me. He was slim and, from his stride, I assumed he was athletic. I knew there was no crash barrier on this stretch of road and wondered how either of us would react if a vehicle veered off the carriageway and came through the undergrowth in our direction. Could we move out of the way fast enough?

I didn't have to wait to find out. Suddenly an elderly saloon car came crashing through the vegetation towards the man in front of me. A wide-eyed young woman, hair in disarray and mouth open, was half in and half out of the driver's seat.

I learned later from the newspapers that her name was Karen and that her employment as a shop assistant selling electrical appliances had ended an hour earlier. Karen's boss, Mr Bigsly, had fired her because he'd had complaints about her manner from customers who had tried to return faulty goods. In these situations her first response was a line she'd learned from a TV program: 'Have you tried turning it off and on again?'

If they persisted with their requests her unbalanced temperament led her to respond with ripe language and insolence. 'It was a sad fucking day when your idiot mother pushed you out,' was one insult favored by Karen. The exchanges had a repetitive quality because she lacked the vocabulary and conciliation skills required to broaden the conversation. Consequently, as her boss noted, the reports from complainants had a similarity that confirmed their veracity.

Mr Bigsly and Karen had had a strident exchange. On Karen's side, this was characteristically unpleasant, even as she tried to point out that she was protecting the company from inconsiderate customers. Fortunately, she and Bigsly did not come to blows. However, Karen was sure that in a just world she would have had the freedom to mince him. She left him to ponder her version of how his conception was enjoyed by his mother.

According to the police, Karen then 'proceeded in her vehicle without due care and attention'—in other words, she drove with a flagrant disregard for the well-being of other motorists and their passengers. The following is taken from the police interview at the scene of the incident. She was quoted thus: 'I don't care what speed I was doing. I wanted my Iron Maiden CD in the glove compartment. That's where I keep the CDs, so I had to stretch over. I have the right to entertainment in my car, don't I? Or do you fascists want to stop that too? I leaned into the steering wheel so it must have turned with me. I suppose you'll say next that I should cut my boobs off—that's sexist. Stop staring at me. All I wanted was my CD, so I reached across like anyone else would. Yeah, I felt the crash as I went through the bushes, but why was that idiot John, as you call him, right in front of me? Some people are beyond belief. No, mate, this is not my problem.'

As the incident unfolded I observed that John, with presence of mind and tremendous agility, leapt up and landed on the car bonnet. He somersaulted over the roof and slid down the back of the vehicle, finishing with both feet together facing the new gap in the vegetation. Perhaps he was a gymnast. The car had been scratched by its path through the bushes and was now dented by his acrobatics, thus adding to its wretched appearance.

I couldn't believe what I had witnessed but I had the answer to my question—such a situation is survivable, up to that point at least.

John walked on without looking back.

Karen swung open the driver's door and jumped out, holding a CD in her hand. She surveyed the damage.

'Hey, dickhead, look at the state of my car.'

'But you drove at me.'

'You shouldn't have been there then, should you? What about my fucking car?'

'I am deeply sorry for you,' he said and continued on his way. I think he hoped an apology would suffice, but I detected ambiguity in his tone. Karen got into her car. I thought it wouldn't start after the crash and, anyway, I couldn't believe she'd drive on a pedestrian path.

How naive of me—tyrants always have luck on their side, have you noticed? The car started. This time, John's stars were not kind and he couldn't avoid his fate. Karen chased him and rammed him from behind. She stopped momentarily to insert her CD. To the ear-splitting sounds of heavy metal music, she drove back through the hole in the hedge.

John survived her behavior, although he now walks with a limp. Karen has been detained at Her Majesty's pleasure.

Postscript

But why me? I mused in the middle of the night. To my surprise, God answered: 'It's nothing personal old chap, it's just the way it is.' And Freud had something to add: 'The element of truth behind all this, which people are so ready to disavow, is that men are not gentle creatures who want to be loved...; they are, on the contrary, creatures among whose instinctual endowments is to be reckoned a powerful share of aggressiveness.' (Freud, S. (1929) p111) Sometimes, whatever you do, bad things will happen. If you meet a hate-filled person, they may well damage you and you won't be able to do anything about it. How is it that tyrants and dictators, i.e. people who project their violent feelings onto others, seem to have luck on their side? At least, that is, until their final comeuppance, by which time they may have murdered their way through hundreds if not thousands of people. How do we allow so many political bullies to run our lives if they are not also a part of us?

Charles Reznikoff wrote a book of poetry entitled *Holocaust*, and one of the commentators on the work, Janet Sutherland, said, 'The scenes of Holocaust unfold in Eastern Europe, but, Reznikoff seems to suggest, they could happen anywhere, at any time, for the nature of man which has given rise to these scenes is constant, unchanging.' (Sutherland, J. (1975)) The book is well worth reading; it is a succinct summary of evidence from the Nuremburg Trials of the Nazis for their brutality.

In the story above, Karen has the kind of narcissistic character that sees the world exclusively from her point of view, without regard for the needs of others. From her perspective, she is not to blame for her behavior, and the feelings of anyone else are irrelevant. In her world, other people exist only to please her or else they are in her way. I'm suggesting she is someone we can find in ourselves.

References

Freud, S. (1929). *The Future of an Illusion, Civilization and its Discontents.* SE XXI. London: Hogarth Press and The Institute of Psycho-Analysis.
Sutherland J. (1975). 'Reznikoff and His Sources', in *Holocaust* by Charles Reznikoff. Biddeford, ME: Black Sparrow Press.

f. The Tale of Jenkins' Ear

'Jenkins?'

'Ouch. My ear, sir.'

'Yes, your ear, Jenkins, and you have two of them. I am only holding one. It's your lucky day—so far.'

'It hurts, sir. Please, Mr Watkins, let go.'

'How did I get this close to you without you noticing, Jenkins?'

'I don't know, sir.'

'You were daydreaming again, Jenkins. Were you not?'

'Yes, sir. No, sir—*ouch*.'

'Would you like to share your obviously engaging thoughts with the rest of us in this classroom?'

'No, sir. I mean, I don't remember them, sir.'

'Don't remember? Don't remember? Who else in this room believes that? Tell us your daydream, Jenkins.'

'COME ON, JENKS, TELL US.'

'There, listen to the chorus.'

'*Ouch!* I was daydreaming of a woman, sir.'

'A woman. Why am I not surprised?'

'I don't know, sir.'

'There's a lot you don't know, Jenkins. There's a long list. So, "a woman". Go on...'

'She was naked in bed, sir, and I was there too.'

'YES,' said the classroom chorus.

'What? Be careful, Jenkins, this is a religious school, even if you're a philistine.'

'She said, "You like that little noise, don't you?"'

'"What noise?"'

'"The sound on the sheets as I move my legs."'

209

'YES,' came again from the classroom chorus.

'Right. Out, boy—to the headmaster's study. Now.'

'What shall I say, sir?'

'You shall say that you were playing to the chorus in defiance of your teacher, Mr Watkins, and he says you deserve a beating.'

'Really, sir? I was just answering you honestly. I'm not responsible for the chorus.'

LOUD GUFFAWS.

'I'm going to beat you myself, Jenkins.'

'Then that will be your second assault on me today, and I think we have reached an impasse, sir. I will not be telling you any more of my thoughts and you will not be beating me.'

'It's 1962, Jenkins. Being queer is still illegal, and I can beat you to a pulp without fear of recrimination. Now, get out.'

And that, dear reader, was nearly the end of my school career. I wish. I wish I had challenged him like that. If I had, I imagine it would have been life-changing. In reality, I suffered my ear being pulled and continued a mediocre school career with the chorus.

I went to the headmaster's study. Our headmaster was Old Perkins. We called him 'The Perv'. I don't know if he was a perv, but he liked smacking bottoms with his hands.

'Ah, Jenkins, just the chap. I understand you have a good eye for color. Why are you here at this time, by the way?'

'Don't know, sir. I mean, Mr Watkins sent me.'

'Yes, yes, I am sure there is a good reason, we will come to that. What do you think of these colors for the walls in my study? My secretary thinks the light blue, because it's modern, I suppose, but I was thinking of something more traditional.'

'I think you are absolutely right, sir, and the school will appreciate the stability that traditional colors engender.'

'That was lyrical, Jenkins. I shall compliment your teacher. Now what was it you wanted?'

'I seem to have forgotten, sir. I should have written it down. I think Mr Watkins was annoyed with me for misusing the chorus, or something like that.'

'Never mind, whatever it was I'm sure you won't do it again. Go and read in the library for half an hour.'

I wish he'd said that. What he actually said was, 'Yes, I can imagine what you said. You are a proverbial heathen, as we all know, with no shame or compunction, so you will get a beating. No, on second thoughts you will get a thrashing but I don't have time just now. Go to the library and wait there. See to it that you do something useful. Mrs Bryant will show you the book of the week—read it.'

In the library was the voluptuous dark-skinned lady of my fantasy who, not fifteen minutes earlier, had been totally intimate with me—in my mind.

'Hello, Mrs Bryant.'

'Hello, Jenkins. You're looking lost and lonely. What can I do for you?'

'I've been sent here by the headmaster. He said you should show me the book of the week. What is it?'

'It isn't anything by D. H. Lawrence anyway.'

'Who?'

'Never mind, you can help me stack. Push that trolley with the books on it. Come along, stay close and you can learn something.'

She started to tell me about the Dewey system of cataloguing books in libraries. Behind the history section was a narrow space between shelves of musty old books. The trolley got caught between two crooked shelves; Mrs Bryant and I were very close. She turned to face me and then her lips were all over my face. Her hands squeezed my bottom. It felt unreal. It stopped suddenly, like a summer shower, wet and refreshing, then suddenly all over.

'Sorry, Jenkins, I don't know what came over me. Don't tell anyone, please.'

'No, absolutely not, but can I come back to the library, after my thrashing?'

'Are you going to get caned? In that case I have a special remedy for sore bottoms.' And she pressed against me and squeezed my, as yet undamaged, bottom again, with both hands. 'Whenever you need me, Jenkins, come in here.'

I couldn't wait for the beating, and the harder the better.

We were in lust, Mrs Bryant and I. Not love, that's really a waste of time. Look what happened to Romeo and Juliet: they would have been better off being in lust and staying there. But they had to do the romance thing and look where that got them.

So, Bryant, thirty-two years of age, and me, sixteen, a right old Oedipus and Jocasta thing we had going, but you've got to get your end away when you can, haven't you? Then she got pregnant, but luckily there was a quiet and obedient Mr Bryant only too pleased to take the honor. And that, reader, is what happened to my school career.

No, not at all. Nothing happened. It never does. School was a boring experience, another instalment in the adult world's attempt to crush the young.

'You are most certainly a philistine, Jenkins. An ignorant infidel.'

And then I was thrashed.

Postscript

Freud has something to say about the behavior of Mr Watkins and the headmaster, 'In matters of sexuality we are at present, every one of us, ill or well, nothing but hypocrites. It will be all to our good if, as a result of such general honesty, a certain amount of toleration in sexual concerns should be attained. (Freud 1898) p266)

Jenkins was goading his teacher, and the class, by his 'honesty'. The class and the teacher were provoking him. Mrs Bryant was provoking Jenkins, who wanted most of all to be provoked by her. But in the end it was all a fantasy and, if Mr Watkins had left Jenkins' ear alone, nothing at all would have happened and you wouldn't have had a story.

Goading is complex, as you see, but the headmaster had the last word (or smack) and put the blame squarely on Jenkins.

Reference

Freud, S. (1898). Sexuality in the Aetiology of the Neuroses. SE III (1893-1899) Hogarth Press and The Institute of Psycho-Analysis

And the next story is another kind of madness, one of fantasy and phantasy in a paranoid mixture.

6

Death by a Thousand Tongues

————◆————

The following story attempts to illustrate a paranoid state of mind in which an ancient method of torture is part of the fantasy. The story demonstrates the protagonist's self-inflicted cruelty, as one aspect of her personality is projected onto another—a strange idea perhaps but a useful demonstration of object relations theory.

The lines in italic describe the unconscious feelings of the speaker, rendered as the speaker's phantasy of a traditional Chinese method of execution.

∽

My name is Ms Whynne, pronounced 'whine', and I have worked for the Magnificent Business Company for years. It's housed in an impressive Victorian building, with long carpeted corridors, original 1890s decor and many rooms, large and small. Sometimes voices are raised as people express their feelings in meetings. Sometimes the corridors are silent after the echo of yet another closing door. Strangely, they seem to close more often than they open. It's lovely to walk in the well-maintained park that surrounds the building, A busy road runs past the gates and I get the bus there sometimes, although I don't go out that way very often.

Many employees smoke cigarettes that they roll themselves, and people talk freely, although a few never speak, keeping their thoughts to themselves. The freedom to speak when you will ensures that our product range just gets better and better.

On this particular day I'd been summoned first thing in the morning to report to Mr Grym, the Managing Director. I didn't know why. Although I thought I was liked and respected I was filled with foreboding. I waited in the foyer, sitting on a bench that was upholstered in dark brown leather.

Far away, in another land a few hundred years ago, businessman Ay Cho was being tied to a stake in the middle of the village of Bu in Shang'Quang province. He faced east.

Ms Authentic, the MD's secretary, a straight-backed woman in a tight black dress, walked towards me. She looked very stern, despite the fact she wore plenty of lipgloss. I think she may sell herself in the evenings, if you follow my meaning. 'Please follow me.' She turned and, with clicking heels and a rhythmic bottom, moved briskly towards the open door of Mr Grym's office.

In the village of Bu, a crowd was gathering around their victim. With the rising sun in his eyes, Ay Cho couldn't see their preparations. But he knew that each person carried a sharp knife. He leaked piss and shit. The crowd pointed and laughed.

As I approached Grym's spacious office I was surprised to see familiar faces, some of whom had been dead for years. How was this possible? I wondered.

I was instructed to sit in a chair at the front of the room. The sun shone directly into my eyes through the east-facing window. Ms Authentic slid the tip of her tongue over her moist red lips. She looked at Mr Grym, who turned to me and said, 'Mrs Whynne, we are meeting today to critically assess your time at the Magnificent Business Company and to present our conclusions.'

Ms Authentic then addressed the group: 'The first person on the left will say a few words and then we will proceed around the room. Address your comments directly to Ms Whynne. Please begin.'

The village chief of Bu read out Ay Cho's crimes. The accusations were old and lacked substance but, despite the lack of evidence, the chief had gone along with the trial. Some important persons wanted Ay Cho out of the way and so the poor man was condemned. The chief made the first cut in his flesh. Ay Cho screamed, but to no avail. The rest of the village eagerly followed suit.

In the boardroom of the Magnificent Business Company, I heard a list of old grievances. There was no way of knowing if their accusations had merit as I could not remember most of the events they described. How could I defend myself? I had to listen and take it.

Alone and despised, Ay Cho called out for his wife and children, his mother and father. He was now empty of pee and shit, but his veins still contained blood, and the crowd wanted every drop.

I was hardly listening any more. In the past, some of these people had invited me into their offices, even offering me tea and a biscuit. Had they just been pretending to like me and lying by omission?

I was fascinated by the animated appearance of those who were dead. I remembered attending one of their funerals. On that occasion, everyone had been whispering about me, cutting me to pieces with their eyes. I'd felt frozen by the other mourners and had made an excuse to leave early. Now what they were saying about me reminded me of their own shortcomings.

After the villagers had each made their cut and some had removed a piece of flesh, they strolled off in groups, forgetting all about Ay Cho and discussing business or shopping. His cries were the unheeded background to their conversations. By midday, Ay Cho's body was a ruin.

The group finally finished accusing me and Ms Authentic turned to her boss.

Mr Grym said, 'I cannot tell you how sorry I am about all this, Ms Whynne. I really do have the greatest respect for you and your work. However, we have decided to try someone else in your position and we are letting you go. Goodbye.'

Ms Authentic, with her bright red lipstick, looked at me as if to say, 'Off you go.'

In the village of Bu in Shang'Quang province the sun dipped beneath the rooftops and, in the fading light, Ay Cho finally succumbed to his many wounds. He died staring at the bloodstained ground, thinking of his family.

217

I found it hard to stand. No one moved to help me and I heard laughter. At last I found the courage to speak.

'You lot are just a bunch of sadists. I know I have a whining voice and I'm no saint but I don't deserve to be treated so spitefully. Your allegations are years old and have no substance. You've obviously been stewing on them for years, even after some of you have died.'

There was more laughter. 'You're not even listening to me,' I protested, as they talked animatedly about the good old days, with jolly comments to each other like 'You look in great shape—considering you're dead,' and that kind of nonsense.

During the night, Ay Cho's remains were torn apart by the village dogs and what was left of him was cremated. The ashes were delivered to his distraught family in a paper bag by the village idiot, who waited by the door to be paid for the service, according to the local custom.

I stumbled to the door and turned to say, 'You should have spoken to me about all this before. It's unfair.' But nobody was listening, so I shuffled out with my hastily grabbed belongings. I had the urge to walk straight out of the building, through the park, and into the traffic on the busy road outside. But I refused to give them the satisfaction of seeing my mangled body.

Now I'm strapped to this bed talking to you. The people here aren't real doctors and nurses—they only dress like them. I know they're going to finish me off. They say I need new medicine to stop my anxiety. But I've never been anxious in my life, because I know how the world really is. Don't let their smiles deceive you; they don't fool me.

Postscript

In this story, Ms Whynne's paranoia is characterized by delusions of persecution, which are vigorously defended with logic and reason. Fantasies and grandiosity are attributed to other people and events.

In general, the paranoid person builds their idea upon some grain of truth. You can take that thought how you will, depending on how paranoid you are. Sometimes you might be right.

I've used the image of Chinese torture to represent the suffering of the paranoid person. It is called lingchi, which translates as the slow process or the lingering death or the slow slicing, and is also known as death by a thousand cuts. This form of execution was carried out in ancient China. A knife was employed to methodically remove portions of the victim's body over an extended period of time (Wikipedia). I found this a good metaphor for the searing pain that accompanies paranoid anxiety.

In this account, an elaborate fantasy illustrates the mind of a person suffering paranoia and every aspect of her story has a back story equally as paranoid as the first. For this poor lady there is no way out of her mental madhouse, the inner room of terror that the paranoid inhabits. Sometimes I think of it as a room with no windows or doors in which a horror movie is always playing, and from which there is no exit. As human beings, our aggression, particularly our capacity for self-destructive behavior, in the form of paranoid states of mind, is a great impediment to creative development.

The next story was written from seminar notes, used in an imaginary setting. It illustrates another kind of suffering in a conscious fantasy that is felt to be real...

Reference

Lingchi, ancient eastern method of execution. From Wikipedia, the free encyclopedia.

7

The Teacher, His Students, and Dream Engine Inc

———◆———

The dual narratives that follow explore some ideas about a state of mind called 'borderline', a word referred to in the well-known term 'borderline personality disorder'. The associated symptoms are more common than we may think. At times there may be a little too much narcissism in all of us. It becomes part of a diagnosis when it reaches overwhelming proportions.

In the following account, a teacher talks to his students about the theory of this emotional condition. The teacher gives a description of a borderline problem during therapy and the students and teacher show some mild signs of behaving in the same way as a client. At the same time, unknown to the teacher and his students, in the office next door a person with a borderline personality enacts her feelings with her work colleagues.

This story within a story attempts to illustrate an emotional condition that is not easy to grasp by showing its symptoms from different positions, and I hope thereby that a fuller picture of the borderline problem will emerge for the reader. It is important to remember how much suffering a person with this problem experiences.

Let's begin our story…

Mr Wiseman, the teacher of psychotherapy, stood at the front of seminar room 5b. An undistinguished room in the Psychology Institute, it smelled of floor wax and the lingering aromas of its most recent occupants: perfume, soap, chewing gum, and garlic. The windows were due to be cleaned soon and one of the blinds hung lopsidedly open, like a fan. The furniture was worn, the tables and chairs haphazardly arranged.

During his seminar, Mr Wiseman's intention was to introduce a psychoanalytic perspective on the theory of borderline states of mind. However, this was the hour after lunch and some people were feeling the effects of what they had eaten.

Mr Wiseman raised his voice slightly, hoping to gain everyone's attention. 'Let's say the client wants to stay on the border between madness and sadness,' he announced. 'This is the so-called borderline state, an uncertain and painful position, like sitting on a fence, always leaning too far one way or too far the other. To avoid the madness of anxiety and paranoia, the person may blame others—in no uncertain terms—for many of his perceived problems.

'He does this to avoid the despair associated with guilt, which he would feel if he accepted responsibility for himself. In addition, he may idealize someone to avoid feeling the pain he would experience if he simply envied them. It's all in the reading list.

'So we can say that projection, denial, and idealization are characteristics of the borderline state of mind. Such behavior, however, is never completely successful and suffering is experienced anyway, not only by those close to the person with this problem but, most importantly, by the person themselves. That is why clients seek therapy, but it's a process in which they may also have the discomfort of finding that they envy the therapist and her abilities.'

Jonathan, a young man in the front row, began to yawn. Mr Wiseman decided to ignore it and continued his talk. 'During therapy, the therapist's insights can threaten the client's mental balance, particularly if she points out the client's responsibility for his own behavior. As a result, the client may try to keep the therapist under his control.'

Jonathan's eyes crinkled at the edges as his mouth widened in another yawn.

'The client must seduce the therapist into compliance or terrify her into silence,' Mr Wiseman continued. 'At the same time, the client wants help because he is suffering.

'I should add that clients generally believe unconsciously that they will suffer more if they experience real feelings of sadness and remorse.'

Looking at Jonathan, Mr Wiseman could see the little pink thing that hangs at the back of the throat. Why couldn't he ever remember the name of it?

The building in which the Psychology Institute was situated was also home to a collection of private companies, one of which—Dream Engine Inc (slogan: 'We Make Your Dreams Come True')—had an

223

office that adjoined Mr Wiseman's seminar room. Neither enterprise was aware of the other.

Patsy Dee ran the Dream Engine office with an iron hand and many people felt bullied by her, yet she insisted that she was the one being bullied. She lived a lonely life, as new friends soon left her.

It was a busy afternoon for Patsy; it seemed that everyone wanted something from her. She sat in her special ergonomically designed office chair while the phones rang non-stop. She enjoyed complaining about work pressure, although she loved the feeling of being wanted.

Patsy was twenty-nine years of age and, never far from her thoughts, was her search for the right life partner. She had currently fixed her desires on Greg, twenty-three, who worked in Accounts. The age difference didn't matter to her. Greg regularly visited her office for materials and she watched him discreetly, particularly his facial expressions. He was perfect: attractive, well-groomed and a fastidious worker; an ideal mate. She had decided that her feelings were reciprocated. The fact that he had not yet made a move towards her was because he was shy, she concluded. So she continued to love him and to wait for the day when he would ask her out.

∞

Next door in seminar room 5b, Mr Wiseman, distracted by his memory lapse about the pink thing in the student's throat, forgot to finish what he was saying. And now another student, Saul, had begun to yawn. *I'll soon be yawning too*, thought Mr Wiseman.

Yet another student was typing loudly on a laptop.

'Trudy, can you stop the typing please? It's disturbing people.' He noticed his tone was sharp.

She stopped.

The other students were clearly relieved but, despite that, he did not feel victorious. Rather, he felt disappointed with himself for being irritated.

Trudy banged the laptop shut and glared at him.

Oh, narcissism, how you are wounded, he mused silently, then continued, a little shaken: 'According to the theory, we all carry our infant with us. I refer, of course, to the fledgling version of ourselves that continues to direct some aspects of our lives, particularly our most primitive feelings. Remember that narcissism is our defense against envy. In other words, putting ourselves first so we don't have to acknowledge how much we need other people.' He was tempted to add, 'This can manifest itself when we fall asleep randomly in class, or type annoyingly.' But instead, and more constructively, he said, 'You remember narcissism? At its most extreme it involves the belief that one's own fantasies are reality.'

Angela, a bright student sitting at the back of the class, nodded. The teacher took that as sufficient acknowledgment and continued with his points quickly, eager to get to an example he had written himself. He hoped it would engage his students' interest.

The office next door was separated from this speculative psychoanalytic theory by a solid wall. Above Patsy's desk was a poster from Spain, which only she liked.

The phone rang. 'Yes, how may I help you?'

'Hi, it's Greg, from upstairs.'

Patsy caught her breath. 'Oh yes, yes.'

'I wonder if you've got time to print out the accounts I've just emailed to you?'

'Yes, of course, absolutely,' she said, aching to add 'my sweet darling.'

'You're an angel, Patsy, thank you so much. I'll be down shortly.'

'You're more than welcome, Greg.'

A little later, Patsy was on the phone to a customer, but she continued to dream aloud. 'He called me an angel—I wonder what he means by it?'

'What did you say?' said the customer.

'Nothing, I was talking to someone else. How may I help you?'

It could only mean one thing, Patsy thought: he likes me too! She was beside herself with anticipation. Despite her excitement, she managed to answer other telephone queries. Multitasking, she called it proudly.

❧

Meanwhile, the teacher was trying to help his sleepy students.

'There's a danger that the therapy gets stuck in an impasse; in other words, it continues without making any progress. The client resists insight in order to avoid change and its associated suffering, which is sometimes called the pain of living. And what is the pain of living? Anyone?'

Silence...

'Shakespeare's *Hamlet*: 'the slings and arrows of outrageous fortune'—do you agree?'

Silence...

'Yes, that's right,' he said, trying to be humorous but hating himself for being sarcastic. 'It means accepting the limitations of life—the truth, in other words. And, of course, suffering the minor depressions that accompany the realization that you have been wrong and your attitudes have hurt other people.'

❧

Patsy next door was absentmindedly pulling dead leaves from a potted plant on her desk, while speaking on the phone to another customer.

'He loves me, he loves me not,' she whispered as she listened. Momentarily she thought the unthinkable: *But what if he doesn't?* Impossible! She could not imagine another tragic end to her dreams. *I know what's right for both of us. Greg won't need to give it a thought.* She dropped a dead leaf into the waste bin.

❧

The teacher noticed that a number of students were now sitting a little lower in their seats, drifting off or daydreaming maybe, but certainly not concentrating. He decided to go to his case transcript immediately.

❧

On the other side of the wall the hoped for romantic connection was unfolding. Patsy could hear the elevator clanking and whirring as it carried someone down—or was it up? A false alarm maybe? No. It started to clank and whirr again. Yes, definitely coming down. She heard the lift doors open, and then came Greg's sweet voice. He was talking to someone. Perhaps a woman has his attention? Oh dear.

Patsy sighed in relief as a deeper male tone appeared to answer Greg. An office colleague no doubt. Thank goodness.

◦◦◦

In the classroom the seminar continued.

'I'll now read you an extract from a session in the ongoing therapy of a person suffering a borderline state of mind:

The client, we'll call him Josh, is eager to meet with the female therapist, let's give her the name Clare. Once in the room, his unconscious need to control her and avoid insight takes over. He feels compelled from within to avoid the pain of knowing the truth about himself.'

Mr Wiseman finished his introduction and, when he looked around for a spark of interest, he saw that Angela was nodding in agreement or approval again.

'Right, let's begin.'

◦◦◦

Patsy could hardly wait for the good-looking Greg to appear. She longed for his shining smile and the loving glances that would illuminate her drab office. She knew he wanted her really.

'Have courage, Greg,' she whispered to herself.

◦◦◦

In seminar room 5b Mr Wiseman was reading from the therapy extract:

'Clare had been seeing her client for only a short time, and in the last session he had raised the issue of a dream he'd had.

Clare believed she had understood its significance quite well in the context of his situation. As this latest session began, Josh commented on the colorful carpet in her room. An apparently neutral remark.'

Trudy was rummaging loudly in her bag. The teacher stopped talking. Trudy looked up and announced, 'I'm just looking for a pen and a notebook, if that's OK?' Then she continued to rummage, muttering, 'I don't know what's so wrong with typing. Other teachers let us do it.'

Mr Wiseman ignored her comment but couldn't help thinking how ironic the situation had become: he was talking about destruction, while she was being destructive. Or perhaps he was now being destructively critical himself. This was a trivial matter—was he being oversensitive? He continued:

Josh told his therapist there was a matter he wanted to take up from last week. Something in his tone made her feel anxious. She thought he sounded aggressive and wondered if he was criticizing her.

'Projection, in other words,' said Mr Wiseman. 'You remember that term, I'm sure. To cause another person to experience a feeling you don't want to feel yourself. That's what was happening to the therapist: Josh was trying to push bad feelings into her.'

Patsy just knew this meeting would be the one that would transform her empty single life. Greg was about to come into the room and declare his intentions. Like a movie, this would be a joining of two loving hearts.

Mr Wiseman continued with his case description:

"'You didn't think my dream was worth much, did you?" grumbled Josh. "You commented on it as if it was just another topic to discuss. In fact, it was the first dream I've told you about and I know that's important in therapy. Or haven't we read the same books?"

'Clare was now struggling to remember last week's session.

"'You said that the dream showed my problem with my mother and father and also with you."

'Clare asked herself if she had really interpreted the dream as transference. She couldn't remember the precise details of the meeting.'

Among Mr Wiseman's students, Saul gave a little snort and woke abruptly. Impatiently the teacher continued…

'The atmosphere in Clare's consulting room was becoming hostile. She was not sure what to say. In Josh's present state of mind, whatever she said would cause offence, she thought.

"'It's interesting that you don't have anything to say. I suppose you're struggling to remember," said Josh.

'Typical, thought the therapist, he's practically reading my thoughts. I'll have to say something that accepts the truth as he sees it.

"'It's clear that I said something that has offended you," she said, "however it's not clear what that is."'

The office door handle turned. Almost choking with anticipation, Patsy gripped Greg's papers. 'Courage, Greg,' she whispered again, 'just say it. However it comes out I will understand and you can leave everything in our new life to me. This is our day, the day we will declare our love.'

∽

Back in the seminar room, Mr Wiseman noted that most of his students seemed to be engaged with the case transcript. Trudy, however, was now asking to borrow a pen from another student in a loud whisper. He wondered if it was some sort of revenge for his comment about her typing. No, he decided, he was being paranoid, and he went back to his description.

'*After a short pause, Josh demanded to know just how much the session was costing. "And yet," he went on, raising his voice, "you don't even remember what you said last time! Let me remind you: you said that I would like to control you, just like I controlled my mother and father!*

'*The therapist was now worried that he might become violent. The fact that she didn't yet know him well made her nervous.*

'*"Well, I can assure you that I did not control them. I thought I've made it very clear to you that it was the other way round. And I don't have any wish to control you either! You are supposed to be helping me but I don't see how that's possible when you accuse me of being a control freak!"*'

∽

Greg entered Patsy's office but he was not alone. By his side was a stranger, a well-groomed young man like Greg. He was also beautiful, in a feminine kind of way, she noted dismissively and assumed he would soon leave. She guessed he was probably a student or a visitor.

⚭

'Clare knew that she had not used the term *control freak*, but the client's vehemence almost literally pressed her back into her seat. However, the irony of his denial that he wanted to be in control struck her forcibly, and she would have loved to have said exactly what she thought. But that would probably lead to a further violent reaction from him as he was bound to resist the insight. Now she was angry herself and feared she could not think of an appropriate thing to say. An inner placating voice suggested that she say sorry. But that wouldn't help, she decided, as she'd be accepting the role of his victim.

'"Don't bother to apologize," said Josh, apparently still reading her mind. I want you to explain yourself. But before you do that, ask yourself how you think I've felt having to carry that insult since the last meeting."'

Mr Wiseman continued: 'Notice this characteristic attack. The client has an advantage over the therapist by exploiting a detail from last week. He exaggerates his version of her comments and all the good in her work is overshadowed. This is his narcissistic defense against feeling sorrow for his behavior and his envy of her insight.'

He looked around the room for a response. Angela nodded, and a few smiles from others indicated some interest. Jonathan was now asleep, it appeared. Trudy was writing noisily with a scratchy pen. *She definitely wants to spoil my seminar*, he thought.

⚭

Next door, Greg said, 'May I introduce my partner, Peter, who is visiting today. He's fantastic with figures and has been a tremendous help with an accounts problem. Peter, this is Patsy. She keeps the whole place going. I don't know what we'd do without her.'

Peter smiled lovingly at Greg. Patsy thought she would vomit. Her senses reeled and a fog descended over her mind.

∽

In the classroom, Jonathan, apparently in REM sleep, made a little noise. The other students sniggered. Mr Wiseman felt the hard work he had put into his prepared example was slipping from their attention.

∽

In the office, Peter said, 'It's so nice to meet you at last, Patsy. I've heard from Greg how important you are to the company.'

Patsy gathered her wits as best she could, although shock had rendered her almost speechless. 'P-pleased to meet you too, I'm sure,' she spluttered. 'I never knew you existed.'

'We're going for some tea in a moment,' Greg said. 'Would you like to join us?'

She gave a false little laugh and said in a bitter whisper, 'No, Greg, I don't want any fucking tea. Why didn't you say something earlier? You knew how I felt about you and now you've cheated me out of a life.'

∽

Mr Wiseman said, 'Actually, the therapist's analysis, as understood by the client, was accurate and clearly unexpected. The client's response is to pin her down emotionally with hate-filled projections of his own helplessness when he hears something which is uncomfortably true.'

Trudy continued to write noisily and Mr Wiseman thought again about the irony of the situation.

'So the purpose of his way of speaking to the therapist is what?' he asked Jonathan, who was just waking up.

∽

The office was silent apart from a telephone that rang and rang. Everyone had stopped what they were doing, frozen in mid-movement. Patsy no longer heard anything in the office. There was only her, that shitty traitor Greg, and his revolting partner. It was indeed a moment from a movie.

Peter looked at Greg, who shrugged his shoulders. Patsy stood up very slowly, lifted her scarf off the nearby clothes hanger, and tied it around her neck. As she pulled on her coat, Greg and Peter took two paces back from her desk. *And so you should*, she thought bitterly.

∽

In the classroom, Jonathan answered the teacher as honestly as he could. 'I've no idea,' he said. 'It's a complete mystery to me.'

'Typical!' muttered Mr Wiseman.

Jonathan appeared not to hear him and continued, 'Why does anyone envy the person who can help them?'

'In this case,' said Mr Wiseman, looking hard at the student, 'in this case,' he repeated, 'the client is trying to get the therapist under his control. If he doesn't succeed, he believes she will say more things that will cause him to have feelings he doesn't want. In addition, despite the fact that he wants her help, he also feels her ability to help him is enviable, so he attacks it. His violent method of communication temporarily stops her thinking.'

'Ah-ha,' said Jonathan. 'So, he makes the therapist anxious, as you said last week. The result of violent projection is that the therapist, for the moment, cannot think.'

∞

Next door, as she slowly put on her hat, Patsy muttered softly, 'I don't feel well. I'm developing a headache, so I'm going home. Please tell the General Manager for me.'

Without looking at either of them, and with exaggerated movements that kept her body well away from them, Patsy left the filing and photocopying department of Dream Engine Inc.

∞

'That's right,' continued the teacher, pleasantly surprised. 'The borderline position is one in which no change is allowed by the client, unless it's what they want, of course. In this case, Josh takes a superior position. He looks down on Clare and mocks her, trying to destroy her insight.' He paused. 'According to the theory, it's a situation where deadliness triumphs over liveliness.

'Does anyone else have examples that can further illustrate this borderline position?'

To his surprise, Trudy said, 'If the client accepts that you have an insight into him, he has to accept you are different. When you show that you think differently, you demonstrate that you are separate and therefore enviable.' She fell silent and looked down at her notes. Mr Wiseman felt momentary shame that he had judged her so harshly.

'Absolutely. Can anyone give me another example of this kind of destructive behavior in which envy and narcissism interact to avoid a relationship?'

'The difficult party guest who is sullen and cynical,' said a now-awake Saul. 'The sort of person who can't eat anything you've prepared and lets you know that he doesn't enjoy dancing. But he won't leave, and instead hangs around making snide and envious comments about other people. He apparently envies their freedom to live in the moment.'

'Very good.'

Trudy added, 'What about the hooligan who idealizes violence and death and despises kindness?'

'Yes, that's a possibility,' said Mr Wiseman. He couldn't believe his unkind judgment of her. 'Any others?'

'The client who gives you a diary of the week, not allowing any space for dialogue or comment. So the contact between you lacks any spontaneity,' said Angela, smiling.

***

Patsy travelled home alone. On a crowded bus, she defended the empty seat next to her with a violent hate-filled glare that kept even the elderly and the pregnant standing.

***

From Jonathan again: 'The client who goes over and over a trauma like the end of a love affair. He will not accept any interpretations about his destructive ruminations. Instead, he focuses on you, the therapist. On how angry you sound, or how bored and tired you look.'

The teacher realized that it was he who had been denying his students' ability and interest. *There's a little bit of a borderline in all of us, including me*, he had to admit to himself.

'What do all these examples have in common?' he asked rhetorically. 'As you clearly understand, they share the deadening of life. And an attachment to being in that position.'

He looked around, wondering if there was anything more he should say.

'Please keep in the front of your minds that, however difficult it can be for the therapist, clients like Josh suffer enormously. They often live shallow and empty lives that keep them at war with the world. What you suffer for one hour, they suffer all day, every day. Not unusually, they have been traumatized early in their lives. This trauma can be repeated during therapy if the therapist is too free with interpretations about their destructive behavior. It's important not to be accusatory.'

Then, remembering his own extraneous thoughts during the session, he added, 'It's easy for us to judge and condemn a client's envious attitudes, even to unconsciously seek revenge. Our task as therapists is to find ways to meet them and their destructive defenses without fear.

'And now', he concluded, 'it's definitely time for coffee.'

The following day, Patsy was off work. No one in the firm could know how much she suffered; how much torment filled her empty life. But they would feel the effects of it. Patsy had to get rid of her pain in her own distorted way. When she went back to work, she was coolly polite to Greg but furious with co-workers over trivial problems. As a result of her bullying, two other people were soon off sick.

A few days later, Greg and Peter received a prettily decorated packet at their home address from an anonymous sender. When they opened it, they found a wondrous gift of dog shit.

Postscript

Excessive and unreasonable rage is characteristic of borderline patients, and we see this in Patsy by the end. Because the story above describes a seminar it explains itself, and gives a few pointers for thinking about the suffering of the borderline state of mind. It is not easy to maintain empathy for someone like Patsy who is violently selfish and hateful at the same time. And yet, as the seminar leader says, her suffering is immense.

Mr Wiseman's Reading List for the Seminar

Diagnostic and Statistical Manual of Mental Disorders (DSM-5). American Psychiatric Association
(It's in the Library reference section)
Hinshelwood, R. D. (1994). *Clinical Klein*, Free Association Books Chapter 14.
Kernberg, O. F. (1975). *Borderline Conditions and Pathological Narcissism*. New York: J. Aronson.

Rey, H. (1988). 'Schizoid Phenomena in the Borderline'. In Spillius, E. B. (Ed.). *Melanie Klein Today*, Vol. 1. London: Routledge.

Rosenfeld, H. A. (1987). *Impasse and Interpretation*. London: Routledge.

Spillius, E. B. et al. (2011). *The New Dictionary of Kleinian Thought*. London: Routledge.

Next come stories of violations via projections that are outrageous in several ways, but you will be the best judge of this, according to your sensibilities.

8

Violations

———◆———

A violation is an intentional or unconscious action that breaks an agreement or a principle and, in the cases below, causes harm by treating another person without respect. The violation is a projection of negative feeling onto the person who is violated. I include unconscious actions because we are all responsible for our unconscious, despite our wish to attribute some errors to accidental actions.

a. The Early Morning Delivery

The paperboy liked his job or, at least, he liked the income it gave him.

Early in the morning, before school, he would cycle around the village distributing newspapers. One of his deliveries was to the Convent of the Holy Virgin. Not all the paperboys liked this stop. On winter days it felt decidedly spooky, involving a long

240

ride up a poorly lit, tree-lined gravel drive, at the end of which sat an impressive Victorian gothic building, boasting fluted granite columns with swirls and gargoyles. It had originally been a manor house and contained an impressive billiard room, among other assets.

The paperboy was not supposed to go into the building—no laymen were allowed—and he had instructions to put the newspaper on a small table inside the front door. But he liked to take a furtive look around. The entrance hall smelled of cleaning materials and something else that reminded him of his auntie's house: feminine, sweet, enticing. The wallpaper looked exotic and expensive, and was left over from pre-convent days. A magnificent central staircase led upwards. From the ornate ceiling hung a life-size crucifix. The blooded, almost naked, figure of Christ dangled high above the marble floor.

The Sister Housekeeper picked up the newspaper at the same time each day. She took it to the Mother Superior for her breakfast read, after morning prayers, meditation, and holy mass. Other senior nuns were permitted to look at the paper later, but the contents were considered too worldly for the tender souls of the younger Sisters.

On this particular morning the early autumnal weather was fresh and crisp. The trees were beginning to take on their lovely seasonal colors: shades of brown, orange, and red.

As the paperboy approached the convent building a siren sounded behind him. An ambulance was racing up the drive. He pedaled harder... and ambulance and bike arrived simultaneously.

The paperboy was determined to do his job and, curious about the medical drama inside, he followed the first ambulance man up the steps. As they approached the grand entrance, they heard muffled cries of distress. The ambulance man pulled open the heavy front door and the paperboy squeezed himself into the building.

In the magnificent hall, the usually serene atmosphere was shattered by a scene fit for a Shakespearean tragedy. Under the life-size crucifix of the tortured Christ, the stocky frame of the Mother Superior was swinging a billiard cue, beating two kneeling, bleeding, and shrieking nuns.

'How could you use his Christian kindness against us, you wicked bitches?' she shouted. 'Are you sisters of the Devil?' She brought the billiard cue down on their heads again and again.

To the right of the Mother Superior and her victims kneeled a man in a black cassock. The paperboy recognized the curate from the local church, who served as confessor to the convent. He was bent double, holding a bloody mass in his arms, sobbing, 'My child, my child.'

Sitting on the floor, a robust nun supported the head and shoulders of a prone young woman, whose thighs were visible and bloody beneath her torn nun's habit. Beside her was the Sister Housekeeper, who collected the newspapers; her sleeves were rolled up and her hands were also bloody. Other nuns were spaced about the scene, clasping their faces, moaning, and sighing: a discordant chorus on the impromptu stage.

Mother Superior screamed at the two new entrants, 'We do not need another man in here.'

The paperboy froze, shocked by her violence. He looked at the ambulance man, who answered calmly, 'No, I think you do.'

What on earth was happening? We have to turn the clock back nine months to the Christmas Midnight Mass and accompanying celebrations; the story is brief and brutal.

Sister Immaculate was the most holy nun to have walked the cloisters. Despite her youth, Mother Superior said she was destined for heaven. However, she had a weakness, and everybody has those. She was contemptuous of anything worldly, warm, and sensual. A layman would have called her a prude. The idea of the sexual act that had created her was far from her consciousness.

But what about the unconscious? you may well ask, and so you should.

It would appear that Sister Immaculate had repressed her sexuality, but it was churning around inside her looking for a way out. The infirmary nuns, Sisters Indulga and Voluptua, had noticed a certain flirtatious excitement, mild but definite, when Sister Immaculate was in the presence of the father confessor.

No one knew what they did in the privacy of the confessional; confession is a divine sacrament, confidential and screened from prying eyes. However, her lengthy visits to the secret cupboard were noted. Other nuns waited outside on their knees, impatient for their minutes in the presence of the intoxicating manly aroma of the kindly Father Youngman.

Sister Immaculate clearly had his interest, they thought, and the heinous sin of envy afflicted the sisterhood. In the infirmary, Sisters Indulga and Voluptua soothed the physical and mental sores of restricted lives and heard many complaints about Sister Immaculate. They listened to fantasies of her not-so-immaculate activities with the curate.

Could these rumors be true? It would seem highly unlikely in the chapel's little wooden confessional box, where man and woman are separated by a wooden wall. But fantasy has an expansive capacity and many frustrated minds have devised ingenious and perverse copulations. The infirmary nuns were overwhelmed with other people's resentment about possible, probable, and most definitely unholy couplings.

Dear reader, you understand no doubt that the infirmary Sisters were receiving what we would call hateful projections. As we know, feelings also have an effect on the recipient's state of mind, unbalancing it in destructive ways. Consequently, the affected person may attempt to pass on their discomfort to yet another.

How could Sisters Indulga and Voluptua relieve themselves of this accumulated resentment? They conceived an awful plan, to be enacted on Christmas night, using their professional knowledge of human bodies, which was more extensive than that of others behind those hallowed walls. Sister Voratia, robust and worldly, who had actually known a man years ago and now worked in the convent kitchen, was enlisted to help them. Their plan was just a bit of naughty seasonal fun, they decided, and they pushed any thought of the possible consequences out of their minds.

After Christmas Midnight Mass the unholy trio took Sister Immaculate aside to ask a favor. They wondered if she could, on this special night, say prayers for a dying nun in the infirmary. They thought God would listen to her. (But He must have been out partying for His son's birthday that night because He didn't help anyone.)

As the holy Sister kneeled in the chapel, eyes closed in silent prayer, the conspirators chloroformed her and carried her away to the infirmary. Laying her on a bed, they discreetly pulled a drape around her to save the blushes of the dying nun—so considerate of them.

Sister Voluptua went to the chapel sacristy and asked the curate to come to the infirmary to give the dying nun the last rites. As he went through the infirmary door, the unholy trio chloroformed him too, and laid him next to Sister Immaculate.

What happened next was unspeakable, a violation of love. The dying nun left this world, and we too must close our eyes.

The curate was returned to the chapel sacristy where, slumped in a chair, and with altar wine dribbling from his mouth, it could be assumed he had been partying alone.

Sister Immaculate was carried back to her place in the chapel and left prone on a bench. She woke up embarrassed that she had slumbered before the Lord and hurriedly went to bed, alone.

In the following nine months she attended the infirmary several times. The nuns assured her that her weight gain was a seasonal adaptation, unnoticeable under her holy habit. But when Sister Immaculate was assaulted by labor pains, she thought she was dying. The robust Sister Voratia was nearby, and her empathy was awakened by her Sister's suffering. She remembered the rude fun of Christmas night and understood the grave consequences. But it was only once! (As many before her have exclaimed.) How could the girl be so fertile? There was no time for that question now. Stricken with guilt and sorrow, and fearful for her own soul, Voratia ran to Mother Superior. She confessed to her part in the Christmas prank and this day of deliverance.

Mother Superior was fascinated then revolted. She called the parish priest to hear several confessions.

Sister Immaculate collapsed in the middle of the entrance lobby. The Sister Housekeeper, with her uncanny skill of knowing everything before she was told about it, had already summoned the curate, called for an ambulance, and rolled up her sleeves.

The enraged Mother Superior indulged in the kind of foul language not heard since the convent was a manor house. She sent Voratia to the infirmary to collect the scheming pair of Indulga and Voluptua and seized a cue from the billiard room. The unfamiliar sounds of a baby being born brought a flock of anxious virgins into the lobby. Everything they were avoiding and yet longed for in life lay before them. Their response was sympathetic, with loud expressions of pain and bewilderment.

The curate was shocked, ashamed, and then delighted when the news of his paternity was passed to him by Voratia. This immaculate conception seemed to solve all his sex scruples at once.

The first ambulance man assisted the new mother, while his colleague picked up the baby and slapped its bottom. The curate's child began to sing along with the dissonant nunnery chorus.

Voratia attended to the head wounds of the infirmary nuns, while the Mother Superior tried to collect herself and prepare for her confession of attempted murder to the parish priest.

The new mother, baby, and father left the convent in the ambulance.

The paperboy had been ignored while he witnessed these events but the Sister Housekeeper smiled when he placed the newspaper in the usual place. She offered him a large bar of chocolate.

'Now, my child, what you've seen in this holy place cannot be talked about.'

'Yes, sister'

'Ever...'

'No, sister'

He gratefully accepted the chocolate and then cycled slowly back down the drive. He couldn't remember where the next paper should be delivered. The autumn leaves glowed brighter, but the coming winter wind felt keen.

He was lost for words—until now.

Postscript

This irreverent black comedy highlights the tragic lives of those who need to deny life in order to have a life, albeit of a limited and restricted nature. Historically, when the surrounding culture is repressive, the tension between human needs and the restrictions of the prevailing moral code proves too much for people who have opted for a pious life with God in order to avoid the inevitable conflicts between the spirit and the flesh.

An illusion of eternal life is extended to those who suffer the consequences of being good on earth and live out their lives in a holy but restricted world. However, the pressure of biology and the need for human contact and love often proves irresistible or, as Freud would say, what is repressed emerges elsewhere in uglier ways : 'Where questions of religion are concerned people are guilty of every possible kind of insincerity and intellectual misdemeanour.' (Freud, S. (1927), p. 32)

This story describes what can happen when frustration and envy take precedence over love. The nuns' Christmas prank was justified as 'just a bit of seasonal naughtiness' without attention being paid to its possible consequences. Or perhaps it was the only way to get back at Sister Immaculate and her envy-arousing behavior. By facilitating their Sister's pregnancy, the nuns perversely achieved what they unconsciously wanted themselves—a child. Their secret wishes had been frustrated by their desire to avoid the anxieties of childbearing and family life, and by committing themselves to celibacy in a convent. However, their mischief inadvertently gave a life to the curate and his lady.

What happened to the curate, Sister Immaculate, and their baby? Maybe something good came out of it. Maybe they were really in love, knowing it only unconsciously and not realizing it until that autumnal day of deliverance. So Father Youngman, his immaculate virgin lady, and their baby had the opportunity to begin a new life together. Amen

Reference

Freud, S. (1927). *The Future of an Illusion*. SE XXI. London: Hogarth Press and the Institute of Psycho-Analysis.

b. The Wayward Angel and Grandad in Another Kind of Christmas Carol

This story introduces the figure of the Wayward Angel, who will make a contribution again in the next book, *Audacities*. For your information, the Wayward Angel is so called because of her naughty behavior. She has been helping people on earth in ways that short-circuit God's desire that everything should take its course according to His divine rules. The Wayward Angel's punishment is to be available at the back gates of heaven, where unexpected arrivals such as accidental fatalities, suicides, murder victims, and so on, are brought. Her job is to assess the suitability of any new arrival for acceptance into heaven. If they don't have a good reason to be there they must be sent back down.

⁓

'What do you want?' said the Wayward Angel brusquely. Then, looking closely at the figure in front of the heavenly gates, she added, 'How can I help you? You are obviously old.'

'Sorry.'

'No, don't be sorry, you are never too old to come here.'

'You have a nice smile.'

'Thanks, it's my magnificent welcome-senior-citizen smile.'

'I don't want to come in just yet. I'd like to be back down there. It's Christmas.'

'Oh, yes, His birthday, thanks for reminding me. I forgot to get Him a present last year and I never heard the last of it until Easter. Then he said, 'Look at me up here on this cross, have you no sympathy?' I do help people in a kind of unorthodox way but I can't change the whole of Christian history on my own, now can I?'

'I hate to interrupt your frustrated diatribe on our Lord. You're actually being quite rude, if not blasphemous,' said the old man, 'but I'm leaving life on earth against my wishes.'

'Sorry, Grandad, I'm getting upset. It isn't easy to think of a gift for the man whose dad made everything, is it? Oh dear, there I go again.'

'I was saying, it's Christmas and I was wondering...'

The Wayward Angel looked down at the house the old man had risen from. It was pretty, idyllic almost, with snow on the roof and evergreens in the garden. A couple were in the kitchen wrapping Christmas presents, children were in their beds, and a dog was asleep in the hallway. There was a tray of sweets and milk for Father Christmas by the fireplace.

She also saw something else, a torn sachet inscribed with skull and crossbones in the waste bin.

'I can understand it's a bit of shock arriving here at Christmas. You have my sympathy. By the way, have you got any enemies down there? In the house.'

'No, not at all. What do you mean?'

'Nothing, get on with your question. You were wondering if you could stay down there for Christmas. "It was Grandad's last Christmas. Didn't he just love that present from the children." Then people can cry over your unused thermal socks.'

'Must you be so cynical? If you could adjust your tone I think I'd feel better about it all. Anyway, I've got plenty of socks, thank you. It isn't easy being in my position, halfway between one place and another. Not to mention the toilet business.'

'What toilet business? We don't have toilets up here you know.'

'I've got a poop bag connected to my large intestine. It hangs around my waist. My bottom doesn't work any more you see. The bag is distressingly smelly at times and the grandchildren won't come near me. I'd like to be clean for one Christmas and leave on a good note, so to speak.'

'I can see the bag is a problem. Since it's Christmas, for this one time only, so long as no one is looking, I can intervene and help you. I'll keep you there on earth for a bit longer, smelling sweet. But you will have to be discreet.'

'Yes, absolutely.'

Just then Jesus walked past, apparently deep in thought, no doubt wondering about his Christmas present list.

'Don't look! If He notices you now and then doesn't see you later there'll be a problem. You understand that if I help you you'll have to stress your way through the January sales because you'll get in everyone's way. Then you've got to worry yourself almost to death over the winter heating bill. Maybe in February or March you can come up with the other oldies, it's a popular time, and then you can go to the front gate. Pearls and gold, choirs of angels—much nicer.'

'Thank you so much.'

And the old man fell through a hole in the clouds whence he was pushed by an angelic hand.

The next morning, in the kitchen of the pretty house with snow on the roof, the wife said to the husband, 'Did you put that powder in Grandad's chocolate last night? I showed you how to do it. That should have finished him off without leaving any incriminating evidence in his blood. I mean, it should have given him the gentle help he needs to send him on his way to heaven.'

'Yes, I did.'

'Then I don't know what has happened. He's using the toilet at the moment, singing hymns and Christmas songs, and his bed is quite clean.

c. A Perfect Collision

A 'perfect storm' is a terrible situation in which bad (and often unpredictable) things happen simultaneously. In this case, the idea is used to describe a series of collisions. The expression originates in meteorology, where it means a weather catastrophe constructed from the concurrence of smaller events.

I took a walk to the supermarket this evening along a popular path used by cyclists and pedestrians. It is built on the bed of a disused railway track, long and straight, and a vehicle traveling along it can gain considerable speed. I wore reflectors on my coat to protect myself from being bumped into by joggers, or wiped out by enthusiastic people on bikes, mopeds, invalid carriages, skateboards, or roller skis.

I heard the whine of a moped approaching from behind. An older teenager was riding it, dressed in black, without a helmet but with earphones and waving both hands as if conducting an orchestra.

Didn't his parents care about him? Or had they bought him the moped to get him out of the house?

He passed me doing at least 45 kph, heading in the direction of a crossroads of four paths behind the supermarket delivery shed.

Subsequently I saw several people approaching each other along these paths: a cyclist with no lights and no helmet, using one hand to work his cellphone (sending an SMS perhaps); an angry-looking woman jogger in tight training clothes wearing earphones and humming as she sweated her way forward (I imagined her partner had walked out on her); and, last but not least, an electric three-wheeled disability vehicle, also with no lights. The driver of the electric vehicle looked young and healthy. I learned later that he had stolen the vehicle, throwing the unfortunate owner to the ground. His right hand had been damaged in the hijack and his left hand was on the right-hand accelerator—an awkward arrangement.

All three, together with the moped rider, were heading on separate paths for the crossroads ahead. I imagined them heading into 'a perfect storm'. In my mind I could see them all approaching their nemesis.

The crossroads was a dark, damp, sad place where windblown plastic bags were snared and tangled by unruly bushes. The paths dipped down to the crossing point, giving each traveler extra momentum. In the last ten meters, as their fateful journeys reached their climax, they saw each other, but none of them could stop. Even if two of them had managed to change course, two more people were arriving fast.

First to reach the crossing was the jogging lady who, on seeing the disability wagon, leapt to her left. Too late, she saw the cyclist looking down at an unanswered SMS. After a glancing collision with the jogger he remained on his bike but swayed to his left, into the arms of the teenage conductor on the moped, who was leaning to his right to avoid the disability wagon.

The bike knocked the thief off the wagon.

The conductor dislodged the SMS-ing cyclist.

The cyclist landed at the feet of the jogging lady.

With the momentum left in his speeding moped, the teenager continued onward, hit the disabled person's electric vehicle, and sped away, still conducting his imaginary orchestra. His moped careered towards the plastic bags in the bushes and an uncertain future as a plaything for vandals and alcoholics.

The jogger stopped to swear at the cyclist, who responded, 'I love your foul language, and your bravery in the face of three vehicles ridden by men. Can I buy you a beer?'

'All right, I think I've earned it. I'm furious with a boyfriend who I need to replace. You've given me reason to hope. But I need a shower first.'

'Come to my place. I've got a shower big enough for two.'

'OK. We can save water that way. Also, I love the idea of mutual lathering. You can be my first new boyfriend. I've decided I need two to avoid being disappointed when one of them leaves me.'

The disabled vehicle thief ran away from the scene of the crash because he thought he might get busted, and he was when he went to the hospital to get his right hand fixed.

He couldn't explain the injury or the cyclist's cellphone, which had landed in his top pocket.

Postscript

All this is true: I saw these people on my walk and felt provoked by their selfish and dangerous behavior. Sadly, they didn't collide but if they had crashed what could the consequence have been? This could have been a life-changing event for them all.

The man who stole the handicapped vehicle could have been rehabilitated and gone on to work for a charity.

The jogging lady and the cyclist could have made several children.

The conductor might possibly have had a career as a moped salesman.

However, life has no meaning without conflict, as we know. In the world of psychoanalytic psychotherapy, each therapist's preoccupation with their theory is based on their identification with the theorist's way of thinking and feeling. This can lead to collisions with other therapists and their states of mind, which may be creative or destructive (let's hope for the former). This may lead to new developments and destructive arguments (let's hope it continues to be the former).

Peter Gay, in his book on Freud, describes the personal nature of some discussions in the 1920s: 'Ernest Jones resented Otto Rank, while Ferenczi thought Jones an anti-semite. Freud was exasperated that Abraham was lending himself to the making of a film about psychoanalysis. Brill, enthroned in New York, tried everyone's patience by not answering letters.' (Gay, P. (1988), p.

466) In addition, during the 'controversial discussions' in London referred to earlier, Melitta Schmideberg openly attacked her mother, Melanie Klein, and some of Klein's followers attacked Anna Freud. As the quote illustrates, there are problems in the best of families, and there were a number of people in psycho-analysis traveling in their own way, disregarding others, who collided with each other from time to time.

Reference

Gay P. (1988). *Freud: A Life for Our Time.* London: JM Dent and Sons.

d. Ronny the Robber

Ronny was at work early, finishing off a job. The weather was dull and damp, and he wanted to be shot of this project as soon as possible. During a recent stint in prison for robbery he had learned a new trade, how to lay paving stones. Now 'going straight' with his own business, he enjoyed the challenge of using his new skills. This morning he was working on a piece of sidewalk outside a bank, by the cash-dispensing machine.

He laid stone after stone. He looked up for a moment to survey his nearly completed handiwork. One of the stones near the cash machine was three millimeters higher than the others. He was distracted and irritated by his error. While he looked at the minor irregularity, he banged in the next stone, which lay diagonally two meters away from the one he was observing.

He didn't want to do anything about the mislaid stone now. He had another job to get to. He was not fully conscious of envious thoughts in his mind: *Rich people are going to use this machine in the future. So does it really matter about that stone? Will someone trip on three millimeters? Probably not, the stone will soon wear in and, if someone falls over, do I care? Not really.*

He banged the last stone harder than usual. He noticed that one corner was smooth and sloped outwards; another detail that made not a bit of difference, he thought. *Why am I worrying now? I'm finished here.* He brushed over the stones with sand and thought about the money he'd earned. He was satisfied. Ronny loaded his van, with a last look at the new sidewalk. In places it gleamed in the light rain. It was a professional job, well done. As he closed the door, he saw a man dressed in a formal business suit and carrying a briefcase heading towards the cash machine.

I bet he had an expensive meal at a smart restaurant last night, thought Ronny. He leaned on the side of his van and observed the man, his envious thoughts continuing, *He ate fresh lobster and drank a fine Chablis, I shouldn't wonder. More than one working man has a bit less in his pay packet this month to pay that bill.* He shook his head in disgust, as if his fantasy of the man was true. *Anyway, me and the lads had a good evening in the pub: fish and chips and a few pints.*

The businessman had reached the bank. He looked at the cash machine on his right and turned his body slightly towards it. He reached into his inside coat pocket with his left hand. As he withdrew his wallet, his body was slightly off balance. The heel of his right shoe slid on Ronny's slightly sloping stone corner. The weight of his expensively upholstered body and the energy of his forward movement slid his foot from under him. His head and shoulders shot backwards. The rest of his musculature could not compensate.

The businessman's body weight made him fall backwards. He tried to put his right hand down to break his fall, but his briefcase interrupted the movement. In his left hand he clutched his monogramed leather wallet. Ronny watched aghast as the man fell backwards and his head connected with the side of the paving stone that was three millimeters proud of the others. Blood spilled onto the newly laid sidewalk.

Poor bloke, what a way to start the day.

Ronnie ran forward to help, feeling guilty.

Postscript

There is not so much conscious violation in this vignette, but Ronny was aware of the small errors he had made and their possible significance in the coming years for some unfortunate person. This experience of envy can be, and often is, unconscious. Envy is characterized by the feeling that someone else has something desirable, and we feel the desire to spoil or destroy it. (E. Spillius et al, (2011) p 166) In Ronny's unconscious his envy allowed him to block his concern for a possible accident by pushing it far into the future. So, he left his small errors unrectified. We could say that the 'violation' was hidden in his unconscious, where he secretly hoped for harm to be visited on another person better off than himself, which might rob them 'accidentally' of their fitness or, in the worst case, even their life. 'If we attribute significance to an external accidental happening, we project to the outside our knowledge that our inner accident is invariably intentional (unconsciously). (Freud, (1900) p.424) If we are to accept the idea that there is no such thing as an accident, we have to assume acute skills in humans which are sometimes unconsciously deliberate. As when a skillful person makes a mistake in their work or an otherwise alert person makes an error of judgment that leads to a fall. Why did they do that? What if their unconscious interrupted their usually adept management of themselves? Did they unconsciously see what was going to happen and allow it to? Did they calculate exactly what should happen and inflict the loss, pain, and injury on themselves? Those are questions I would ask. Or am I going too far?

Reference:

Masson, J.M. (1985). The Complete Letters of Sigmund Freud to Wilhelm Fliess, 1887-1904, v-492. Cambridge, MA, and London, England: The Belknap Press of Harvard University Press.
Spillius, E. et al, 2011, *The New Dictionary of Kleinian Thought*, Routledge

In the next story lies another kind of provocation: one party has to tolerate an anxiety that another is not prepared to accept. The story represents a client's mixed feelings about the importance of not determining the length of a therapy at the beginning. It takes the time it takes...

9

Can You Fix It? (A Metaphor for the Length of a Therapy)

––––––◆––––––

I had a client who wanted to know why his analysis should take an indeterminate time. The discussion continued over a period of time until he came to a session with an account of his car troubles. I have revised it to make it into the following story.

∽∾

The smell of warm oil, do you know it? When you visit your local garage and walk into the mechanic's holy of holies, a large draughty shed whose oil-splattered walls seem to display the work of a demented graffiti artist. Pin-ups on out-of-date calendars and bits of old cars confirm that this is a place of mysterious activity. You hope that something good might happen to your faulty car, and yet you have the certain knowledge that it won't, not today anyway.

I stepped into the shadow of the half-open corrugated door and peered into the gloom.

A pair of legs extended from under an old Jaguar. The socks didn't match, and one trouser leg had ridden up to show a dark hairy leg above the sock. The legs belonged to a middle-aged man known as Greasy Harry who, at that moment, hollered 'Bloody fucking shit' and slid out from under the car, where he was lying flat on a trolley with small wheels. His face was covered with at least a pint of black engine oil. His younger colleague, Jimmy, rushed forward with a roll of kitchen paper covered in oily fingerprints. Jimmy was a wry, energetic man with a permanently surprised look on his face. His overalls were covered with grease, mostly around the thighs, where he wiped his oily hands. Some oil had even found its way onto his unshaven face.

'Is this a bad moment, Jimmy?' I asked.

'I don't know. Why are you here?'

'Can you fix it?'

'Fix what, mate?'

'The car I left here a week ago.'

'Really? Hmm…' He looked around the workshop and out into the yard, then he turned back to the nearest vehicle.

'Look at this,' he said, leaning in under the bonnet of an old black car. 'This is a 1955 P4 Rover 90 Sedan. Beautiful. I can climb into the engine space to work on it. What have you got?'

'It's a Honda Jazz.'

'Japanese, and a lot of trouble they were in the last war. We don't talk about that but the cars are no better, are they, Harry?'

Harry was sitting on the dirty concrete floor, silently unrolling kitchen paper.

'That's a bit harsh. It takes two in any fight.'

'Don't get philosophical with me, mate. It was all those people over there what started it.'

260

'Look, the history and politics of South-East Asia are not really my concern at the moment.'

'Not exactly South-East Asia. It's Japan, ain't it?'

'All right. Anyway, I've a wedding to get to and it's out in the country so...'

'Don't get me started on rural bus services, shocking disgrace. We don't support the cuts, do we, Harry?'

Harry said nothing. He was leaning against the Jaguar, wiping his face with crumpled paper towels. I looked at Jimmy.

'He never talks if the answer is negative.'

'What about my car?'

'I remember now. I've looked at it.'

'I should think so too. You've had it a week, as I've said.'

'Don't be snarky. It needs a new part, a B3897, and I don't think we've got one at home.' He turned towards Harry.

Unwisely I muttered, 'That's not all that isn't at home.'

'Now listen here, mate, I understand you're annoyed. But no need to be rude just because I don't have a posh job like you.'

'I'm sorry, you're right, that was uncalled for. But you understand my frustration? Anyway, my job's not posh, I'm a...'

'Never mind. Apology accepted. As I was saying, the part— Harry, do we have any B3897s in the shop?'

Silence. Oil trickled down Harry's neck.

'No, we don't. It will have to be ordered.'

'How do you know you don't have any? He didn't answer.'

'Yes, he did.'

'No.'

'All right, I'll ask again. Harry, do we have any B3897s in the shop?'

'I've fucking told you all-fucking-bloody-ready,' Harry said, 'we don't have no bloody-fucking B3897s in the shop.'

'Satisfied?'

'I didn't hear him before.'

'I can read him, it's an art. Believe me, he answered the first time. Look, I'm telling you, mate, parts from Japan? Three weeks minimum.'

'I understand. Have you ordered it? So I've only got two weeks to wait?'

'We've only just discovered the problem and, in addition, it depends if the part has a blue bit or a red bit on the end.' Turning to Harry, he said, 'It was a blue bit, wasn't it, Harry?'

Silence.

'It was a red then. I'll write it down. We made an order once and forgot to specify. We had a right old ding-dong. Long-distance phone call, which we had to pay for, mind you. And trying to understand each other wasn't easy.'

'I'm sure it wasn't, but you've had the car a week.'

'Don't blame me, mate, you have a word with them. Anyway, we have to write a note so it takes the time it takes.'

'What? You're joking!'

'No, mate, it's the truth. It takes the time it takes. We're not joking are we, Harry?'

Postscript

This story features unconscious provocation by the mechanic with his nonchalant attitude, but the basic message is that most things that are worthwhile take time to develop. 'To shorten analytic treatment is a justifiable wish… unfortunately, it is opposed by a very important factor… the slowness with which deep-going changes in the mind are accomplished—in the last resort no doubt, the 'timelessness' of our unconscious processes.' (Freud, S. (1913), p. 130)

We can all remember circumstances when we were frustrated by the slowness of a process but had to tolerate it. In addition, we can identify with the customer who is suffering the experience of being in the hands of a professional who has expert knowledge they are not sharing.

Reference

Freud, S. (1913). *On Beginning the Treatment*. SE XII. London: Hogarth Press and The Institute of Psycho-Analysis.

This little book now finishes with a story from childhood. A story of making the best of the situation you find yourself in and finding the inspiration to rebuild a life from an unlikely source…

Epilogue
Revelation

———◆———

I was ten years old, a reluctant pupil in a school run by religious people. They were devoted to their God and what they believed He said, but the teaching was excruciatingly boring. Who was I to them? Another child reluctant to be disciplined and cowed by religious fervor. I thought it was pointless to listen. I was caned for talking during lessons and moved to sit with the girls, in the hope that I could be shamed into silence. I learned to chat to them as well and was caned again.

I didn't know the meaning of the word suicidal, but I knew school life was driving me crazy. The corridors smelled of cleaning fluid and yesterday's vegetables. The toilets were dark and stank of urine. Why didn't the caretaker use a hosepipe in there every evening? Perhaps he did. The playground was a whirl of activity I couldn't understand, and I hated it all. I felt like an inmate in an educational asylum. I dreamed during lessons and I resented the teachers' efforts to pull me out of my fantasy world. I waited for life to return after school.

On London's perimeter were a number of hospitals for the mentally ill built by generous Victorians, who believed in fresh air for the patients. They were situated in the surrounding countryside, often with a farm attached. By the time I was a child, the city had almost grown out as far as the hospitals.

We lived in a village on the edge of the city. It had been expanded by post-war housing projects and the local mental hospital was adjacent to the community. Every day, ambulatory patients wandered the high street. Like an ancient order of monks walking in their private cloister, they patrolled the paths with downcast eyes. They were refugees from ordinary life: in our world, but not of our world. I watched them, fascinated by their deliberate movements and apparent lack of interest in everyone else.

One day I followed a man the length of the high street; he was picking up discarded cigarette ends. I wanted to see what he did with them. His hair was long for those days and stuck out in all directions, his forehead a mass of frown lines. He seemed elderly but, looking back, perhaps he was no more than forty, maybe even younger. He wore a dirty military greatcoat and walked with a stoop, one foot on the sidewalk, the other in the road. When he looked in my direction, he seemed to look right through me.

At the side of the road, smokers would drop their cigarette ends in the gutter. He stopped from time to time to pick one up. Then, after removing the lid from a rectangular tobacco tin, he'd drop in the dog-end and close the lid. He held the tin close to his body—a habit, I imagined, intended to protect his treasure from the other anxious men of his hospital ward.

When, after a time, he rested on a wooden bench, I sat at the other end. He glanced at me, aware perhaps that I was no threat, and then opened his tin and inspected the contents. One by one he carefully opened each stub of a discarded cigarette, tore away the scorched paper, and dropped it on the ground, where the pieces formed a little heap. He rubbed the tobacco between thumb and fingers to separate the strands. The tin was soon half full of dark brown tobacco, which must have been heavy with nicotine, having served as a filter for the smoked cigarettes.

Every movement was slow and deliberate, as if he was savoring a pleasurable experience, like eating an ice-cream. From his coat pocket he took a flat red packet and removed a thin cigarette paper, then carefully returned the packet to its place. He dropped a line of tobacco onto the virgin white sheet and, with a deft movement of his fingers, rolled the paper around the tobacco strands. Then he licked the glued edge slowly, from side to side. He seemed to take pleasure in every part of this remaking.

Now was the moment he had worked for. He placed the new cigarette between his lips, took out a box of Swan Vesta matches, and struck the red tip of a match on the bench. Cupping the flame with his grubby hands, he raised it towards his creation. The end of the paper flared and the tobacco lit up. Extinguishing the match between thumb and forefinger, he returned it to the box. Then he closed his eyes, leaned back on the bench, and drew the smoke deep into his lungs. Perhaps appreciating a memory of the days before the urine-and-cabbage stink of the corridors of his current home, he puffed for a moment of sanity.

He looked at me again, and this time he smiled. For a moment, we lived in the same world. I understood without words that I had to make something of the scraps of knowledge I could pick up in school if I wanted to live.

Postscript

This vignette of life in a village in the 1960s is based on a memory. I have used it at the end of this book to introduce hope. We do not have to be crushed by other people's provocations. The patient in the story was unknown to me. Maybe he had been suicidal and was finding his way back to life. There is an obvious link in the story to the idea of making the best of whatever life has to offer. I suppose as a child at that time I thought something better should be available as a package: a new school, with better people, good food, clean rooms—an ideal place. The anonymous patient was reminding me of a brutal reality: I had to give up being provoked by my environment, find what was good, and make it my own.

Reference

Gibson, C. (2021). *Revelation*. Short story in Schmidt-Hellerau, C. (Ed.), *The Analyst as Storyteller*. New York: International Psychoanalytic Books.

Book Three

Audacities

Death, where is your victory? Death, where is your sting?
1 Corinthians 15:55

Introduction

———◆———

'So shalt thou feed on Death, that feeds on men,
And Death once dead, there's no more dying then.'
William Shakespeare (*Sonnet CXLVI*)

A suicidal person hopes that the above quotation is true and that death will kindly relieve them of pain. But their pain is not lost: it is passed onto others, who experience the loss of a life many times over. The suicidal action lives on as a disturbing memory, and sometimes as unmodified rage.

How did this book of stories about suicidal behavior come about? Some of them are written in a light-hearted way: why is that? I will come to that below but, first, what is meant by audacity?

Audacity is a bold and arrogant disregard of normal restraints, it is associated with courage or confidence, and with what other people find shocking, presumptuous, insolent, or shameless.

In this collection of stories about audacious acts—the audacity of suicide—that affect many lives I try to show how cruelty, unkindness, and envy creep into all aspects of life. Nothing is sacred to the suicide: love and creativity do not always have a chance to

271

modify destructiveness. After a suicide nothing is resolved, nothing is settled, no remembering can become mere memory.

My experience is that we humans are capable of unlimited love and of its opposite: hate and cruelty. We control ourselves through what we call civilization, which can break down under stress. One of those stresses is murder. Once a suicide has occurred, civilization seems to leave the field: repetitions occur; people around the suicidal victim lose their balance and are capable of great injustice. This is particularly so if they hide the truth and allow others to suffer the unconscious knowledge they carry of the self-murder of a relative, friend, or therapist.

With these stories I try to illustrate how we humans are ruled by envy as much as love. Although we try to keep love dominant over our envy, life does not always work out as we wish. Or maybe it does work out according to some of our darker unconscious wishes. When we are motivated by hatred, nothing is sacred. There is no limit to the cruelty we can inflict on each other and on ourselves.

'It is (this) sadism alone that solves the riddle of the tendency to suicide which makes melancholia so interesting—and so dangerous.' (Freud, S. (1917), p. 252)

If we accept that our ability to destroy is ubiquitous, we have a chance to feel sad about who we are and to try to avoid repeating ourselves. I am writing this partly from the experience of a friend and colleague who, in her better moments, would have laughed heartily at these stories but was unable to find her way out of her last depression. For her, mental health was an objective too far removed. The book also addresses her situation and the culture of silence that surrounds suicide. I think this arises because the self-idealization that accompanies the status of therapist and analyst is felt to be damaged by the tragic mental disturbance of a member of a professional organization. However, we all need to accept our responsibility for each other's well-being. Perhaps the suicide victim's chosen end indicates that their plight was unnoticed, by colleagues and friends.

I'm inviting you to read with an open mind and to see where your feelings and thoughts take you. These stories can be viewed like abstract paintings that provoke feelings by reminding us of experiences in our unconscious. Like when you watch a film, or listen to a piece of music, or look at a piece of art, allow yourself to register your reactions and thoughts. The stories are not always a comfortable read because they remind us that, however our lives have developed, we are responsible.

Reflections on the audacity of suicide require an audacious approach; in other words, laughter. There is a defiance in using comedy in the face of fear and tragedy. So many feelings arise at the same moment when one is informed of the suicide of someone close, and the experience of something irresolvable dominates, but life goes on and, in the end, that person's choice was their responsibility. The experience of everything happening at once is a part of reading a story about suicide that contains humor. Laughter creates a space for hope.

In some cultures, and possibly also in our own personal culture, there is a taboo concerning jokes about suicide. Freud, in his book *Jokes and their Relation to the Unconscious* (Freud, S. (1905)), says that, in humor, the conscious allows the expression of thoughts that society usually suppresses or forbids. The superego allows the ego to be humorous in relation to a sensitive subject. Freud goes on to say that our enjoyment of the joke indicates that we understand the truth of a message that is otherwise repressed, and that our sense of humor allows us to overcome our inhibitions. Humor allows us to express our outrage and fury at someone who has tried to murder or has murdered someone we love and care about, someone who is important because they are our parents, family member, friend, or even therapist. It is the murder of a friend or loved one by another friend or loved one who lived in the same body. On the one hand, the suicidal person is a victim; on the other, they are overwhelmed by a part of themselves that was sadistic enough to commit a murder.

Humor gives an outlet for feelings that may block our thinking. The point of the humorous stories in this collection is to give the freedom to express negative feelings when convention invites us to live in a passive sorrow; humor opens a door through the rage that binds us and inhibits.

When coming to grips with your feelings about what you read don't forget the inner quality described by John Keats (1795–1821) (Bion, W. B. (1984), p. 125), which is so useful in most situations, that is, *negative capability*; this is when a person is capable of experiencing uncertainties, mysteries or doubts without restlessly chasing an answer. We need humility in the face of unknown forces in others and ourselves otherwise, as we get older and more experienced, we reach a point where, if we are not careful, we think we know the truth. I hope these stories are a reminder that we are never free of our unconscious, that we are all ruled as much from within ourselves as without by an unconscious that is only partly knowable and is always one step ahead.

References

Jones, A. (Ed.) (1974). *The Jerusalem Bible*. London: Darton, Longman and Todd.

Clark, W. G., and Wright, W. A., (Eds) *The Complete Works of William Shakespeare*. Garden City, NY: Nelson Doubleday Inc.

Freud, S. (1917). *Mourning and Melancholia*. SE XIV. London: Hogarth Press and The Institute of Psycho-Analysis.

Freud S. (1905). *Jokes and their Relation to the Unconscious*, SE VIII. London: Hogarth Press and The Institute of Psycho-Analysis.

Bion, W. B. (1984). *Attention and Interpretation*. London: Karnac Books.

1

The Interpreter

———◆———

In my fantasy, the building in front of me was a crumbling, forbidding castle. Cold water dripped from its high walls. A feeling of doom possessed me. I crossed a broken wooden bridge. A creaking door was opened by a hunchbacked guard.

The remand center, an imposing building built in red brick, probably in the Fifties, was surrounded by two rows of high fence. It had been repainted in pastel colors; sugar coated in innocence.

At the main door I was greeted by a smiling uniformed young woman who led me through the building. One heavy door after another answered to her swipe card. She showed me into a plain, gray interview room. 'I'll collect Josef for you. Wait here please.' She disappeared into the maze of corridors.

The new prisoner appeared younger than his thirty-five years. He was tall and slim, dressed in a blue tracksuit. He held his gaze on the corner of the room.

'Hello Josef, my name is George. I'm a psychotherapist, and I consult for the prison service. The director called me; she says you expressed a wish to talk to an independent professional. Is that so?'

'Yes, I did, and I know what a therapist is,' he said bitterly. He bent forward, his forehead almost touching his knees, and began to sob quietly. 'I've done a terrible thing. I can't be forgiven and, worst of all, I've lost the love of my life.'

'Why don't you start at the beginning and tell me why you're here?'

Josef moved restlessly, then started to speak softly. 'I was born in a country far from here. My parents had strict traditional values. There was little affection in the home. I longed to have their arms around me, but it rarely happened. At night I lay alone in my bed, looking at the blank screen of a TV. My parents had put it on the wall adjoining their bedroom. Despite their religion, which could have denied me such a luxury, I think they wanted to distract me from something else. Sometimes in the middle of the night I awoke to noises that sounded violent, and exciting. My mother seemed to be in pain. Then, as if by magic, two messages appeared on the TV screen in large, bright letters: 'They are making babies in there' and 'They are partying next door and you're not included.'

'I felt it was ugly, and I was powerless to stop it. That was my trauma. That's the right answer, isn't it? That's what you're looking for, isn't it?'

I began to think he was delusional. The messages on the TV screen sounded like a version of hearing voices. He was seeing voices.

He continued to cry.

'When you're ready, tell me about "the terrible thing".'

Josef sat up straight and took a breath. 'As I grew up, I enjoyed learning from books, especially languages. I studied rigorously. I wanted to speak another language, two if possible. I was sure they were my ticket out of my cold home. I left the TV alone, and I didn't follow the news. I didn't understand why the schoolteachers and children were anxious, but soon I understood that my country was engulfed in a civil war.

'One day, men dressed like soldiers came to the house, and took my father. I never saw him again. I don't feel any regret, but they beat my mother, and I heard those sounds again, like the ones from the bedroom.' He stifled a sob. 'Mother said, "Save yourself, get out." I hid in the garbage, where I belong now. I travelled for months through many countries, until eventually I landed here. Your language is so complex, so different; it's beautiful. I studied until I could have the job I'd always wished for. I'm a professional interpreter, you know.' He straightened his body and lifted his chin. He looked at me for the first time.

'While I studied, I took a part-time job in a slaughterhouse cutting up dead animals. It was horrible, but it paid my bills. I've misused those skills.'

He returned to his account, as if escaping from an uncomfortable thought. 'In my work I've met many interesting people, some I would have liked to have as friends, but some I could have hit on the head with a frying pan. My father did that to me. I have a bump here, see.'

He lowered his head and, through his cropped hair, I could see a long scar. For the first time, he smiled a little.

'I was asked to do a special job two months ago. It turned out to be interesting, exciting, and infuriating. It was the beginning of the end of my life.'

He paused for breath, restraining his tears. I felt I was with a brave and determined man who had a weakness he could not understand.

'I was called to interpret in a psychotherapy clinic. I'd never done that before. The therapist was a young woman, Charlotte. She too seemed nervous. I felt unprepared for what I would hear, and I was. Charlotte explained that the coming interview was confidential. She told me to say exactly what she said, and to convey as exactly as I could the meaning of the other person's reply. That's what I do all day; I don't know why she needed to say that. I suppose it was her routine comment to any interpreter. Perhaps she was worried about the client, and the effect he could have on both of us.

'She said, "There are many powerful feelings in a situation like this. You will need to be strong and hold to the truth. You have to put your feelings aside and convey only the message." Afterwards, I understood what she meant.

'The therapy room had no windows. The colors were plain, and there was a dull landscape painting with too much green in it. The room was like a prison cell. My future was in front of me, but I didn't know it. The therapist was young, fair, and sweet. She looked as if she tasted nice. I felt I shouldn't have those thoughts, or look at her like that.

'The man who came into the room called himself Bobby, but he obviously came from my country. Maybe he had taken the name to try to soften other people's experience of his personality. He was short and thickset; he didn't seem to be familiar with being nice. He forced a smile through much of the interview. I didn't like him; he was overconfident, with an undertone of aggression in his manner. When I looked at his eyes, I could see that he was eating up Charlotte. Had he no shame? I felt protective and competitive. I changed his attitude after a while!'

Josef looked at me with satisfaction.

'The therapist remained calm, but I thought I could see fear in her eyes. I was determined to help her. Once we were sitting, and the introductions had been made, Charlotte said to the new man, "This is an assessment interview, requested by the social services. You understand that I will be writing a report for them. You will be able to read it too." He nodded.

'"You have been accused of being unkind, and at times violent, to your wife and daughters."

'Bobby smiled, and said the accusations were untrue. He didn't understand why anyone would say that. He loved his wife and family. His home was well known in his neighborhood for its caring, family atmosphere.

'"However, several people have given witness statements about your behavior. It will help me to understand if you tell me your story," said Charlotte.

'Bobby smiled again and continued his denials. I felt annoyed by his insulting demeanor. I spoke to him roughly in our language. "You know the truth... the lady is being nice to you... stop avoiding her questions... and you can stop your lustful scrutiny of her body."

'Charlotte hadn't asked me to say that. It was wrong of me, but I couldn't help myself. I realized my central position: I was the only person in the room who knew what the other two were saying. It was intoxicating to have control. I wasn't excluded any more from the activities in the bedroom. I thought this was my chance to really do some good. I could save her and put him in his place. Metaphorically, I could hit him with a frying pan. I gave into my wishes and used my power mercilessly. Finally, the smile left his face.

'At first I only added one sentence to her question. Gradually, I became bolder, and soon I was adding a paragraph. She looked at me quizzically, but she was polite; she didn't challenge me in front of Bobby.

'Later, she asked if I was saying other things because he didn't react as she expected. I lied: "Not unusually, one sentence in your language takes several in mine."

'He admitted that he had hit his wife and daughters. Charlotte reported that she was satisfied with my work. I didn't say anything. I was the winner. I'd got the truth out of him. I'd saved Charlotte and his family from him.

'I didn't hear what happened to the rest of that assessment but, two days ago, something unfortunate happened. I was in the same clinic for another job. When I was leaving, the administrator called me back. She asked me if I could work late and stand in for a female interpreter who could not attend. The lady to be interviewed came from my country. We have taboos about meetings between men and women who are not of the same family. She said it was a sensitive case. I said, "Of course I can stay." I'm single you see, so my evenings are empty.

'The therapist, Julia, was an older woman. She appeared calm and experienced. She was not troubled by me being a man. The interviewee, Amira, seemed surprised and shy. When I came in, she avoided eye contact with me. She nodded her acceptance of me as interpreter, but maybe it was her habit to say yes to the authorities.

'Julia's questions were clear, and she kept an eye on me. Perhaps she had heard from her younger colleague that I appeared to say more than was necessary. Amira talked about her life: her childhood family, her schoolfriends, how she came to be married by arrangement. I found myself fascinated. I tried not to be emotionally involved, but my heart swelled, I felt sure they could hear every beat. I thought it would burst out of my chest. I breathed slowly, drank some water. Julia asked me if I was all right.

'I said, "Of course." What else should I say? "I am wildly in love with your client?"' He laughed ironically. I hoped it was a good sign. Perhaps he could laugh at himself.

'Then Amira talked in detail about the daily domestic abuse she and her daughters were subjected to; both verbal and physical violence. It became clear to me that I was meeting the wife of the man I had helped to interview a few months earlier. I wasn't sure if this was professionally correct. I mean from the confidentiality point of view. I should have said something, but my feelings were too strong. I could think of nothing else than to be in her presence for every second possible. I thought I had finally found the love missing from my parents' home. That place had been violent to me in another way, without love, or affection.

'We came to questions I dreaded, but wanted. "How was their private life?" I could hardly get the words out. Julia said that Amira didn't have to answer, but that it would help if she could. With some reluctance, she answered. I wanted to know, and I didn't want to hear anything. I wanted to shout, "Stop."

'In our language, her account was so intimate. In my mind we were alone in the room, only her face and mine. The images of his violence and stupidity burned and tore my soul. I could hardly control my feelings.

'As she finished her description she said in a whisper, "I've asked my friends, and the experience I've had during some of these events they call an orgasm. My body felt it, but I was not there. I feel ashamed. I never want to see him again."

'I thought she had said that last part because she wanted to let me know that she understood sexuality. Then she said, "My heart is locked in a box, and the key is nowhere to be found. I put it away the day I was forced to marry him, and I do not know where I left it."

'Her tears dripped onto the soft, pale-green fabric of her long dress. She made no effort to stop them. She was humiliated beyond words, and I was a part of it. But I was sure I knew where the key to her heart lay. I was staring at the client, and she was looking at the floor. I wanted to wrap her in my arms, love her, and beg her forgiveness. Julia cleared her throat. I was shocked by my absence from reality. I gave the briefest description of the client's answer. I said I was making a summary, and that it amounted to the following: they did have a private life, but always at his demand; there was violence involved; she felt things she did not want to feel; she was horrified that her body reacted with pleasure at times because her heart was locked up somewhere else.

'Julia looked at me as if she would like to give me therapy. I had no time for that; in my mind, Amira and I were together. I didn't think that I was repeating the behavior of her husband by mentally possessing her without her agreement, but I was.

'I can't remember how the session ended. I think Julia ended it prematurely, perhaps because the patient was upset, and maybe because she understood what had happened to my mind.

'That night, alone in my apartment, I was afflicted by memories of Amira's descriptions of their violent intimacy. I was tormented by longing, and by my wish to know everything they had done. I could hardly breathe. I couldn't think. The TV in my room started to work. The screen said, "The beautiful Amira needs you; the key from your soul will unlock the box that holds her heart." But the final message was my undoing: "She wants you, but Bobby lives."

'Early this morning I went to the kitchen for a glass of water. Looking through the kitchen window at the still night, I conceived a plan to remedy everything. During the interview with Julia and Amira I had broken a rule of confidentiality by taking her husband's address from the client notes. I had read it upside down on Julia's table. I'm quite good at it. I felt moved to break the laws of the land, and those of God. I took a long, sharp knife from my kitchen. I went to his apartment.

'He didn't make a sound. There was blood on my clothes and hands. It was as if I was looking at a murder scene that was someone else's responsibility. I called the police and, before they arrived, I went home to make preparations for my arrest.'

Josef sobbed, overwhelmed, I imagined, by his sorrow for taking the life of Amira's husband, the family's father.

'I've lost her for sure, and she didn't even know I was involved with her. I suppose she'll hear all this at the trial. It would be better if she didn't know my thoughts. I'll remain silent.'

The meeting was almost over. I did my best to round off the interview and to help Josef with this pain. Without much success I feared, as he looked devastated. The guard knocked on the door to indicate the end of our time. I assured Josef that I would return in three days. He seemed calm and grateful for the chance to talk.

Over the rickety wooden bridge, I left the dark, forbidding castle building, and walked out towards my freedom. I was returning to my comfortable life, but a chilling feeling afflicted me. I couldn't find the words to raise it into consciousness.

A few days later I was called to the prison to meet the director. Josef was dead. He had managed to strangle himself in his cell. He had hidden a long bootlace in a condom in his body.

'He must have planned it,' the director said.

'Yes. He said he went home after the murder to prepare himself for his arrest. I wondered what that meant.'

'Maybe he only wanted to meet you to get the events coherent in his mind. But then, of course, the full weight of his crime was too much for his conscience. I'm sorry it had to be you.

While you are here, you could help in another way if you have the time. The guard who found him is a young woman. I think you met her a few days ago. Could you listen to her?'

Postscript

Freud, quoting Plato, said, 'The virtuous man contents himself with dreaming that which the wicked man does in actual life.' (Freud, S. (1900), p. 620) The above story is, as you will understand, a metaphor for infatuation and a countertransference enactment. Countertransference may be described as a misperception of the other person caused by our unconscious wishes and needs. It is the response of the therapist to their client, 'a misperception of the patient caused by the analyst's own psychopathology.' (Spillius et al, (2011), p288)

The story plays on the idea that the therapist is also an interpreter. She or he interprets the relationship in the room between the client and the analyst. Should the therapist become too involved in the conscious fantasies and unconscious phantasies expressed in the sessions, she or he loses their position as an independent observer and commentator. 'It is that we are never so defenseless against suffering as when we love, never so helplessly unhappy as when we have lost our loved object, or it's love.' (Freud, S. (1929), p. 82) In a situation such as that described in the story, a so-called acting out may occur. The therapist enacts their part in the client's fantasy, instead of describing it. Naturally, it is difficult to keep a balance in the work. The therapist has to know the client's fantasies through her feelings and then figuratively step back in order to observe and describe the client's experience.

What do you think about this?

References

Freud, S. (1900). *The Interpretation of Dreams*. SE IV. London: Hogarth Press and The Institute of Psycho-Analysis.

Freud, S. (1929). *The Future of an Illusion, Civilization and Its Discontents*. SE XXI. London: Hogarth Press and The Institute of Psycho-Analysis.

Spillius, Elizabeth Bott, et al.,(2011) *The New Dictionary of Kleinian Thought*, Routledge, 2011, p. 288.

The next story takes a more light-hearted approach, but with a serious point about the effects of memories...

2

The Bloody Audacity of It

———◆———

'That dark-green corduroy jacket makes you look like a free-thinking academic, but without the relaxed sexual boundaries of a true artist,' said my wife, followed by, 'Help me with the laundry.' Whose job is that? And then there was the purple-shirt incident. 'Why did you buy that?' she said with contempt.

I decided to end my mental anguish by falling for a few seconds. What could be simpler? So I went up to the bridge. In my disturbed state of mind, I believed I would live on without her. I didn't even stop at the bakery cafe on the way up to the bridge. I'll eat a cake later, I thought. How mad is that?

Soon I was on the other side of the fence, reaching out to the sky, like a character in some Hollywood romance. I heard a tight, nasal voice and looked around. Behind me on the sidewalk I saw a woman wearing a floral-patterned orange headscarf, perhaps to stop the cold wind blowing her wig off, and an oversized yellow woolen coat. She was carrying a green plastic shopping bag. Her silver-framed glasses were shaped like butterfly wings. So blatantly vulgar, I thought. Her complexion was gray.

'Hello. Excuse me, I'm Elaine Ratchbull.'

'Yes, pleased to meet you, but I'm occupied at the moment.'

'Do you have a name?'

'No.'

'Why are you hanging over the edge?'

'What's it got to do with you?'

'My friend Janet Crams is over there, checking the other side of the bridge. We met up here a few years ago, and we come here regularly. We're suicide spotters.'

'You're what?'

'Don't sound surprised. We come at the weekends to look out for anyone who is planning to do it. But you're so sullen, and you appear incapable of a conversation.'

'That's insulting.'

'I know, but if you can't hold a conversation by the time you reach your age that's a sorry state of affairs. It's an art, you know. They should teach it in schools. And don't get me going on the national school curriculum, I've had thirty-five years of that. Anyway, this won't get anything done. Where were we? Oh yes, your probable imminent departure from the life that God and your mother gave you.'

'What the fuck are you talking about?'

'Don't play the innocent with me and mind your language. You need to think this through, but I suppose you're using all your energy to hold on. Perhaps you're ambivalent, and you'll let your fingertips decide when they've had enough. Sometimes it takes a while before you see one give up. I mean, start the final journey. But it's quicker if you're overweight.'

'I'm not overweight, it's muscle.'

'You look a bit puffy to me. Self-indulgent, are we? You'll make a good thud at the bottom, you wait and see. No, hang on, sorry, you won't hear it. But you might. Janet knows more about those details. You know, those last uncomfortable sounds you can't control, like the intensive-care nurse saying, "It's the other plug, Doctor." Sounds that really drive into your soul—or drive your soul out, perhaps I should say? Anyway, no need for philosophizing, we have more immediate excitements to concern us.'

'How can you talk like this?'

'I'm just explaining. You asked what I'm doing. It's like fishing: you wait and wait, but when you get a bite it's great. Usually, there's someone late on a Saturday evening or early on a Sunday morning. After the football and before church: what a tight little window that forms, doesn't it? You don't know Julie-Anne, do you? Slight little girl, funny hair. She was up here last week, but not for long.'

'No, I don't. Should I? I don't understand you.'

'Just asking. My life is empty since Mr Ratchbull crossed over. Reginald Ratchbull was my husband, you know, God rest his soul.'

'My condolences, but I'm thinking about something else.'

'You're not thinking at all. So, as I was saying, even the few seconds it'll take you to fall to the bottom will fill an empty hour in my mind. A real tingle in the nerves. It's amazing to see some of you wiggle as you go down, and then the splash as you hit the bottom.'

'Splash? On concrete?'

'Yes, it's in gray and scarlet. For the artists, it's a nice flourish at the end of a failed creative life, don't you think?'

'I don't care.'

'I think you do—you look worried. Most of the jumpers look up as they fall. Like a baby looking for their mother. It's quite touching.'

'That's an unbelievably cruel thing to say at a moment like this.'

289

'Indeed, "at a moment like this". Listen to yourself, young man. Can you imagine how long a second is when you realize what you've done? You look bothered. Are you? My friend's crossing the road now; she's probably keen to see you get started. We've been here all night, and it gets cold you know.'

'This is obviously tough for you. Haven't you got a Thermos of tea?'

'Irony, eh? It's in my bag, and sandwiches, with ketchup of course—we try to keep it themed. Here she is.'

'Hello, dear. I'm Janet.'

Janet was dressed like Elaine, and had dark rings around her tired red eyes. The preposterous behavior of these ladies was clearing my head, strangely. My position on the side of the bridge was not as bad as it looked to them; I was standing on a girder they couldn't see.

'Won't you shake hands? That's better, be friendly. Oh, your hands are cold, at least that one is. Are you all right holding on with one hand? You're strong, aren't you? I imagine you've got firm muscles. Is she getting at you? I don't know why we do it really. And what's your name?'

'He doesn't have a name, but he wants the encouragement. Don't you?' said Elaine.

'I've got a name, as it happens.'

'You got it from your mother, I imagine,' said Janet. 'It's the name you're about to kill, and probably your mother too if she's alive, poor woman. What an end to a life, burying a squashed son. The things people have to go through these days.'

'Stop dribbling out these stupid words. I have a mother, and my name is Roger, if you must know.'

'It isn't that I *must* know, but if you have a mother it's just more personal, isn't it? You should remember who you're killing. Roger what? What's your family name?'

'I'm not saying.'

'Don't insist, Janet, we've taken ages to get this far. His poor little fingers will give up soon.'

'Getting tired, are we? But we need the family name, Roger dear. You know your mother won't recover from your early exit, don't you?'

'My wife, you mean.'

'Well, all the people you know. And now he tells us he's got a wife.'

'Who'll soon to be a widow,' said Elaine.

'A nice how-do-you-do for a Sunday morning, isn't it? Some people say they get over it, but they don't. They'll be haunted by your untimely exit.'

'That was poetic, Janet, "untimely exit". I like that.'

'I've had enough of this. You two are heartless. I'm leaving.'

'You're not the first one to say that. Mr Ratchbull used to say that all week, until we got to Saturday evening of course. I'm quite partial to a 'bit of the other' occasionally. Don't you miss it, Janet?'

'Oh yes, I do. My Mr Crams, my George, was a real man of a Saturday night.'

'You're mad: the pair of you.'

'Oh yes, of course we are, and who's the one hanging off the bridge? Is it me or Janet? No. Mind you, Janet, those last few months with Mr Ratchbull were empty of excitement. He hated himself.'

'I know what you mean. My George was the same, and he hated me as well of course. Upsetting it was.'

'I've had enough.'

'Oi, now stop that. Where do you think you're going? You've got a show to put on.'

'Another one saved then, Mrs Ratchbull. He was strong, lifted himself right up and over the fence.'

'You know where he's going now, don't you? They all do it,' said Elaine.

'No.'

'To the bakery.'

'Really? Let's sit down here on the curb for our tea. There isn't any traffic to speak of.'

'That girl last week, remember her?' said Elaine. 'What was her name, Julie-Anne? She insisted on that double name. She had pink and purple hair, and a lovely summer dress. Sweet-looking girl. I told her how her face would look at the bottom, and what a pretty picture her dress would make as it ballooned around her in the wind on the way down. "And we'll see your knickers. I hope they're clean for the occasion," I said. She didn't like that.'

'Yes, I remember now. You've got such a way with words, haven't you, Elaine? Her dress would "balloon around her". That has a ring to it, and no one likes to expose their knickers, even if it's for the final time. Is there any tea left?'

'In a minute. Listen, when we were walking back down, didn't you see her in the bakery?'

'Who?'

'That Julie-Anne. Leave the Thermos alone.'

'Oh, yes.'

'It's that bakery that's a cake shop too. And don't say how ironic that it's opposite the graveyard,' said Elaine.

'I wasn't going to.'

'"Ironic" is a bad word. They don't like it. I said it to one of them once and he let go.'

'Yes, that was terrible. But we were learning then, weren't we?'

'Anyway, Julie-Anne, bless her, was in that bakery stuffing herself with chocolate buns; the cream was all around her mouth.'

'That's ironic.'

'Don't.'

'I mean, she was so skinny, she needed plenty of calories.'

'It's a gamble though, isn't it? I mean the way we talk to them.'

'Sometimes I think we go too far.'

'No, we don't. You've got to use the skills you've got. I wish someone had done it for my Reginald.'

'And my George too. I wonder what his last thought was.'

'Now then, we mustn't be maudlin. But they're so sensitive these 'early leavers', and how they complain about their mothers. So ungrateful. And the bloody audacity of it, that's what really gets me. Do you want a chicken or a beef sandwich?'

'Beef, thanks.'

'Oh, a bit of sunshine. Turned out quite nice, didn't it? And it's a lovely view from here.'

'That Roger was a lovely view in this morning light, didn't you think? Have you ever had a younger man?'

'Must you, Janet? Eat your sandwich, it's got ketchup on it, how you like it.'

'I'm still here, you know.'

'Oh yes, so you are, hiding behind us. Now sit down properly Roger, or whatever your name is, and stop sulking,' said Elaine.

'I'm not sulking.'

'And your poor wife, what's she done to deserve you? There's an extra sandwich here. You're probably quite peckish after all that hanging about.'

'Oh, don't make me giggle. "Hanging about"—I'll spill my tea. She's such a laugh, isn't she? Don't you think so? I love that purple shirt, by the way. It suits you,' said Janet.

'Thanks. You two are bonkers, aren't you?'

'Hasn't he got a way with words? Just like you, Elaine.'

'You never get over it, Roger dear. Never.'

Postscript

'Yet one word more: grief boundeth where it falls,
Not with the empty hollowness, but weight:
I take my leave before I have begun,
For sorrow ends not when it seemeth done.'
William Shakespeare (*Richard II*, Act I, Scene 2)

In some situations, especially a suicide, sorrow never seems to end, and this story illustrates that experience for the two ladies who have clearly lost their men to the bridge. And indeed, the experience seems to have driven them a little mad. In their own strange way, they try to help other possible jumpers, in this case by reminding Roger who he's going to hurt and harm.

It was Freud who pointed out that sadism solved the riddle of suicide, and made it interesting: 'We have long known, it is true, that no neurotic harbors thoughts of suicide which he has not turned back upon himself from murderous impulses against others.' (Freud, S. (1917), p. 252) He went on to say that the self-

294

murder can occur if the ego can treat itself as an object, and is able to direct to itself the hatred and aggression it has for an object in the outside world. In this case, we see that Roger hates his wife and, as the ladies point out, his mother too. He is not conscious of this and believes, in his temporary madness, that by getting rid of himself he will solve his problem with his wife, and live on without the part of himself she dislikes.

'In the case of *repressed* memory-traces it can be demonstrated that they undergo no alteration even in the course of the longest period of time.' (Freud, S. (1901), p. 274) The unconscious is timeless, and so is the cruelty of a suicide. As Elaine says at the end, 'you never get over it'.

Those who are witnesses and mourners of the tragedy must live with the knowledge that the suicide wanted to cause pain, at least unconsciously. Is this true? Was Freud right when he said, 'it is sadism alone that solves the riddle of the tendency to suicide, which makes melancholia so interesting and so dangerous.'? (Freud, S 1917) p252) Or are there other more important factors?

References

Freud, S. (1901). *The Psychopathology of Everyday Life*. SE VI. London: Hogarth Press and The Institute of Psycho-Analysis.

Freud, S. (1917). *Mourning and Melancholia*. SE XIV. London: Hogarth Press and The Institute of Psycho-Analysis.

Clark, W. G., and Wright, W. A., (Eds) *The Complete Works of William Shakespeare*. Garden City, NY: Nelson Doubleday Inc.

In the next story we have a tragedy in the school environment that illustrates an aspect of Freud's basic theory of neurosis, the Oedipus complex.

3

Babies in School

———◆———

'What I love about you, Axel,' said Phoebe, 'is that you are so gorgeous. I want to eat you up.'

'Ouch! You don't have to bite my ear every time, do you? I nearly choked on this bit of toast.'

'Oh, my poor little boy, don't you like being loved? I'm going out to the shops now. Do you want anything?'

'No thanks.'

'Off you go to school. You'll be late if you don't move your pretty bottom soon.'

There was a window open in the dining room and, in the draught, the front door banged shut. Axel sat alone, feeling empty, as if he'd lost her. He realized what time it was, shouted 'Bye Mum' and rushed out to the bus, late.

The headmistress, Pamela Strump, enjoyed the sight of teenage bottoms, despite her fierce morality. She was middle aged, dumpy, and bad tempered.

Seventeen-year-old Axel, an athletic guy with the casual arrogance of one who is aware of his sex appeal, stood outside Ms Strump's office. His rugged features, dark hair, and pale-blue eyes attracted attention. When he felt challenged he could be impulsive and aggressive.

In his previous school, he'd hit the headmaster. Against the school rules, he'd been running in a corridor. The headmaster had seen him approaching, shouted, and tripped him as he ran past. Axel had jumped up and landed a punch. At the resulting internal investigation, the headmaster was sanctioned, and Axel had to change school. Now Axel had another kind of trouble.

The school secretary, a quiet woman with her hair in a bun, greeted him. 'Hello, Axel. Ms Strump will be with you shortly.'

'Thank you. Do you know why I've been called?'

'No, I'm sure I don't, but you can sit down if you wish.'

'It's all right, I'd rather stand, thanks.' The secretary was wearing a flattering summer dress, and Axel studied the engaging lines of her mature body while she focused on her typing. Then he remembered her children, also at this school. He looked out of the window at the gray-black playground tarmac, and at the untended bushes on its perimeter. There was always some kind of trash that had been blown into them: potato-chip packets, sweet wrappers. He remembered a piece of paper on the floor of the delivery room. He'd studied it while trying to avoid listening to the distressing sounds of the birth. He wondered if he was to face more recriminations from Strump about begetting a baby. Or was it his routine lateness at school? That couldn't be it; it was trivial. Anyway, not everyone has a duty of satisfaction to a lover at home. A smile crossed his face.

Strump called him in and sat down heavily in her office chair. Her desk is her shield, thought Axel. She didn't look at him, nor she did she invite him to sit down. Axel looked at her plush carpet, with its jolly colors. What a fuss she had made when she'd laid that in her office, but now she looked pale and angry.

'She's dead,' she said by way of a greeting, and began to sob.

'What? Who?'

'Your beloved math teacher, Phoebe. She was hit by a car. What a wretched thing to happen to me and the school—again.'

'But I saw her this morning. What will I do?'

'Always thinking about yourself, Axel. You have a baby daughter, the poor child.' She stood and moved around her desk towards him.

'Don't touch me, not ever.'

'I'll get you a cup of tea.'

'Tea! I don't want fucking tea. It's your fault, you fucking bitch, you said you'd ruin her.' He wanted to whack her, beat her to a pulp on her precious carpet.

'Now just a moment… I understand you are upset but–'

'Upset?' She moved towards him as if to hug him. He gave her chest a shove with his elbow as he pushed past, and fled the building.

He walked randomly. It must be true, he thought, even Strump wouldn't tell such a lie. He couldn't cry… He felt empty. Was this what shock felt like? His cellphone rang, and by reflex he answered.

'Hello, Axel, it's Melissa from social services. Your headmistress phoned me.'

'Yeah, and?'

'I'm so sorry you heard the news like this. We're all upset and Pamela, I mean Ms Strump, is mortified she hurt you, she is really. I know she's said hard things about the situation and everything but–'

'What happened to Phoebe?'

'It seems she wasn't paying attention when she crossed the high street this morning. Apparently, the car involved was not travelling fast, but she hit her head on the corner of the sidewalk. She died right there. When the police report arrives we'll know more.'

'Death in the gutter... Huh, she said she belonged there.'

'Would you like to meet me? Come to my office. I'm here all day.'

He walked distractedly, unable to find the social services building for a while. When he arrived, Melissa hugged him. He liked her long blonde hair and round body. He felt her press against him. He breathed her in and, for a moment, a living woman was in his arms, and he in hers. It was a relief. He accepted her tea.

'Phoebe drinks tea, you know.'

'You like the same kind, don't you? You said so the first time we three met. This is a disaster. The teacher-and-pupil romance drama aside, I saw you were in love, and were delighted with the baby, the poor child.'

'Phoebe thought her career was finished. She said it was her fault totally. She couldn't let it go, I mean blaming herself. I should have been more careful.'

'I understood she was determined to keep the baby. Maybe she wanted it from the beginning. Sorry, I shouldn't interrupt. Please go on.'

'She said, "I'm keeping this one." I didn't understand.'

He sobbed. His body reacted, but not his soul; he couldn't feel anything. 'I don't know where I am. It's so unreal. I'll go now.'

'We can meet tomorrow,' said Melissa, as he went through the door.

Axel walked home, certain that people were looking at him. It was embarrassing. His parents were upset and were kind to him. His mother clearly loved having the baby. He wept intermittently, still without feeling, all evening.

The next day he returned to the social services office but, when Melissa gave him another hug, he felt unfaithful to Phoebe, and let go before she did. Why is she being so friendly and comforting, he thought? I'm her case, not a relative.

'I've spoken to Phoebe's family. You know their home is quite a distance away. They are not so well off. I don't think they can manage a new baby. But your parents are more than happy to take her, they say.'

'Why can't I cry properly or feel anything? Why not?'

'It's natural when you're in shock, Axel. Give yourself time. It might be helpful to tell me the story of how you became involved with Phoebe. Perhaps it will put things in perspective.'

'Maybe.'

'Take your time.'

'Where shall I start?'

'At the beginning. How did you meet?'

'On my first day at this school the headmistress gave me the once-over—you know, *really* looked me up and down. I thought the bitch fancied me and, to be honest, I enjoyed the attention. Anyway, she told me to follow her and we walked down a corridor where children's art covered the walls—patterns and pictures in crayon, charcoal, and watercolor.' He felt his eyes well up again. 'We went into Phoebe's classroom at the end of the corridor. She didn't look much older than her pupils, but I knew she must be. She was the prettiest teacher I'd ever seen. Her hair was full, dark, and curly.'

'Like yours.'

'Her body was slim; her eyes were wide and brown. When she looked at me, she took my breath away; she looked right into me, and I looked back. Usually, a look doesn't mean so much, but with her it was different, like love. I couldn't believe it. It seemed weird.'

'The headmistress said something about how good I was at math. Phoebe said, "I'm pleased to meet you, Axel, I've heard you are good with puzzles."'

'I do like puzzles; they distract me from everything else. Then she asked me if we'd met before and, when I said no, she wondered if she'd met my parents somewhere.

'I had no idea. It was really embarrassing, standing in front of the class like that.'

Melissa pushed a box of tissues over the table that separated them.

'I could feel the whole class looking at us. The headmistress left; she seemed a bit put out. Phoebe showed me to a desk and gave me a book open at the right page. She was soon by my desk again, leaning over me to show me something. She smelled lovely; not only her perfume but her.

'At every lesson she found a reason to be close to me. Other boys talked about me being the teacher's pet. One afternoon, Phoebe asked me back to the classroom to look at a problem I'd missed. That was untrue: I never miss problems. She offered me a lift home. In the car, while changing gear, she accidentally touched my thigh, and smiled. I liked it. I didn't react, but I felt something. She stopped a few streets away from my house. I was surprised she knew where I lived. As I moved to leave, she touched me again. I sat back. She was smiling, looking into my eyes. I couldn't resist running my fingers through her hair, it was so soft. She released the seat and leaned back. I kissed her.'

'A romantic start,' said Melissa, fidgeting with a lock of hair.

'We started to meet at her flat: "After-school activity" she joked. She said my dark hair and pale-blue eyes turned her on. It was fast

302

and wild every time, like when you make up with someone after a row. I never thought about condoms or the pill.

'When she got pregnant, she told people that the father was an old friend, or that it was planned by her at least. But I knew it had to be me. It didn't stop our sex life, until near the end, when it began to feel strange. She got so big, and I felt the baby move sometimes, like a third person in the bed. It didn't feel right.

'Water keeps coming out of my eyes.'

'The tea must be cold by now. Let me get you another.'

'It's all right, I want to finish. She was alone in the hospital when the birth got difficult. The staff asked for the father. They rang me at home—you know I'm adopted?'

'Yes, of course.'

'My parents wondered what it was all about, and when I said that a school mate was in hospital, my dad drove me there. I couldn't say the truth, so I asked him to leave. I didn't want him to see me searching for the maternity department.'

'That must have been uncomfortable.'

'Yes, my dad is old and kind, and I didn't want to upset him. In the delivery place, the midwife looked at me with a question mark in her eyes. But I felt proud to be a father; they could think what they liked. Soon there were lots of staff. I was pushed to one side. The birth was brutal and bloody, with forceps. Phoebe was screaming, and I felt responsible. The baby looked like she'd been in a serious fight. I'm looking out of the window now but I don't see anything. I did the same then: looked around the delivery room to try to avoid the horrible sights. I switched myself off.'

'How did your parents take it?'

'I had to tell Mum and Dad, of course. They were shocked at first but they controlled it, and they supported me. They didn't blame me or go over the top with the "How could you?" business. It was like they knew. Perhaps they suspected. They went with me to see the headmistress, and defended me too. They didn't blame Phoebe either, not like that old bitch Strump. They even invited Phoebe to our house, and said she could live with us. I think they want a grandchild.'

'They're lovely people, really supportive.'

'I'd like to go home now.'

'Of course, but do you feel up to it? You can sit here as long as you like. You don't have to say any more. I can drive you home later.'

'No thanks, Mum and Dad are babysitting. I need to walk; I don't want to meet them looking upset. Now I can't stop this crying.'

'You know, it might help to see her—Phoebe, I mean.'

'I haven't seen a dead person before but yes, I'd like to see her.'

'We can meet again tomorrow. I'll go with you to the undertaker's.'

The next day, Axel went with Melissa to see Phoebe's body. They were shown into a quiet room that looked like a chapel. It was cold. She lay in a coffin that rested on a trestle with wheels. Her hair curled around her face, and her hands were crossed over her stomach. A candle flickered on the far side of the room.

'She looks so peaceful and beautiful. She isn't smiling, but she isn't upset or angry. It's weird that she doesn't breathe,' said Axel.

He felt Melissa's arm round his shoulders.

'Thanks. It's so strange to see her like this. I'm glad you're here.'

'She's wearing a lovely summer dress.'

'It was her favorite. My mother had it dry-cleaned. It's unreal. I wish we had one more moment together, warm and alive.'

Melissa pulled him closer. Their hips touched. He wanted her comfort and he didn't. Axel stepped forward quickly. He felt Melissa's arm slip from his shoulders. He lowered his head and kissed Phoebe gently on the lips.

'I wish I hadn't done that. She's so cold. I'll remember it all my life.'

'You'll remember other loving moments too, and soon they'll take over,' said Melissa. He felt her hand make circular movements on his back.

'I hope you're right.'

The rest of the day he spent with his parents and daughter. Should he call her Phoebe? He had a lot to learn about babies. At the diaper change he was glad his mum was there.

Later in the afternoon, he was sitting on the living-room floor. The baby was lying on a blanket in front of him. He heard his mother talking in the kitchen. 'Did you know she's thirty-one years old?'

'Shush,' said his father.

'Who?' called out Axel.

'Oh, that woman down the road, the one your dad says looks like a pop star.'

'Hmm.'

'By the way, Axel, I've been in touch with Phoebe's parents. They're coming to the funeral.'

'I know. Melissa told me. I'd like to meet people who look like her.'

His mother hugged him. He felt little again. That evening, he lay on his bed and tried to remember Phoebe's warmth.

Two days later, Melissa rang. 'How are you doing? These are terrible days, waiting for the funeral.'

'I know, I'm part of it.' He remembered her arm on his shoulders and wanted to shake it off. Or did he? He needed her. 'Any news from the police?'

'No, they can take a long time. I'm ringing because we need to have a meeting before the funeral. There are a few formalities to go through.'

When he returned to the social services office, Melissa gave him a quick, firm hug. She looked serious. She offered him tea again.

'Always tea—it's like crisis equals tea.'

'It's nice to see you smile, Axel. We have to talk about a couple of things today.'

'Oh yes, child custody and another school for me, I suppose.' He was distracted by a memory of Phoebe. 'When we went to see her, she looked so lovely. I couldn't see any marks on her. Wasn't that strange?'

'It's true. She looked peaceful.'

'I couldn't understand how she died. She showed no signs of injury, but she was so cold.'

'I know that's distressing, but the undertaker covered her head wound very well.'

'And she didn't smell of anything. When we first met, she smelled so good, I felt as if I knew her already.'

'Really? Did I tell you her family are coming?'

'Yes, I'm glad. Why didn't they come immediately? I know it is a long way but...'

'Do you think they might be ashamed as well as distressed?'

'How should I know? What's the matter?'

'I've spoken to a social services colleague in her hometown.'

'Yes, and?'

'Did Phoebe tell you her age?'

'No. I guessed about twenty-five. She looked young for a teacher, but she wouldn't let me see her passport. We tussled over it once. Then she kissed me, and I forgot about it.'

Melissa was silent.

'It wasn't thirty-one, was it? I overheard my parents talking about someone.'

'Yes, thirty-one. Did she tell you she'd been pregnant before?'

'No.'

'She'd had a relationship with an older man, when she was fourteen, and she became pregnant. The man seems to have been an unpleasant character.'

'Oh.'

'Phoebe's wish to keep the baby provoked him. He went to prison for beating her up. Phoebe's family couldn't support her, but we don't know the whole story. Her social worker helped her to put the baby up for adoption. After that, she seemed to have been determined to make a career. When she became a teacher, she moved away.'

'Is there a point to this?'

Melissa took up a picture from her desk and sat beside Axel. 'This is a picture of the father of her first child, a boy.'

'Oh shit, he looks like me. Am I that baby? It can't be true—why me?'

She put her arm round his shoulder. 'You know I'm here for you.'

'Fuck off.'

Postscript

FRIAR LAURENCE:
    'These violent delights have violent ends

And in their triumph die, like fire and powder,
Which, as they kiss, consume.
William Shakespeare, *Romeo and Juliet*, Act II Scene 6

The story is an example of the above quotation: the excitement of the couple's passion leads to a tragedy, as it did in Shakespeare's play. Clearly this story is about the Oedipus complex, and particularly about the unconscious experience of wishing to destroy one parent and possess the other. Oedipus complex: 'Organised body of loving and hostile wishes which the child experiences towards its parents.' (Laplanche, J., and Pontalis, J.-B. (1980) p 282). These mixed feelings are often experienced unconsciously. The couple in the story can be criticized for their relationship within a school setting, but they are not conscious that they are mother and son. Sometimes we think of this symbolically when one partner is much older than the other, or when there is an imbalance in dependency, when i.e. one person controls the other, as in the teacher–pupil relationship. In this story, the fact that they really are mother and son, and are involved in an incestuous relationship, gives emphasis to the illustration.

A distasteful situation is described in the story. It is not easy to accept, but of course it happens. Perhaps it is a little too grim for many people. A passion on both sides of a relationship, even a professional relationship such as that between a teacher and pupil, is not strange. This scene is repeated in a relationship where one person has emotional power over the other. This is what is known in psychoanalysis as 'transference': each person transfers to the other an experience of someone else they have known and carry with them as a memory. In a school classroom, as in a consulting room, the pupil (client) is dependent on the teacher (therapist). A situation of dependence requires responsible behavior from the

308

person being depended on. They should not misuse the other's wishes to form a physically satisfying relationship, for example. From the psychoanalytic perspective, the story carries a double prohibition when we include the love between a child and a parent described by Freud in his exposition of the Oedipus neurosis. (Freud, S. (1905))

Axel's sexual interest is clearly in overdrive but, because he's only seventeen, this is easy to understand. And, as we learn during the story, he's particularly keen on older women, like the school secretary, as well as Melissa and Phoebe of course. Although, having said that, his relationship with Melissa is fascinating and his rejection of her at the very end is perfectly fitting.

The situation described of a mother unwittingly meeting her son and having an affair with him is unusual but, in line with the theory of the Oedipus complex, it is a situation that may be played out with surrogates in ordinary life. For example, men who have an affair with a younger woman without being conscious that the new woman reminds them of the daughter at home who they would never wish to harm. But their feelings are so strong that they feel compelled to act them out with someone.

In addition, the situation in the story describes the love felt by Phoebe, which has its roots in her unconscious knowledge of who Axel is. And vice versa of course. Was this an unconscious suicide?

Do you believe that unconscious reminders of people previously loved, like parents, play a part in new relationships? Do you think the Oedipus complex is ubiquitous?

References

Freud, S. (1905). *Three Essays on the Theory of Sexuality*. SE VII. London: Hogarth Press and The Institute of Psycho-Analysis.

Laplanche, J., and Pontalis, J.-B. (1980). *The Language of Psychoanalysis*. London: Hogarth Press and the Institute of Psycho-Analysis.

In the next story we witness another school tragedy in the name of love that is scarred by religion...

4

The Tragedy of Brother Jules

——◆——

I'd received a detention for my comments to the religious knowledge teacher about Jesus possibly having had a bisexual nature. 'First, Jesus had Mary Magdalen, a fallen woman.' I pointed out that this information is in some gospels, but not those approved by the church, I had to concede. Then, unwisely, I'd added, 'And second, has anyone looked at the Leonardo painting of The Last Supper lately? Clearly he also had a thing for John, the disciple.' This was not appreciated. 'It's unassailable evidence,' I said, and this increased my punishment from half an hour to one hour.

Later that afternoon, as I crossed the playground on my way home, I saw steam billowing from the shower room vents. The school caretaker, Mr Rudge, walked briskly towards the changing rooms. He's calm and friendly and doesn't usually do anything quickly. He wore a white shirt under a tidy blue boiler suit. 'You've got to look smart, Jonathan. Whatever you do in life, self-respect, that's the thing. Be yourself; never mind what other people think.' I thought he should be the headmaster.

'Everything all right, Mr Rudge?'

'I don't know, I'm going to check. You've been in trouble again, I hear. I hope it was worth it. Come with me and make yourself useful.'

Good old Rudge, always willing to see the best in someone. He was gray-haired, with crow's feet around his eyes. His shoulders were hunched in his near-retirement years, and I wanted to tell him to straighten his back, but I had no desire to embarrass him. He probably would have smiled anyway. He seemed to love his job, although I didn't know what he thought about the religious community that ran the school, or their morality; he'd kept his views to himself, until today.

Almost at a run, we continued to the gym. He opened the door to the changing and shower rooms in the basement. A cloud of white vapor engulfed us.

Earlier in the day, Brother Jules, our English teacher, had held a lesson about the poet Shakespeare. Brother Jules is a young monk of the holy order that run this boys-only school. He's a slim man, always well turned out, and his holy cassock is stain free, unlike that of some of the older members of the community. He's clean shaven, pale skinned, with a neat haircut. A fit-looking bloke with a gentle manner, I suppose you could say. Why he chose a celibate life heaven only knows, but he's a dedicated professional.

He asked Butts, fifteen years old, to read aloud a sonnet. We should have read it as preparation for this lesson. Butts was described by his class teacher as 'A cynical and cheeky youth, prone to the cruel bullying of weaker pupils.' Butts proudly told us all; strange guy.

He pretended to struggle to find the right page, as if a book was something unfamiliar. He sniggered as he fumbled, and looked around the classroom for approval from his mates. Brother Jules sighed; Butts finally settled down and read aloud, "Sonnet Eighteen by William Shakespeare.'

'Thank you, Butts, we know the author,' said Brother Jules, glancing at the pretty boy of our class, Mackenzie. Every class has one it seems: a teenage boy with an angelic face and a feminine manner. Our class was no exception and Mackenzie was beautiful. No one would deny he could pass for a girl if he used a bit of make-up. Butts turned again and grinned.

'Read on, Butts,' said Brother Jules.

'*Shall I campare thee to a summer's day?*'

Brother Jules glanced again at Mackenzie. I wondered if he thought that no one noticed, or was he so infatuated with the boy that his judgment had gone out of the window? Another mate of Butts, Kelly, cleared his throat loudly. Butts knew what the sound meant—they were mocking Brother Jules.

'*Thou art more lovely and more temperate*:

Brother Jules looked at Mackenzie. Kelly coughed again.

'*Rough winds do shake the darling buds of May*

And summer's lease hath all too short a date:' Butts laughed.

'Now, read those lines again, Butts, and the rest, without interruptions.' Brother Jules looked sternly at Kelly. The rest of the class groaned.

"*Shall I campare thee to a summer's day?*,' said Butts emphatically.

Mackenzie returned Brother Jules' loving gaze and held it for a second too long, while the rest of us smiled at each other. The bell sounded for a change of lesson. Time for a gym class. Butts said, 'It's 1967, it'll all be legal soon lads.' His voice was drowned by the squealing and scraping of chairs and desks being moved. Brother Jules looked quizzical, then raised his voice, 'I'll expect you all to know this sonnet by the next lesson.' After the gym lesson, he was to supervise the changing room and showers. The gym teacher had to rush to an urgent dental appointment.

An hour later, Brother Jules stood by the door of the changing room, which was in the basement under the gym. From his position, he could observe the boys changing and showering. He looked over the heads of the group, and appeared to be interested in the maze of hot-water pipes attached to the ceiling. I thought he was trying to be modest, and to keep an eye on the group without seeing too much of the half-naked bodies in front of him.

I was near Butts and Kelly. We were behind Mackenzie. Butts shouted, 'Oi!' Jules looked at us and turned away.

'Fun time, lads,' said Butts.

'Don't torment him,' I said, but without conviction.

We knew Mackenzie was easily aroused in the company of other naked teenagers, and that was a laugh. Although it can happen to anyone, I think we sneered at him instead of suffering our own embarrassment about unruly hormones and physical responses in a communal shower.

Mackenzie walked towards the shower, a towel around his waist. Brother Jules looked away. Mackenzie hung up his towel. Brother Jules turned back. Mackenzie walked into the shower. Butts placed himself between the loving pair.

I felt sorry for Mackenzie. When he moved to hide himself in the corner of the shower, Butts grabbed his arms from behind, griping his biceps firmly. He pulled and pushed him into Brother Jules' line of sight, then let go. Mackenzie tried to get back into the crowd. Butts pushed him out again.

I couldn't count the feelings on Brother Jules' face. He seemed excited, shamed, and frightened. He blushed and moved forward, as if to protect Mackenzie. The changing-room pack howled with delight. Brother Jules took a step back.

Mackenzie was flayed by the eyes of the group as he was forced to play the scapegoat for our shame. He bent double trying to hide himself. Butts grabbed his biceps again, Kelly put a foot into his back to straighten him up, then pushed him forward again, while Mackenzie unsuccessfully tried to drive his heels into the unyielding floor.

The classroom chorus chanted, 'Look, look.'

I wanted the speechless Brother Jules to take Mackenzie into his arms to save him. But I didn't think his religious training allowed him such courage. He turned sharply towards the door and bumped his head on a low pipe, which resonated with a clang.

'Homo,' shouted Butts. Guffaws of crude laughter followed.

Brother Jules pulled open the door and shouted, 'Sod you, Butts.'

Amid the jeering, Butts called after him, 'Not me who's the sod, is it? What would Jesus think?'

I heard the door of the gym equipment cupboard slam shut. It's a windowless room opposite the shower room, used as walk-in storage for the physical education kit: small weights, training balls, skipping ropes, and the like.

Mackenzie was alone, at the mercy of the homophobic mob. Butts let him back into the shower area. Mackenzie crouched in a corner. His tears ran away with the soapy water.

Now, a few hours later, Mr Rudge and I tried to see into the shower room. We hesitated, mocked by the hiss of escaping steam.

'This is a mess, Jonathan. Come on, we'll have to crawl in.'

We groped our way forward on hands and knees. The floor was damp and puddled. Slumped in the corner, where Mackenzie had

315

suffered his agony, we found Brother Jules. He had a skipping rope around his neck. Above him the hot-water pipe was torn in two.

Mr Rudge was calm and determined. He deftly removed the rope. 'Help me pull him out.' We took one arm each and dragged Brother Jules across the wet floor. 'What these people do to young minds,' Mr Rudge muttered. 'It's wicked.' In the corridor he started to press on Brother Jules' chest. 'Come on, come on. Call another teacher and an ambulance, Jonathan, he's not dead yet.'

I ran upstairs, towards the school office, wondering what the hell we'd done.

Postscript

There are a number of topics for discussion here: religion as a system of controlling the faithful's sexuality and other behavior; the desperate and painful experiences of unfulfilled love; the persecution of homosexuals by society in some places, and by religions in particular; and not least the subject of bullying in a school or any other organization.

In this story, Brother Jules is overwhelmed by his love for the boy Mackenzie. However, his love is constrained by the morality of misusing a position of trust as a teacher, and by his religion, which forbids homosexuality. Psychoanalysis takes a different view:

'It is a great injustice to persecute homosexuality as a crime, and cruelty too.' (Freud, S. (1935) pp. 423–425) The subject of homosexuality, combined with an illicit love between teacher and pupil in the context of religion, needs to be treated with delicacy, even tenderness.

This story could easily leave a sour taste but, by the end, I hope you, the reader, will empathize with the cleric and with Mackenzie, his would-be young lover. A sprinkling of light humor helps a story like this, and I hope I've got the balance right.

And religion was also not a favorite of Freud's. He thought that it was a form of wishful illusion that was coupled to a denial of reality: 'religion is an illusion and it derives its strength from its readiness to fit in with our instinctual wishful impulses' (Freud, S. (1933) p. 175)

Freud had no time for religion, except for trying to understand why a large number of people need the illusion of a god in order to manage daily life. And the morality attached to some religions aligns with a harsh superego in many people, which is a hindrance to natural development, said Freud. In particular, the development that occurs if we can accept that death is real and final and that there is no safety net of a kind deity after we die. We are forced to accept reality in a new way.

School bullying is seen in this story as the heartless and cruel behavior it is. However, we humans seem to need to do it. What are we doing? Are we passing bad feelings we do not want on to other people? Bullying is particularly common and interesting, as young people repeat with each other their experience of some adults' attitudes towards them. In this case, the bullying occurs in an institution dedicated to the development of the mind. Sadly, it is not a liberal place, as it is strangled by the dictates of religious conviction and dominated by narrowmindedness. The young people in this story were simply echoing the attitudes of their elders.

And what do you think about the several issues raised? Is there one that strikes you as most relevant?

References

Clark, W. G., and Wright, W. A., (Eds) *The Complete Works of William Shakespeare.* Garden City, NY: Nelson Doubleday Inc.

Freud, S. (1933). *New Introductory Lectures on Psycho-Analysis.* SE XXII. London: Hogarth Press and the Institute of Psycho-Analysis.

Freud, S. (1935). *Letter from Sigmund Freud to Anonymous, April 9 1935. Letters of Sigmund Freud 1873–1939*, pp. 423–424. *Ernst L. Freud (ed) (1961) Basic Books*

The next story picks up the theme of bullying in a business organization, and the consequences are devastating...

5

Miss Playne and Oliver

———◆———

Hello, my name is Jonathan Crunchy. I know, strange name. In addition, I've always been overweight and have suffered jokes on both counts. I know what it's like to be bullied for personal peculiarities, and there can be tragic consequences. Such a situation occurred in my workplace. I used to work in the HR department of the Outstandingly Just Company. You have experienced, no doubt, that people and organizations may live up to their names, or the opposite. We worked for justice in the workplace, but our office was not a good example. I've pieced together the following account from my conversations with the victim, her diary, and the inquest documents. I suppose writing this is my trauma debriefing.

I had a colleague called Jane Playne. 'Miss Plain' as her petty line manager loved to say, loudly. The office nasties gossiped about her. 'She's a virgin, surely. Who would have her? How could anyone want her?' I could see how she suffered, as if their manicured fingernails tore her skin.

Jane's private life was lonely and barren: her parents were dead, and she was estranged from her younger brother. Jane was thirty-nine last birthday and wanted a family, but a baby appeared to be out of the question. I couldn't help her; I'm gay and our colleagues didn't like that either, of course.

'You know where my diary is hidden, Jonathan,' she said to me at lunchtime one day. 'If anything happens to me, read my story.' Looking around nervously, she added, 'I'm glad you're with me. I'm afraid they'll tamper with my food.'

'I don't think they would go so far. They're only shifting their own anxieties about being alone onto you. That's what bullying is you know. Try to ignore it.' Wise words but not much consolation for me and, indeed, there was salt in the sugar bowl that day. I couldn't believe it.

'These spiteful attacks from my so-called colleagues are getting to me. I can't cope with much more. I want to die most evenings but, don't worry, I won't do it. If I do, I won't go alone.'

'That sounds ominous.'

'I'm only joking,' she said.

'You need a friend and a partner.'

'We could be friends in the same apartment, it could be fun, but we'd be competing for the same people, wouldn't we?'

It was a relief to laugh but I regret I didn't agree to the idea. After the events I describe below, I read her diary in full. It wasn't funny. She'd made plans for the last day of work before the Christmas holidays. Her 'instrument of exit', as she called it, was locked in the lower drawer of her office desk. It had been left to her by her recently deceased dad. Actually, his death from a nasty cancer was believed to have affected her state of mind.

Jane wrote: *Knowing I have Dad's wartime souvenir with me is a comfort. I can leave when I wish and I'll make them (female co-workers) my witnesses.*

320

Monday morning (12th December). Jonathan and I were busy placing young recruits to the company in various departments. Today, just before lunch, a young man called Oliver was brought to me by a person from the front desk. At the sight of the newcomer, heads turned, they seemed unable to take their eyes off him. He walked, poised and handsome, through the open-plan office landscape of desks and postcard-decorated screens. The gossips were muttering and, from every workstation, I felt their envy like a green malodorous mist floating towards me. I signed the reception papers and looked up into the soft eyes of Oliver. His clothes were an unnecessary formality in my fantasy world; my hands caressed his perfect black skin. I imagined the baby I would deliver in excruciating ecstasy, with joyful tears—bonkers, I know. Distracted, I reached for my glass of water. It was empty. Oliver picked up the glass. The eyes of the office followed as he walked. Jonathan, of course, pointed out the kitchen. I think he was a bit jealous too. Oliver returned and, wiping the bottom of the glass with his pink palm, he set it down in front of me.

Yes, I was watching her. Well, him mostly. With a trembling hand, she lifted the glass to her lips. The office crew looked at each other, sneering. The young man leaned forward and said something to her.

Jane's diary entry recorded the following: *He said, 'I find you attractive. Do my paperwork, I'll enjoy watching you. Then please take me to lunch and back to your home for an hour. I have a present for you.' This was outrageous. He was misusing his beauty to improve his job chances, but I'm so lonely I couldn't resist. I didn't care about the morality of intimacy with a young employee. When we got home, his tenderness overwhelmed me. I let go. I even thought I might stay alive for the coming year, then I slept. When I woke up, evening light dimmed my bedroom. Oliver was gone. He'd left a thoughtful note. He thanked me for the meal and my love. He said he understood that we might not be able to meet like this again. I didn't think there was anything unethical about it, but maybe it was. I'm disappointed and elated. Two hours with Oliver is a memory no one else in the department can compete with.*

I observed whispered conversations in the office, with eyes looking in Jane's direction. Two days later, I was helping her with some files and discovered a used condom inserted among her papers. Jane gasped. I cleaned up for her, but I think that was the last straw.

At midday, Jane came into the lunchroom. The bitches were sitting at their usual corner table, where they could observe the rest of us. Instead of coming to me, she walked slowly towards them. I stood up and leaned against one of the pillars in the wide room. I was afraid there would be a scene, and there was. I had a clear view of what happened next. When Jane drew back the only free chair and sat down, her tormenters looked surprised, and then arrogant. The Christmas decorations hanging loosely around the room twinkled merrily.

Jane raised her voice and said, 'In my soul, Oliver, the beautiful new employee you saw briefly the other day, is mine forever. He gave me the gift of himself.'

They sneered, and some laughed aloud.

'Now I want to share with you a sweet Christmas present from my late father.'

They looked at each other, tight lipped. Jane reached into her fine leather bag, lifted out an object that filled her hand, and placed it in the sugar bowl in the middle of the table. Her enemies recoiled. With a theatrical gesture, she pulled the pin on an old grenade. I ducked behind the concrete pillar.

It was a tragedy that the wartime souvenir was so durable. There was a white flash and then the room was splattered with lunch

322

food, splintered china, and Christmas decorations. I couldn't hear anything for several days.

The inquests concluded that her father had illegally brought home a grenade from the last war. Perhaps he had thought it was a dud. In her diary, Jane wrote that she didn't know if it would work, but at least she could frighten her enemies.

As it transpired, Oliver was not out of the question as a partner for Jane. He was thirty-five years of age, although he looked much younger. He was disappointed about her sudden death but found his place in the Outstandingly Just Company's structure. He lives with Ms Tweek from accounts. She's a lovely lady, smiles a lot. I'm not jealous.

Postscript

Hello, this is Jonathan again. I'd like to make a few points while you think about this story. It's an account of social torture with a shocking and bloody end. I'm sure you're grateful that I didn't describe the human contents of the dining room after the bang. Anyway, I wrote this to emphasize the destructiveness of bullying, the power of envy, and the rage it may engender. And there is Jane's response to the death of her father. It was impossible for her to find the peace of mind to go through the mourning process while work colleagues were hacking at her.

'Every one can master a grief but he that has it' said my favorite writer, William Shakespeare, in his wonderful play, *Much Ado About Nothing* (Act III, Scene 2). It is easy to give good advice to someone else, but would I be able to cope with such a situation? I don't know that I would. I know I said that I've had my problems but, for Jane, this was a kind of 'perfect storm' of stresses that she couldn't control.

It hadn't occurred to me until writing this account that perhaps Jane was furious with her father for dying. Perhaps she loved him deeply and wanted to join him. Maybe she hated him for leaving her but couldn't admit it. What better way to express that than to use his grenade against someone else instead. Now I sound like a psychologist, but I've read about this kind of thing in serious books, Freud for example, he's very serious. It might be relevant to your ruminations.

I miss her too, you know; it's nice for a gay man to have a friend like Jane. She was loyal and she could think, it's just that the circumstances were too much for her. Maybe Oliver, who gave her an hour of freedom, was the trigger for her breakdown. He made use of the situation too, by exploiting her need for physical affection. Perhaps he was a stark reminder of what was missing in her life and she couldn't bear it any more.

If Freud is right, then Jane had loved her father and was furious with him for not loving her back and, in that way, mocking her desire for him. This is somewhat like the contemptuous way in which her boss in the office mocked her name, and her appearance. She lived in hell.

It's true that, in this account, I've signposted the ending almost from the beginning, but there is a spell running through the narrative in the person of Oliver, who is the catalyst for the final act of destruction. Jane's attraction to Oliver is more or less inevitable, given her stressed situation.

I mentioned the subject of bullying in the opening paragraph, and this was the overriding factor, as we learn about Jane's treatment at the hands of her workmates. Without them, she might have managed her hidden grief for her father, and her loneliness. It is easy to hate bullies, but perhaps they are in us all at times.

As I said at the beginning, writing this was my way of dealing with shock and grief. That's all from me, Jonathan, but if you happen to have any wartime souvenirs around the house I should give them up, if I were you.

Reference

Clark, W. G., and Wright, W. A., (Eds) *The Complete Works of William Shakespeare*. Garden City, NY: Nelson Doubleday Inc.

In the next story is a universal fear, neglect, which is a silent kind of bullying...

6

A Gray Day

———◆———

'When sorrows come, they come not single spies,
But in battalions.'
William Shakespeare (*Hamlet*, Act IV, Scene 5)

Gerry sat in his armchair at eleven o'clock in the morning. The TV had been on all night, but not loudly; he never wanted to disturb his neighbors. Now, horse racing was in progress and betting odds rolled across the screen, although he hadn't placed a bet today.

To avoid a reflection on the TV screen the thin drapes were drawn almost closed. His faded armchair had once been a bold red, but now only its rear showed its original color. The material on the arms was shiny from constant use. Whenever he stood up, a spring in the seat climbed a little further past the restraint of the canvas upholstery, like a determined dandelion forcing its way through asphalt.

Balanced on the left arm of the chair was an open can of beer. On a low stool beside Gerry was a dessert bowl; a bottle of ketchup without a lid lay on its side. The faded carpet was patterned with autumn leaves, well trodden and worn down by the open kitchen door.

Ketchup stained the pale-green cardigan he wore over a gray T-shirt. His trousers were too big and sagged. He bought his clothes from second-hand shops and hadn't found anything with a better fit; in truth, he didn't have the energy to search the racks of unsorted offerings. Gerry was seriously overweight, and his double chin was pronounced. He sat with his head tipped slightly forward to gain a better focus on the TV screen through his bifocal lenses. They were in need of cleaning and upgrading.

The apartment was poorly ventilated; the sweet smell of old food and unwashed clothes prevailed. Gerry never complained about his wretched environment; it was familiar, a comfort. It was a daily reminder of his childhood home and of his constantly exhausted mother.

'Be a good boy, Gerry, and go down to the shop for me. One loaf of white bread, a packet of cigarettes—you know the kind—and a bottle of Guinness; take a few pennies for yourself.'

'Yes, Ma.' Later, he ate white bread and dripping for his tea. He made a pudding by sprinkling sugar on another slice. They sat in front of the TV together and, while she smoked and drank the beer, they watched the children's programs. He felt safe.

His present home was at the top of a block of flats. He liked to be out of sight, with a view over the busy streets, but he hadn't looked out yet today. He avoided his neighbors, because he never knew what to say. He was irritated by the small exchanges about nothing that accompanied unexpected meetings.

His wife had left him when he had gone bankrupt. Their children were apparently too busy to visit him. Gerry hadn't worked for three years. He'd enjoyed his profession as a plumber. At fifty-five, after years of hard work, his knees had given out. He couldn't crouch over pipes, nor reach under floorboards. He'd employed a few nice people, who he thought were friends. They used to go to the pub on Friday evenings but, when his management skills had not been able to save the company, the social contacts had ceased.

His doctor had said he would have to find work that was less physically stressful, but he didn't want to do anything else and he had no other skills. He lived on sick pay and a small private pension. He ate cheap food with beer every day. Occasionally, he bought a bottle of whisky, which quickly disappeared. He couldn't walk to the pub any more, and he needed a hip operation. He was on a waiting list, but the thought of a successful operation followed by blessed relief felt like a fantasy. Today another month had gone by.

The TV program changed: it was time for the midday news summary. More fighting somewhere in the world, less money for healthcare, and a heart-warming reunion between family members from the two Koreas. Then came a cookery program. The smiling hostess promised viewers they could easily make a luxury chocolate cake; a treat to cheer themselves up. Gerry liked chocolate cake, but he didn't move.

Early afternoon sunlight seeped through a gap in the fabric covering the window, and a thin stream of sunlight moved slowly across the screen. Gerry didn't adjust the drapes. His beer was at room temperature. His dinner plate rested on one of his feet. Half a sausage and a few chips lay strewn in front of him. Ketchup had spilled on one slipper and the carpet. His vanilla-and-chocolate ice-cream sat in the bowl by his chair. A spoon stuck out of the melted mass, spots of blue mold forming on the surface. An empty medicine box lay on the floor.

The finishing touches to the chocolate cake looked delicious. The program hostess smiled and wished everyone a productive afternoon in the kitchen. Gerry didn't blink.

Postscript

'In me thou see'st the twilight of such day
As after sunset fadeth in the west,
Which by and by black night doth take away,'
William Shakespeare (Sonnet LXXIII)

Like the sonnet, this dark vignette is a sorrowful requiem for Gerry. It illustrates the anxiety everyone feels about dying alone and unwanted. Was it a suicide? We don't know. If not a direct self-killing then perhaps a death by self-neglect. Too many things went wrong in life, one after another, and Gerry was not able to recover from one loss before the next weighed down on him.

It's not only a requiem, it's also a call for compassion towards people who have weaknesses we share. Our childhood, and our temperamental reactions to our early experiences and phantasies about them, have laid down a pattern of behavior that we need to take account of each day. According to psychoanalytic theory, we are inevitably guided by unconscious processes. We require the insight achieved through self-reflection if we are to avoid repeating our childhood histories.

Reference

Clark, W. G., and Wright, W. A., (Eds) *The Complete Works of William Shakespeare*. Garden City, NY: Nelson Doubleday Inc.

What can lift a person into insight about their destructiveness? A direct intervention? Possibly, and the next story is an illustration…

7

The Ferry Crossing

———◆———

The ship's chief engineer prowled his engine room. His highest priority was the smooth running of *his* engine room on *his* cross-Channel ferry. He was furious. Last night's scheduled oil change on engines two and three had been missed by the night crew. His life experience was broad, and he knew how disappointing human beings can be. The chief, as he was called, was dedicated and determined. He'd been a successful amateur boxer in his youth; a southpaw with a good reach. He was of average build and weight, and kept himself trim; despite his fifty-two years, he could land a hefty punch. If he had something to say he didn't spare anyone's feelings. On the other hand, if he valued a person, he could not do enough for them. The weather this morning was chilly, an icy wind blowing through the decks. The ship lay by the quay, loading goods and passengers. The chief went up to the bridge and made his presence known immediately.

'There's a bloody cock-up in the engine room, Captain. Several fucking idiots have been asleep on the maintenance jobs. For some reason, engines one and four have been done, the oil is clean, but engines two and three are a mess. What's it all about?'

Captain Goodturn was a large and jovial man with a positive view of humanity. In general, he had an optimistic view of life. He felt that most things would work out all right in the end if he focused on the human relations aspects of his job. He was wise enough to listen calmly to the chief's robust complaints.

'I'm sorry, Chief, I didn't realize the oil change had been missed on those two. I really cannot explain why. I'll talk to the relevant people when they come on duty again. I'm sure those engines will hold until this evening. They've all had a service recently. Isn't that so?'

'That's as maybe, Captain, but engines two and three need regular attention, as I've said before.'

'Indeed you have, Chief, and I respect your professional judgment. I'm sure there will be a reasonable explanation.'

'If you don't mind me saying, sir, I think that sounds like misplaced kindness. There will not be a reasonable explanation, and in fact the people involved, as you also know, are a complete waste of space.' The chief paused his character assassination, a far-away look in his eyes. 'I can feel the result of their failure now, vibrating through my feet, even on this deck. Engine three is playing up again.' He rushed off the bridge.

Captain Goodturn shouted after him, 'I'll buy you a drink in the mess at the end of this journey, Chief.'

Despite the engine problems, the cross-Channel ferry left the quay on time. The chief and his apprentice, Robby, endeavored to keep engine three ticking over, while the ship reversed and turned using engines two, one, and four. Robby, seventeen years of age, wasn't big, but he was strong and resourceful. The chief called him 'a good lad', and that was high praise coming from him. He'd said to the captain some weeks ago, 'The lad is as good as gold, just what I need down there. He's bright, quiet, and interested in his new job. I can trust him.'

While they worked, the chief talked above the thunderous engine noise.

'The engine room of a ship is like an orchestra. Each machine is an instrument. If one of them starts to play out of tune, I know it. Keep that in mind, Robby. You should learn to feel that too.'

'Yes, Chief.'

A shadow passed the open door. 'See who that is, Robby. Find out what they want.'

Robby moved quickly, and looked down the narrow corridor. 'It's a bloke,' he shouted.

'And?'

'Oi, you, what do you want?' He strained to listen before turning back to the chief. 'He says he's looking for the top deck.'

'He's an idiot. Come back here, Robby.'

They struggled on with their engine maintenance using spanners and a big hammer.

'Now, listen to that, the orchestra has changed pitch. Number two has begun to sound strange again. I'll deal with it. You carry on with this one. And give me that hammer.'

After an hour of determined work, the chief said, 'I think the hammering helps, but I don't know how long they'll hold. I need a moment to think. Four and one are keeping us steady, so I'm going up top for a smoke. I won't be long. Keep doing what you can.'

'Yes, Chief.'

The chief went out into the corridor and through a stairwell door labeled 'crew only'. He enjoyed this privilege of exclusive use.

His footsteps clanged on the meshed metal treads as he labored up several flights, cursing the night crew's ineptitude all the way. He climbed through the last narrow door onto the top deck. The cold air felt fresh and clean after the oily warmth of his engine room. He took a worn leather pouch from the top pocket of his overall. It contained a little mangle-like machine, cigarette papers, loose tobacco, and a box of Swan Vesta matches. Standing on the upper deck with feet parted to steady himself, the chief prepared to roll a cigarette. It was part of a meditation that momentarily raised him above the pain of life. He put a thin paper into the roller machine and sprinkled in some tobacco, taking care to level the quantity along its length. He pushed the rollers until the glued edge of the paper was visible. He licked it with a sweep of his tongue and turned the mangle another half turn. Satisfied, he lifted his new cigarette out of its cradle, squeezed it gently by running two fingers along the shaft, and then put the new cigarette to his lips.

Looking up, he saw a man at the rail watching him. The newcomer was dressed in a winter coat of fine gray wool, a pale-blue T-shirt, jeans, and worn training shoes. He had no hat, despite the cold wind.

'I used to do that when I was a student,' the man said, 'before I got married. I wasn't very good at it, and I've messed it all up now of course. I mean the marriage part.'

'You're the bloke from down below, aren't you?' said the chief, his cigarette wobbling up and down between his lips. 'My lad had a word with you. Don't wander about like that, it's dangerous.'

The man nodded and looked out again over the water and the drifting ice floes. He didn't move.

The chief put his cigarette-making equipment back in its pouch and into his inside pocket. 'I see you're looking at the water. It's deep of course, and dark. There's plenty of broken ice scraping by the ship.'

The man turned towards him. 'My name is Justin and my wife is called Monica, or my ex-wife, perhaps I should say.'

'That's more information than I need at the moment. You'll hear my name when you've earned my respect.'

'Oh, I see. Are you upset?'

The chief made a protective windshield by holding the matchbox between his second and third fingers and his thumb. He cupped his palm, struck the match on the underside of the box, and put the flame in the space between the round curve of his palm and the box. Then, lifting the arrangement up and bowing his head, he joined the end of the cigarette and the flame. He sucked air through the cigarette to get the tobacco burning. He drew in the smoke and sighed out a cloudy vapor. Shaking the match to extinguish the flame, he squeezed off the charred end and put the remains of the stick back in the matchbox. Looking at Justin, he took a shred of tobacco from the end of his tongue with the thumb and forefinger of his right hand.

'I've had a stressful morning so far. It isn't easy to keep an old bus like this afloat, let alone keep it going forward. You've had your breakfast in the restaurant, no doubt. In that time, other people were working hard to keep the electricity on and the hot water running.'

Justin nodded and said something the chief didn't catch. Then, raising his voice, Justin added, 'I see you've wiped oil on your forehead, and you've got hard-worked hands. Your face is lined with stress.'

'I don't understand why you're making these personal comments. Perhaps you're not right in the head.'

'And you're very direct. I mean, you don't pull your punches, do you?'

'I'm known for it. I get things done.' He took another drag on his cigarette. 'Now, there is something to be understood between us. I'm out here to collect my thoughts.' Smoke came out of his mouth and nose. 'The captain, the night crew, engine three and now number two have given me trouble this morning.' He paused and pulled again on his cigarette. 'I believe you may be thinking of jumping into the drink. At this temperature, you'll have about eight minutes to live. Believe me, when you hit the water, your terror will make you regret your action. They all feel it.'

'They all feel what?'

'Regret. In the water, you will think that a thousand needles are penetrating your skin. And you'll be watching this ferry steam on. You'll scream in desperation.'

'Is this your business? My thoughts and plans are my own.'

'Indeed they are, Justin. However, if you jump, I won't do anything about it. Do not think for a single second that I care. I won't even look at you.'

'That's a cruel and callous declaration of indifference.'

The chief drew on his home-made nicotine stick, while he looked Justin in the eye.

'Yes, mate, you've got a nice turn of phrase. However, notwithstanding that, your jump will clear my view, and I can have this space to myself.' He looked up and blew smoke into the clear, cold sky.

Justin was quiet for a minute, then said, 'I'm profoundly shocked by your attitude to my possible fateful choice. You don't hold back, do you? But you've made me think about my wife, Monica. I've really hurt her, and I regret so many things I've said and done.'

'Landed one on her did you, mate?'

Justin's head went down.

'That's not right, you've got something to sort out there. You can take the return journey and all, as long as the bloody engines are running.'

The chief stood up straight, as if struck by an outside force, his eyes smiling but unfocused. 'My orchestra is almost in harmony. Almost. Robby has fixed number three. Good lad, *he's* not a waste of space.' He turned towards the 'crew only' door.

Justin smiled too. 'It's a long time since I made a cigarette like that. I wonder if you could spare me one? I can pay for it.'

'No need to pay me, Justin. You can have one as long as you make it yourself.' He reached into his inside pocket and took out his leather pouch. 'Here's the kit, you can bring it down to the engine room when you're finished. I'm the chief, that's my name.'

Postscript

Well, this story is obviously raising the question of how we speak to people in the throes of suicidal considerations. Some people might find what I've written a little rough. It isn't how you'd talk to just anybody, although the chief probably would. He would talk to anyone in the same way. Or perhaps he was a shrewd judge of character and said what was needed. We cannot know, the story does not say more.

The everyday expression, 'It's no use beating about the bush,' says it all. What is the value of direct intervention? How direct should it be? Here I use the brusque chief engineer as the figurehead for my point. Would you do this?

There is another issue in the story: personal responsibility. When Justin admits that he has wronged his wife Monica, the chief becomes a little conciliatory and offers Justin a ride home on the ferry. And as if to confirm this, when Justin wants to pay for the cigarette, the chief reinforces the idea of dealing with a problem yourself by saying he can have the cigarette if he makes it himself.

This fatherly role we see in Shakespeare's play *Romeo and Juliet* (Act III, Scene 3) when Friar Laurence is very direct with Romeo about his first suicide attempt. That speech also ends in a conciliatory way.

And what is the point of the Robby character? He shows the stability of someone who is serious about his work, and demonstrates a quality that the chief admires, namely persistence. So part of the message in this story is that Justin should not give up either.

Reference

Clark, W. G., and Wright, W. A., (Eds) *The Complete Works of William Shakespeare*. Garden City, NY: Nelson Doubleday Inc.

There follows a series of vignettes about experiences at the gates of heaven...

8

Five Whimsical Tales of Angelic Intervention from Genevieve the Wayward Angel

———◆———

Heaven, hell, God, the Devil, yada yada... but, hey, you know this religion business is true, don't you? If not, you're in for a surprise. I'm Genevieve the Wayward Angel—yep, I *really* am an angel—but despite being an angel I occasionally float outside the boundaries of acceptable heavenly behavior. God likes life, death, and eternal life to flow naturally and, when I intervened in earthly lives once too often, His Splendid Angels took the chance to punish me.

You've never heard of Splendid Angels? Every organization has them in one form or another, doesn't it? Those people who enjoy being idealized accept and encourage the adulation of those who need a strong leader. The Splendid Angels have a big following; self-styled God's police I call them.

Now, to explain: I'm not a fallen angel, I'm just a bit naughty. As I said, I've intervened on earth and helped people when I shouldn't have. For my misdemeanors, and to redeem myself, I have an extra job from God. I have to manage the back gates to heaven, which are made of silver, and I hope you never see them. Round the front, the gates are pearly white and gold.

The back gates provide an entrance to heaven for those who have departed earthly life by their own hand or by accident, if you believe in accidents. I have to check their stories and prepare them for what's coming. Higher authorities want them to take responsibility for their actions but, if they won't, they may have to go back down to acquire more experience. I'm not allowed to make that decision, but sometimes I do and then I'm in trouble for running my own afterlife.

The Splendid Angels don't like me. They've been complaining amongst themselves that my robes are too colorful, and they don't like my hairstyle. It's not easy to be creative wearing a white gown every day so I introduced a rainbow fabric. I like to stay loose, if you know what I mean. I don't think God minds: He smiles when He sees me, and even turns a blind eye to some of my interventions. At least I think it was Him, or His son, or their ghost.

The following are some stories from my experiences at the back gates to heaven. You'll get more of an idea about how I landed the title 'Wayward' if you continue reading. But don't believe it all, not even from an angel. You might be shocked by some of the following material: don't forget what the author has said about the use of humor in other stories as a way of managing and understanding your rage at a suicide.

There are some more quotes from Freud and his friends, and from Shakespeare. I'm sorry about this—who needs psychoanalysis when we have religion? But the narrator is insistent, so we indulge him.

a. Leaving the Earth

'No love toward others in that bosom sits
That on himself such murderous shame commits'
William Shakespeare (Sonnet IX)

A number of people turned up at the back gates to heaven on a particular day. It doesn't matter which day, just read on. As I've indicated, if people are waiting for me, the chances are that they've suffered a self-inflicted traumatic ending.

'Hello, you're a motley crew, aren't you? You realize this is the gate for people we're not sure about?'

They shuffled their feet for a bit, avoiding my eyes. One person spoke up, 'Listen to me. I'm General Frank Tucker. I don't know why I'm here; none of this is my responsibility. I only do things for the good of the regiment. However, it is the case that my staff told me I was putting myself in danger.'

'So, you had something to do with it and the rest of you shouldn't be here either, but you've gone too far for me to send you back. Look at the state of you all: blown to bits, a hole in the head, drowned, hanged, poisoned. What were you thinking? Never mind, don't answer that. I don't want a list of sob stories.'

They looked at the floor.

'Embarrassed? You should be. I'm Genevieve the Wayward Angel and, for my sins, I have to teach you something you've missed.'

'Hello,' said the group reluctantly.

340

'Finally, a response. But speaking together is annoying so don't do it again please.'

'Why are you called 'Wayward'?' asked the general.

'It's a long story but I can say—'

'The gates are locked,' they chorused.

'I told you not to speak all at once, and you know why they're locked.'

An elderly lady with a walking frame appeared and the locking mechanism on the silver gates disengaged with a whirr. The group took a step forward.

'Hold it, you lot are not going anywhere. Come along, dear. Cheryl, isn't it? Nearly there.'

General Tucker continued his rumination. 'I sat in the car, and the windscreen began to wobble backwards and forwards; it moved slowly like a wave, in and out, until it shattered. The floor bulged upwards and split; flames rose up; there was enormous pressure. I had time to think about everything. I regretted getting into that car. I don't know why I did.'

The old lady stopped. 'Hello, Frank. I'm the collateral damage. I was passing your car when it blew up. The moment of dying takes a long time, as you say. It isn't pleasant, is it?'

'I remember the click of the revolver hammer,' said one of the group. 'It seemed slow and drawn out.'

'It felt like I took a year to hit the water,' said another.

'I chose the wrong rope,' said a girl with a bruised neck.

'The tablets were tasteless, the brandy was good but, when I changed my mind, I couldn't be sick. I didn't even have fun at the end of my miserable life,' said a fourth person.

'How do you know my name?' said the general.

'I heard people calling you. No one knew me. I felt so lonely.'

'Come in Cheryl, you won't be lonely now.'

The gates swung open. Cheryl pushed her walking frame aside, and choirs sang joyfully as she walked unaided. The entrance clunked securely behind her. The group were crestfallen.

'I don't want to hear any more self-pity,' I said. 'I've a job for you. If you can help someone else, maybe He'll let you in. Look down there.'

Far away, down on earth, they could see a red-faced figure rising towards them. He had a rope around his neck and was trying to hold it with both hands, to relieve the pressure on his neck.

'That chap is hanging himself.'

'Why?'

'It doesn't matter, he's changed his mind.'

'We all did that, but it was too late. My eternal moment of regret only lasted a part of a second,' said the revolver man.

'Don't start whining.'

'I'll bloody well deal with this,' said the general. 'I say, down there.'

The young person looked up.

'It's my son, Frank Junior. This is my fault. Now look here young man, stop that immediately and go back down.'

'Don't be ridiculous,' said the revolver man.

'He's swinging over a stool,' said the general.

'I know what ropes feel like,' said the bruised-neck girl. 'I'll help him. Oi, you. When I tell you, put your left foot down.'

'I feel sick,' said the brandy girl.

'Only fifteen seconds left before he's here.'

The swinging man spoke. 'Put a foot down? Where? Are you real? I wish I'd bought a less prickly rope. I feel worse than before. I thought I'd ease my guilt about hating my dad.'

'Now! Oh, Christ—sorry, I shouldn't use the holy name in vain—wrong foot, he's missed.'

He swung over his launch point again.

'You're a bloody idiot,' shouted General Frank, 'you always were.'

'Calm,' said the revolver man.

'What you did wasn't calm and that was no way to handle a gun. You should have–'

'Focus. Ten earth seconds left,' I said.

'Try again, with the other foot. I'll say when,' said the rope girl. 'Now,' she shouted. 'Yes, he's made it, but he's fainted on the garage floor. Oh, God! Sorry, I don't mean God, I mean sorry he fell so hard.'

'I've seen men get over worse than this,' said the general. 'He's tough: he's my son.'

The spirit of Frank's son appeared with them.

'No, no, you're not supposed to be here,' said the rope girl.

'It's OK,' I said, 'he's dreaming. I'll talk to him now. This won't take long.' I lifted his head by the jaw, and spoke firmly. 'You know now that the experience of dying takes place in super-slow motion.'

'Yes,' said the sleepy young man.

'And you will always regret it?'

'Yes.'

An hour later, in the garage of General Frank Tucker's former residence, the young man's best friend found him sitting on the stool.

'What the hell have you been doing? Look at the state of your neck!'

'I was just experimenting. You know, it takes forever to die, and you meet all kinds of strange people.'

Outside the heavenly silver gates, the motley crew heard the lock disengage. They were jubilant: in unison.

Postscript

The dilemma of the suicidal people in this story is that, at the moment of self-execution, when they acted on what they thought was a good decision, they realized they were wrong. They changed their minds and wished they hadn't tried to leave their earthly life.

We can speculate that their hatred of life temporarily inhibited their love for life and that, once the act of departing was set in motion, they saw the truth and were overwhelmed with regret. People with depression suffer a lot, but most do not try to kill themselves. As Freud says, in *Mourning and Melancholia* (Freud, S. (1917)), if they have too much sadism in their personality, they can well take the law into their own hands and execute the bad person inside them. Or at least try to. 'It is sadism alone which solves the riddle of the tendency to suicide which makes melancholia so interesting—and so dangerous.' (Ibid., p. 252)

So, we have two ideas that are often repeated in different ways in most of these stories: ambivalence about life; and sadistic wishes to hurt someone else, i.e. a person located in a fantasy in the internal world of the suicidal person. In addition, there is a wish to hurt people who witness this action and its consequences.

By the way, ambivalence has positive uses as well. This attribute helps to heal a split in the mind. What I mean is that, when we move between two opposing positions, we can sometimes weigh up the value of each and decide to make modifications to achieve an acceptable middle ground. For example, do I only hate someone or only love them? Can I find a place in my mind for loving them and hating them too sometimes? That's what is meant by facing up to reality about humanity, and it is one of the qualities of maturity that we can feel sad that we have hated a person we have also loved.

References

Clark, W. G., and Wright, W. A., (Eds) *The Complete Works of William Shakespeare*. Garden City, NY: Nelson Doubleday Inc.

Freud, S. (1917). *Mourning and Melancholia*. SE XIV. London: Hogarth Press and The Institute of Psycho-Analysis.

b. Alexandra's Ride Over the Edge of Reason

My husband, as usual, gave me a detailed description of his day at work: his meetings, both business and private; conversations with colleagues; what they were wearing and ate for lunch; followed by the content of numerous phone calls. I felt the final straw land on me when he related the struggles of a potted plant in his office. The one his maiden aunt had given him five years ago, not the parting gift from his last workplace, which was now in a terminal state after a few months struggling with the air conditioning. All this exceeded my ability to bear his anxieties as well as my own. I didn't scream, although I wanted to. At least he didn't make a wallchart—it has happened. Meanwhile, I was trying to attend to the children. We have two young ones and they also like Mummy's attention.

'Finish this pasta for the kids, Adrian, please. I'll be back in half an hour.' I didn't consciously think I wanted to step out of our life forever but... Sorry, I should say that I'm dead, at least for the moment.

We all live there at some point, don't we? I mean, standing on the edge of the abyss, looking into madness. Haven't you had that experience? It's the place that's represented by artists, writers, musicians. They show us what we dare not see. I live with a cinema in my head, I think a psychoanalyst would call it my unconscious. It's a large room with no doors or windows. On the walls, ceiling, even the floor, a horror movie plays twenty-four hours a day. I'm anxious all the time, although Adrian doesn't seem to notice.

Oh dear, this is boring. Stories are supposed to start with something that catches your attention and makes you want to go on. But perhaps you realize that I want to get out of that room in my head.

I have to admit that I think I'm mad, temporarily I hope. But, in my present state, there seems to be only one solution—jump. I didn't understand that until I met the character in front of me. She appeared to me just now. She said, 'What's all this then? Oh dear, now I sound like a policeman.'

'Hello. Yes, you do sound like a policeman.'

'Who are you?'

'I'm Genevieve the Wayward Angel. I'm in trouble with God for interfering in life on earth.'

'That doesn't sound good. And you don't look like an angel, although you're glowing somewhat. I think you look like a rainbow.'

'Are you being rude? I believe you need me at the moment.'

'No, I mean yes. I need you, but if you are wayward I'm not so sure. How did you get that name?'

'I intervened and saved someone from hell who wasn't supposed to be saved. It's a long story. I'm sort of banished from the good places in heaven: the celestial sports center, Cafe Paradise. I have to work at the back gates to heaven. *Twenty-four seven*, as the Americans say. I'm bored. That's why I'm cruising around the earth this evening. I saw you might be on your way up to me so I thought I'd come over and look for myself before you start floating upwards.'

'I didn't know there was a back gate to heaven.'

'Yes. Sometimes, we're quite busy. It's the place for the 'intentionals and accidentals', but God agrees with Freud about accidents.'

'Accidental and intentional what?'

'Deaths.'

'Is this the beginning of my eternal journey?'

'Possibly.'

'Oh dear. I'm Alexandra, by the way. I should have said earlier: pleased to meet you.'

'I know who you are.'

'Yes, of course. You're an angel. I wonder if you could help me? I don't think I want to be separated from my body.'

'You don't sound too worried.'

'I can't make up my mind. I should be at home for dinner, but family life is becoming... well, sort of... I don't like to complain, but I think I've had enough. I mean, the children's demands feel huge and my husband's incessant chatter drives me mad every evening. I can't find the energy to live any more.'

'I know.'

'I feel anxious, as if something terrible will happen at any moment.'

'And now it has.'

'I went out for a walk before dinner, but a cyclist ran into me. I'm usually so careful.'

'You didn't look both ways this evening?'

'I wasn't attentive enough. My body is lying there on the wet tarmac; he must have hit me on the back of the head with the front of his helmet.'

'Yes, he's called Edwin, and he lives in a fantasy that he's training to race in the Tour de France. He was cycling head-down, admiring his thighs, with no lights, dark clothes— unconscious suicidal behavior in my book. When you didn't move after he hit you, he thought he'd be construed as a murderer. In terror, he rode away. I'll catch up with him later. His behavior might be an excuse to let you off. We'll see. What's the rest of your story?'

'When I went out, I said to Adrian, my husband, "I'm going out for a breath of fresh air before dinner." He said, "All right, dear. We'll eat when you come back. Are you taking your usual route, just so I know?" I told him yes, and that the food smelled good. I wanted to reassure him that I'd return soon. I didn't complete the thought that perhaps I wouldn't. And now I won't be back, unless you help me.'

'Please stop crying. I can't bear it.'

'I wasn't conscious of my wish to disappear. Honestly, I didn't mean it. I donned my tweed autumn coat, and my blue woolly hat is over there in a puddle. I arranged my hair nicely. I don't know why now.'

'You wanted to look attractive for someone who might save you from your unhappy life. Was that another motive for leaving the house?'

'Yes. No. You're judging me, aren't you? You're deciding if I'm morally reprehensible. I want to go in through the heavenly gates, as described in the Bible or somewhere, but not yet. The children are too young.'

'Go on.'

'I carried on up the road towards the bus station, intending to take a walk around the neighborhood. As I approached, I thought it'd be fun to take the next bus to another stop and walk back.

'The next bus came. The driver was pale, like one of the undead, I thought. How cruel of me: maybe she'd had a bad day. Or did my wish to escape my life prompt that image? I felt free as I rode away, and began to forget my children, my partner, the aroma of food.

'The bus route is familiar but, from another perspective, it felt exciting, as if I was really leaving. I got off at the stop on the other side of the road. As the bus left, its warm interior looked bright and friendly. I was alone in the patch of light around the bus stop; I felt lost and wanted to move.

'To get here, I had to cross the pedestrian bridge. I don't know why, but I thought of a story I'd heard last year of someone we knew slightly, who'd jumped in front of a car. It was unexpected, terrifying, and exciting.'

'Perhaps you wanted that when you heard the story.'

'I don't know. Please stop interrupting: this is upsetting. Every time I look down, my empty body isn't moving, and I want it back with me to love and dance and hold my children again.'

'All right, sorry, I understand.'

'I was hypnotized by the noise of the traffic. The wind blew my hair. The cars seemed to be moving slowly. I felt possessed by a wild part of me that made black into white and yes into no. I thought I could jump over the rail and leave my gnawing anxiety on the sidewalk. I looked at the traffic—soon it would screech and hoot as I lay like a rag doll with the sounds fading in my ears.'

'You'd be coming to me.'

'I'm not sure I like your tone. You seem keen to take me with you.'

'On the contrary. I'm here to help.'

'At that moment, a jogger came over the bridge. She brushed my coat as she passed, music leaking from her earphones. She said, "Wake up. You love them" and faded into the dark. Was it an old friend or a work colleague? Was it the image of an inner voice of protest? The traffic was loud again, and I realized where I was. It's true: I do love them. I continued over the bridge but my anxiety and the urge to jump returned. I lifted myself up in one move. Halfway over, my coat fluttered in the wind and my hair blew out. I regretted it deeply. Bang! A male jogger made full body contact with me, and we landed on the sidewalk. He was on top of me for a moment. A sweaty person, yuck! But I liked it. You're right, in my mind there's an imaginary person I want to look nice for.

'He apologized, calling me by my name as he lifted himself from my body, and asked if I was OK. Then he told me I needed to go home.

'"How do you know what I need?" I said. "Why can't you look where you're going? How do you know my name? Do I know you? Are you my husband's friend Peter, or is it Tony?" He didn't answer. Perhaps he didn't hear me. He continued his run. I looked at the rhythm of his sweaty bottom; he was wearing a multicolored Lycra second skin, it looks quite nice on some. I'm glad Adrian doesn't jog.

'Outraged, I walked off the bridge. I felt confused, unsure if I was angry or grateful. I didn't know what to make of it. I continued my walk and turned onto the cycle/pedestrian path. It's pleasant to walk here during the day but, in the evening, foliage obscures the lampposts. I looked right. The path seemed clear, and so I turned left to walk home. I didn't see Edwin, as you call him.'

'To be fair to you, he was moving fast, so he might have come into view a few seconds after you looked.'

'Thank you. He crashed into me, I suppose. I heard a man's voice shout "Merde! Mon Dieu!" as I fell forward and lay face-down on the path.'

'I didn't realize Edwin was taking the Tour de France so seriously he's even swearing in French. Here's a tissue.'

'Thanks, that's kind. As I lay there, I could smell our evening meal, as if it was coming back to me in a dream. I was thinking, *When I get up and I can see you, whoever you are, you're going to get such a telling off.* Then, like a dramatic end to a movie, my vision faded to black, my knowing became nothing and now I'm here with you looking at me, lying there, absorbing that puddle in my clothes.'

'You're not saying anything. Do you know all this? You were those joggers, weren't you? You've been intervening. You're also a risk-taker, aren't you? You know I should be at home, and my coat will be ruined if I don't get up quickly. Could you please repeat your kindness on a huge scale and put me back into me? I miss Adrian and the children so much. I promise I'll never do anything like this again.'

'This has come to you like a surprise attack, an ambush that resulted in the idea of jumping in front of a car. Metaphorically, you hold a gun you didn't know you owned. You thought it couldn't happen to you, but at the same time you wanted to disappear. You should get some help, talk to a professional.'

'That was a bit of a speech. All I'm saying is that I've decided to stay on earth and tolerate what I feel.'

'Sorry about the speech but now you've decided to accept your life I can help you. This next bit will probably get me into more trouble, but close your eyes.'

351

'They're already closed.'

'Don't be clever. I'll put you back outside your front door in a clean coat, with your blue woolly hat on your head. When I say the word, count to three.'

'Thank you so much. I hope you won't be badly treated. This is goodbye then?'

'We'll meet again, but we don't need to think about that at the moment. I'm off to surprise Edwin. Count…'

'One, two, three…'

Postscript

Of all the whimsical tales, this is perhaps the one with the most whimsy. Although it may be amusing, I'm trying to make a point that a suicidal state of mind does not only belong to people in psychiatric wards. Quite ordinary events in life, if there are too many of them, can be overwhelming for anyone sometimes. In this case, Alexandra is torn between her love for her family and other feelings of the pointlessness of all her efforts. The Wayward Angel intervenes to help her but, in the end, an accidental event which Alexandra contributes to by not looking properly leads to her original wish being fulfilled. Then, as I said about ambivalence above, she regrets her situation. It must be the most horrible experience to regret the decision halfway through an irrevocable event like suicide, as we saw in story (a) 'Leaving the Earth'.

Alexandra is also making the point that sometimes it is possible to be in a state of mind where nothing matters, and that this is so strong that any other feelings of concern are blotted out. The experience is eternal because its root is in the unconscious, which is timeless. The person knows there can never be an end; as a result, the only way to erase the experience is to die.

The Wayward Angel speaks: 'the Splendid Angels did indeed come after me and I was given even more time looking after the back gates to heaven. Ridiculous—how can you have more time in eternity?—but that's bureaucracy for you. By way of consolation, I've been joined by a couple of freethinkers: Sigmund Freud and his friend Charlie. When they arrived at the pearly gates they said, "But all this is an illusion," and were promptly send round here. I'm supposed to teach them something and set them right. We'll see how that goes. I'm not optimistic.

I'm sure people who ride the Tour de France are nice people and not at all like Edwin but, to be kind to him, we can all panic in an unexpected situation.'

c. Jenny

Freud, Charlie, and I, Genevieve the Wayward Angel, were standing by the back gates to heaven. Who are Freud and Charlie? Of course, as you are well aware, Freud has written a lot of books. He's quite a genius: ideas just flow out of his head. He looks like the old pictures of him in his middle years, if you are familiar with them. He's thoughtful and kind.

Charlie is a character. He just says whatever comes into his head. I'm not sure what he did on earth and I'm not sure he is either. Freud seems to know him though. His hair is all over the place. I think he had a frightening end to his life, but I don't ask, I don't want to upset him. His clothes are crumpled, but not his spirit. I think he used to hang around the psychoanalytic crowd in Vienna. They all went to Freud's Wednesday meetings; in those days, everyone was welcome.

We were warming ourselves by the golden brazier. A brazier is a large metal container, like an old oil drum, that burns all sorts of rubbish. Believe me, it's cold up here. The pearly gates round the front have central heating and choirs of angels in matching robes, not a single blond hair out of place. Our eternal fire makes us look like a welcoming alternative to their 'ever so good' entre. I digress. I'll continue with my account. And I should just add, in what should be a footnote, that when people arrive at heaven's gates they look like they did on earth.

A teenager appeared at the gates. 'Good evening, young lady, I'm Genevieve. I like the floral print on your dress.'

'Yes, thank you, my mum made it for me actually. Um, my name is Jenny and I'm surprised to be here, but not, if you see what I mean. It was my intention, but I didn't expect silver gates and an angel, especially not in a rainbow nightdress. Who are those two standing by the fire?'

'Old friends, Freud and Charlie. I'm a Wayward Angel, so called for historical reasons, and my fashion choices are my business.'

'Absolutely. The nightdress comment was rude, I'm sorry. I've heard of Freud at school. Didn't he listen to hysterical ladies, hundreds of years ago?'

'Not exactly hundreds of years, was it, Sigmund?' said Charlie.

'Never mind them. Why are you here, Jenny?'

'I should say in my defense,' said Freud, 'that what I discovered first was the value of listening to people without interruptions or asking questions and, most definitely, not to interfere in their lives.'

'That was a wounding remark,' I said.

'But an important point,' said Charlie.

'Go on with your story, Jenny.'

'My boyfriend kept on about sex, and how he needed it to love me more. In the end I said he could do it, I mean fuck me, if he stopped whining. Sorry, I shouldn't use the F-word up here, should I? It's heaven here, isn't it? You are merciful though, aren't you?'

'Not quite heaven yet, but yes to the merciful part. Please go on.'

'In the end I gave in, to make him shut up. It wasn't nice. I discovered pimples with blackheads on his back. How could I have my first sex with a boy with spots? Now he's left me, and he didn't even say thanks.'

'You have my sympathies.'

'Then he described how we had screwed on social media, and how much I had loved it, which was untrue. I decided to kill myself, while my parents were out. I'm fifteen years old. Everyone will be angry with me. This is such a mess. I want to go back, and I don't. I live down there in that house. See, I'm still lying there in my bedroom.'

'I agree. You're too young. You shouldn't be here. We'll have to think of something.'

'Please let me finish my story.'

'Sorry.'

'Told you,' said Freud.

'Shush.'

'I poured out two boxes of acetaminophen, a packet of my mum's sleeping pills, and my dad's angina medicine on the floor. I took a bottle of sweet wine from the kitchen and filled a glass tumbler. It smelled awful. I looked up at the half-drawn drapes, where a faint light seeped through...'

'So much detail?'

'You asked.'

'And you heard what Sigmund said. Come over here by the fire, dear, and tell us,' said Charlie.

'This is the afterlife preparation interview. I'm the one who decides.'

'Now who's being splendid?' said Charlie.

'Ignore those two, Jenny. Just the basic story will be fine.'

'I took the first of forty pills. The wine was disgusting. There was a meow outside my room. We call our cat Bulimia. We renamed her after a visit to the Child Guidance Clinic. We only went once. Terrible place: they talked about eating disorders. I don't have any, but the cat does.

'She scratched at my door, I opened it, and she glided in. I took some more pills and wine. I fainted, or died, maybe I'm dead-ish. And look down there: the cat is eating the tablets and licking up the rest of the wine. I must have knocked the bottle over. My mum and dad are coming through the front door now. I think they're early. I'm not completely dead, surely?

'No, time is on your side, so to say.'

'Look, Mum is talking to Dad.'

I don't know what happened to this afternoon, do you Reggie? Time seemed to fly by. Three hours just disappeared in a flash. I can't remember what we were doing.

'What's happened to the time?' said Charlie.

'Nothing to do with me,' I said.

'It must have been you—they shouldn't be back home until seven o'clock,' said Jenny.

'I adjusted the clocks a bit. It's nothing.'

'But it must have been a big bit. How could they be here, I mean there? That's my dad, Reginald, he's looking for a coat hanger. Look at my mum: she's distracted, the house is too quiet. She always wants to know what's happening. Now she's calling for Bulimia. She's going upstairs and opening the door to my room. Now she's found my body. She's screaming. She's so upset. What have I done? I didn't think she cared. She's backing out of the room. Oh, God (sorry for using the holy name), she's falling down the stairs.'

'Don't worry, it won't be fatal.'

'How do you know?'

'I know.'

'Listen to her, Sigmund, omnipotence itself,' said Charlie. 'And what does she think she looks like in that rainbow outfit?'

Freud said, 'I don't think how she dresses is relevant.'

'Do you mind? I'm speaking, and this is the drama of my life so far. Can you be serious?' said Jenny.

'Sorry.'

'Look, my dad's having an angina attack and his tablets are in the cat. He's in pain but he's calling an ambulance for us. I didn't realize he's so brave and determined. What have I done to them?'

There was a clap of thunder and one of God's own heavenly police, a Splendid Angel, appeared. Freud and Charlie moved to the other side of the burning brazier.

'Something has happened to time on earth. This is just the kind of thing you're being punished for. You're a celestial vandal, and you look strange in that outfit—really.'

The Splendid Angels are such bitches sometimes. I ignored her rudeness. 'Everything is under control, your splendidness. An ambulance will arrive soon and take them to hospital. They'll receive medical help and family therapy to work through their grief for Bulimia who, as we speak, is overcome by drug and alcohol abuse. They'll understand the fate of the cat is a metaphor for their family

357

life. Soon Jenny will be going to school again, with friends. A calm and sadly cat-less family will support her.'

'Big success. But sacrificing Bulimia is no consolation for cat lovers.'

'I hoped He might let that go.'

'Nothing is ever lost or forgotten,' said the Splendid Angel.

Charlie turned to Freud. 'Isn't that one of your lines?'

'We can think of a few things ourselves. In point of fact, he took it from us.' Freud shrugged his shoulders.

Jenny was sent home.

Postscript

A sad and jolly tale, perhaps, to illustrate some aspects of the teenage experience: the feeling that Mum and Dad don't care, and nor does the ex-boyfriend. Jenny takes the only course she thinks possible. And again, ambivalence (the coexistence of love and hate), comes to the rescue as she regrets her action. The fantasy story is a metaphor for a voice inside her who could help her not to do it. In this story, she had gone too far without divine intervention but, in reality, maybe not. She says she thinks she is dead-ish. Perhaps with an intervention from her parents and the hospital she would have made it without the imaginary angel. The change in the clocks that brings the parents back represents the kind of accidental event that sometimes saves a suicide from completion. Or was it an accident?

d. What Do You Have to Say?

Genevieve, the Wayward Angel, let Johnson, a road-accident victim, pass into heaven through the silver gates. Her duty done, she then floated back to the heavenly brazier to warm her hands and to continue her early morning chat with Freud and his friend Charles.

'That was an interesting case,' Genevieve told them. 'He said his car flew through the air and landed upside down. He was a bit unclear about how it actually happened—said he couldn't remember.'

'"Nothing is ever lost or forgotten." That's what you say, isn't it, Sigmund?' said Charles.

'Yes, I suppose I did. Actually, Johnson looked a bit guilty to me. I wonder if there is more to it. I think I'd listen carefully to anyone who comes up next,' said Freud.

'What were we talking about before Johnson arrived? Oh yes, how you can influence people with the things you say, even though you don't realize how,' said the angel.

'Yes,' said Freud. 'In the unconscious, ideas are collected and reworked. You might hear something from someone else who doesn't think what they say is important at all.'

'I remember those discussions years ago about the unconscious making new ideas from lots of bits and pieces we pick up each day. It's still fascinating to think about,' said Charles.

'Precisely. But what you say could hurt them too of course. You have to be careful.'

The heavenly doorbell rang, and a voice called out. 'Excuse me. I wonder, if it would not be too much trouble... I mean, when you have time, and you're available to talk to me... I've been waiting for some time down there.'

Genevieve floated over to attend to the new applicant. She met a man in his sixties, white haired, with damaged spectacles balanced on his broken nose. His mid-gray suit was muddy and torn in places. His old school tie hung awry.

'What did you say?'

'I mean, to summarize my words, I was wondering what I have to say in order to get in. If I may ask so without offending.'

'A little pedantic, aren't we? Yes, all right you can probably come in. You look like you've had a bad experience, and you're old enough. What happened?'

'My name is Dobbs, by the way. Actually, Johnson was the fellow in the car who put me here. Apparently, you've let him in before me.'

'Yes, Dobbs, 'apparently' I did let him in, thank you. Perhaps I was too hasty. There is no need for a long story, but tell me how it happened.'

'I think he drove off the road deliberately, accidentally running into me in the process. I must be fair, although perhaps he meant to run into me. Maybe he didn't like me. But I don't think I know him. I was struck from behind and flew over the handlebars. It must have been quite a scene.'

'It's no laughing matter, Dobbs.'

'Sorry.'

'Strange. You don't seem too bothered that you've ended up here.' Genevieve turned and called out, 'Hey you, Johnson. Hold up. Stop.'

The melodious sounds of heavenly choirs died like an old-fashioned gramophone player in a power cut.

'Come back here,' Genevieve instructed, and Johnson slouched over, looking at the ground as if he was a child who'd been caught with his hand in the biscuit tin. He was a tall and gangly figure, with a dour expression.

'This man here, Dobbs, tells me that you drove off the road deliberately. Is that true?'

'I said I *think* he did,' Dobbs piped up. 'He probably didn't mean to hit me. I don't want to be cast in the role of an unfair accuser.'

'Yes, thank you, I've got the idea.' Turning to Johnson, Genevieve said, 'You told me it was an accident caused by a bus driver.'

'Uh, well, I didn't know what to do, my business went bad and I thought–'

'No, you didn't think, and let me tell you...'

At that moment, there was a commotion by the gates. The new arrivals were a crowd of people in shorts and T-shirts, carrying buckets and spades, souvenirs, and duty-free goods.

'What are you lot doing here?'

A man in a bus driver's uniform pointed at Johnson. 'When he drove across the road, and then off it, I lost control of our vehicle. We from the front of the bus have recently died of our injuries. But we prefer to travel in groups. We waited for each other. It'll be cheaper for you with the choir-of-angels thing. Only one grand entrance.'

'Yes, very thoughtful, this was a quiet day. OK, look here, I'll have to keep some of you, the oldies, but you others have not said what you're supposed to say on earth yet. So you will have to go back down, unless there is divine intervention because He likes you. But I wouldn't count on it.'

'What do you mean?' asked Dobbs.

Freud and his friend Charles remained by the heavenly brazier. They looked to be deep in discussion.

'A little help, gentlemen? Please.'

They continued to chat. 'All right, I know who you are the next time you ask me to fast-track an old friend.'

With their hands in their pockets, Freud and Charles floated over to the group.

'Now then, you can all listen to this,' said the Wayward Angel. 'In answer to your question, Dobbs: everyone has something to say on earth. It gives your life meaning.'

'That sounds a bit right-on and spiritual,' they all said together.

'That was irritating. What are you, a choir? Don't do that again, please. And as regards 'spiritual', if you have a problem with that, look around you. Those of you who are unbelievers have a few more seconds to reboot your souls. After you've crossed the threshold it'll be too late, and there'll be consequences.

'Now, where was I? Oh yes, on earth everyone has something to say. You were supposed to be looking after the person next to you, and you may be surprised how important some words can be, even those you think are trivial. It's a bit like performance art. You will have an effect one way or another.'

The group looked taken aback by this little speech. Freud and Charles seemed bored. The Wayward Angel addressed Freud: 'And don't give me any "Been there, done that" comments. Remember what I said about your old friends.'

To the group, the Wayward Angel said, 'I can see who has spoken already. It's an angel's business to know that. OK, you, young man with the scraggly beard, and you, the girl in the hippy dress hanging on his arm. And you over there with a tie—on holiday? You three are going back down, immediately. Some people will be surprised at your return, some happy, and a few disappointed. Sorry about that. Goodbye.' The clouds under their feet parted and out they went into the blue.

'Now then, as for you,' said the Wayward Angel to Johnson, the secret suicide, 'you've caused a lot of trouble.'

Freud and Charles turned away.

'Just a minute, you two can talk to him.'

They took him by the arms, one on each side, and floated him gently back to the heavenly brazier.

To Dobbs, the Wayward Angel said, 'In answer to your question that started this sad tale, you cannot come in. Sorry.'

'Oh well, I'll have to admit that my apparent early departure via my bicycle accident with a suicidal person, Johnson over there, was actually quite convenient. I was thinking about an early exit, but I didn't have the courage to do it. You see, I live alone, and my cat died recently. I was given early retirement from my job at the city archives. I don't know why, perhaps it was unconscious, but I decided to cycle regularly for my health, and I went on roads that are actually quite dangerous. Contradictory really. I should have realized that, if I went there three times a day, as I did, eventually someone would run me down. Perhaps I had hidden motives; it was my private win–win. If I disappeared via a car accident, it wouldn't be my fault and people would have sympathy for me.'

'You seem a little confused but that tragic game is over. This is reality. Believe it or not, your unscheduled departure is your responsibility and you still have something to say down there.'

'I don't talk to anyone. You're the first person to talk to me for months.'

'Give an interview to the local radio station—tell them about today. You'll be surprised how many people will want to speak to you. And I'll get you another cat. She'll be waiting by your front door when you get back.'

Dobbs floated away with a smile.

Postscript

Again, we are in a situation of ambivalence: people who have behaved in a stupid and possibly suicidal way want to reverse their decision and start over. Sometimes we might get a chance to do this, but unfortunately not always. And everyone has to take responsibility. There is a bit of a sermon in this story about the words everyone has to say on earth before they have done their job; however, it is usually the case that life goes on more smoothly if we look after the person next to us; kindness will rarely go amiss.

This is also a tale about the unforeseen consequences of a suicide, which is similar to the way in which we don't know who we influence when we speak because it may have a ripple effect, like small waves on water. The suicidal person doesn't know who they will hurt, and how it will affect others for the rest of their lives.

The last of these five stories is about recovering from a state of stupidity, one which had unconscious suicidal motives, apparently.

e. Stupidity Redeemed

Hello, Wayward Angel here again and, before you ask, let me remind you why I'm called the Wayward Angel. I've had trouble with The Splendid Angels, those fabulous creatures with amazing wingspans and whiter-than-white robes who float among us. They try to enforce the rules of heaven.

One of those rules is that angels should not interfere with what happens on earth. We can listen and reflect, but that is all.

I have a tendency to intervene, as you'll see again. After one such incident, a Splendid Angel called me 'Wayward', and the name stuck. It was a bloody cheek, but I quite like the notoriety.

I have the apparently unenviable job of looking after the back gates to heaven. These are for unexplained or self-induced exits from life on earth. Those people are not allowed through the pearly gates at the front. It's one of those niggling bits of red tape. It's an interesting job, and I meet all kinds of people. You should know that, after death, nothing changes: the same people who think they have the ear of God have a lot of power. It's tiresome; don't think you're escaping anything when you cross over to us.

You've got to have a good reason for getting into heaven by the way. I don't let everyone in. Being dead is not enough; we can fix that.

Anyway, on this day, Charles, Freud, and I were warming ourselves standing around the golden brazier. It stands by the back gates to heaven and it's got automatic climate control, not like the ones on earth.

Freud is with me because he's kind and wants to help but, perhaps more importantly, he's not ready to accept where we are. He always said that the whole business of heaven and hell was an illusion. He even wrote a book about it in 1927, *The Future of an Illusion*. Well, he knows that future now: how could he have been so wrong?

Charles is a shortish, round man with a twinkle in his eye. He's one of the psychoanalysis gang from the 1920s. Not many people have heard of him, but Freud likes his company.

We were discussing our evening entertainment. Should we go to Freud's favorite establishment, Café Landtmann, again? (According to Wikipedia: 'During its long history, Café Landtmann served as a meeting place for many of the leading industrialists, politicians, thinkers, and artists in Austria, and was the preferred coffeehouse of Sigmund Freud'.)

You see, we go to the best place: it's incredibly posh. It's fun to be there, unseen, watching everyone. Yes, of course we're spirits: people can't see us. By the way, if you can see me at the moment then you have a problem.

So, there we were standing by the back entrance to heaven, as I said, when there was a rattling at the gates.

'Oi, you over there: what the fuck is this all about? Why are these gates locked? It's cold out here, let us in. Come on, get a move on, are you deaf?'

I floated over and found a decimated young couple. You should know that, when spirits come up to heaven, they look like the body they have left behind. That's true.

'What on earth have you two been doing? You look like you've seen a ghost, your bodies are mangled, and where are your feet?'

'Yes, indeed,' said Charles, from his warm place by the fire. 'Good start. Good joke. *What on earth?*'

'Leave this to me. It isn't funny.'

'Yeah, who rattled your cage?' asked the young woman.

'Temper, temper,' grumbled Charles, as he and Freud looked down at the earth. 'There on that motorway, a wrecked motorbike.' Charles pointed. 'Cool-looking machine, Sigmund. Much better than we had.'

'Hmm.'

I turned to the new arrivals. 'You're a bit young to come in; we prefer oldies, or at least mature adults.'

'Is that a fact? Well, for your information, I'm Tracy and he's Ronny, just in case you're the slightest bit interested.'

'Yes, point taken. Politeness. You're a very direct young lady, aren't you?'

'I'm stressed. Ronny was showing off, again. He went too fast and lost control—just like he does at other times.'

Ronny shifted his weight, from one broken leg to the other.

'He said, "Feel my cock at one hundred and eighty" and I did—touch it, I mean—and he said, "Oh, nice," and we left the fast lane and crossed over to the other side.'

'Was that wise? I mean, you're really on the other side now, aren't you?'

'Yes, that's good—*the other side*, that's us all right.' Charles nudged Freud, who was looking down and didn't respond.

'You over there, whatever your shitty name is, shut the fuck up.'

Charles said, 'That's a bit rich, young lady, you're in no position to—'

'Don't test me. When I get in there, I'll sort you out, no trouble.'

'I'm sure you will,' I said, 'but the question remains: was your behavior on the bike wise?'

'It's a bit late to ask that now, ain't it? What about dealing with the situation as it is? And who are these two old blokes you're hanging around with? Call yourself an angel, I suppose. I've met tarts with that name.'

'I'm called Genevieve and I'm an angel, even if I'm wayward.'

'That's what I said. You've got a tart's name.'

'And the "old blokes" are Sigmund Freud with the beard and Charles.'

'Pleased to meet you, gentlemen. No response. Of course they're deaf when it suits them, I suppose. A moment ago, we crossed over the central barrier. I was screaming, and a truck hit us. I was still holding his cock. Look, see, he can't feel anything now, can yah, Ronny? Just as well, ain't it, you stupid suicidal bastard?'

'Sorry, Tracy.'

She looked at Freud and Charles, who were apparently studying the bike and commenting on the scene below.

'And you two over there, I know you can see my smashed-up, half-naked body. I don't want no sexist remarks.'

'What's sexist?' asked Charles. Freud shook his head.

Tracy looked down at the bloody scene. 'People are filming us. We're broken into pieces. What a mess. And my hair: half of it's missing. I look like a rag doll after the dog's been at it.'

'Sorry, Tracy. I should have given you the other helmet.'

'What's the point of a different helmet if we hit the front of a truck? You should have thought about me before you twisted that throttle.' She slapped him with the broken stump of her arm. 'You think speed means manly, don't yah?'

'Sorry, Tracy.'

'You're not taking much responsibility, Tracy. You said you touched his private parts. You don't think that had something to do with it? You don't have to do what he says. Are you suicidal?'

'Listen to me, Genevieve. Tarts like you don't say "private parts". It's a cock and don't be righteous. I thought you called yourself 'Wayward'. In answer to your accusation, I love 'im, so I want to please him. You don't know what love is, do yah?'

I knew she was right. I was sounding like a Splendid Angel.

'I think we should be a bit polite in this situation; I mean we're on the outside of these gates.'

'Ronny: shut the fuck up. I can handle this.'

Charles chipped in, unwisely I thought. 'Are you really so sure of yourself, young lady? You are aware, I hope, that your unconscious wishes have now been played out. I mean the wish to die as represented by your choosing a speed-hungry boyfriend. As Sigmund over here would say, I'm sure.'

'You can stop talking all that psychoanalysis shit. It won't get us anywhere in this situation, now will it?' said Tracy.

Freud looked sheepish, and Charles said, 'Now look here…'

'And don't give me "Now look here", you fucking voyeur. Stop staring at my boob down there.'

'No, well yes. There are two actually, but one is less than it should be, I think.'

'What? Told ya. You're looking at me bits, you pervert.'

Freud floated over to me and drew me to one side. 'Can't we do something? We—or rather you—could fix this by a minor miracle, and get the traffic flowing again. I mean, there's no one else around.'

'If one of those Splendid Angels comes by, it'll be awkward.'

'But do you want her in here? She's got a mouth on her all right. It could be your good deed for the day. Take a chance. God likes kindness. It's a 'win–win', as they say these days.'

'Yes, true, point taken. Tracy, I think it's too early in your life for you and Ronny to be here, so we'll do something to help you.'

Dark clouds appeared on the horizon.

'Ah, the superego of the Splendid Angels—or is it God, raising a protest?' said Charles.

'Stop playing about with my ideas. My psychoanalysis is a constant joke to you, isn't it?'

'He's touchy, isn't he, that Freud bloke?' said Tracy. 'A bit oversensitive. All quiet and kind and then suddenly edgy. But he's being nice to us.' She turned to Freud. 'I said, you're being nice to us, aren't you?'

'You don't need to shout, I'm not that old.'

Tracy was distracted by a young couple nearby. 'Who are they?'

'Who?'

'Them over there in the fancy dress, kissing and cuddling, and all that.'

'Ignore them, you'll only encourage them. We've been trying to move them for ages.'

'But they're so romantic. Look: they keep touching hands, smiling, and saying something.'

'They've been here for hundreds of years. They say it is so delicious with first kisses. They don't want to give up nice human feelings. I can't put them back on earth again: look at their clothes. Their parents have never been interested; they're always fighting each other.'

'But who are they?'

'Romeo and Juliet. Have you heard of them?'

'Is that possible? I mean, an eternal romance?'

'Don't get any ideas. You're not getting into another mess.'

'What do they do?'

'They met at a fancy-dress party.'

'And?'

'Listen to them, Romeo, he's holding her hand:

If I profane with my un-
worthiest hand
This holy shrine, the gentle sin is this:
My lips, two blushing pilgrims, ready stand
To smooth that rough touch with a tender
kiss.

Juliet answers:

Good pilgrim, you do wrong your hand
too much,

Which mannerly devotion shows in this;
For saints have hands that pilgrims' hands do
touch,
And palm to palm is holy palmers' kiss.
William Shakespeare (*Romeo and Juliet*, Act I, Scene 5, ll, 95-102).

'And it goes on from there.'

'Oh, lovely. I get the general idea. What then?'

'They meet the next day and get married. They have a first night together. It's wonderful, ecstatic.'

'I want that. Ronny, why can't you talk like that?'

'Sorry Tracy, I wasn't listening.'

'Typical.'

'Ouch.'

'Stop hitting him, Tracy. You should know the story ends in a double suicide.'

'Now you're being cruel.'

And with that I jumped out into the blue, taking them all with me. As we made a controlled descent towards the earthly horizon, blue lights were approaching. The crowd continued to film the bloody scene.

'Unbelievable. That's going to stop.' I immobilized the spectators, temporarily, and emptied their cameras' memories.

We landed. No one could see us of course. We're divine. Some disgusting reparative scenes followed, as I put all the bits and pieces of the real Tracy and Ronny together. I had to retrieve some parts of Ronny from the radiator grille. Their boots had traveled quite a way from the scene of impact. Funny how that happens. In this case, the feet were still in them. Don't worry. The witnesses will forget, and so will you.

Fiddling with things keeps boys quiet, as we all know. Charles and Freud were no exception as they repaired the broken bike. With my help, it went quicker than expected. Soon the couple were complete. They lay sleeping in each other's arms on a soft, patterned blanket by the side of the motorway. The bike was parked next to them, as good as new.

'The poor truck driver,' said Freud, looking at a pale, trembling man.

In no time I had the driver intact again in mind and soul, continuing his journey on the motorway, listening to music. He didn't remember anything unusual about his journey.

There was a commotion as police cars, fire engines, and ambulances arrived. The remade couple from the blanket were in trouble for sleeping together on the side of a motorway. They couldn't remember how they had got there. An efficient police sergeant stood over them.

'Are you the owners of this vehicle?'

'I am,' said Ronny.

'You're so polite, aren't you?' said Tracy, yawning.

'Someone phoned us to say a truck had hit a bike and there were fatalities, but there's nothing wrong with that bike. Why were you two sleeping here, and why is the central barrier damaged? It looks like someone went over it. And there is oil on the other side of the road. Incriminating evidence, I'd say. People always film these events. Where are the film clips? Where's the truck?'

'I had the most amazing dream. Did you, Ronny? Someone was helping us to be together. I could feel angelic hands all over me. Was it you? Were you doing some naughty touching? It was lovely.'

'Shush, Tracy, this isn't the moment.'

'Shut up. You're always saying that. When is the fucking moment?'

'Excuse me, young lady, but I'm asking the questions, and mind your language.'

The sky darkened and an almighty storm with buckets of rain—not to mention 'cats and dogs'—poured down on the scene. The sleepy couple and the police sergeant jumped into his car. The motorway was soon as clean as a whistle. People sat shivering in their cars, trying to press life into their cellphones.

'Who d'you two think you are? Romeo and Juliet?'

'I wish.'

'I wish it too, Tracy.'

'You know how that story ends, I suppose,' said the police sergeant.

'I thought that last comment was unnecessary,' I said to Freud and Charles, as we floated back to heaven's back gates and our warm fire.

The dark clouds had moved on. Had God been helping us? We'll never know. He's always so discreet.

'It turned out quite nice in the end,' said Charles. 'Do you think we can sit on the back of that bike sometime? They'll never notice.'

'Now you're being silly,' said Freud. 'How do you think that would end?'

Postscript

'Of course accidents happen young man, you just need some craziness to get you out of whatever you've landed yourself with.'

That was said by my school teacher when I was ten years old— an unforgettable piece of wisdom.

To what extent Tracy and Ronny were suicidal is a moot point. They behaved stupidly, but not with a conscious wish to die. We could argue that getting a buzz from near-death experiences is part of a suicidal frame of mind. But were they more suicidal than Romeo and Juliet? Those two reacted to understandable stress, without parents to help them think. Tracy and Ronny responded, also without thought, to excitement. Can we say that their death instinct temporarily overwhelmed them? 'the perpetual activity of the death instinct, though never eliminated, is counteracted and kept at bay by the power of the life instinct.' (Klein M. (1948), p. 123)

In this story, the craziness that gets Tracy and Ronny out of their so-called accident is the craziness of the Wayward Angel and friends. But we don't all have them around when we need them. We have to hope for something else in ourselves, i.e. the creative power of the so-called life instinct. Which may of course be a little crazy; let's hope so.

The idea of a death instinct is part of Freud's late theory. I mean late in his life. Many of his colleagues did not agree with him. They thought he was being pessimistic because of his age, the outcome of the First World War and, perhaps most importantly, the loss of his favorite daughter, Sophie, to the Spanish influenza. But Freud was not moved. When his colleagues would not accept his theory he thought they were behaving like children who didn't like a tough reality.

Melanie Klein took up the idea of the death instinct and clarified it when she characterized envy as the active partner in the theory. Like Freud, she argued that we are born in a struggle between two wishes; to embrace life and to destroy it. The extent to which we can allow life to dominate over death determines the outcome of our creativity.

The person who first described the concept was a woman, Sabina Spielrein, in her paper 'Destruction as the Cause of Coming Into Being' (Spielrein, S. (1912)). Her original paper was written ten years before Freud's 1920 paper, 'Beyond the Pleasure Principle' (Freud, S. (1920)). Freud explicitly mentioned her paper in a footnote, acknowledging that it had started the train of thought that led him to conceptualize the death instinct.

So, in summary, the theory of the life and death instincts means that there is a tendency towards destructiveness in all of us, which is modified by love, affection, kindness, and compassion.

And, in my view, this is the meaning of life: look after the person next to you.

References

Clark, W. G., and Wright, W. A., (Eds) *The Complete Works of William Shakespeare*. Garden City, NY: Nelson Doubleday Inc.

Freud, S. (1927). *The Future of an Illusion*. SE XXI. London: Hogarth Press and The Institute of Psycho-Analysis.

Freud, S. (1920). 'Beyond the Pleasure Principle', in *On Metapsychology*. SE XVIII. London: Hogarth Press and The Institute of Psycho-Analysis.

Klein, M. (1948). A Contribution to the Theory of Anxiety and Guilt. *International Journal of Psycho-Analysis* 29:114–123.

Spielrein, S. (1912). Destruction as the Cause of Coming into Being. *Journal of Analytical Psychology* 1994;39(2):155–186.

Epilogue to Audacities

———◆———

An epilogue is a comment on or conclusion to a book and should reveal the meaning of the book's title, which in this case is *Audacities*. I think the meaning has been revealed several times so far, but to recap: in this case it is the brass-necked, shameless mistreatment of those who love you and depend on you when you decide to murder the person they care about. It's rude and unkind, not to say vicious.

Would you agree with Freud that it is sadistic to murder oneself? He may have a point. Of all the people who are depressed on any given day, relatively few actually kill themselves. As I have described above, Freud thought that it was an excess of sadism in the personality that explained the ability of a few people to do it. (Freud, S. (1917), p. 252)

Are there other, more acceptable, reasons for a suicide, even if we think they are based on a misperception? For example, the violent action may be connected to fantasies of trying to protect the suicidal person's loved ones from him/her. This is particularly so if the suicidal person judges themselves to be truly terrible, and a danger to everyone else.

Another question in relation to some of these stories is: do you agree with the use of humor on this sensitive subject? People who have suffered the loss of a loved one by means of suicide may not think there is anything to laugh about. How did you feel about this?

I am resisting saying anything more, because a suicide is the end of an unfinished life, and only questions remain for those who live on. Those people carry memories and often suffer the torture of self-blame. There is no end to thinking about the lost loved person. I think this ending should reflect that abruptness, and the silence that follows. What remains are the thoughts and questions for discussion at the end of each story.

Reference

Freud, S. (1917). *Mourning and Melancholia.* SE XIV. London: Hogarth Press and The Institute of Psycho-Analysis.

Epilogue to Tales from the Unconscious

———◆———

A nd to finish this collection of three books, an example of a six-word story about psychoanalysis and psychotherapy, that I use as a teaching aid.

Why? accept reality?
Or madness prevails

Postscript

The six-word story is a brief literary form: a six-word narrative. It gives a beginning, a middle, and an end to a story, the idea is believed to have originated with Ernest Hemingway.

Why? is the central question in any psychoanalytic therapy.

To **accept reality** is the final aim and achievement of an analysis; it is the resolution of the Oedipus complex, and the Kleinian depressive position.

'Why accept reality' is perhaps the clients' question and the answer comes in the last three words of the story: **Or madness prevails.**

If reality is not accepted, the individual is forced to live as if fantasy is reality. And that is a psychotic position.

Reference

Freud, S. (1957, 1986). *The Standard Edition of the Complete Works of Sigmund Freud.* SE I–XXIV. London: Hogarth Press and The Institute of Psycho-Analysis.